Praise for *Just the Nicest Couple*

"You won't know who to trust in *Just the Nicest Couple*, a domestic thrill-ride which grabs you on the first page and doesn't let go until you reach the end. A riveting tale about marriage, trust, and secrets, this is Mary Kubica at her best."

—Laura Dave, *New York Times* bestselling author
of *The Last Thing He Told Me*

"*Just the Nicest Couple* is Mary Kubica at her twisty, mysterious best. Every character brims with secrets. Every page holds a surprise. It's entirely unputdownable and everything a reader is looking for in their next read."

—Sally Hepworth, *New York Times* bestselling author
of *The Younger Wife*

"In *Just the Nicest Couple*, Mary Kubica is writing at the top of her game. She wastes no time dropping her characters into an impossible situation and then ratchets up the tension, one twist after another, until the last, shocking conclusion. *Just the Nicest Couple* is propulsive, addictive, and impossible to put down. But be warned: nothing—and no one—is as they seem."

—Julie Clark, *New York Times* bestselling author
of *The Last Flight*

"Mary Kubica's *Just the Nicest Couple* is a masterfully written thriller about deception where we least expect it and the danger of a lie tumbling out of control. Taut and incredibly suspenseful, every moment is perfectly crafted to keep us wanting more. An engrossing, spine-tingling read!"

—Ashley Audrain, *New York Times* bestselling author of *The Push*

"Rich with detail and a mounting, almost suffocating sense of dread, *Just the Nicest Couple* is a dark and twisted exploration of loyalty, family, and how far we'll go to protect the ones we love."

—Andrea Bartz, *New York Times* bestselling author
of *We Were Never Here*

"Kubica is a master of unnerving domestic thrillers. Fans will devour [*Just the Nicest Couple*] in one sitting."

—*Booklist*

"In Kubica's twisted tale of deception and falsehoods, readers will relish the shock factor in an ending they didn't see coming."

—*Library Journal*, starred review

Also by Mary Kubica

MARY KUBICA

JUST
THE
NICEST
COUPLE

PARK
ROW
BOOKS

PARK
ROW
BOOKS™

Recycling programs
for this product may
not exist in your area.

ISBN-13: 978-0-7783-3406-4

Just the Nicest Couple

First published in 2023. This edition published in 2024.

Copyright © 2023 by Mary Kyrychenko

TM is a trademark of Harlequin Enterprises ULC.

Park Row Books
22 Adelaide St. West, 41st Floor
Toronto, Ontario M5H 4E3, Canada
ParkRowBooks.com
BookClubbish.com

Printed in U.S.A.

For Rachael

prologue

I gasp and stagger backward. My hand goes to my mouth, bearing down.

My brain screams at me to run. *Run.*

I can't at first. Shock and fear hold me captive. They keep me from moving, like a ship that's dropped anchor. I'm moored to this spot, my eyes gaping in disbelief. My breath quickens and I feel the flailing of my heartbeat in my neck, my throat and in my ears.

Run, my brain screams at me. *Go. Fucking run.*

There is movement on the ground before me. The sound that comes with it is something heathen and raging, and some part of me knows that if I don't go now, I may never leave this place alive.

I turn away. It's instantaneous. One minute I'm unmoving and the next I'm moving so fast that the world comes at me in vague shapes and colors, streaks of brown and blue and green. I barely feel the movement of my legs and my feet as I run. I don't feel the impact of my shoes colliding with the earth, moving quickly across it. I don't look back, though I want more than anything to steal a look to know that I'm alone. That I'm not being followed. But I don't look. It's too risky. Looking back would cost precious seconds that I don't know that I have. If I do, those seconds could be my last.

Sounds come, but I'm so disoriented that I don't know where they come from. Is it only my pulse, the rush of blood in my ears?

Or is someone there?

I feel something tangible against my hair and then my spine. My back arches. I jerk away, pitching forward, landing hard on my hands and knees.

The world stops moving.

I have only two thoughts in that moment: staying alive, and that this isn't the way it was supposed to happen.

CHRISTIAN

Lily is sitting on the leather chair in the family room when I come in. Her back is to me. I see her from behind, just her long brown hair spilling down the back of the chair. She stares toward the TV on the opposite wall, but the TV is off. It's just a black box, and in it, I see a murky reflection of Lily on the screen, though I can't tell if her eyes are open or shut.

"Hey," I say, coming in through the garage door, closing it quietly and stepping out of my shoes. I set my phone and keys on the counter, and then ask, "How was your day?"

It's getting dark in the house. Out the window, the sun is about to set. Lily hasn't bothered with the lights, and so the inside of the house is colorless and gray. We face east. Any pretty sunset is the other way. You can't see it from here, if there even is one to see.

Lily says nothing back. She must have fallen asleep, sitting upright in the chair. It wouldn't be the first time. She's been extremely tired lately. The pregnancy is getting the best of her, not to mention that she's on her feet teaching all day. These two things in combination exhaust her. It used to be that Lily would be in the kitchen, cooking dinner when I got home, but these last few weeks, she comes home from work ready to drop. I don't mind that she's not cooking. I've never been the kind of person to need a home-cooked meal after work, but that's the way Lily was raised. Her mother did it for her father, and so she thinks she should do it for me. She's been apologetic that she hasn't had it in her to cook dinner, but she's been queasy, too, and the last thing she needs to be doing is cooking for me. I called from the car and ordered takeout already; it will be here any minute.

I step quietly into the family room. I come around to the other side of Lily to face her. Lily isn't asleep like I thought. Her eyes are open but her expression is blank. Her skin looks gray, washed-out like the room, and I blame the poor lighting.

Lily's head turns. She looks up at me as if in slow motion.

"Hey," I say again, gently, smiling. "You okay? Did I wake you?"

I flip on a side table light, and she winces from the brightness of it, her eyes taking time to adjust. I apologize for it, realizing that her pale face had nothing to do with the lack of light.

In the warmth of the lamp's glow, I see that Lily's hair is wet. She wears maroon-colored joggers and a sweatshirt. She's showered and changed since coming home, which is more than she usually does. Usually she falls flat on the couch and doesn't leave until it's time to go to bed.

I drop to my knees in front of her. I reach forward and run a hand the length of her hair. "You look exhausted, babe. Do you want to just go to bed? I can help you up. Takeout should be here soon. I'll bring it up to the room for you when it gets here."

Lily blinks three times, as if to clear the fog. She finds her voice. It's husky at first, dry, like after a day of shouting at a football game, which is not that different than a day of teaching rowdy high school kids math. "No," she says, shaking her head, "I'm fine. Just tired. It was a long day."

"You sure? I wouldn't mind dinner in bed myself." I had a long day too, but it doesn't seem right to compare them when only one of us has another human growing inside of them.

"That sounds messy," she says.

"I promise I'll be neat."

Lily smiles and my heart melts. I love it when she smiles at me. "When are you ever neat?"

"Never," I say, feeling better if she can still poke fun at me. I've done my research on pregnancy and childbirth. I've read that the fatigue women feel during the first trimester is maybe the most tired they'll feel in their whole lives. Growing a human is exhausting. Caring for one is too, but we're not there yet.

"You need anything?" I ask, and she shakes her head.

Takeout comes. I convince Lily to come sit on the couch with me, where we both fit. We watch TV and, as we do, I ask her about her day and she asks me about mine. She's quieter than usual tonight. I do most of the talking. I'm a market research analyst, while Lily teaches high school algebra. We met in college over of our shared love of math. When we tell people that, it makes them laugh. We're math nerds.

When it's time for bed, Lily goes up to the room before me. From downstairs, I hear the sink run as she washes up. I clean up from dinner. I throw the takeout containers in the trash. There is a package waiting on the front porch. I step outside to get it, where the night is dark, though the sky is clear. It must be a new moon.

Lily is standing at the top of the stairs when I come back in. She's there in the upstairs hall, standing in the dark, backlit by the bedroom light. Gone are the maroon sweats she wore earlier. She has on my flannel shirt now. Her legs are bare, one foot balanced on the other. Her hair is pulled back, her face still wet from washing it.

"Don't forget to lock the door," she says down over the railing, patting her face dry with a towel.

I wouldn't have forgotten to lock the door. I never do. It's not like Lily to remind me. I turn away from her, making sure the storm door is shut and locked, and then I push the front door closed and lock the dead bolt too.

Our house sits on a large lot. It's old on the outside, but has a completely revamped, modern interior. It boasts things like a wraparound porch, beamed ceilings, a brick fireplace—which Lily fell in love with the first time she laid eyes on the house, and so I knew I couldn't say no despite the price—as well as the more modern amenities of a subzero fridge, stainless steel appliances, heated floors and a large soaker tub that I was more enthusiastic about. The house is aesthetically pleasing to say the least, with an enormous amount of curb appeal. It practically broke the bank to buy, but felt worth it at the time, even if it meant being poor for a while.

In the backyard, the river runs along the far edge of the property, bound by a public hiking and biking trail. We were worried about a lack of privacy when we first moved in, because of the trail. The trail brought pedestrians to us. Strangers. People just passing by. For most of the year, it's not a problem. The leaves on the trees provide plenty of privacy. It's only when they fall that we're more exposed, but the views of the river are worth it for that small sacrifice.

"Done," I tell her about the locks, and she asks then if I set the alarm. We've lived here years and hardly ever set the alarm. I'm taken aback that she would ask.

"Is everything okay?" I ask.

Lily says, "Yes, fine." She says that we have an alarm. We pay for it. We might as well use it. She isn't wrong—it's just that she's never wanted to before.

I set the alarm. I make my way around the first floor, turning off lights. It takes a minute. When I'm done, I climb the stairs for the bedroom. Lily has the lights off in the room now. She stands at the window in the dark, with her back to the door. She's splitting the blinds apart with her fingers and is looking out into the dark night.

I come quietly into the room. I sidle up behind Lily, setting my hand on the small of her back and asking, "What are you looking at?" as I lean forward to set my chin on her shoulder, to see what she sees.

Suddenly Lily reels back, away from the window. She drops the blinds. They clamor shut. I've scared her. Instinctively, her hands rise up in self-defense, as if to strike me.

I pull back, ducking before I get hit. "Whoa there, Rocky," I say, reaching for her arms.

Lily's hands and arms remain motionless, suspended in air.

"Shit, sorry," she says, knowing how close she came to impact. The realization startles us both.

"What was that?" I ask as I gently lower Lily's arms. Lily isn't usually so jumpy. I've never seen that kind of reaction from her.

She says, "I didn't know it was you."

"Who did you think it was?" I ask, as a joke. She and I are the only ones here.

Lily doesn't answer directly. Instead she says, "I didn't hear you come up the stairs. I thought you were still downstairs."

That doesn't explain it.

"What are you looking at?" I ask again, gazing past her for the window.

"I thought I heard something outside," she says.

"Like what?"

She says that she doesn't know. Just something. We stand, quiet, listening. It's silent at first, but then I hear the voices of kids rising up from somewhere outside. They're laughing, and I know there are teenagers clowning around on the trail again.

It wouldn't be the first time. They never do anything too bad, though we've found cigarette butts and empty bottles of booze. I don't get mad about it. I was a stupid teenager once. I did worse.

I go to the bed. I pull the blankets back. "It's just dumb kids, Lily. There's nothing to be afraid of. Come to bed," I say, but, even as she turns away from the window and slips under the sheets with me, I sense Lily's hesitation. She's not so sure.

NINA

must have fallen asleep with the TV on. Whatever I was watching has given way to the ten o'clock news, which glows garishly in the darkness of the house, the volume obnoxiously loud. Lying on my side on the sofa, my eyes half-open, I watch it. Today, a midrise apartment building in the city caught fire and collapsed. There was a shooting on the south side. It's all bad news. The news puts this on because it's what people want to see. It's a sickness. It's not that the world is innately bad or that bad things happen more often than good things. It's that we're drawn to bad things. Death sells. I turn the news off. I hate watching it.

I push myself upright on the sofa, into a sitting position, rubbing at a kink in my neck. I must have been lying on it funny. Despite the nap, I don't feel any more rested. If anything I feel more tired. I just need to carry myself up to bed, but Jake isn't home yet and I don't want to go to bed before he is. I want to talk to him. I want to talk things out. Things got heated last night and I feel bad for it now. Looking back on it, it was mostly my fault, but, in the moment, I was being stubborn. I didn't see it that way. I said things I shouldn't have said and it's been eating at me all day. I thought over and over again about calling him at work to apologize, but I didn't want to interrupt him because he's so busy when he's at work, doing things that matter, like saving lives. He never likes it when I call him at work.

The papers I was grading are fanned out on the coffee table; I only got through a few of them before nodding off. They're for my honors English classes. We've just finished reading *1984* and the kids were asked to write about ways in which our modern society is Orwellian. I love reading their responses. I didn't mean to sleep for as long as I did. I told myself I was just going to close my eyes for a bit, and then get back to grading, but I must have slept for hours. I feel guilty now because I promised the kids I would have them graded by tomorrow. They put so much work into them and are anxious to know what they got. The honors kids are hard on themselves. But now it's dark outside and I'm tired, worried about what happened with Jake and needing him to come home so that we can talk.

I stand from the sofa and go to the kitchen for coffee. It's been a long time since I've pulled an all-nighter but a good night's sleep is not in the cards for me. I fill the Keurig's water reservoir, replace it on the unit and let it warm, checking my phone to see if I missed a call or a text from Jake. It's ten thirty-five at night. I don't know why he isn't home.

Jake saw patients in his office today. These days tend to be his shorter days because there's a predictability about them. Patients come in for consults or pre-op appointments. They have set appointment times, which may run over a few minutes if a patient is late or Jake gets behind, but never by more than a few minutes. The rest of the time, Jake spends these days catching up on paperwork. If anything, he's said, nonsurgery days

JUST THE NICEST COUPLE

are boring. Jake prefers being in surgery because that's when he's at his best.

Despite that, the days he performs surgeries are astonishingly long. He wakes up at four thirty in the morning when the alarm goes off on his watch. The workday starts just after dawn with rounds, prechecks and discussing patients on his list with the rest of the surgical team. They end sometimes as late as nine or ten o'clock. Surgery days are the most unpredictable too. While surgeries are sometimes planned, like removing a tumor, sometimes, like last week, a patient comes in with a gunshot wound to the head and Jake has to spend unanticipated hours trying to save a life. That gunshot victim died. She was practically dead to begin with. That's how Jake phrased it. There is a detachment in the way he speaks of his patients because there has to be. He can't get all emotional about it, otherwise he wouldn't be a good surgeon. There is a whole psychology about how doctors like him get through the day. It started in med school for Jake, where he referred to cadavers as things, not people, so he could cut into them more easily. For most people, seeing a dead body is a defining moment in their life; for Jake, it's frequent.

With this gunshot victim, Jake said that, even before she landed on his operating table, before he cut into her, she was fucked. Her odds of survival were infinitesimal, something like 5 percent, with even smaller odds of her having a good quality of life if she survived.

"That must have been hard for you, then, knowing she was likely to die and still doing the surgery anyway. It must feel futile," I'd said, trying to be empathetic because there's been a rift between Jake and me these past few months. He says it's my fault, and I've been trying so hard to be present in the moment, to not be distracted by other things when I'm with Jake.

He was drinking a whiskey sour. He lowered it to the table, his eyes watching me intensely over the glass. I think he took offense at what I'd said. I wasn't trying to suggest that what he did for a living was futile, but that was what he heard. What I did often felt futile too: talking for hours to students who were half-asleep and not listening.

"How could you be so sure she wouldn't survive?" I asked.

"With gunshot wounds, it depends mostly on the location and trajectory of the bullet," Jake said, sounding smart. "This bullet entered her head at the anterior temporal lobe. It traveled from one side of the brain to the other, crossing the midline, which is not ideal," he said, as if there was an ideal way for a bullet to travel in one's brain. "The bullet went in, but it didn't come out. It tore through both hemispheres, all four lobes of the brain before getting lodged in there."

"Did she die in surgery?"

"After."

"How?"

"Brain stem death."

"What does that mean?"

"The brain stem." I could see him thinking in his head how to dumb this down for me. I was grateful, not offended. Sometimes he throws out words like globulus pallidus and acoustic neuromas as if I should know what they mean. He's so used to tossing them around with ease among colleagues, he forgets I'm not one of them, that I didn't go to med school for years. "It's responsible for all the things that keep us alive. Breathing. Blood circulation. Digesting food. When the brain stem is dead, you are too."

"Like being in a vegetative state?" I'd asked.

"No," he said. He took a sip of his whiskey sour while I waited for an explanation. "It's different, because a person in a vegetative state still shows signs of brain stem function."

"How old was she?"

"Twenty-nine."

"Who shot her?"

"Her husband."

I wished I hadn't asked. I didn't want to know any of it. Un-like Jake, I couldn't be detached. I thought about it for the next twenty-four hours at least, wondering what happened between them to precipitate her husband shooting her in the head.

On surgery days, there is never any telling when Jake will be home. If an emergency surgery comes in, he stays until it's done. But today isn't a surgery day. He should have been home hours ago. I try calling him now, but Jake's phone is off or dead because it routes straight to voice mail. It's not like Jake to let his phone die. I leave a voice mail for when he has a chance to charge it, keeping it light, asking him to call me when he can. I don't say that I'm worried or that I'm wondering where he is because maybe I've mixed up my days and today was a surgery day after all. I've been distracted lately. My mother's health is failing. She's going blind and then, if that wasn't bad enough, the doctors recently found a mass in her left breast. We need to do a biopsy and see if it's malignant or benign. I'm a pessi-mist and so, in my head, I've already decided. It's malignant. If that's the case, we will have to decide what to do: keep the breast or get rid of it. My mother can't make a decision to save her life, which leaves all the decision-making to me. She's not that old to be going through all this but both things, macular degeneration and breast cancer, are in her genes, which means they're in my genes too. The doctor's appointments are endless: the general practitioner, mammographer, ophthalmologist and soon, a surgical oncologist. I've had to take days off work for them. The appointments fill the hours when I'm not teaching and, when I'm not with my mother, I'm thinking about and worrying about her, obsessing over decisions like lumpectomy or mastectomy, knowing if I make the wrong choice when the time comes, my mother will die for it.

Because of it, Jake and I have grown distant from each other. It was the impetus for last night's fight, how I care about everyone and everything but him. It's not true. But I can see why he would think it. Except that last night I'd turned it around on him. I devalued his feelings and made him feel bad for the way he felt. After screaming at each other, Jake took his pillow and slept on the sofa. He left this morning after hardly speaking to me and without really saying goodbye. Now he's not home and he's not answering his phone, and I'm worried I know why.

CHRISTIAN

In the middle of the night, Lily is crying.

"What is it, baby? What's wrong?" I ask, curling myself around her. Her crying is a quiet whimper that she tries to suppress. But I'm a light sleeper. It doesn't take much to wake me. I hear her cry, but more than that, I feel the vibration of her body against mine.

Lily is turned away from me in bed. Her back is pressed into me. She doesn't tell me what's wrong. "Bad dream?" I ask, feeling the back of her head nod against my chest. "Here," I say, "let me get you some water," pushing against the weight of the quilt, which levels us in bed.

"No," Lily says, reaching for my hand. "Please just stay here, Christian. Just stay with me."

I lower my head to the pillow. I sink back into bed and wrap my arm around her.

If I didn't know any better, I'd think Lily was scared.

★ ★ ★

In the morning, Lily is awake before me. She always is. She's showered and dressed and she's downstairs, standing at the kitchen island in the dark, eating a piece of toast, while I just rolled out of bed.

"Will you tell me about it?" I ask, coming to stand at the island opposite her. "About the dream."

Lily stares back, her brown eyes reluctant. "I didn't have a dream," she confesses.

I cock my head. "What were you thinking about, then? Why were you so upset last night?" I ask.

There's a long pause before Lily tells me.

"I went for a walk yesterday after work, at Langley Woods," she says. Langley Woods is a large forest preserve. Lily and I have been there before. We've gone together to run or to take our dog for walks, when we had one. It's not far from our house. There is a waterfall, though it's small, more like a dam than anything, and over ten miles of hiking trails. "The doctor said walking would be good for me. Safe," she reminds me, as if defending something she hasn't yet said, asserting that what happened isn't her fault.

Lily is a distance runner, but she's laid off running since she found out she was pregnant. There were three miscarriages before this, each pregnancy ending before the end of the first trimester. Lily blames herself for them, as if something she did or didn't do is what led to the miscarriage.

"That's good," I say. "A little exercise, a little fresh air. That's good." My voice is calm, encouraging, supportive, but inside my heart is beating a little faster than it was a minute ago because I'm wondering if Lily is going to say that something happened to the baby, that she lost the baby yesterday. My palms are clammy now; they start to sweat. The last time it happened, she was nine weeks along, like now. We'd already been to the doctor. We'd had an ultrasound and heard the baby's heartbeat.

The doctor had told us that the risk of miscarriage went down after detecting a fetal heartbeat for the first time, to something like a few percent, 4 or 5, I can't remember. Still, the doctor was wrong. She filled us with false hope. We didn't think anything bad could happen at that point. Shame on us. Lily had a history with recurrent miscarriages by then. She wasn't like other women the doctor saw. That small 4 or 5 percent included Lily, because she lost that baby even after hearing a heartbeat.

Lily was at work when it happened, sitting in on an IEP meeting when she felt the rush of blood between her legs. She sat there until the end of the meeting, until everyone else had cleared the room. When she stood up, she looked down and saw the blood on the chair. It came as no surprise, but was no less devastating.

Now Lily's hand shakes as she reaches for her water bottle. She unscrews the cap, brings it to her mouth and takes a long swig. She lowers the water bottle slowly back to the countertop and replaces the cap. It's dragged out. She's searching for the words to tell me the baby is dead, that she lost it yesterday when she was at Langley Woods. She came home. She showered, washing the blood away. The baby's gone. That's why she was so upset last night. There will be a D&C to clean out what's left of it. It's old hat. We've done this before. This is nothing new for us.

Lily's voice shakes when she speaks.

"Jake Hayes was there," she says. It's not what I expect to hear. It takes a second to regroup, to replace thoughts of miscarriage with Jake's face.

"Oh yeah?" I ask, flooding with relief that this has nothing to do with the baby. I let out a breath. I feel my body sag, my shoulders droop forward. I didn't realize how much tension I was holding in until I release it. They say that emotional pain is far worse than any physical pain you can experience, which makes the relief from it all the more profound. The baby is fine.

I'm still going to be a dad. Everything is okay. "Did you talk to him?" I ask, my tone turning optimistic. "How's he doing? We haven't seen him in what—six months?"

Nina Hayes teaches at the high school with Lily. She and her husband, Jake, are mutual friends. Lily sees Nina almost every day, but it's been a while since either of us has seen Jake. He's a surgeon. He's too busy saving lives to hang out with us.

What I realize is that Lily's whole body is now shaking. What started as a shakiness in her hands and her voice has spread. "You look like you're freezing," I say, coming around to her side of the island, reaching forward to run my hands along Lily arms for friction. Up and down, up and down. It's not cold in the house, but I run warm. Even in December I've been known to crack a window. But it's September still. It's too early to turn on the heat, not when the temperatures still reach eighty some days, even if they do drop to the upper forties and fifties at night. "Are you feeling okay?" I ask, touching her forehead with the back of my hand. She doesn't feel warm, but still I say, "Why don't you call in sick today? Take the day off. Rest."

"I can't," Lily says. "I'm giving a test tomorrow. I promised the kids we'd go over their study guides today, so they're ready for it." Lily is far too conscientious. It's her one weakness, if it's even a weakness.

"Can't a sub do it?" I ask.

Shaking her head, Lily says, "No. The subs are good, but they're not me. They don't always know the answers. They don't always explain it right. I don't want the kids to get stressed. If I call in for the day, I'll have to push the test back, and then we'll be behind."

"So?"

"It's not worth it. I'm okay," she says decisively, pulling away from my hand. "I can go. I'll just nap when I get home."

"Tomorrow is Wednesday already," I say to try and brighten her mood. "Two days down, just three days until the weekend and then for forty-eight hours, you don't have to get out of bed. I'm at your beck and call. Anything you need—back rub, foot rub, breakfast in bed—I'm your guy."

Three days until the weekend is almost the most pathetic consolation prize ever, but I'm trying. She humors me with a smile. "Sounds amazing," she says.

Lily leaves her plate with half a piece of toast behind. She takes her water bottle and moves toward the garage door to leave. She mostly wears pants these days, as the days get cooler, and because she feels more comfortable in pants. Today they're leggings, with a stretchy waist. She's gained maybe a pound or two, the kind of weight gain noticeable to her but no one else. She hasn't told anyone we're pregnant.

The leggings look incredible on her, but then again, anything would look incredible on her.

Lily picks up her bag by the door. She lifts it onto her shoulder. It looks heavy and I go to take it from her, to carry it to her car for her, but she says she's fine.

"You sure?"

"Yes. I'm sure. Have a good day. Love you," she says.

"Hey."

"What?"

"You never told me about seeing Jake," I remind her, remembering then. She stops with her back to me, her hand on the garage door handle. "Is he doing good?" I ask.

Lily wheels slowly around. She looks at me, and then she looks at the clock above my head. I glance back over my shoulder. It's a big, oversize clock, the little hand pointing at the Roman numeral six. School starts before seven for her, which is ridiculous if you ask me. What high schooler is up and functional at seven in the morning? It's black outside when Lily leaves for work, the only saving grace being that she's home before three o'clock, hours before me. I don't envy her in the mornings, but I do when afternoon comes.

"I have to go," she says, "or I'll be late. I'll tell you tonight, okay?"

"Okay," I say. "Love you." Lily leaves. I move to the front of the house to watch her headlights pull out of the garage and off down the street.

The day gets away from me. For the next eight hours, I don't think again about Jake Hayes or what Lily was going to say to me about running into him.

NINA

Jake never came home.

It's all I can think about.

I stayed awake until after two in the morning, grading papers, or trying to anyway, but I didn't get through all of them. I had my phone beside me the whole time, in case he tried to call or text. He didn't. I wanted to call or text him again, but I'd already sent three texts and left the voice mail. I told myself that he would call when he was ready to talk. I didn't want to make things worse by annoying him. He didn't come home for a reason and that reason was me. He didn't want to see me. He didn't want to talk to me. I messed up, but Jake is notorious for holding grudges. I worry what happens if he doesn't forgive me.

Now it's third period and the kids are energetic and overexcited. Someone in the foods lab started a fire by accident that just triggered the alarm. The fire department came and we had to go outside. It was all relatively quick. We couldn't have been outside for more than fifteen minutes, but now that we're back in the classroom, there's a frenetic energy to the room. Only some of the kids are in their chairs. The rest are moseying around the room, taking their time getting back to their desks, going the long way so they can stop and chat with friends.

"Let's focus, people," I say, clapping twice, though I myself am anything but focused. I've practically given up on teaching for this period, maybe for the day, and if it wasn't for the student teacher at the back of the room watching me, I'd put on a movie and be done with it. "We only have a few minutes to get through the rest of these notes." Third period is one of my regular English classes. They're good kids but not as driven, not as conscientious or well-behaved as my honors kids. I have to ask three times for them to get back to their desks and another time for them to be quiet. It's a wasted effort. No sooner are they quiet than the bell rings.

The kids bolt from the room for their next class. I head straight for my phone in the top drawer of my desk to see if Jake has called. At the same time, the teacher from next door, Ryan Schroeder, pokes his head in. "Sounded like a circus in here."

I've already pulled my phone out of the drawer. I look at it. My face must give away my disappointment. I hear Ryan but I can't look at him and I can't answer him because I'm so upset by the blank screen. It's just the home screen image, a photograph of Jake and me. Ryan gives me a minute, and then he asks gently, "Is everything okay, Nina?"

Jake hasn't called. My heart sinks and I fire off one more text, telling myself this is the last one I'll send until he calls me back.

Please call me, Jake. I'm so sorry. Let's talk about it. You were right. I was wrong. I miss you. I love you.

Jake would have had to stay at a hotel last night. He isn't the type to impose and sleep on a friend's sofa or something like that, not to mention that he isn't the type to air his dirty laundry. He'd much rather splurge on a nice room and room service. I think about him enjoying room service while I stayed up, grading papers and worrying about him all night long. I'm practically dead on my feet now, just trying to get through this day, but already worrying about what happens if he doesn't come home again tonight. For how long will he freeze me out, and refuse to acknowledge my calls and texts?

I wonder, though, what he would have done for clean clothes. Would he have gone home this morning after I left for work to change? Would he have gone to the store and picked up something new, or would he have just worn scrubs from the hospital? It's not only clothes either. Jake would have needed toothpaste, deodorant. If I get home and they're not there, I'll know he's been by the house when I wasn't home.

I said things the other night that I didn't mean, the worst one being *If you hate it here so much, then why don't you just leave?*

As they say, be careful what you wish for.

You'd like that, wouldn't you? Jake had asked. We were in the bedroom, standing on either side of the bed, squared off. I should have said no, that I wouldn't like that at all, that I'd hate it actually, but instead I'd stayed silent, glaring. He took my silence as a yes. It wasn't the first time we ever fought, but it was the first time it escalated to that level. Fighting about the time I spend with my mother has become something common between Jake and me. It used to be that he didn't want me to spend any time with her—he wanted me all to himself, and I'd be lying if I said some part of me didn't find pleasure in this—but when her health began to fail, I couldn't exactly neglect her, nor did I want to. She's my mother.

"Nina?"

I come to. I snap out of it. That mental image of my husband's angry face disappears and is replaced with Ryan's empathic face. He's stepped into the classroom now, and he studies me with his dark eyes, his head cocked and curious. He asks again, "Is everything okay?"

My student teacher still sits at the back of the room, scribbling away in a notebook, pretending not to listen. Despite being twenty-one or twenty-two, legally an adult, he's a boy in a man's body, with close cut blond hair, dreamy green eyes, newly emergent facial hair and a forgivable amount of acne. The kids like him, though he could just as easily be one of them.

"I'm sorry, Ryan," I say, shaking my head. "I got distracted. What were you saying?"

"The fire drill," he says. "I said it sounded like a circus in here."

"I'm so sorry." I apologize again. "The kids were so wound up. I didn't have it in me to fight them, not when the period was so close to being done."

"Hey," he says, "you don't have to be sorry. I was just checking that they didn't have you tied up somewhere." Ryan laughs. I force a smile, but I still feel embarrassed that he could hear the mayhem all the way next door, even though my door was closed. My student teacher must think I'm an idiot. I should have made more of an effort to quiet the kids, if not for me then to set a better example of classroom discipline. I glance down at my phone again, in case I somehow missed a notification. It's not lost on Ryan. "Are you sure everything is okay?"

"Yes, fine. I just need to run and see Lily, if you don't mind?"

"Of course not. Not at all."

Ryan steps aside so that I can leave, brushing past him on the way through the door. I don't have a class fourth period. I tell my student teacher I'll be right back, and then I head to Lily's room, which is in the math hall. It's still passing periods, and the hallways during passing periods are mobbed with kids. They're elbow to elbow and practically impenetrable, even for a teacher. High schoolers are also adult-sized. Aside from the way I'm dressed, it's sometimes hard to tell us apart. Even at five foot seven inches, I look just like any other student. They don't make room for me to pass in the hall.

Once I get to Lily's room, I peek in the open door. Unlike me, Lily has a fourth period class. There is about a minute left of passing periods and maybe only a third of the desks are filled. The kids are still out in the hall, chatting with friends. They like to cut it close.

Lily stands at her desk. She's talking to Colin Miner, a student we share. Lily is teensy, and so he dwarfs her. She's also incredibly beautiful, wearing these plaid leggings that only someone like her could pull off. She wears a mock neck sweater that's loose without being sack-like. She has the figure for it. The sweater hangs down to her upper thigh, her long brunette hair lying in waves down her back. She wears almost no makeup. Lily doesn't need makeup. I've overheard girls say things about how pretty Lily—Mrs. Scott—is and how nice. She's a favorite among teenagers, which is a major triumph, since teenagers are notoriously hard to impress, especially as the math teacher. It's no secret that almost no one likes math. Almost no one likes English either—teenagers like nothing but their phones and their friends, I've learned—but English at least tends to come easier than algebra for most students.

Lily smiles when she sees me hovering just inside the door, waiting for her to finish up with Colin. She tips her head and waves, and I see the concern in her eyes, the question. She's wondering what I'm doing here. Our classrooms are in different halls, though they're on the same floor. Still, it's not that easy to get from one room to the other, not in the four minutes the kids are allotted for passing periods. It's not that often that I stop by Lily's room during the day.

"Nina. Hi," she says, coming to me as Colin Miner returns to his seat.

"Hey." Up close, Lily doesn't look as perfect as she did from a distance. She looks beat, as if I'm one to talk. There are bags under her eyes and she wears only one earring, the same small silver hoop with a drop pearl that she wears every day. "Can I talk to you for a quick sec? In private?" I ask.

"Yeah, of course. Just give me a minute," she says.

The bell rings and the last few kids run in and to their seats, practically diving into them. Lily gets the kids started, and then she and I step into the hall, where she pulls the door to, but not closed, so that it doesn't lock on her and so that she can keep an eye on what's happening inside the classroom. "What's going on?" she asks.

"You're missing an earring," I tell her.

Her fingers go to her earlobes, touching them. "Oh," Lily says, her expression changing. She looks sad, upset I think, that she lost the earring. "Thanks," she says, frowning as she takes the other earring out, fastens the back and folds it into her hand. "Is everything okay?" she asks, crossing her arms against the mock neck sweater.

"No," I say, "I don't think so." I don't mean for them to, but my eyes fill with tears. I'm not one to cry. But I'm so tired and the lack of sleep as well as what's happening with Jake is a lethal combination. Lily is sympathetic and crying is contagious; for a second, Lily looks like she could cry too.

"Nina," she says. Lily unknots her arms and reaches for my hand, squeezing it. I squeeze back. "What is it?" she asks. "What's wrong?"

I don't hold back because it's Lily. Lily and I have been friends for years and not just work friends, but real friends. We tell each other practically everything. Lily isn't one to judge. It's not like she and Christian have the perfect marriage, because no one does. Everyone fights sometimes. Every marriage goes through hard times.

"Jake and I got into a stupid argument the other night. Stupid but nasty. I said some things I shouldn't have said. He did too, really hurtful things. It's not like we haven't fought before. But this was different, worse."

"Why?" she asks, willing to talk despite having a classroom of teenagers waiting on her. I'm grateful for that.

"Because, Lily," I say, hesitating a beat, almost ashamed to admit it, even to Lily, and because saying it out loud makes it real, "he didn't come home last night."

Lily's mouth parts. Her eyes get wide. She lets go of my hand, her arms going to hang stiffly at her sides. It's unintentional, I think, because she realizes quickly that she's made this very obvious reaction and she tries reversing it because she doesn't want to make me feel worse than I already do.

"Oh God, Nina. I'm so sorry," she says, blinkingly slowly, and then she hides her surprise behind a sympathetic smile and reaches again for my hand.

"It's bad, isn't it?" I ask. "That he didn't come home." Lily goes to shake her head, to say no, when I ask, "Has Christian ever not come home?" hoping her answer is yes. I mean, it can't be that uncommon. People fight. Feelings get hurt. It's not like you want to see that person the next day and pretend everything is okay. You need time for the situation to defuse. If he had come home, Jake and I would probably have just wound up fighting again because our emotions were still high. What good would that have done?

Lily is brutally honest. "No," she says. "I'm sorry. I almost wish the answer was yes. But no, he hasn't ever not come home. But that's just Christian, Nina. He's always the first to cave when we fight. I don't even know that he's always sorry when he says he is. He just hates conflict. He would do anything to avoid it."

That's sweet. It sounds like Christian. Christian is a good guy. But it makes me feel exponentially worse about myself and about my situation with Jake. I wish Lily would have just lied and said the answer was yes to appease me. How would I have known it wasn't true?

"Have you tried calling him?" she asks.

"Yes. Many times. It goes to voice mail."

"What were you fighting about?" she asks, but before I can explain, there is an eruption of noise from inside the classroom. Someone must have done something, and the class exploded into raucous laughter. A few kids are out of their seats and almost no one is doing what Lily asked them to do.

"Listen," she says, "I have to get back to my class. Let's talk about this later, okay?" She gives my hand a final squeeze, and I say yes, of course, that I'm sorry to have kept her so long.

But later, at the end of the day when I go back to Lily's classroom to talk it out, she's already gone.

CHRISTIAN

It's two twenty in the afternoon when Lily texts. I'm in the middle of a meeting. A handful of us sit around a conference table working on a survey for a client. I look down at my phone. Lily's text reads:

> Can you leave early? Can you meet me at home? If not, that's ok.

This is so classic Lily, to not want to put anyone out.

"Hey," I say to my colleagues, still staring down at Lily's text and thinking the worst again, that Lily has lost the baby, if not yesterday then today. I push my chair back and stand up, glad this isn't a meeting with a client. It's not a huge deal if I leave. "I hate to do this," I say, packing up my things and pushing my chair in, "but I've got to run."

I'm in my car, pulling out of the parking lot within five minutes. Two minutes later, I'm heading eastbound on 88, where my speedometer reaches eighty-five miles per hour.

Lily is in the leather chair again when I come in. It's a swivel chair. Today it's turned to face the garage door, so she sees me arrive, having to use my key to unlock the door because it's locked, which it never is. We always leave that door unlocked. Lily must have locked it by mistake.

"What is it? What's wrong?" I ask, tossing my keys on the island and practically running to her. As expected, the day got warm. As soon as the sun came out, the temperatures rose by thirty degrees. Now the sun streams in the wall of windows on the back of the house, falling across Lily's lap. She's stripped down to a tank top and leggings because of the heat, and sits with her legs pulled into her, cross-legged in the chair.

There are scratches on her arm and shoulder, some quite deep. This is the first time I'm seeing them. "What happened?" I ask, lowering myself to the floor, running a finger over them before gazing benevolently up at her, into her eyes. "Did you fall?"

Her eyes are wet and I know that she's been crying. Lily is reluctant to speak. I leave her and go for the antiseptic and antibacterial ointment, and then I come back and clean her arm. She's like a rag doll lying limp while I manipulate her arm to get to the scratches.

"Tell me, Lily," I say as I take care of the wounds. "Tell me what's wrong." I think she must have fallen and landed on the baby. The baby is dead. It has to be.

She doesn't say.

"Lily," I say. "Why did you need me to come home?"

"I'm sorry. I should have just waited until after you were through with work. I shouldn't have asked you to leave."

"It's fine. It was a quiet day. But I'm here now. Please tell me."

It wasn't exactly a quiet day. Besides the meeting with colleagues this afternoon, I spent the morning liaising with clients, getting to know prospective clients and updating existing ones on progress. I'm working on multiple projects right now and need to make sure that, at any given time, they all run smoothly. Mine is usually a nine-to-five job, but there are things I didn't get done today—because I was in meetings all day and because I left early—that I'll need to do tonight. It doesn't matter. Lily is what matters.

She closes her eyes. She takes a deep breath.

"Please, Lily."

Her hands are on her lap, folded into fists. She unfolds one. There on the palm of her hand is an earring. I gave Lily those earrings years ago, on our fifth anniversary. The fifth anniversary is, traditionally, supposed to be wood, and so I hid the earrings inside a wooden jewelry box engraved with her name. She said she loved them. I think she's worn the earrings every day since, which is how I know she does love them and is one of the many ways I know she loves me.

"I'm sorry," she says. "I'm so sorry. I lost one."

I look up at Lily in disbelief that she's so upset about the earring.

"It's fine," I say, shaking my head. "It's no big deal. They were cheap, Lily, like twenty-five dollars or something." I lie. They're white gold, with a small pearl. That pair of earrings cost two hundred dollars, but it really doesn't matter as long as Lily and the baby are fine. "I'll get you another pair. Is that what you're so upset about?" I ask, but I realize it's not, because there are also the scratches on her arms and the empty look in her eyes.

She shakes her head.

"I told you I saw Jake Hayes at Langley Woods," she says carefully, and again I'm thrown because I thought this was about the baby. I thought something bad had happened to the baby. I'm surprised to hear Jake's name again. To be honest, I'd forgotten all about Lily seeing him yesterday on her walk.

"Yes," I say, nodding. "Yes, you did."

She looks away, out the windows at the river. The sun shines down on it, turning the water blue. There is a gentle breeze outside. Tiny ripples form on the river's surface. Seagulls fly above it, swooping down for fish.

Lily won't look at me when she says, "I didn't tell you everything."

"Okay," I say. I set the antibiotic ointment aside. I put my hands on either side of her face and force her to look at me. "You know you can tell me anything, Lily. There's nothing you could ever say that would change the way I feel about you."

"I was just there walking, like the doctor said to do. She said gentle exercise might help with the nausea and fatigue."

"Right. I was there. I remember her saying that."

"It was such a pretty day too. I was happy that I thought of taking a walk. I was happy I had a little energy for it, because I've been so tired, you know?" I nod. I know. She's been so tired. "I parked in the lot off Riley Road. I was just going to walk a mile or two and then turn back. I didn't want to overdo it. There were other people there, you know? It wasn't crowded, but I wasn't alone either. There were a half dozen other cars in the lot. I passed people on the trail. I didn't think it was unsafe."

I swallow. What does she mean when she says *unsafe*?

My eyes go back to her arm.

"What happened, Lily?"

I see the movement of her throat when she swallows. "I saw Jake, and at first I was glad to see him. Surprised but glad. It had been so long. We started talking, and he got to telling me how it had been a bad day for him. A patient had died. He'd lost a few patients this week. I didn't know he ever lost patients. I thought he saved them all. I was wrong. It was getting to him, losing patients. He said usually it didn't, but the patients he lost this week were harder than most. Jake told me about it. It was why he was there, I think, to clear his mind, to blow off steam. We walked together for a while, just talking, catching up. And then, I don't know, he said we should go down one of those unmarked trails, into the woods. He'd seen deer on the path earlier and he wanted to see if they were still there, so he could show me. It was a mother with two spotted fawns, he said. I should have said no. But it's Jake, you know? I know Jake. It's not like he's a stranger."

Lily pauses. The anticipation builds, the suspense killing me. I know what she's going to say, or at least I think I do. I still need her to say it.

"What did he do, Lily? Did he hurt you?"

"I'm so sorry, Christian," she says, a spasm, a vibration to her voice as she says it. She isn't crying, but she is on the verge of it. Her chest is heavy when she breathes, her lungs falling into her with each breath, practically gasping.

I cup her face in my hands. I tell her, "You have nothing to be sorry for."

Lily talks faster now, her words rushing out like water from the tap. "He said he and Nina have been having trouble. He started telling me about it, about how she's been distant lately. Her mother has been sick. They found a mass, among other things. I think I told you that. It's an emotional burden. And Nina has been caring for her mother, which leaves her emotionally unavailable for Jake. Jake said that he needed affirmation and affection from Nina that she wasn't providing, that she couldn't provide because she's always with her mother. He understood—he was sympathetic, but that didn't mean that, as a man, he didn't have needs of his own. That's what he told me. I didn't know what to say. It was so personal, Christian. It was awkward. It didn't feel like he should be telling me any of it. Nina is my friend, not him. It's the kind of thing women tell their girlfriends. I said nothing back, I just listened, and then

Jake told me what a good listener I was, how he was so grateful for me. If only Nina could be more like me, he said." She pauses. "He tried to kiss me, Christian," she says, and I stand up and fly into a silent rage, not at Lily but at him. I know him. We've had dinner together, a handful of times. I've been in their home and they've been to ours. I recommended him to a friend whose wife needed surgery to have a brain tumor removed. I vouched for him, and then he makes a pass at my wife.

"That son of a bitch," I say, going to stand at the window, looking out. In my head, I think that I could kill him.

I'd always mostly liked Jake. He'd been cocky, if anything, a little overconfident, but a good guy, I thought.

"The thing is, Christian," Lily says, rising up, coming to me, reaching for my arm, "that I might have hurt him."

"What do you mean?" I ask, turning away from the window to face Lily.

"Nina said today that he didn't come home last night. She doesn't know where he is. She hasn't seen him since he left for work yesterday morning. She's worried."

"Hurt him how?"

"I pushed him away when he tried to kiss me. He didn't like that, being refused. He turned on me. *You think you're better than me? That I'm not good enough for you.* That's what he said, and then he said something like how I was sending the wrong signals and leading him on. He called me a whore. He was angry, Christian. So angry, and I was… I was scared. We were down one of those paths, far away from the main trail. There wasn't anyone else there. He grabbed me by the arms, like this," she says, fastening her tiny fists around my upper arms, and I see on hers now, when the light hits them, how there are the marks of Jake's hands, his fingerprints bruised on her skin, some made black-and-blue. Lily is upset as she describes how he pushed her and how she fell to the ground, and how she wasn't sure that he might not try and rape her. She got onto her hands and knees and tried crawling away, but he grabbed her by the ankles and pulled her back so that she fell to her face, and not just her face but her abdomen where the baby, our baby, my baby, is.

I don't breathe as she describes it for me.

"There was a rock. I could reach it. It was large, big enough that it fit my whole hand. It was partially buried and I didn't know if I was even going to be able to get it out of the dirt. I didn't think about what I was doing. I just had to get away from him, you know?" she asks, and she's crying now, and she doesn't have to tell me how she hit him with the rock.

"It's okay, it's fine," I say, running my hand the length of her hair, pulling her body into mine, comforting her. "You did the right thing, babe."

"His eyes went wide, like this," she says, showing me with hers, "like I'd surprised him. He staggered, and then fell away from me, to the ground. There was blood coming from his head."

"How much blood?" I ask.

"A decent amount."

"Was he conscious?"

"Yes. I think so. His eyes were open."

"But he fell?"

She nods. "Yes."

"How many times did you hit him? Just the once?"

"A few times, maybe," she says. "It happened so fast. It was a reflex. I felt like I had to do whatever I could to get away. For me. For the baby." She's talking so fast now. "I didn't think about what might happen to him. He fell, and then I ran as fast as I could. I kept running until I got back to the car. I didn't look back. I didn't know if he'd gotten up, if he was coming after me. Why do you think he didn't come home, Christian? Do you think I—" And then she gasps, and her hand goes to her mouth.

"No," I say decisively. She didn't kill him. I take her hands into mine, only now seeing dirt wedged beneath her finger-nails, the broken nails from where she clawed that rock out of the earth. "No. No, Lily. I think that fucking coward was too afraid to go home. There would have been a gash on his head. A bruise. Right? How would he have explained that? And he probably thought you'd tell Nina what he'd done. Did you tell Nina what happened?" I ask, and she shakes her head errati-cally, her hair falling into her eyes, and says no, that she thought about it, but that she couldn't bring herself to tell Nina because she didn't want to hurt her like that. Nina would have been devastated if she knew what Jake tried to do.

Later she shows me the marks left behind from Jake. It's not just on her arms. Her knees and a shin are skinned from crawl-ing away from him. A palm is bruised from where she caught herself when she fell, when he pushed her to the ground. The emotional wounds are worse. Lily is scared. She's haunted by what happened. She thinks he might be out there somewhere, angry, seeking revenge. I tell her no. But I don't know where Jake is, and I don't know why he didn't go home to Nina.

"You should have seen his face, Christian," she says, trem-bling. "I've never seen anyone so angry. His face was red. He was sweating. There was spit coming from his mouth. He just…" She shakes her head. There's fear in her eyes. She's re-living it.

"Lily, stop," I say gently, but she keeps talking.

"I don't know, Christian. He just snapped."

Jake snapped. That's one way to put it. We've all been there before. We've all had those moments where we freak out, where we act aggressively, in a way that feels beyond our control. It's a rage response. Once I cursed out some twenty-year-old kid on the side of the road who rear-ended me. I almost broke a computer because the page was loading too slowly and I didn't have the patience to wait. In high school, I punched my fist through wired glass after missing a shot that would have won us the conference basketball game. We lost the game. I needed stitches. I still have a scar. But Jake Hayes took it too far.

As night falls, Lily moves away from the wall of windows that face the river, telling me she feels exposed in our home. I dim the lights, but short of turning them off, we're still visible from the outside. There is a vaulted ceiling in the family room, with two floors of windows. We couldn't figure out how to cover them when we moved in, so we didn't. We left them bare. We preferred the undisrupted view at the time: the river, the trees.

But now I wonder if it's possible that Jake is out there somewhere, watching her, watching us.

There are really only two options: that Jake didn't go home last night because of Nina and because he knew he could get into serious trouble, maybe jail time, for what he'd done, if Lily pressed charges.

Or that Lily hurt him so much that he couldn't go home.

"Should we call the police?" Lily asks.

"Why?" I ask. I don't mean it to be hostile. I'm wondering if she wants to call the police to press charges, or if she wants to call the police and confess to something she did. It's not a silly question. I'd been wondering it too, but I never came to a decision. I want Lily to call the police, to press charges. I want Jake to pay for what he did, or for what he tried to do, for his intentions.

But if Lily hurt him or worse, if she left him there bleeding, if she waited twenty-four hours to report what happened, then, on some level, she's also in the wrong.

"Let's not," I tell her. "Not yet."

"I should text Nina," she says.

"Why?"

"To see if he came home. To see if she's okay." I think it through. She's probably right, because that's what she would do if Jake was missing and she had nothing to do with it. She would check on her friend.

I go through the clothes in the hamper after she's in bed. I find what Lily was wearing yesterday, buried beneath other things. The pants are black, but the shirt is white. It has dirt on it and debris like from leaves. One of the buttons is missing, a white thread hanging loose. All of that enrages me.

But the thing that worries me most is how the right cuff is wet with blood.

NINA

I have to take my mother to the ophthalmologist after work. She has macular degeneration. She's losing her central vision, which is what she needs for things like to read and to drive. She's only sixty-two. She's not old. She has trouble recognizing people's faces. That's how we knew there was a serious problem, though I thought at first that it was something like Alzheimer's, so when the diagnosis came in, I was somewhat relieved. She can't even to go the grocery store anymore without help, because she can't see well enough to get there or to find the items she needs. The thing that's totally infuriating is how capable and sharp she is despite the declining vision. She has her wits about her still. It's not fair. Until recently she was completely independent and now she relies on me for everything. It feels sometimes like that changed overnight. She has the wet form of macular degeneration, which is maybe worse. There is blood leaking into the retina. She receives anti-VEGF injections in the eye to stop or slow the progression; it's horrible to watch. It makes me never want to get old, to want to die young. My mother has her peripheral vision still. It's not that she's blind. She doesn't run into things. She can somewhat see. It's that, from the way she describes it, there is a blind spot in the center of her field of vision, like someone took a crayon and scribbled over it.

I drive my mother home after her appointment. I walk her into her house. "Why don't you stay for dinner?" she asks.

"I can't. Sorry. Not tonight, Mom."

"Why not? It's not like Jake will be home," she says, because Jake is at work and because my mother knows how Jake gets when I spend too much time with her. Still, I say no again, that I can't, because I'm anxious to get home and see if there is any sign that Jake has been there. I don't tell my mother this. She doesn't know about Jake's and my fight and I won't tell her about it because ultimately what we were fighting about was her.

"I have too many papers to grade," I say instead, and my mother says okay, but she looks sad, as she always does, when I go. I hate leaving her.

I don't get back to my house until close to six. When I do, there's no sign that Jake has been home. None of his clothes are obviously missing, and his toiletries look untouched. It comes as a punch to the gut. I stand in the bathroom doorway, holding on to the doorframe, not sure what to do with myself. It's getting darker outside. The sun is going down. I can't stand the idea of another night in this house alone, and wonder how long Jake plans to be mad at me.

I'm used to coming home and Jake not being here. This is nothing new. I'm used to being alone, knowing that eventually Jake always comes home. I've never minded being alone before, especially after work, because it's my me-time, my time to decompress from the day.

But now, standing in the empty house, knowing Jake might not come home all night, I feel more alone and lonely than ever. The house feels suddenly vacant. It's too large of a house for us because one day, Jake and I think we want kids, though I'm getting older and time is running out. We're not there yet, because of Jake's work schedule. The last thing he wants, he's said, is to be an absentee father, like his had been. He wouldn't even entertain the idea of kids when he was doing his residency. But now that that's through, he's started to ponder it, or at least indulge me when I bring it up. We have three extra bedrooms in the house. I don't know that I need to fill them all with kids, but at least one would be nice, to experience being a mother once in my life.

I turn on the TV to delude myself into thinking I'm not alone. The sound of voices brings comfort.

I find my laptop. At some point during the day, I figured out that if I check the credit card statement online, I'll be able to see where Jake spent the night. I don't know what I'll do with this information. I don't think I would go to the hotel and make him talk to me. That might make things worse. Jake doesn't do anything Jake doesn't want to do, but it will be good to know where he is.

I sit down at the kitchen table. I go to the bank's website and log in, scrolling through the most recent purchases. I'm expecting to see some upscale hotel because Jake would die before sleeping at a Holiday Inn. But, to my surprise, there are no recent hotel stays. I try telling myself there is only a delay in posting, but I don't think so because I think what usually happens with hotels is that they post pending charges the minute you check in, and then, later, refund that incidentals deposit if you don't spend it.

Even more worrisome is that there are no charges in the last thirty-six hours at all, other than my own. There is a charge for a Starbucks near Jake's office from early Monday morning but, after that, it's as if Jake has gone off the grid and I wonder if it's deliberate.

I navigate to the checking account to see if Jake took out cash. Maybe he's using cash so that I can't track him. Can you even pay for a hotel with cash?

I feel sick inside at the growing possibility that Jake is trying to stay hidden. He doesn't want me to find him. He doesn't want to fix our marriage.

What if Jake has left me for good?

There are no recent withdrawals from the checking account. How can Jake be getting by without the use of cash or credit cards? How is he paying for things?

I'm relieved to see our accounts intact, that Jake hasn't transferred our money to some offshore account to spite me. He doesn't hate me that much. I earn a teacher's salary. He is a neurosurgeon. It's no secret that Jake is the breadwinner in our marriage. I feel lucky for it, that I can do what I love for a living and still never have to worry about money. I grew up with a single mother who worked the night shift as an LPN. We didn't have much. Sometimes even the cost of gas was too much to afford. I started working when I was fifteen, to be able to contribute to the cost of groceries, the mortgage and utilities. Since getting married to Jake, I've gotten used to being able to buy things without having to think twice about the price. I don't know that I could go back to the lifestyle I grew up in, not that I would ever have to because I have Jake. And because, even if, God forbid, he left me, we'd split everything down the middle.

My cell phone rings. I practically fly out of my chair at the sound. It's the first time in two days that it's rung and, after all this time of begging and pleading with it to ring, it finally is.

Thank God. Jake has come to his senses. He's ready to talk it out. He's forgiven me.

I reach for my phone, lying facedown on the table. I flip it over and look at the name on the display, expecting it to say Jake. My heart sinks. It's not Jake. It's our friend Damien.

I answer the call, though my first instinct is not to answer, but to leave the phone free for if Jake calls. But maybe Damien knows something that I don't. If Jake would sleep on anyone's sofa, it's Damien's.

"Hi, Damien," I say.

"Hey, Nina. I'm sorry to bother you," he says.

"You're no bother," I tell him. "You're never a bother. How's Anna?" I move from the kitchen table to the butler's pantry for the wine fridge. I pull out a chilled bottle of white and pour myself a generous glass, lifting it to my mouth without putting the bottle away. My nerves are frayed. I balance the phone on my shoulder, bringing both the open bottle and the glass back to the table with me.

Damien's excitement is palpable. "She's pregnant!" he announces, and I'm so happy for Damien and Anna because they've been trying to get pregnant for years. It wasn't happening. It was one failed attempt after another. They went through fertility drugs, and then artificial insemination. Damien and Anna were always very candid with Jake and me about the process and the struggle, mainly, I think, because Jake is a doctor and because we're their only friends without kids. It was easier to talk to us about it than with other friends. Jake and I are at that point in our lives where almost everyone we know has or is having kids, except us.

The last I heard, Damien and Anna were trying in vitro, which is obscenely expensive. They don't have the income for it. The cost alone was almost enough to make them give up. They had agreed they would try one time, but that they didn't have the savings to go for it more than once.

"That's amazing!" I say. "I'm so happy for you both." I am happy for them, so happy, though I have to force the enthusiasm into my voice because I'm not in a happy place myself.

"You want to hear the best news?"

"What could be better than that?" I ask.

"Twins. It's twins, Nina."

I feel so happy for them. Anna is amazing, the kind of woman who radiates kindness and warmth. "Anna will make the best mom," I tell him. "She was born to be a mother. How far along is she?"

"Thirteen weeks. It was mum's the word until after her first trimester, but now I'm stopping strangers on the street to tell them."

I smile. I wouldn't put it past him.

"Listen," he says. "Is everything okay with Jake?"

I have to catch my breath. "Why?" I ask.

"I've been trying to get a hold of him since Monday morning, but he hasn't returned my texts. It's not like him." Damien waits as if I should say something, but I'm at a loss for words. "Anyway," he says in response to my silence, "I'm just wondering if he's there and, if so, if you could put him on for me? It will only take a second."

"Jake isn't here," I say, slightly stunned that Jake wouldn't answer Damien's texts either.

"No?" he asks.

"No. He's not. He's at work," I say because I don't know what else to say. It's not a lie. It's seven now. It's a surgery day. Jake is at work. It's crossed my mind to go to the hospital and make him talk to me, but I worried that would make things worse. When Jake is ready to talk, he'll come to me.

"Of course he is. Could you tell him I called? Could you ask him to call me back?" Damien says that he wants to tell Jake the good news, about his and Anna's babies. Damien and Jake are incredibly close. They went to college together. They were in the same fraternity. They've been friends for two decades. Damien was Jake's best man at our wedding, and Jake was the best man at theirs. He gave the the most hilarious speech. He had people doubled over, laughing. I still remember it, though sometimes that feels like a lifetime ago, like an entirely different Jake, one who was more happy and carefree. Still, I can't understand why Jake wouldn't answer Damien's calls or texts when it's me he's mad at.

"Yes, of course I will," I say, short of breath because of how fast my heart is beating. "He's just been so busy at work," I say, feeling like I need to make excuses for Jake's behavior. I reach for my glass and take another long sip, and then reach for the bottle and top off the glass.

Damien and I say our goodbyes. I promise again to tell Jake to call him. Easier said than done.

I can't tell Jake anything when he won't speak to me.

CHRISTIAN

In the middle of the night, I shake Lily awake.

"Hmm?" she asks, half-conscious.

"What'd you do with the rock?"

I've spent the night lying awake, wondering where it is and if it has blood on it like Lily's sleeve, and if so, if it has Lily's fingerprints on it too.

She rolls over onto her back. My question forces her eyes open. I see the whites of them in the darkness. She sleeps in my old shirts at night, ones she took out of a Goodwill bag and laid claim to. This one is flannel. It's soft beneath my hand. The shirts are long because I'm that much taller than Lily, who is five foot three, relatively petite. They hang down to her upper thigh, meaning her legs are bare. I press my leg against hers, feeling her skin next to mine. Under the weight of the quilt, she gives off heat.

"I dropped it, I think," she says, her voice slow with sleep.

"Would you remember where?"

"I don't know."

I say okay. I wait until Lily's breath slows and evens out as she falls back to sleep. I slip quietly from bed, careful not to wake her. I sort through the hamper in the closet for the clothes Lily wore yesterday: the white shirt mostly, but also the pants, her underpants, a pair of socks. I carry the clothes downstairs, and leave them in a plastic bag, knotted tightly, by the garage door.

I'll have to get rid of them.

Early in the morning, I convince Lily to take the day off work. I've already called my own boss and told her I wouldn't be there. A sub can give Lily's math test. The kids can live without her for a day. I listen as she calls in sick, saying that she must have eaten something that didn't sit well; her stomach is bothering her. Lily rarely, if ever, misses work. Whoever is on the other end of the line is understanding, sympathetic even. She can't use the pregnancy as an excuse because no one knows we're pregnant.

Lily says that she slept better last night. I hardly slept. Still, she wears a bemused expression on her face, as if lost in thought, and I can only imagine what she's thinking about and if she's reliving the moment Jake Hayes pushed her to the ground.

I pour myself a cup of coffee. I sit and watch from over my mug as Lily forces down a piece of dry toast. The key to staving off morning sickness, she's told me before, is to eat. Hunger is what makes it worse. I watch Lily from across the kitchen table. Even in this state, she's a sight for sore eyes. She has a round face and full cheeks, with features that are soft, nothing overly angular or sharp though her eyes are large. Her skin is like satin; I imagine it staying that way even when she's sixty or seventy and we're growing old and gray together.

"What?" she asks, looking up from her toast as she catches me staring at her.

I lower my mug to the table. "If you did anything to him, it was only to protect yourself."

I say it to soothe her, to quiet the voices in her head.

I make it worse. I shouldn't have said anything.

"Do you think I killed him?" she asks, her eyes widening, and I think of the blood on her shirtsleeve, the shirt in the bag by the door, trying to quantify it, to work out how much blood it really was, and if it only looked worse than it was. I minimize it, telling myself if Lily broke his nose when she hit him, that would explain the large amount of blood. Broken noses have a tendency to bleed a lot. And they're not fatal.

"I'm just saying you shouldn't feel guilty for anything you did or didn't do. He put you in a difficult situation. He left you no choice but to fight back. You know that, don't you?"

Her conscience deceives her.

"I keep thinking," she says, "that if I had just screamed, someone might have heard me. If not, the sound of it alone might have scared him off." She shakes her head, her eyes getting wet, the toast in her hand shaking so that she sets it down before she drops it. "I don't think I screamed, Christian. I keep going over it again and again, trying to remember. I don't think I said anything. Why didn't I just scream?"

"Because you defended yourself, Lily. Which is better than screaming. You didn't let yourself become a victim."

She stares at me, saying nothing. She nods, but she doesn't believe me.

I pack things in the trunk before we go: a shovel, gloves, garbage bags, just in case. Lily doesn't notice.

As the sun rises, we leave the house and drive to the forest preserve just as traffic is starting to back up on the roads and expressway.

"Why did you want to come here?" Lily asks.

"I want you to show me where it happened."

"Why?" she asks.

"I want to see it with my own eyes."

What I don't tell Lily is that I need to find the bloody rock, the thing that puts her here. I also wouldn't mind finding her missing earring because I think it must have come out when she was trying to get away from Jake. I want to get rid of any evidence that she was here.

"What if he's here?" she asks, scared.

"He won't be," I say. She doesn't buy it. We both know that I don't know. But if he is here, then he's not alive or he's not in good condition, and then there is nothing he can do to hurt her. Either way, she's safe. I grab her by the hand and say, "Listen. That's a lie. I don't know if he will be here or not, but either way we'll know, okay? Not knowing is the hardest part."

Lily's eyes hold mine for a long time, trying to decide if I mean it this time.

I park in the lot off Riley. We get out of the car, moving like prisoners on a death march. We don't say much. What we say is out of necessity, things like "This way" and "Watch your step." We're not alone at the forest preserve. There are other people here, but it's 7:00 a.m. and the path is far from crowded. This early in the morning, the people here are runners and bikers. They're a different breed, almost aloof and detached as they slip on headphones and take off down the trail alone, lost in worlds of their own.

Lily and I move down the path at our own pace. We hang back, letting everyone else go first. We're in no hurry. We don't want to be here. It's only of necessity that we are. We hold hands as we retrace Lily's steps from the other day. We kick up pebbles as we walk, moving to the right as a biker comes soaring by, passing us on the left. The man rises to stand on the bike pedals as he passes, his calves like steel. Lily is jumpy. She doesn't hear him approach. Only I do because he gives no warning. Lily doesn't know he's there until he's directly beside her, and then she falls nervously back, her hand pulling from mine and going to her heart. "It's okay," I say. "It's just a bike." The biker doesn't notice Lily's reaction. He says nothing to us as he flies past, disappearing over a flat, wooden bridge and around a bend in the trees. I take Lily by the hand and we keep walking, watching the biker until we can't see him anymore.

"Do you know where you were when you met up with Jake?" I ask Lily, my voice low in volume, looking down at the soft sunlight on her face. The sun is low, still rising. It's beneath the treetops so that the light it gives off is subdued and serene. The trees are pretty this time of year, their color just barely starting to turn. Everything about this is serene except for the reason we're here.

Lily looks around. She's quiet, contemplative, trying to decide. The problem is that everything looks the exact same.

Lily knows this place well. If she can't pin down an exact spot, no one can. The last marathon she ran, she trained here. That summer, it was her home away from home. Sometimes I came and ran with her, though I couldn't keep up and I couldn't run as far as she could. Inevitably, we got separated, which is how I know it's almost impossible to get lost if you stay on the trail, which is a loop. Eventually you come back to where you started. Lily knows this trail like the back of her hand, and yet, except for the obvious landmarks—where it crosses the street, the part of it that overlooks the creek, or where it runs parallel to train tracks—it's indistinguishable. You can't tell one tree from the next.

"Maybe up here somewhere. It looked something like that," Lily says. She points at an unmarked trail sitting just off the main trail, where the trees part ways and a small beaten path leads into the woods, disappearing. There are a vast number of unmarked trails that crisscross the forest preserve. I remember seeing them before. They're the kind of thing that don't get much, if any, foot traffic. They're not on the map and they don't always connect to any of the main trails. I know with 100 percent certainty that, if it wasn't for Jake, Lily would never have stepped foot on one. She's much more shrewd than that. She has good judgment. She would have stayed on the main trail, where there are people and where she wouldn't get lost. But Jake is a friend and she didn't have any reason to believe he couldn't be trusted. He led her to believe there was something worth seeing down the more remote path. He took advantage of this, of her, of her trust in him. He led her away somewhere he knew he wouldn't be seen.

"Do you think this is the path you took?" I ask gently.

"Maybe," she says. Lily takes a closer look, trying to decide. I know she's trying. She shakes her head, disappointed in herself. "It all looks the same, Christian," she says.

"I know. It all looks the same to me too. Would you remember if we walked a little ways in?" I ask. From here, the trail aggressively thins so that only one person can pass through at a time.

"Maybe," she says, but I can sense her hesitation. It's darker down the trail, chilling in light of what's happened. "I could try."

"You sure?" I ask, and she nods. I don't want to make her do anything she doesn't want to do.

"I'll be right behind you," I say. I hold the tree branches back with a hand and let Lily go first. We have to walk single file. I don't know that I want Lily to go first because I'm afraid of what we'll find. I don't want her to see something she can't handle seeing. I want to see it first, so I can prepare her and protect her from it. But I also don't want to lose her if she's the one following behind.

The terrain is uneven. Lily has to use her hands to clear the brush as she walks. "I don't remember it being this wooded," she says.

"Maybe this isn't the right path."

"I don't know. Jake went first and I followed. Maybe that's

why I don't remember. He was blocking my view of it." Lily followed him blindly into the woods. Jake is a big guy, something like six foot one and two hundred and ten pounds. His body would have filled the path.

He would have easily overpowered Lily.

"You want to go a little further?"

"Maybe," she says. "Just a little."

Lily walks awhile further. After some time, she stops walking and decides, "I don't think this is it."

"No?" I ask. "It still doesn't look familiar?"

"I just remember that after a while, there was a clearing in the trees. I don't see it."

"Could the clearing be further down?"

"I don't remember going this far."

"Okay," I say.

"I'm sorry."

"There's nothing to be sorry for, babe. Let's go back. We'll try another path. We'll keep looking. It's fine."

What are we looking for exactly? I don't know. A body, blood, the bloody rock, or maybe nothing more than peace of mind.

I hang back and let Lily pass in front of me. We follow the footpath back to the main trail. From there, we walk further along the trail until we come to another one of these unmarked paths about a quarter mile down.

"What about this one?" I ask.

"Maybe." Again it's hard to tell. This one looks no different from the last. But we try. Same as last time, I let Lily go first and I follow behind. This path is different in that it isn't narrow for long. A hundred feet into the trail, it widens so that Lily and I can walk side by side. It's better this way. I like having her by my side.

Lily is quiet, but there's a change in the way she walks, more mindful, more alert. "You recognize something," I say. It isn't a question.

"Yeah," she says. "I do."

"Do you think this is where you were?" I ask. She never has a chance to tell me.

"My God," she says and she stops.

About ten feet away, the grass is discolored. The discoloration is clearly blood. The redness of it is a disturbing divergence from the greenish-brown grass. There looks to be a large amount of it, enough that I swear under my breath. A small smear heads deeper into the woods, though the blood in the grass, like the blood on Lily's shirt, is still hard to quantify. It may just look like more than I think. Maybe. It's possible.

Lily and I see the blood at practically the same time, Lily just a millisecond before me. Our feet come to rest a few meters before it. We say nothing at first. We stare down at the blood, Lily's hand rising to her mouth like she might puke. "You can't be sick, Lily," I say, offering her water, because vomit contains DNA. The last thing we want to do is leave any more evidence that she was here.

She takes a tentative sip of the water, her hand shaking on the bottle. I help guide it.

"Are you okay?" I ask, watching as she struggles to swallow.

She nods. "It was here," she says, as if that much isn't obvious. She takes another sip of water and this one goes down easier. She can't bring her eyes back to look at the blood. "I remember. I remember this clearing. This is it." The clearing is still thick with trees, but there's a small break in them. Still, the trees stop the sun from getting in. The sunlight on the ground is mottled at best, patchy through the treetops. The land here is more woodchips and dirt than the soft bed of grass I'd imagined when Lily described how Jake pushed her to the ground and how she fell on her hands and knees. No wonder her knees were so torn up.

"The deer, he said, were in there," Lily says, crouching down and pointing to a place where the trees stand a little further apart and you can see inside, into the forest, like through a peephole. I come to stand beside her. I crouch down like her, following the direction of her finger.

"Did you see them?" I ask, and Lily shakes her head, sad, because we both know there were never any deer here.

"He got close to me," she says, "like this," pressing the side of her body into mine. "He wrapped his arm around my waist, like this." Lily's hand wraps around me from behind, her cold fingers coming up under the hem of my shirt, touching skin, stroking me somewhere just above the hip. My whole body tenses, not because my wife is touching me, but because some man touched my wife like this.

Lily is talking fast now, like she does when she's scared. "I could feel my pulse in my neck, Christian. I wanted him to get his hand off me. I wanted to go back, to the main trail, but I didn't know what to say, how to make that happen. He kept pretending he was looking for the deer, and I thought that if I just played along, he'd eventually give up on looking for the deer, and then we could go back."

A noise from deep in the woods startles us. Lily flinches. She jerks, backing away from the trees, grabbing onto my arm to feel protected. Her fingernails leave little crescent moons in my skin.

I press a finger to my lips to keep her quiet. I wiggle my arm free, and then I step closer to the woods, gazing deeper inside, acutely aware that, though we found blood, we found no body.

The trees are the kind with white trunks and bark that flakes off. They stand in a line like soldiers. The trunks are even, equidistant from one another like a man's legs. There is no end to the number of trees. I stare into them so long that they become an optical illusion. It becomes almost impossible to tell if the trees are moving, if they're coming closer, or if they're rooted to the earth.

The noise—like the rustle of leaves, the crackle of footsteps—gets closer.

Lily whimpers. The sound of it is a scared puppy.

The leaves are still thick on the trees. The trees themselves are thick, wide enough for a person to hide behind. It's dark and shadowy deep in the woods. I have no idea how far we've walked away from the main trail. Maybe a quarter mile. Our car is even further. I think of Lily tearing away from this place and how desperate and terrified she must have felt running back through these woods alone and away from Jake.

I part the boughs of the trees with my hands. I take a step deeper into the woods. Branches reach out, scratching at my arms. The noise gets closer and closer until it's upon us, and yet I still can't see what it is.

"Christian," Lily moans.

And then, suddenly, a chipmunk beetles out from the trees. It crosses between us. I jerk back and almost step on it. "Shit," I say, exhaling loudly. Lily's hand is pressed to her mouth, holding back a scream. It takes a second to catch my breath. I let go of the trees and fall back. "Fuck. It's okay," I say to Lily. She's gone white. I go to her. I wrap my arms around her and pull her into me, feeling the beating of her heart against my chest. "It's nothing, just a stupid chipmunk."

What did we think was going to happen?

"Christian?" Lily asks when she catches her breath.

"What?"

"Where do you think he is?" she asks.

I release her so that I can see her face. "Honestly? I think he left. I think he's fine."

"But the blood," she says.

"It's not that much. It's deceptive. It looks like more than there is. You've donated blood before," I remind her. "They fill a whole bag with it. You can lose a lot of blood and still survive."

I try to decide if the blood on the ground was more than a blood bag's worth. I don't honestly know.

I spew bullshit. I have no idea if anything I'm saying is true.

"What should we do about it?" Lily asks about the blood on the ground. I take what's left of my water bottle and pour it over the splotch, weakening it, watering it down. Lily and I gather leaves and lay them on the ground, hiding what's left of the blood. When we're done, it's not overly noticeable.

On the way back to the trail, I say, "Let's look for the rock. We should try and find it just in case."

Lily catches me in my lie. She stops suddenly, and turns to face me. "In case he's dead?" she asks point-blank. "You just said he was fine, Christian." Lily isn't dumb and she's much stronger than she looks. "In case I killed him?"

The answer is yes. She might have killed him. Or he might have left, he might be fine, just like I said. Absent a body, I don't know.

Let's be clear: I don't want to find a body here.

But not knowing where he is is so much worse.

As it turns out, looking for a rock or an earring in a forest preserve is no different than a needle in a haystack. We never find either of them.

"What do we do now?" Lily asks as we walk empty-handed back to the car.

"I was thinking that he would have had to drive here from his house, right? Did you see his car in the parking lot when we got here?" I ask, because if not, then we'll know he left, that, despite Lily hitting him, he was well enough to drive.

"I don't think so," Lily says. "But I wasn't looking for it."

We backtrack to the parking lot to look for Jake's car. I take Lily by the hand as we walk. She's gone quiet and I wonder if she's thinking of the blood in the grass like I am, about how viscous it was, and about how there was more of it than I would have expected for a man who got up and walked away, despite what I said.

Jake drives a BMW 7 series. They start at close to a hundred grand, though some are more like a hundred and fifty grand. I know what kind of car he drives because the last time we met for dinner, months ago, the car was new and he was totally stoked about it. It was all he could talk about: how quickly it accelerated and how well it handled. After we ate, Jake and I left the ladies at the restaurant, and he took me for a drive, to show it off, to prove how fast it could go. Jake wanted me to envy his car and, by association, him. It hadn't bothered me at the time.

Lily and I had laughed about it later, how he couldn't shut up about that damn car.

Would you love me more if I was rich like him? I remember asking Lily in jest. I didn't mean it. I knew Lily loved me regardless of how much money we had or didn't have in the bank. Lily and I have never been rich, but we do just fine. Our house was way out of our price range when we bought it, but we made the decision to buy it anyway because, for the price and for the land it was on, with the size of the property and the river views, it felt absurd not to. We knew we'd grow into it. We both knew the next few years after buying the house would look different, and they have. But we felt okay with that because the house was an investment and eventually, our decision to buy it will prove fruitful. It just means that I drive a Honda for now and, unlike Jake, there are no BMWs in my immediate future.

Only now, all these months later, in light of what's happened, does Jake rubbing his car in my face get under my skin.

When we get back, there are maybe ten cars in the parking lot, none of which is Jake's. I feel relieved because it's better, of course, if his car isn't here. It means that Jake left on his own, that Jake is fine, that Lily didn't kill him.

In which case, I might.

"He's not here," I say. "He left."

I look at Lily. I expect for her to look relieved, but she doesn't. She's quiet.

Lily's holding something back.

"What is it?" I ask.

"There is another lot," she says, "off Feeney." She knows this place better than me.

Lily and I get back in my car. We say nothing as we take the frontage road to Feeney Avenue, where we look for the second parking lot just off Newcomb Road.

The parking lot is round. Slowly, I make my way around it, not seeing Jake's car. "He's not here either," Lily says, finally warming up to the idea that Jake Hayes is actually fine. "His car isn't here."

I gaze over at Lily in the passenger's seat. "No," I say, shaking my head, feeling a smile come on. "It isn't."

"Thank God," she says, exhaling heavily, relaxing back into her seat. "Where do you think he went if he didn't go home?"

"I don't know. Maybe he's crashing on a friend's couch while his head and ego heal." What I said that first night is right. Jake couldn't have gone home with a gash on his head. How would he have explained that to Nina? He would have been worried, too, that Lily would have told Nina what he'd done or tried to do.

Lily's relief is palpable. The very real possibility that she might have killed him, no matter how justified it was, weighed heavily on her. Lily never would have been the same if she'd taken a man's life. She never would have forgiven herself.

I leave the parking lot. I go to pull back out onto the street. It's as I'm about to accelerate onto Newcomb, that I see it.

"Fuck," I exhale, seeing Jake's car before Lily does. It's parked on the street, which is for overflow parking. It's also for people who come to the forest preserve early, before it opens. When Langley Woods is closed, barricades stop people from pulling into the lot, but that doesn't deter them from using the trails. There is nothing that says you can't park in the street.

"What?" Lily asks.

"It's there," I say.

She leans forward, looking out the window, but she doesn't know what she's looking for. "What's there?"

"His car." I point at it.

Jake's BMW isn't alone on the street. Far from it. There are at least eight other cars there.

It takes a second for the realization to hit Lily, and then her hand goes to her mouth and she falls back in the seat, quiet, deathly still.

"It doesn't mean anything, Lily," I say, but it does, because Jake never would have spent the night—two nights now—at the forest preserve by choice. I bring my hand to her thigh. It's been cold these last few nights. The temperatures get down to about fifty or fifty-five degrees at night, but it doesn't have to freeze for a person to become hypothermic. If Jake was bleeding, if he'd lost a significant amount of blood, if he was wet or if it was windy outside, it would have made him more susceptible to hypothermia.

I pull out onto Newcomb and pass by Jake's car on the way back to the expressway.

"What are you doing?" Lily asks.

I tell her, "Going home."

"Why? No."

"What are we supposed to do here?"

"We have to look for him," she says. "We can't just leave him here."

Yes, I think, *we can*.

It isn't that I don't want to help. But if Jake Hayes is here, then he's beyond helping. This place is huge and he or his body could be anywhere. We already know he wasn't following the main trail. He'd gone off it, with Lily.

There are plenty of places to hide, plenty of places to go to die.

If he's here, we'll never find him.

And yes, there is a small part of me that says he did this to himself. That he had it coming to him. That none of this would have happened if he hadn't done what he did.

"Please, Christian," Lily begs. "Please can we go back and look for him?"

I do it for Lily and maybe to assuage my own guilt. I make a U-turn, go back to the parking lot and park. Together Lily and I walk the ten miles of trails. It takes hours. When we come to a bench, I make her sit down and catch her breath and rest. She shouldn't be exerting this much energy, and again I worry about the baby. I worry that this will be the thing that makes her miscarry. If that happens, I will kill Jake Hayes myself if he isn't already dead.

We look for any sign of Jake, so that later, when we leave solemn, empty-handed and alone, we can at least say that we tried.

NINA

I wake up Thursday morning groggy and with a headache.
I shower and even as I step out of the shower, I feel warm,
sweaty, feverish. I'm not myself because I drank too much last
night and because, despite a bottle of wine, despite being unconscious for six hours, it didn't translate to a good night's sleep.
I'm not rested. I feel like shit. I don't bother with breakfast because my stomach is off and my nerves are completely frayed.
I run through a drive-through on the way into work to get
coffee because in my fraught state, I left mine at home, and I
won't get through the day without caffeine.

Where is Jake?

It's all I can think about. Where the hell is Jake?

Another day and night have passed and still he isn't home.
I tried calling him. Texting. The calls go to voice mail. The
phone doesn't even ring. Around midnight, drunk, I left another message for him, which must be something like the fifth

or the sixth voice mail I've left for him now. The message must have been completely incoherent too. I don't know what I said exactly. I don't know why I keep calling, but, more importantly, I don't know why he won't call me back. The only text I received all night came from my friend Lily, asking if I was okay and if Jake was home yet. No and no, I'd typed back with the sad face emoji, and she replied,

I'm so sorry. I'm thinking about you, Nina. Please let me know if there is anything you need or anything I can do. Anything at all. xo

I drive to school. I just happen to pull in at the same time as Ryan Schroeder, the teacher whose classroom is next door to mine. Years ago, Ryan and I were first-year teachers together. We've come up through the ranks together, getting tenure at the same time. I follow him around the lot, to where we usually park. Ryan pulls in first and I slide into the spot next to him. He steps out of his car, waiting on the curb for me to gather my things and get out. I wave, but he can't wave back because he's holding two coffees.

"Good morning," he says as I slip out of the car, setting my coffee on top to reach into the back seat for my bag. I hoist my bag over my shoulder and slam the door.

"Good morning," I reply. I grab my coffee from the top of the car and together we turn and walk toward the building. The students have begun to arrive en masse. At this time of day, it's mostly the bus riders and the kids that get dropped off by their parents. The line of parents dropping off wraps around the building, spilling out onto the street, creating a bottleneck in traffic. I always feel badly for cars that get caught up in the traffic by mistake. It's mayhem, though after school is even worse. "Rough night?" I ask, because of his two coffees.

"Only one is mine. The other is for Pam," he says. Pam is the school secretary and a godsend.

"Sucking up again, I see," I tease, but then I sober and say, "No, really. That's sweet of you, Ryan."

"She does so much for me, it's the least I can do. You look tired," he says, looking sideways at me. Ryan is tall and built like a basketball player. He coaches the boys' basketball team and is the kind of teacher that everyone likes and yet who commands respect.

"I am. I didn't sleep well," I say, longing for a caffeine drip. I don't know that this one cup of coffee is going to do the trick and am envious of the two in Ryan's hands. "And," I admit sheepishly, looking up at him, "I may have drunk an entire bottle of wine before bed. My head kills."

"Ouch. Fun night?"

"I've had better."

Ryan gets serious. "I've been meaning to ask, how has your mother been doing? I haven't heard you mention her in a while."

"The same. No worse but no better either. We went to the ophthalmologist the other afternoon and she has a biopsy coming up, on that mass the doctor found in her breast. She's so worried about it," I say, letting him think the bottle of wine was on account of my mother's health.

"I bet. That's understandable. You must be worried too."

"I am. Very. But once we know what we're dealing with, we can figure out how to treat it."

"She's lucky to have you," he says. "But this is a lot for you to be dealing with on your own. You don't have siblings? Anyone to share the burden?"

"No, it's just me. My dad left us when I was six and my mother raised me alone. Growing up, it was only the two of us. We're close as a result." Ryan and I approach the building. As we do, he stacks one coffee on top of the other to reach out and pull the door open for me. It's awkward and I'm sure the coffee will spill. "Let me—" I start to say, reaching out for the door myself, but he says, "Nope. I've got it." He beats me to it.

"Though I don't know that I'd call taking care of my mother a burden," I say as he pulls open the door and I make myself as small as possible to squeeze past. "I'm happy to do this for her, but it is hard. It's time-consuming and emotionally draining. I just worry about her so much, all the time. Thank you," I say, about him holding the door open for me, as a call comes through on my phone. The sound of my phone ringing sets me off again. My heart starts beating faster, and I think again that it could be Jake, that Jake has finally come to his senses and is ready to talk, to forgive me. I drop back. Ryan keeps going, bringing Pam's coffee to her in the office so that he doesn't see at first that I've fallen behind. I reach into my bag for my phone. Ryan turns and notices he's alone and he tries waiting up for me, so we can finish our conversation. "Go on without me," I call out. "I'll catch up with you later."

I find my phone. I look at the display and deflate. It's not Jake. It's not anyone I know. The air collapses out of my lungs like from a balloon.

Before I even answer the call though, I have a foreboding feeling, a sense of doom. Something bad is about to happen but I don't know what. It's not seven in the morning. It's far too early for someone to be calling with anything other than bad news. Even robocalls and telemarketers don't call this early. I step back outside the building for privacy, scooting past kids in the door, going the opposite way of traffic like fish swimming upstream. I clear my throat and answer the call.

A woman's voice comes at me through the speaker. "Hello," she says. "Can I speak to Mrs. Hayes please?"

"This is she."

"Mrs. Hayes," she says. She says that she is the chief surgeon at the hospital where Jake works, and my heart accelerates quickly. Why is the chief surgeon at Jake's hospital calling?

"Dr. Hayes has you listed as an emergency contact," she says, and with that, my whole body goes numb. I lose feeling in my legs and hands.

Emergency contact.

Oh my God, he's dead, is all I can think. Jake is dead.

I lean against the exterior brick of the building, letting it support me. A bus pulls up to the curb. Its engine is loud. I have to press a finger into my ear to hear this woman's voice over the noise. I watch as kids climb out of the bus, down the steps. Half-asleep students walk like zombies past me and into the building.

"Are you there, Mrs. Hayes?" the woman asks.

"Yes," I say, my voice weak.

"Mrs. Hayes, we're concerned about Dr. Hayes. He hasn't shown up for his surgeries in a couple days, and his office staff reported that he didn't make it into the office for his afternoon appointments on Monday. His staff has tried to contact him, but hasn't been successful. Is everything alright at home?" she asks and, for the first time I realize that not only has Jake not been coming home to me at night, but he hasn't been going into work. He hasn't returned my calls, but he hasn't returned the hospital's calls either.

Jake hasn't just left me.

Something has happened to Jake.

"Jake hasn't been coming home either. I thought…" I say, but then I let my voice drift off because I don't want to say more than I need to say. This woman is a colleague of Jake's, but she's a stranger to me. I recognize her name, Dr. Morris. I recognize the names of most of the people Jake works with because he talks about them at home, but that doesn't mean I know them. She doesn't need to know about the fight I had with Jake. "Jake is missing," I breathe, and as I say it, it has such a different implication than that Jake left me or that Jake didn't come home.

Jake is missing.

Oh my God. Jake is missing.

As soon as I hang up with the chief surgeon, I go straight toward my car in the parking lot. I don't go back into the building. I call the school office from my car and, when Pam answers, I tell her an emergency has cropped up and that I'll be late.

"Is everything okay, Nina?" she asks, and I say only that I don't know.

I slip the car into Reverse. I pull out of the parking spot and onto the street. Traffic is getting even heavier on the roads. It's starting to build, not just school traffic but morning rush hour, which backs up at intersections. Even worse, the police station is located on the other side of the Metra station from here. The commuter train, during rush hour, comes by with some frequency. I have to wait for not one train, but two trains to pass. I get upset at a car in front of me that doesn't immediately go as the gate lifts. The driver is on her phone. If she waits too long, another train will come and we'll be forced to wait even longer. I honk my horn and the car goes.

The police station is a squat brick building. I've driven by it a thousand times, but I've never been inside because I've never had a reason to be. The building is unremarkable and dated, reminding me of an old elementary school.

My hands are shaking as I pull into a parking spot. I put the car into Park and step from the vehicle. I try closing the door but my seat belt gets in the way, and I have to open the door and push it back in.

"I need to report a missing person," I say with a shaking voice to the front desk officer once inside. The lobby is practically empty. Other than the front desk officer and me, there is only one other person here, a man who sits in a chair facing the windows, looking out.

I'm worried about Jake. But I'm also feeling guilty and ashamed that I waited all this time to come to the police. It never crossed my mind that something might be wrong, that something might have happened to Jake. I only thought that he was upset with me, that he was avoiding me.

"Who's missing?" she asks.

"My husband," I say. "Jake Hayes. Dr. Jacob Hayes."

"Okay, ma'am." She pulls something up on the computer screen. "When did you last see him?" she asks.

"Monday," I say.

I think back to Monday morning. Jake and I were both up and getting ready for work. That is the last time I saw Jake. Because it wasn't a surgery day, he didn't have to be in the office until eight, which meant we were getting ready at the same time. Usually on mornings like that, Jake and I would talk, catch up. I looked forward to them. There was less of an urgency on nonsurgery mornings. We would have breakfast together and talk about our plans for the day. But not this Monday because, this Monday, we moved in silent circles, giving each other a wide berth because we were angry with each other, and hurt. We didn't speak to one another, at all. We didn't say a single word, not until Jake left, leaving me with three final words that got under my skin. It wasn't so much what he said but the way he said it. What if those are the last words he ever speaks to me?

Instead of talking that morning, chair legs scraped against the floor. Doors slammed. Drawers were flung noisily shut. Tension hung low and heavy in the air like fog.

I'd spent Sunday with my mother. She needed things like groceries for the week, and a new fall coat because the days are getting cool. I'd taken her to the mall and the grocery store, in that order, but first we went to church because that's another thing my mother can't do without me and, for the most part, she's a devout Christian and loves going to church.

Later, when we got back to her house, my mother asked me to stay for dinner. She didn't say so, but I know she hates being alone. She gets so lonely. "Let me make you dinner to repay you for taking such good care of me," was how she phrased it, but I knew she wanted me to stay because she didn't want me to leave. She was desperate for company. I said okay and I stayed. I texted Jake to let him know. He never replied to my text. My mother made my favorite meal, like she did when I was a girl and she had a rare night off work. I could tell she enjoyed having someone to cook for again, other than herself. It was a struggle, because of her vision, but she did it mostly by herself, cooking from a recipe she had memorized. Her mother, my grandmother, also had macular degeneration. It's hereditary. If someone in the family has it, then you're far more likely to get it too. It's hard, watching my mother struggle and knowing this is very likely my own fate.

The problem was that Jake doesn't work on Sundays, unless he's on call. He wanted me home with him. He didn't tell me that. I was just supposed to know, to use mental telepathy I suppose, to read his mind, though lately, even when we are both home, he likes to be alone and not with me. It seems like whenever I come into a room he's in, he finds a reason to leave it.

When I came home after seven, he stared icily at me from across the room. He didn't speak. He was drinking a whiskey sour. At first I felt threatened by the lowering look. For whatever reason, I thought of that patient of Jake's who died after surgery. The one he told me about. The young woman who was shot dead by her husband. The one with brain stem death. I don't know why I thought of her just then, but I thought again about why her husband might have shot her, and then wondered if she did something as innocuous as spend the day with her mother.

"Is your husband considered high-risk?"

I come back to the present.

"Meaning?" I ask.

"Do you have reason to suspect foul play?" the front desk

officer asks, inexpressive, staring at me from the other side of a large reception desk, seated behind bulletproof glass.

"Such as?"

"Such as evidence of a struggle, or a home or vehicle in disarray. Blood. A weapon."

I shake my head. "No, no, nothing like that. But I don't know where his car is."

"Make and model of the car?"

I tell her.

She nods. "Okay, ma'am. Is your husband in need of medical attention that you know of, or does he take prescription medicine that he doesn't have on him?" Again I shake my head. Jake doesn't take medicine, only his supplements, which he can live without. She breaks her gaze to type something into the computer, and then looks back at me to ask if Jake is mentally impaired.

"No," I say. I understand where she's going with this. High-risk persons and minors understandably get more care and attention than an almost-forty-year-old, able-bodied man like Jake.

"Is it possible your husband's absence is voluntary, Mrs. Hayes?" she asks, looking up at me.

"What do you mean?"

I know exactly what she means. I don't know why I ask, other than to delay answering.

"Is it possible he willingly left?"

"Yes," I say, being completely honest because it is entirely possible Jake willingly left. Until that woman called from the hospital, I was sure that was the case. But it's uncharacteristic of Jake to miss work. In all his years of practicing medicine, he has never missed work, even as a resident when he was working grueling eighty-hour weeks and was exhausted beyond belief. He still showed up every day as scheduled. Jake's work means everything to him. It's the one thing more important to him than me.

MARY KUBICA

I take it back. I say, "It is possible he willingly left, but I don't think he has because he hasn't shown up for work in days, and my husband would never not go to work. He's a doctor. A neurosurgeon. People's lives depend on him. He's extremely conscientious, but also, he just loves what he does. He wouldn't do anything to botch his reputation at work. Something has happened to him, I think."

"Did you and Dr. Hayes have an altercation, Mrs. Hayes?" she asks and, at first, the question comes as a punch to the gut. I'd hoped she wouldn't ask something like this. Still, I say yes, because I have to be honest, but I worry as I do that if, God forbid, something terrible has happened to Jake, they'll think I did it now that I've confessed to an altercation with him. But finding Jake is what matters.

"Have you tried calling him?"

"Of course. He's not answering his phone."

Jake's phone is dead. It has to be. Jake wouldn't have just turned off his phone.

She asks for a photograph of Jake before I leave. On my phone, I find my absolute favorite, and I find myself staring down at his blond hair, cut short on the sides but longer on top, spiking upward; his chiseled cheekbones; the strong jawline that bristles with days old, prickly facial hair; his breathtaking blue eyes. I'd taken the picture of Jake over a year ago, on a rare few days off. It was more of a staycation than a vacation because Jake couldn't get away for more than a few days, but still, we booked a hotel in the city and did things like go to expensive restaurants and charter a yacht and take it on the lake. He's on a boat in this picture. Lake Michigan surrounds him. He looks so relaxed, the blue of the lake and sky rivaling the blue of his eyes.

The front desk officer also asks for things like an authorization to release dental and skeletal X-rays, and a DNA sample, like from Jake's comb at home, which I'll have to bring later.

My imagination goes wild. The words skeletal X-rays are perhaps what do me in, though I somehow manage to hold my tears back until I make it to the car and only there, bent over the steering wheel, do I convulsively sob.

I leave feeling more than a little disheartened. Because Jake isn't high-risk, he won't be given the same attention someone else might, like say a diabetic or a child. Never was that explicitly said, but I'm not naive. It was implied. He'll be on the police department's radar, but I'm not certain they'll actively be looking for him.

"Most missing people come home on their own within three days," was the last thing the front desk officer said to me as I left, meaning there is nothing for me to do but go home and wait.

It's third period by the time I finally make it into work. It was too late to call in a sub, and so other teachers divvied up and covered my morning classes for me. I thought about just going home after I left the police station, but I couldn't stand the idea of being in that big, quiet house all alone.

I left my student teacher in the lurch too. He's sitting at my desk when I come in, while Mr. Schroeder teaches my class. The student teacher isn't ready to be left alone with the kids; if he was, we could have gotten through the morning classes without a sub.

"Thank you for covering for me," I say to Ryan. "I can take it from here."

"What happened to you this morning?" he whispers back, as my student teacher stands up, making space for me to sit at my desk. "I was waiting for you, and then you were just gone. I tried calling you, to see if everything was okay. Is it your mother?"

I shrug out of my coat. I set it on the back of my chair and hide my purse under the desk.

"I know. I'm sorry. No, not my mother, she's fine," I say,

but I don't want to tell him what happened. I don't want to talk about Jake with Ryan or in the presence of my student teacher because I'm not sure I want everyone knowing what's going on. Gossip runs rampant in schools, not just among the students, but teachers too. I can't stand to think about them sitting around the teacher lounge, talking about Jake and me and our marriage.

"We don't have to talk about it," he says, seeing my reluctance, and I'm grateful. He reaches forward to give my arm a bolstering squeeze. "Just know I'm here. I'm just next door and the door's always open, anytime you need."

"Thank you," I say, "for that, and for covering my class for me. I appreciate it."

"Anytime."

I somehow manage to get through the rest of the day. It's not my best day. Physically I'm here, but I'm not mentally present. The kids don't even notice. I'm glad. I assign them work and let them do it in small groups of their choosing. Half of the students don't even do the assignment, but I don't have the bandwidth to deal with that now. All I can think about is Jake. I'm a mishmash of emotions. I'm no longer only worried that Jake has left me. Now I'm worried something bad has happened to him, which makes me incredibly scared. But if something bad hasn't happened to him and he's just intentionally gone missing in spite, then I'm angry. I'm confused. I don't know what to feel.

I race to see Lily at the end of the day before she leaves. The other day, she left so quickly after work that I didn't have a chance to talk to her, and then yesterday, she wasn't here. She'd called in sick. Other than exchanging a few texts, I haven't talked to her in two days.

Lily is standing at her desk when I come in. She's putting things into her bag, getting ready to leave. "Thank God I caught you," I say, short of breath from walking so fast to her class. "Are you feeling any better?"

She turns to look at me. Lily looks drained, colorless. It could be the fluorescent lighting in the school, or it could just be Lily.

Still, she says, "Much. Thanks for asking."

"Stomach flu?"

"Just something I ate, I think. But it's all better now."

"Good," I say, watching out the window as school bus drivers start their engines and get ready to leave. It's a process. The buses go first and then, when the buses are gone, the student parking lot empties, newly licensed drivers spinning out of the parking lot without looking where they're going. It's terrifying to watch. It's only a matter of time before someone gets killed.

"I was just about to text you and see if everything is okay. I thought I heard you weren't in school today," Lily says.

"I wasn't earlier," I say. "I went to the police station."

Lily stops what she's doing. "Oh," she says. She lowers her papers to the desk and turns to face me. "Why?" she asks, looking concerned. "What happened?"

"It's Jake. He still isn't home," I say.

"But the police, Nina?" Lily asks, as if suggesting it was a bit over-the-top to go to the police. "You said you had a fight, right? I thought you were thinking he was just mad at you. Has something else happened?"

"Yes," I say, pushing up on the sleeves of my shirt because it's hot in Lily's classroom. "Something has happened," I say. "I heard from the hospital this morning. They said that Jake hasn't been going to work. And a friend of his called looking for him. Jake hasn't been returning his calls or texts either. Why wouldn't he call him back?"

The temperature in this building is mercurial. The HVAC doesn't work right, so that it's hot as hell in some rooms, freezing cold in others. The kids always complain.

Lily must be hot too. She looks suddenly flushed. Her expression changes. She knows I'm right. It would have been irresponsible not to go to the police after all that. "Oh wow. Oh my God. I'm sorry, Nina. What did the police say?" she asks as she comes closer to hug me. "You must be so worried."

I shrug. "The police didn't say much."

"Where do you think he is?" she asks, releasing me and stepping back to look at me. "Could he just need some space?"

"If I knew, I'd go to him." At first I wanted to give him space. It's the reason I never went to the hospital looking for him. But now I want to see him with my own eyes, to know that he's okay.

"What are the police going to do?"

"I don't even know, Lily," I say, on the verge of breaking down. I lower myself into one of the student desks, cross my legs and say, "Maybe nothing. The truth is that people have a right to disappear. So I don't know if they're looking for him or not. They say that they are, but I don't believe it."

"I'm sure he's fine," says Lily. "He'll come home."

"How can you be so sure?" I ask. I know she means nothing by it. She's only trying to make me feel better, but her words are empty, meaningless. I don't hold it against her. She's trying to be kind, but her words ring hollow.

Before Lily can respond, there's a light rapping on the small window on the classroom door. When we look, Denise Brady's face is pressed to the glass. Denise is another teacher at our school. I wave her in, giving Lily a look so that she'll know to keep what I've told her between just her and me.

"Just the two ladies I was looking for," Denise says, and I force a smile.

"Hey, Denise."

Denise is older than either of us. She's married and has kids of her own who are in college now, making her an authority on teenage behavior. Now that her kids are out of the house, she has time on her hands and is the kind of woman who hates to be bored. Denise leads the faculty book club and likes to plan things, like birthday dinners and the annual holiday and end-of-the-year parties. Today she's here because one of the other English teachers is turning fifty in a couple weeks. Denise wants to get a small group of us together for a dinner out to celebrate. It sounds nice, but my head is light-years away from making dinner plans when all I can think about is Jake. Still, I go through the motions. I get out my phone and check my calendar for dates and we settle on October 10, as long as everyone else is free. Denise will check with the others and let Lily and me know. I put it down on my calendar in case but, even as I do, I'm wondering things like if Jake will be home by then or if he will still be missing or worse, and either way, I don't think I will go.

"It's a date, then!" says Denise before waving goodbye and moving toward the door to leave. She almost gets to the door. "Oh hey," she says, and then she turns back to Lily. "I almost forgot to tell you, Lily," she says. "My husband, Jim, says he saw you the other day."

Lily makes a face. "No. I don't think so," she says.

"No, he did. He saw you, but he didn't want to be a nuisance and so he didn't stop you and say hello."

"That's silly. He should have just said something. I'm surprised he even knew who I was." I can see Lily running through her mind the places she's been this week and trying to picture Jim there, because that's the same thing I would do. I'm terrible with faces. I don't know that I'd know Jim if I saw him. I only met him once.

"He remembered you from that holiday party a few years back, the one at our house. He remembered both you and your husband. Christian, isn't it?" Lily nods. "He had a long conversation with Christian that night. He remembers it still. He really enjoyed talking to him."

People say kind things about Christian and Lily all the time. Everyone thinks they're just the nicest couple.

"Where did he see me?" Lily asks, and then she turns away from Denise, going back to packing up the rest of her things.

Denise says, "That forest preserve, out near Lemont. I can't remember the name of it. It's just off Feeney, if I remember right. Gosh," she says, looking up toward the ceiling as if the answer is written there somewhere on the tiles. "I haven't been there myself in years. Something Woods."

She can't put her finger on it.

"Isn't that Langley Woods?" I ask, despite having never been there myself. I've just heard of it.

"Yes!" she exclaims. "That's it! Langley Woods." She says how it's beautiful and peaceful, a great place to hike and clear the head.

Lily looks over her shoulder at Denise, but I can see in her face that Lily's mind was momentarily somewhere else, that she wasn't listening.

"Where?" she asks, blinking.

Denise says it again. "The forest preserve. In Lemont. Langley Woods."

"Oh," says Lily trying, I think, to remember whether she was there or not. "I did go there," she decides. "The other day. For a walk. It was such a pretty day. But I don't remember when."

Denise knows.

"It was Monday," she says.

The days of the week are starting to blend together. I have to think through what day it is. Tomorrow is Friday. Today is Thursday which means that Monday was three days ago.

Monday was also the first night that Jake didn't come home.

I walk back toward my classroom to get my things and leave. Already I'm dreading the thought of going home to an empty house. It makes my physically sick to think about. I don't know what I'll do with myself, how I'll pass the time.

The hallways are vacant now. The kids are gone and practically everyone else has left. The building is much different at this time of day. It's almost unrecognizable without kids. The halls are hollow and the classrooms are empty, the only sound the tapping of my heels against the terrazzo floors. The emptiness overwhelms me. I feel so lonely I could cry. Before coming to my own classroom, I stop by Ryan's. I've changed my mind. If he's there, I think that I'd like to talk to him about Jake after all, because I feel so alone and confused, and wouldn't mind a man's take on what's happening with Jake. I go to the door, which is shut, though the classroom light is on. I don't bother trying the handle. The classroom doors are always locked from the outside; it's a safety precaution. It makes sense, but it also makes it difficult when students need to use the restroom and have to be let back in. I press my face to the glass, looking for Ryan, but he's not inside the room. I must have missed him.

Disappointed, I turn and go to my own classroom. My door is also closed; I have to use my key to get in. My student teacher closed the door before he left. I'm grateful, because my purse is still in the classroom under the desk. I only brought my keys with me. I'm wondering if the janitors have already been through to clean, but when I come inside, I see that they haven't. Everything is almost exactly the way I left it, except that on my desk now is a vase of flowers. They're wrapped in cellophane with a bow, as if from a florist. I physically stop in the open doorway, taken aback by the flowers.

What have I done to deserve them? It's not anywhere close to my birthday and I wonder where they came from, who gave them to me. Jake isn't the type to give flowers. It's not that he never has. It's just that he hasn't in years. I remember him giving roses to me when we were first dating, leaving them in unexpected places like beside my coffee in the morning or flattened inside a book I was reading, which was always a nice surprise, to turn the page and find a rose waiting for me inside. It's just that he hasn't given flowers to me more recently. He thinks they're impractical because they die—Jake doesn't have a romantic bone in his body, he's far too pragmatic for that—though I've told him before that everything dies, it's just a matter of time. But Jake thinks flowers are uninspired. These days, he prefers something unexpected and longer lasting like jewelry or my Tesla, which came on my birthday, also wrapped with a bow.

I go to the flowers, thinking, hoping that maybe they're from Jake. For a second, my heart feels lighter. I cut the cellophane off with a pair of scissors, looking for a card. The flowers are gorgeous, an arrangement of roses, carnations and eucalyptus in a glass vase. I sink my nose in to smell them. They're divine. They make me smile. I read the card, hoping for answers, to see Jake's name on the card and a simple but sweet message—*Love you always*, or something like that—but instead I find myself at a complete loss. My smile disappears. I turn the card over to see what, if anything, is on the back and then stand, pouting at the vase.

Pam, the school secretary, is still in the main office when I go to check. She's alone, pecking away on the keyboard. "I wasn't sure you'd still be here," I say, coming into the empty office. She looks up at me, over the computer, and smiles.

"Hi, Nina," she says over the noise of the printer, which springs to life at the same time, spitting out pieces of paper.

"You work too hard, Pam. You should go home."

"Look who's talking," she says.

I smile. "The flowers in my classroom. Do you know where they came from?"

"Some florist," she says offhand, shrugging. "He delivered them today, during seventh period. I didn't want to bother you when you were in class, so I walked them down after school," she says, rising from her chair to go to the printer. "You weren't there, so I left them. I hope that was okay."

"Yes, of course. That's fine. Thank you for bringing them down."

"No problem," she says. She takes the document from the printer. She looks at it to be sure it printed correctly, and then, satisfied, she goes back to her chair to sit. "That sweet husband of yours," Pam says with a wink from behind the large desk. "Lucky you. Hell will freeze over before my husband ever sends me flowers at work. Is it a special day or did he do something he needs to make up for?"

I do a double take. Why does Pam think the flowers are from Jake? I ask her, "How do you know the flowers are from Jake?"

Pam doesn't, I realize. She's just speculating. She giggles. "How many men do you have sending you roses at work, Nina?" She's right. None. But Jake never has either.

A look on my face must give me away. Pam realizes that I don't actually know who the flowers are from. "Well, what did the card say?" she asks, her eyes narrowing.

"Nothing," I tell her.

"Nothing at all? It was blank?"

"No, it wasn't blank. There was a message," I say, but the message didn't help. If anything the message was so cryptic, it made it worse. "It said something like *I hope these make you smile, because I love to see your smile.* But the card wasn't signed."

"It wasn't?" Pam's face practically lights up. She says, "It sounds like either the florist forgot to include the sender's name or you have a secret admirer, my dear."

I leave the flowers on my desk when I go. I have too much to carry, and I don't know that I want them going home with me anyway because what Pam said got under my skin. A secret admirer. It's not that much different than a stalker.

I walk across the parking lot. I stayed so long after school that the teacher parking lot has cleared almost completely out. It's close to four thirty now. School ended over two hours ago.

I walk quickly. I pay attention to my surroundings, but the solitude and the vastness of the parking lot suddenly overwhelm me and I feel anxious to get to my car.

I think again about the flowers. I should feel flattered by them. That was the sender's intent, but I don't feel flattered because I don't know who they're from. Someone knows something I don't. Whether it was Jake or not, I don't like that. And if it was Jake, then I don't like this game he's playing with me.

The content of the note was bothersome too. *I love to see your smile*, it said, which tells me someone is watching me.

CHRISTIAN

Lily is standing in the family room when I come home. I'm later than usual because Thursday nights I meet some guys at the gym to shoot hoops, and then we go and get a drink. Tonight I considered not going with them but coming home to Lily instead, though ultimately I decided to go because, after thinking about it, it seemed like the best thing for me to do—for both Lily and me to do—is to not break from routine.

Now Lily stands at the windows, looking away from me, out into the yard. Her arms are crossed, her brown hair hanging long and wavy down her back. I can tell from the way she stands that Lily is anxious about something, and I feel guilty for sticking around for a second beer.

I come up from behind. I set my hands on her shoulders and massage them, feeling the tension she carries in her shoulders and neck.

"Hey," I say. Lily turns around, and I know something is

wrong but, for the first time in a while, my initial thought is not that something terrible has happened to the baby. "What happened?" I ask.

"Nina went to the police," she says.

"And?" I ask, slowly, drawing it out.

"She told them that Jake is missing."

"Okay," I say. "And what did they say?"

"They weren't too worried about it. They think he may have left voluntarily."

"Okay," I say again, nodding. "That's good, right? For us." I smile. I reach for her hands. I try and stay optimistic. I'm not actually worried about this at all. I can see that Lily is upset but I think I knew that inevitably Nina would one day go to the police. She had to. She couldn't let her husband be gone forever and not say anything. It would be cruel if not suspicious. Lily nods, but I can tell she's not so sure this is a good thing. "It's okay, babe. Don't worry about it. It's a formality."

"There's more," Lily says.

"What?" I ask, growing serious again because the tone of her voice scares me.

"Someone saw me there."

"Saw you where?"

"At Langley Woods."

A knot rises up to my throat. I swallow it back. It takes effort. I can feel my heartbeat in my ears, pounding.

This changes things. A witness now puts Lily at the scene where Jake was killed.

My words are slow, thought out and staccato-like. "What did they see?"

She shakes her head. "Nothing," she says, quiet as a secret, as if someone might be listening to us. "I don't think. Just me, walking alone, I guess because nothing was ever said about me being with someone. It must have been before," she says, stopping there, leaving the rest unsaid. Before she met up with Jake.

Before they went walking together. Before he coaxed her down that isolated trail. Before he assaulted her. Before she fought back. Before she killed him. Before she ran.

"Who?" I ask.

"The husband of one of my coworkers. Jim Brady. You met him once at a faculty holiday party." I shrug. If I did, I don't remember. Lily's faculty parties happen with some frequency. Sometimes I remember colleagues of hers or their spouses, but sometimes I don't.

"You didn't see him?" I ask.

"No. I don't even remember what he looks like, Christian. I wouldn't know him if I did see him."

"How do you know he saw you?" I ask, and she tells me how this coworker came to see her when Nina was in her classroom this afternoon. What makes it worse is that Nina now knows too that Lily was at Langley Woods.

Later, I decide that we need to find a way to move Jake's car from the street. His car on the side of Newcomb Road is the only thing that puts him at Langley Woods, and it's only a matter of time before his car rouses suspicion and people go there looking for him. That in and of itself wouldn't be a big deal. But the fact that a witness now puts Lily at Langley Woods on the same day Jake disappeared worries me.

Presumably Jake's key is on him, wherever he is. Lily keeps a copy of my car key with her in case a need arises. It's possible Nina does the same.

We're eating a late dinner, or trying to, but neither of us has the appetite for it. I make an attempt to eat, but Lily only stabs at hers with a fork, pushing her food to the sides of the plate like I used to do as a kid and didn't want to eat something my mom had made.

"Do you think you could get into Nina's bag at work to look for a key?" I ask.

Lily's head comes slowly up. She stares at me from across the table. It's dim in the house. We only turned on a couple lights and even those glow amber, not white. "Why?" she asks.

"I think it would be smart to move Jake's car."

She sets her fork down on the side of her plate. "What do you mean? Move it where?"

"I don't know exactly. I'm thinking that if I just move it, to a parking garage or to some other random street, we'll throw the police off when they go to look for him. They'll be looking in the wrong place. We can get ahead of this."

Lily chews over the next words in her head before letting them out. I see her wheels spin. "What will happen if they find him dead? Will I go to jail?"

My saliva turns thick. I swallow it back, with effort. "Of course not," I say, but I'm lying. She knows that I am. I have my tells, like how I can't make eye contact when I lie.

I think there is a very real possibility she could go to jail. I know lawyers, but it's not the kind of thing I can outright ask somebody without it raising alarm. If Lily hit Jake so forcibly with that rock that it gave him a traumatic brain injury that he later stumbled off and died from, she did so in self-defense. But there is no actual evidence to this. It's only her word that she fought back in self-defense. And, skeptics would ask, if it happened like she said it did, why didn't she call for help when she got back to her car, why didn't she go to the police?

I know why. She didn't think she had hurt him as badly as she did. She thought she'd only slowed him down so that she could get away and she didn't say anything because she didn't want to hurt her friend.

It wasn't until the next day at work, when Nina said how he didn't come home, that Lily started to worry. But by then twelve or sixteen hours had passed. It was too late to call for help.

These things in combination make her look guilty.

I think about what might have happened when Lily hit Jake

with the rock. I've thought about it many times, a repeating circuit in my mind. Lily said that she didn't hit him just once. She hit him repeatedly. She said he fell. He may have lost consciousness. But even if he didn't, if he remained conscious, he may have experienced symptoms like blurred vision or a ringing in the ears. Symptoms of traumatic brain injury can set in within seconds, hours or days. Without medical intervention, they get worse. He would have been disoriented, uncoordinated. Confusion with TBIs can be profound. What happens is that there is bleeding in the brain, from blood vessels getting hurt. The blood collects in the space between the skull and the brain. I know because these last twenty-four hours, I've spent an excessive amount of time researching brain injuries. That collection of blood is called a hematoma. It expands, putting pressure on the brain, causing death. But it's not always instant.

Even for someone perfectly fine, that path into the woods is easy to get turned around on. It's easy to get lost. The trees limit the view. There are no landmarks and it's easy to misjudge distances. I, perfectly fine, felt disoriented walking in the woods. Jake may very well have stumbled off in the wrong direction, going deeper into the woods instead of back to the marked path. Who knows how far he walked before he collapsed. It's hard to imagine a person could just completely evaporate somewhere around here. It's the suburbs of Chicago and not the wilds of Alaska, but still, the forest preserve encompasses twenty-five hundred acres of land. You can fit something like eighteen hundred football fields in that space, and most of it is heavily wooded, which means that I could search for Jake for years and never find him.

The thing is that Jake is an upstanding citizen. He's a doctor. He's never been in trouble with the law, as far as we know. There is no reason for anyone to believe he's a predator.

Lily has physical wounds: the scraped knees and the impressions of his hands on her arms. But even that is circumstantial at best and healing. It's only a matter of time before they're completely gone.

Jake's blood and bone fragments on a rock with Lily's fingerprints also on it—that's evidence. Her blood-soaked clothes in the bag still hanging on the garage door handle—that's also evidence.

What Lily did isn't murder. It's maybe manslaughter. There was no intent to kill him. But manslaughter comes with jail time, and I won't let my wife and the mother of my child go to jail.

I can't live without her, no matter for how long.

Years ago, Lily's identity was stolen. It was a nightmare. Whoever did it opened credit cards in Lily's name and bought expensive but ridiculous things with them. They changed her address so that the credit card bills went somewhere else, not to us. We had no idea any of this was happening until we went to apply for a loan for a car, and realized Lily's credit rating was incredibly low. It took years to restore.

I got smart and locked down our internet and accounts. I downloaded VPN software and figured out how to go undetectable on the web so that we couldn't be hacked. What that means for me now is that my search history can't be monitored. I can google things like what a BMW 7 series key looks like without it being traced back to me. I show Lily the image. It's not your standard key, but a key fob. I tell her that it would have the BMW logo on it, and then remind her what the BMW logo looks like. Our best bet at moving the car comes down to Lily finding this thing. "That's what you'll be looking for," I say. "Check a key chain. Or purse pockets."

Lily nods and says okay, but I can tell that she's nervous. She doesn't know how she's going to pull this off. Lily isn't used to breaking rules. She's rule abiding to a fault. She doesn't speed. She always wears her seat belt. She won't look at her phone when driving, even at red lights. When a lane is about to end and she has to merge, Lily is the first to do so, no matter how many times I tell her that the laws of physics say it's better if she waits until the last second to merge, like me. She doesn't, because it pisses other drivers off. Lily doesn't like to piss people off. If a restaurant menu says no substitutions, she won't even ask, no matter how much she wants or doesn't want something.

Later that night, lying together in bed in the dark, we talk through ways for Lily to search Nina's purse for Jake's key. "Where does she keep her purse?" I ask. Lily faces away from me in bed. I spoon her from behind, my hand under her shirt, across her abdomen where our baby is.

Outside it's raining, the rain like fingernails tapping against the glass, and I think of that rain washing any last remnants of blood from the rocks and grass.

I want more than anything for it to be a downpour.

"I've seen it in her classroom, under her desk," Lily says, about the purse. "She closes the door when she leaves the room. They lock automatically."

"Is there any way you can get into the classroom if the door is locked?"

"Yes," she says. "My classroom key unlocks all of the classroom doors."

"That doesn't seem safe," I say, surprised but also relieved because it makes things easier on us. I didn't expect it to be that easy.

"Teachers have complained."

"I would too. So you'll go when she's not in the room. Does she take her purse with her to lunch?" I ask.

"I don't know," Lily says. "She might just bring a lunch and eat in the classroom, like me."

"But eventually she'd have to leave?" I ask, hopeful.

Lily says yes. I ask her when she personally leaves her classroom, leaving her purse behind. When she goes to the bathroom, the copy room, or for things like department and team meetings, she says. My hope for that key hinges on Lily's ability to pull this off, and that worries me because it's not in Lily's nature to break into places and steal things. "You just have to be confident and calm and quick. Do you think you can do this?"

"I don't know, Christian," she says. She's scared of getting caught. She's scared of being seen. "What happens if I can't?"

"Then we'll find another way," I say, because the last thing I want to do is make her uncomfortable and scared. "Just do your best. If you can't, you can't."

Lily turns around in bed to face me. "Christian?"

"What?"

"Why are you being so nice? Why are you helping me like this when I did a terrible thing?" she asks. I made a vow to Lily once. For better or worse. I never imagined that the worse would look anything like this, but life is unpredictable at times, and there is nothing I wouldn't do for her.

In the dark, I just barely make out the outline of Lily's face. I run my fingers along her hairline, her cheek, seeing her with my hands. I lean forward into her, close. She does too. For a minute, we breathe each other's air. I feel her breath on me. Her hands slip around me, pulling me toward her so that we're flush, one continuous being.

Lily brings her face somehow even closer to mine. She hesitates, and then she kisses me. It's sedate, slow, deep. I feel that kiss everywhere. I've been too afraid to touch Lily. I've wanted to. God, how I've wanted to. But I've been walking on eggshells around her, not wanting to do anything she didn't want to do, not wanting to do anything that would be uncomfortable for her, after what she's been through both with Jake and the baby.

I pull gently back from her kiss, though our faces still touch. "Because I love you," I whisper, sliding a tentative hand beneath her flannel shirt, stroking her softly, and she sighs quietly at my touch, like a breeze moving through leaves. Her body responds.

Lily rolls onto her back. Her legs fall open. She reaches for me. I rise above her, slowly lowering myself between her thighs. "Because I would do anything for you," I say. "And because what you did wasn't terrible. It was necessary."

It was necessary.

I just don't know that everyone would see it that way.

NINA

I drive to Jake's office, which is the last place anyone saw him before he went missing. His office is located about thirty minutes from the high school where I teach, on the third floor of a four-story medical building. I leave straight from work, driving to it, not getting there until close to five o'clock.

I circle the lot first. I do so slowly, leaned forward in my seat, searching through the window for Jake's car. His car isn't here and, though I'm not surprised, I am disappointed; there was a part of me still holding out hope that it would be.

I park in the lot and walk into the modern glass building, taking a wide, open staircase up to the third floor where Jake's office is. I follow the signs on the walls, moving down the hall and into the neurology office at the end of it, the one with Jake's name on the door along with two other physicians' names.

The receptionist looks briefly up from her computer when

I come in. She smiles and asks for my name, as if to find my appointment on the schedule.

I say, "I don't have an appointment. I'm Nina Hayes, Dr. Hayes's wife. I was hoping to speak with someone about him."

Her face changes. She straightens her back, sitting more upright. "Mrs. Hayes. Yes, of course. Just a minute please." She gets up from her desk. She excuses herself and disappears somewhere that I can't see, behind a partition. A minute later another woman, a doctor in a white coat and low heels, peeks her head out from behind the same partition. "Are you Mrs. Hayes?" she asks, coming closer, clutching a tablet to her chest, a stethoscope wrapped around the back of her neck. "Of course you are," she goes on to say. "I recognize you from the picture in Jake's office." Her hair falls over her shoulders and down the front lapels of the coat. Her hair is long and ginger and I'm taken aback though it's silly that I am, but for all the times I've thought of Jake at work, I've pictured middle-aged colleagues— all of them, in my imagination, inexplicably male—and not a woman this attractive. When Jake mentions colleagues by name, they're almost always Dr. Winter and Dr. Caddel, and it's my fault that I never thought to ask more about these people he works with.

"Nina," I say, extending a hand as she shifts the tablet to one arm to reach out and shake my hand. "I'm here about Jake."

"Andrea Caddel—Andi," she says, and I realize my mistake. I'd just assumed the *Andy* that Jake sometimes mentions was a man and not the short form of Andrea. "Dr. Hayes isn't here, Mrs. Hayes. I thought someone from the hospital called and spoke to you?" she says.

"Yes," I say, "they did. I'm sorry. I should have clarified. I know Jake isn't here, but that's why I've come. I was hoping to speak with someone who would have been working with him on Monday. I'm trying to figure out where he might be. No one has spoken to him since Monday. No one has seen him either."

She nods. "Yes, of course," she says, softening. "Let me grab his nurse. We've been trying to reach him for days," she says, as the receptionist returns, slipping back into her chair. "Everyone here is just so worried about him."

"I know. I appreciate that. I'm worried about him too."

"You must be completely beside yourself," she says.

"I am."

"Have you spoken to the police?"

"Yes. I've been to see them and I've filed a missing person's report."

"I just hope that, wherever he is, he's fine. Let me see if I can get Tricia, Dr. Hayes's nurse, for you. I wasn't working on Monday, but she can tell you more about what happened that day. The last I saw, she was in with a patient, but maybe she's through."

The receptionist takes me to Jake's office to wait, so that I don't have to stand in the waiting room with patients. "Thank you," I say as she unlocks the door and lets me in, and then leaves me alone with Jake's things. His office is bland. The furniture—a desk, a slender bookshelf with books and potted plants that someone else must be watering and keeping alive—is laminate and ordinary. If I know Jake, he probably hates it. It's nothing like his office at home, which is high-end and done by a professional designer. I haven't been to this office of Jake's before. I've been to the building only once to meet him for lunch, though Jake met me in the lobby that day. It's not strange that I haven't been here before, I don't think. But it strikes me now how Jake and I have the life that we share, and then we have entirely separate lives.

It takes a minute, but Dr. Caddel finds Tricia.

"Hi, Tricia," I say as she comes into Jake's office wearing light blue scrubs, her hair pulled back into a ponytail with loose curly pieces that fall from her hairline. "I'm Nina Hayes, Dr.

Hayes's wife. I was hoping I could talk to you for a few minutes about Jake."

"Sure," she says. "What did you want to know?"

"Dr. Caddel tells me you were working with Jake on Monday."

She nods. "I was."

"Can you tell me anything about that day? Was it a typical day?"

She thinks back. "Yes, for the most part. Dr. Hayes worked Monday morning as scheduled. But then around, I don't know, maybe two or two thirty, he said that he needed to run out for a while and that he'd be back."

"Was that unusual?" I ask. "For Jake to run out in the middle of the day?"

She considers this. "Yes and no," she says. Dr. Caddel stays and listens, leaned against the wall. Her tablet is gone now so that her arms are empty. She crosses them against herself, nodding slowly, listening intently. "He doesn't do it often, but he's done it before. He had a cancellation too, so there was a gap in his schedule. His next appointment wasn't until four, and the morning had been so busy that neither of us had time for lunch. I didn't think anything of him leaving. I thought he was just going to get a bite to eat or that he had an errand to run."

"But then?" I ask, leading.

"But then," she says, "the next thing I knew, it was four o'clock. Dr. Hayes's patient was here, but Dr. Hayes wasn't. The office manager, I believe, tried calling him, but as far as I know, he never answered. Someone told me he hasn't come home."

"No."

"It's so unlike Jake," Dr. Caddel says.

"It is," I say, because Jake is always so punctual and so conscientious. "How did he seem when he left?" I ask, my eyes going back to his nurse, Tricia.

"Fine," Tricia says, "for the most part. He had a difficult appointment in the morning, a follow-up meeting with the family of a patient who died."

Dr. Caddel says, "Those are never easy."

"I can imagine they're not. Was Jake upset about it?" I ask, looking to Tricia, but again it's Dr. Caddel who speaks.

"With every surgery comes risk, which is why patients are required to give informed consent before we operate on them. Sometimes a surgeon can do everything right, the surgery can be incredibly routine, and still a patient dies. Despite his efforts, Dr. Hayes could not stop that particular patient from bleeding out. From what I've heard, the family was devastated and they took it out on Jake. For as hard as we try, it's impossible for a surgeon not to feel shaken when something like this happens."

"So he was upset, then," I suggest, and she nods, though Jake is a master at keeping his emotions at bay, of not letting on to what he's thinking or feeling inside.

After I leave, I drive to the hospital where Jake also works and where he operates on patients. The hospital, like most, has a parking garage and it worries me because parking garages have notoriously lousy security. Generally, they might have a camera at the entrance and exit, but within the garage itself, there are too many blind spots, too many obstructions to install cameras everywhere.

As I circle the multistory garage, climbing the endlessly round ramps, not finding Jake's car, I think of everything terrible that could have happened to Jake.

My imagination is my worst enemy in this moment.

Friday afternoon, after work, I decide to call the florist to see who sent me flowers. They sat on my desk staring at me half the day. I tried not to think about them, but they were there, within my line of sight. No matter how much I tried, I couldn't stop thinking about them or wondering where they came from. I didn't want to get rid of them—because what if they were from Jake?—but after lunch I moved them to a shelf on the other side of a tall cabinet, so that my view of them was obstructed.

The name of the florist is on the card. Cell phone service inside much of the school building isn't great—it has something to do with the thick brick walls and the insulation; my classroom is practically a dead zone. I take my phone just outside, waiting until the student parking lot has emptied so that I don't have to contend with the noise of cars and kids when I call the florist.

I dial the number and a woman answers. "Hello?" she says.

"Hi. I was hoping you could help me," I say. "I received a flower delivery yesterday afternoon, but the card didn't include the sender's name. I'm wondering if you can tell me who purchased the flowers? I'd like to be able to say thanks."

The woman is at first quiet. "There was no name on the card?" she asks, and I tell her no.

"There was a greeting with the card," I explain, "but either the sender's name was inadvertently left off the card or the flowers were sent anonymously. Would you be able to tell me who purchased the flowers?"

"I'm so sorry, ma'am," she says, "but I can't give that information to you."

"Excuse me?" I ask, pulling a face, finding it odd that she wouldn't be able to tell me the sender's name. She must have it there on the order form or, if nothing else, a credit card receipt.

"If there is no name on the card," she says, "then the sender chose to remain anonymous. The information you're asking for is personal. We have a strict privacy policy when it comes to giving out our customers' personal information. We can only give out as much information as is written on the card."

"But surely you must have his name on the order form or the credit card receipt."

"Even if we did, that information is private, ma'am," she

says again. "I can't disclose the customer's name without his or her permission."

"There must be some way to get that information," I say.

"I'm sorry, but no."

"I'd like to speak to your manager, then, please."

"Ma'am, I am the manager. I own this shop."

"This is ridiculous. I'd just like to say thanks to whoever gave them to me. It's not like I'm trying to steal someone's identity. How do you expect me to do that if I don't know who the flowers are from?"

"Well," she says, "you could ask around and see if anyone you know will admit to the flowers, but the only way I'm able to give you that information is with an order from the police."

I actually laugh out loud. "You can't be serious," I say. "You want me to go to the police to find out who sent me flowers?"

"I'm sorry, ma'am, but I am serious. The information you're asking for is private."

I hang up with the florist. I let myself back into the building, feeling agitated as I walk down the hall for my classroom. I turn a corner and there is Lily. Her back is to me and she's moving quickly away from my closed classroom door. "Lily," I call out for her.

She turns to face me. "Hey," she says. "There you are. I thought you'd left."

"I was outside, making a call. Did you need something?" I ask.

"Yes," she says. "I had something to tell you."

"What?" I ask.

Lily racks her brain, but already she's forgotten what it is.

CHRISTIAN

Lily has no luck finding the key. She's visibly upset when I get home from work. She's pacing barefoot when I come into the house, having to use my key to unlock the garage door because Lily locked it again. "It wasn't there," she says, bringing her pacing to an abrupt stop as she turns to face me. "I looked on her key chain and in the pockets of her purse, like you said, but it wasn't there. I'm so sorry, Christian." Lily's face is red and she's on the verge of tears.

She thinks she's let me down.

"It's okay, babe," I assure her, reaching for her. "It's not your fault she didn't have the key on her. We'll figure something else out. What's she saying about Jake?" I ask.

"He's still not home," she tells me. Of course he's not home. I don't say that aloud. But I think it. I also think that Lily still harbors some hope that Jake might actually come home, that he's not dead, that she didn't kill him. I know she wants to believe that.

"I thought of something as I was driving home," Lily says.

"What?"

"I know their garage code. I watched their cat when they went away for a few days last summer, remember? Unless they changed it, I can get into the house. Maybe the key is there. I can get it when she's not home."

It's brilliant. I take Lily's face in my hands and kiss her. "You're a genius, Lily," I say. Except Lily shouldn't be the one to do it. Lily should be a decoy. She should be the one to make sure Nina doesn't come home while I go inside to search for the key. I tell Lily this. "Text her," I say, "and see if she wants to meet for breakfast in the morning. Tell her you're worried about her and thought it would be good for her to get out for a while and talk about Jake."

It serves two purposes: getting Nina out of the house, but also making Lily look like the good friend that she is.

Nina had already been working at the high school when Lily got her job. Nina and Jake are older than Lily and me by a few years. Nina was assigned as Lily's mentor that first year. The school always assigns mentors for first-year teachers, for guidance and support. It was how Lily and Nina became such good friends. That was years ago. Now Lily has been teaching long enough that she has tenure and, last year, got the educator of the year award for her district.

The year that they met, they spent the last few days of summer together at a new teacher orientation, Nina running it, Lily attending. I remember how, when Lily would come home at night, all she could talk about was Nina. How nice she was, how funny and easy to talk to. Lily's first year of teaching was rough. She went into it with the best intentions. By the end of the first day, she'd discovered that learning to be a teacher and being a teacher were two very different things. It was harder than she expected. Burnout was very real that first year. Lily would cry when she came home and more than once, said she wanted to quit. Teenagers are jerks. They're little assholes. No matter how many times I told her that, it didn't make a difference. I didn't have to deal with them every day. They didn't listen to her. The girls, especially, were mean. She would overhear them, whispering about her and making fun of catty things like her clothes. Somehow Lily persevered. She and Nina commiserated with each other about how hard it was and the asshole kids they had in common. It helped. Nina got her through it. Lily grew stronger, more tenacious. She made the kids respect her somehow. By her second year of teaching, Lily was a pro.

When all this is said and done, Lily and Nina's friendship will be over. It makes me sad for Lily, for how much she will lose before this is through. But you can't have a relationship built on secrets and lies.

"Do you know if they have a home security system?" I ask Lily before she leaves. I've been up for hours. I got up early to catch up on work from the week. I took one day off and left early another and, even when I've been physically there, I haven't been mentally present. I sat at the kitchen table preparing for a meeting with a focus group on Monday, and then, when Lily woke up, I went back up to the bathroom to shower.

Lily has plans to meet Nina for breakfast at ten. I'll leave after she does. I'll drive to Jake and Nina's house, and then wait a couple blocks from it, until she texts to let me know that Nina has made it to the restaurant to go in. It's foolproof.

"No, they don't, or they didn't last summer when I watched the cat."

"What about a video doorbell?"

Lily shakes her head. "I don't know. I went in through the garage. I never used the front door."

"Okay."

"What are you going to do?"

"Don't worry about me. I'll figure it out. It will be fine."

"Please, Christian, just don't get caught," she says. Moving Jake's car feels like the finish line at the end of a marathon, if we can just get there. Once his car is far away from Langley Woods, no one will know he was ever there. No one will know he and Lily ever ran into each other that day. For all intents and purposes, Lily was there, but Jake was not.

"I won't," I promise her. The stakes are high. This isn't some high school prank. I'd be lying if I said I wasn't nervous as hell, but the last thing I'm going to do is tell Lily that. Lily is nervous. She's so worried that she'll slip up at breakfast and say something she's not supposed to say. She's been trying to avoid Nina as best as she can this week. Now she has to talk to her, without interruptions. She's worried Nina will see right through her and that, even if she doesn't verbally slip up, that her eyes, her body language will somehow betray her. It took longer than normal for her to pick out something to wear. She was indecisive, doubtful, as if there might be some hidden message, some unspoken truth, a confession in a pair of jeans.

"Deep breaths," I say to her now, forcing her eyes on mine. We breathe together. In and out. I make her hold her inhales. It helps the oxygen settle in the lungs. We do it three times, and I watch as Lily visibly calms before me. "Just be you. If you start to panic, excuse yourself. Go to the bathroom and breathe."

Lily nods. She hasn't talked much about the nausea or the fatigue this week. I guess it's hard to distinguish between pregnancy nausea and what it must feel like knowing you've killed a man. Lily has nightmares. She doesn't say it. But she makes sounds in the middle of the night, like she's running, gasping for air, trying to get away. Sometimes she cries, and I think that's for what she's done. Lily would never intentionally hurt anyone or anything. I, myself, have been having heartburn. It feels like there's acid pooling in my abdomen and chest, weakening the abdominal wall, forming a hole. Lily and I are running on adrenaline, but it's running low.

I can't wait for this to all be through.

For a long time before we go our separate ways, we hold on to each other.

I take the bag of Lily's bloody clothes with me when I go, the ones I pulled from the laundry that first night after she told me what happened. For the last few days the bag has hung on the garage doorknob, in full view.

Lily first noticed the bag hanging there last night. "What's this?" she asked. I said nothing back, though in retrospect I should have just said it was garbage and been done with it, because then Lily wouldn't have had to look for herself what it was.

Lily asked, "Christian?" when I said nothing, because I couldn't think of a lie fast enough. My silence roused her curiosity.

"Lily, don't," I said as she took the bag from the garage doorknob, untied the handles and looked inside, to see for herself what it was, because I still hadn't told her. Lily's face turned white and her body recoiled.

"What is this?" she asked at first, and then, taking the items out of the bag, recognizing her own clothes, "Is this—"

I could almost see the passage of bile going from her stomach back up through her throat. It wasn't necessarily the sight of blood that did it, but the knowledge of where the blood came from.

She went to the sink for water. As she did, I reached to take the bag from her and she let me, glad, I think, to be free of it.

"You don't need to see that," I said. "I'm sorry. I didn't want you to see that."

I looked in the bag myself, to see what she saw. Blood gets

darker over time, turning it more brown and less red. Still, there was no denying that what was in the bag, all over Lily's clothes, was blood.

Jake and Nina Hayes live in an upscale neighborhood that's all custom homes, each house trying not be outdone by someone else. They must be something like four or five thousand square feet, with brick and stone exteriors, turrets, cathedral doors, things like that, which make me think of castles. It's the kind of place that also makes me wonder how, exactly, people can be this rich. It's envious, but it makes me think about people in developing countries dying from things like starvation. The discrepancy is shocking, and I think if the Hayeses or their neighbors gave more instead of keeping it all to themselves, this world might be a better place. The only thing that I find surprising is how small their lots are. If I had the kind of money that Jake and Nina have, I'd want privacy and land.

The weather today is advantageous. It's a windy, gray day. It's not raining, not yet, but there is a threat of rain, which keeps everyone inside.

I park a few houses down from Jake and Nina's house. I wait a second, and then I get out of the car and walk back, along the sidewalk. It's late September. The days are getting cooler but the trees are mostly still green, only a meager few leaves starting to turn. Over the next few weeks, the rest will change colors and fall.

I wear a baseball cap. I pull it down low. I walk confidently, with my hands in my pockets, as if I have as much right as anyone to be here.

When I get to the Hayes's long driveway, I go straight to the front door. I don't hesitate. I've been thinking about the very real possibility of a video doorbell and need to know what I'm up against. When I get to the door, I make like I'm going to press the doorbell but I don't press anything. For a second, I stand on the stoop, accessing the button. Ring, Nest and the rest—they all look the exact same, part doorbell, part camera. The cameras are meant to be visible, not hidden. The intent is to deter people from vandalizing property or breaking in, rather than to catch them in the act. If the Hayeses have a video doorbell, I need to know. I have a story in my back pocket for if I get caught on camera now, ringing the doorbell, one I made up about how I misunderstood and thought Lily was here. I'd come looking for my wife, because I needed her for some reason. Family emergency. She wasn't answering her phone. I didn't have all the details worked out, but I could make them up on the fly if I needed to.

I won't need to. The Hayeses have a traditional doorbell. There is no camera attached. It's just the button. I relax.

I make my way back along the front walkway for the garage. I enter the pin number into the keypad. The garage door lifts open and, as soon as I can, I duck under the overhead door and watch it close behind me. When it reaches the ground, I turn the door handle and let myself into their home.

I find myself standing in a modern mudroom. I hold my breath, counting, waiting for an alarm to go off because maybe Lily was wrong. Maybe Jake and Nina got a home security system after last summer when Lily watched their cat, or maybe they had it all along, but didn't ask Lily to set it. Lily and I have a home security system. I never felt we needed one. It was a luxury and just another bill to pay. We didn't have one in our previous house. But this alarm came with our house and, until this week, we almost never used it. I set it off by accident once and the sound was enough to bring me to my knees. You don't make that mistake twice. I practically had to offer up my firstborn child to make the security company believe that Lily and I were safe, that no one had broken in and was holding me at gunpoint.

Now, every night for the last five days, Lily has asked me to set the alarm.

Neither of us has put into words how, though we know Jake is dead, absent a body, there is nothing concrete to say that he's dead.

I'm a numbers guy. As a market research analyst, my life's work is all about qualitative and quantitative research. Data. I like proof. In the absence of proof, my imagination goes wild. Lily's does too. She has fears that she hasn't much articulated to me. But I know she feels them. Last night, as we made love, I caught a glimpse of her face in the moonlight. Lily was beneath me. She suddenly stilled and I looked to see if she was okay, if I had lost her. Lily's eyes were open. She was staring somewhere over my shoulder. She wasn't with me. She was somewhere else, her eyes on the open bedroom door and she was waiting, I think, for him, for Jake, to come in when our guards were down. Lily shows signs of PTSD. There are times she goes mentally back to that moment with Jake in the forest preserve. She thinks about it still. Sometimes, she's said, when she closes her eyes, she can see his face, she can see the rage in his eyes. She hears him spitting his words at her. She feels the spit on her face. It terrifies and traumatizes her all over again.

In her head she knows that he's dead. She just can't make the rest of herself believe it.

Sometimes she wakes up crying from nightmares. In her dreams, she can't run fast enough. He catches her this time, yanking her by the ankles, pulling her back, dragging her face-down across the hard earth. She feels it on her skin, on her face, as he hauls her over rocks and debris, further into the trees where it's dark as night, the sun eclipsed by trees. He uses the palm of his hand to press her face into the earth. She inhales dirt as she tries to breathe. She's always gasping for air when she comes to.

When I'm convinced there is no alarm in the Hayes's house,

I walk further inside, into a kitchen, which is overwhelmingly large and modern and white. I've been here before. I've stood in this very kitchen, around the island, talking to Lily, Nina and Jake, laughing and drinking to excess. I'm no stranger to their house, but still, it's peculiar to be in someone else's house when you haven't been invited in. It feels as if the walls have eyes. I feel a phantom presence, like I'm not alone, though I am. I tell myself that no one else is here. It's not possible. Nina is at breakfast with Lily and Jake is dead. Neither of their cars was in the garage or on the driveway. I *am* alone. I just don't know why it feels like I'm not. Maybe it's my guilty conscience.

In the kitchen, a cat comes from out of nowhere, meowing at me. It curls itself around my ankles. I go to touch it and it hisses at me. I jerk back, my elbow knocking into a glass of water by mistake. The glass slips from the edge of the countertop and falls. I catch it on the way down. I don't even know how. Quick reflexes. The glass doesn't break, but the water spills, running down the face of the cabinet and pooling on the floor.

"Fuck," I mutter. The cat runs away. I've never liked cats. They're mercurial. One minute they're your friend, the next they're biting you.

I quickly unroll paper towels from a holder by the sink. I sop up the mess. I can't throw the paper towels in the trash, because I have to leave no evidence that I've been here. I force the paper towels in my jacket pocket so I can take them with me when I go.

I look at my phone. Lily said she would text when they left the restaurant. They haven't been gone long enough to be seated, much less have eaten. I have plenty of time. Still, I don't want to be here. I want to find what I need and leave.

Lily and I made a plan before she left our house. We talked about it. I told her I didn't want her texting things like *Leave now* or *Nina is on the way*, anything that would make us look guilty of wrongdoing or suggest that I was here, in case later someone, like the police, looked at our texts. I'm trying to be smart about this, to think five steps ahead. Lily and I have code words. *Pizza tonight?* means Nina is on her way home, but that I have a couple minutes to spare. *Thai?* is a code red. In other words, get out now.

It's like we have our own secret language.

I think about where, if Lily didn't carry my spare key, we would keep it.

A junk drawer comes to mind. I search the kitchen drawers for a junk drawer, finding one, but without a key fob in it. Instead batteries, an eyeglass tool kit, birthday candles and matches. The dining room or living room don't make sense. I step back into the mudroom and sink my hands into the pockets of a jacket on a coatrack, coming up with only gloves. A bag also hangs from the rack. I unzip the pockets of the bag one by one but they're mostly empty inside, with things like tissues and coins.

The master bedroom, maybe. My dad used to keep his wallet and keys on his dresser at night. Jake could too. I start to head for the stairs when I remember that Jake has an office. It's toward the front of the house. It's one of the rooms you see when you first come in through the front door. The first time we had dinner here, he showed me his office. He and Nina had just moved in and we were getting the grand tour of the house, the massive master bedroom, the finished basement with wet bar, the workout room. Jake was most proud of his office. It was masculine and luxurious and more importantly, all his, like a man cave but with prestigious diplomas and a bar cart full of top-shelf liquor.

I remember that Nina and Lily skipped the office part of the tour. They went back to the kitchen for more wine and appetizers, which they took out onto the patio that overlooks a golf course. Jake and I stayed for a while in his office, him sitting at the incredibly large executive desk and me on the small leather chair opposite it, feeling just as small as the chair. We sat there, sipping some kind of gin that he told me sold for almost three hundred dollars a bottle. "Good, isn't it?" he'd asked, gloating from behind his lowball glass. I wasn't impressed. I didn't tell him, because that's not me. Instead I said it was good, the best gin I'd ever had.

I leave the kitchen for the office now, cutting through the foyer. I let myself in through the frosted glass door, which is closed but not locked. I leave the door open behind me.

At first I carefully float around the room. I run my fingers over things. I want to know Jake Hayes. Not the Jake Hayes who was arrogant but funny and fun to be around, like a rich frat boy, but the one Lily bumped into this week. That's a man neither of us knew.

Jake was a man who was hard to get a read on. Lily and I talked about that and agreed. For a doctor, he wasn't compassionate or empathetic. After a few drinks, he had a tendency to make light of things that happened on the operating table. Maybe it was his way to cope with the stress of it all or maybe he was just cold. I've read his reviews online, mostly because I was curious and they were there, public and easily accessible. Patients complained about things like appointments being rushed or feeling not listened to, but they said that he was highly competent, that they trusted his decisions. I've also read that people with a higher IQ have a lower emotional intelligence than people with a lower IQ. Jake is the classic example of this. Smart but emotionless. The red flags are more obvious now, in light of what's happened. They're less easy to dismiss. From the things Nina has told Lily, smart but emotionless is not an unfair assessment of him. It's practically spot-on. Even in their marriage, he could be cold.

But now, moving around his office, I want to know the side of him I never knew, this other side of him that thought it might be okay to try and come on to my wife, to exploit her trusting nature, to force her to her knees on the dirt and attempt to do things to her that I can't stand to imagine. Jake isn't just arrogant and cold. Now I know that there's this violent, brute side of him that keeps me up at night, wishing I had been the one to bash his head in with a rock, although maybe it's better that it was Lily because sweet, little, one-hundred-and-ten-pound Lily would have been less forceful about it than me, dragging it out, killing him slowly. I like to think he died slowly. That it was painful. That he suffered.

I don't try to be particularly quiet as I riff through the desk drawers, sliding my hand along the inside of them and beneath piles of notebooks and paper, feeling for the key. I take things out, looking under and behind them. I keep thinking I might find something damning among Jake's things, but it's all harmless, files and such. I sit in his executive chair for a second, swiveling around, letting my eyes wander around the room, considering the file cabinet or a safe. Is a key fob the kind of thing you keep in a safe? If you don't want to lose it, maybe.

I rise up from the desk to go to the file cabinet.

It happens at the same time. The phone, in my pocket, vibrates against my thigh. I take it out to look. It's Lily. Thai tonight?

From upstairs, above my head, comes a noise like footsteps. It crosses above me, and then stops. I hold my breath. Not ten seconds later I hear the rush of water like through pipes. My eyes follow the movement of water as it snakes across the office ceiling and then descends behind the wall, down to the basement.

Someone, upstairs, has flushed a toilet.

My instincts were right.

I'm not alone in the house.

Someone else is here with me.

NINA

The restaurant where Lily and I meet is one of my favorites. It has a rustic farmhouse feel to it, while still being modern at the same time. The decor is all black-and-white and wooden, with things like white shiplap walls; wide, wooden floorboards; painted, black exposed pipes that run along the ceiling. The fabric of the chairs and booths is all black-and-white, in geometric designs. It's visually pleasing and the food is divine. A line of people wait for a table, but Lily was smart. She thought ahead. She made a reservation so that we're able to skip the line, much to the chagrin of those who see us come in and get immediately seated.

"Thank you for suggesting this," I say to Lily as we settle into a small table, sitting across from each other. "I can't tell you how much I appreciate it."

"Yes. Of course. I wanted to talk to you, just to make sure

you're hanging in there and that you're okay. It's so hard to talk at work, when we're always in a rush or getting interrupted."

I put my bag on the floor beneath me and say, "I'm sure this comes as no surprise, but Jake still hasn't come home."

Lily sighs, sympathetic as she reaches across the table to set her hand on mine. "I'm so sorry, Nina. Have you heard anything from him?" she asks.

"Nothing," I say. "I spoke to his colleagues the other day and drove around looking for his car at both the hospital and his office. I don't know where he is, Lily. It's like he's just completely gone."

"I wish you would have told me you were going to Jake's office and the hospital," Lily says. "I would have gone with you, to keep you company at least, or to help you look for him."

"That's sweet of you."

"I can't imagine how hard this must be, Nina." Lily offers a commiserative smile. She is a good listener. She's always been. It's one of the reasons I find it so easy to talk to her. Lily's secret, I think, is that she actually listens. She doesn't offer advice like other people feel the need to do. People always want to fix things. They want to make them better, which is sweet and well-intentioned, but not everything can be fixed. Sometimes a person just wants to find an outlet for their feelings.

"It is. You don't even know. I can't sleep. I can't think. All day and all night I think about him, wondering where he is and if he's okay, if he's dead or hurt or if he's just intentionally avoiding me. I don't even know what would be better," I admit, "if he's hurt or if he's avoiding me, because if he's hurt then at least maybe he doesn't hate me."

"I'm sure he doesn't hate you," Lily says.

The waitress appears and asks if we're ready to order. Lily asks for toast and scrambled eggs and I get an omelet. We order coffee. Lily asks for decaf.

When the waitress leaves, Lily says, "Have you heard anything more from the police?"

"I went back to the police station last night. They had told me when I filed the missing person's report that most people come home on their own within three days. It's now been five."

"Do they have any leads?" she asks.

"Not yet."

"Have they tried tracing his phone?"

Last night, I asked the police the same question. Phones can be traceable. But, from what the police told me, it can be hard to find a phone if the battery doesn't retain some of the charge. Even if Jake's phone isn't somehow dead—which I'm sure it is—the carrier can ping the phone, asking it to reply with its location but still, the results are imprecise. They can track a phone to a broad area, but not a specific location.

But that doesn't matter, because Jake isn't a minor, he isn't high-risk and he isn't on my phone plan. The cell phone carrier won't perform a warrantless search, and only now have the police issued a warrant. They were reluctant to do so because it's not a crime to disappear, though, now that so many days have passed and Jake hasn't once accessed our bank accounts, gone to work or spoken to anyone, the police have started taking his disappearance more seriously.

I say, "They're working on that now. But every time I call Jake's phone it goes to voice mail, which tells me it's dead. I don't think the police will ever find him that way."

"I'm so sorry," Lily says as the waitress drops off our coffees with a little bowl of cream and a sugar dispenser. I reach for my cup, emptying cream and sugar into it.

"I know you are. I keep wondering if something has happened to Jake or if Jake just doesn't want to be found. He'd been so different lately, Lily. He was stressed at work, and distant with me. We'd been fighting for a while before this happened."

"Why was he distant?" she asks.

"Because of my mother, I think. Because I've been spending so much time with her and not enough with him. He didn't like that."

"But your mother needs you," Lily says, and I'm glad that she at least understands.

"I know. I tried to make him see that it was all beyond my control. I've felt torn, like I can't be in two places at one time."

"Have you talked to anyone else about Jake? Family or friends?"

"I've called his parents, his brother and some friends, but honestly, Lily, I don't know what else to do. I feel helpless. Jake has to be somewhere. I feel like someone, somewhere has to know where he is."

"What did his family say?" Lily asks.

"That they don't know where he is. That they haven't spoken to him."

Lily asks, "Do you think they're telling the truth?"

"Honestly? I don't know. I can see Jake's parents lying for him. I suppose he could be staying with them. They say no, but I don't know what to think or who I can trust anymore."

Lily gives me a genuine smile and says, "You can trust me."

I appreciate that. I know that I can. I say, "You're a good friend, Lily. I'm really so grateful that I have you."

A few minutes later, the waitress comes back with our meals.

"Can I get you anything else?" she asks.

"No," I say, "thank you," and she leaves. I reach for my fork, though I don't know that I'll be able to eat. My eyes were bigger than my stomach, and I don't have much, if any, appetite of late. "My mother is staying with me now," I say to Lily, apropos of nothing other than that I want to talk about something other than Jake for a change. These days, he's monopolizing all of my thoughts, my conversations and my dreams. I can't breathe without thinking of Jake.

Lily looks up from her plate. "Oh?" she asks, visibly surprised. "You didn't say."

"Well, not for good. I just couldn't stand to be alone in the house. I needed the company and my mother probably shouldn't be alone either. It's just until Jake comes home," I say, trying to stay optimistic about him coming home. The thing that I find the most worrisome of all is how he hasn't gone to work. To me, that's more alarming than him not returning my calls or taking money out of the bank. Jake has spent twenty years of his life training to become a surgeon, from college, to med school, to his residency. He's living his dream, following in the footsteps of his own father, who is also a neurosurgeon, close to retiring now. Jake wouldn't risk losing all that. There must be something physically preventing him from going to work.

"How long has she been staying with you?" Lily asks.

It was just yesterday that I invited my mother to come stay with me. I hadn't told her until last night what was happening with Jake. I tried keeping it from her because she isn't wild about him. It didn't help that, before she got sick, Jake gave me an ultimatum: him or her. If I didn't stop spending so much of my free time with my mother, he said, he would leave. He was jealous and also, I don't think he's ever been a huge fan of her. My mother can be outspoken at times and Jake didn't like her putting ideas in my head. When we were both home, he wanted me all to himself, which meant on the weekends I could never visit her. It was okay. We made it work. I told her what Jake said, what he wanted—about his stipulation that weekends were reserved for spending time with him—and my mother and I made more of an effort to see each other during the week, in the evenings, after school, but when he was still at work. Except that the evenings were never long enough, and after work I was sometimes too tired to visit. But then her vision started to go and it was all beyond Jake's and my control. When she needed me, I had to go to her. I had to be with her.

When Jake didn't come home Monday, I didn't want to give my mother another reason not to like him. I thought this would all blow over in a couple days and that she wouldn't have to know that he was ever gone.

My own father left us when I was six. He and my mother had a tumultuous marriage to say the least. I remember falling asleep every night listening to them fight. It wasn't ever physical, but it was hurtful. They would scream at each other and call one another names. And then one night, in the middle of the night, my father left because he'd fallen madly in love with some other woman and he wanted to be with her. Growing up, my bedroom faced the front of the house. I remember waking up that night to the sound of him leaving, and creeping to the window to watch him go. For a while he would send me cards on my birthday or Christmas, but eventually that stopped. I haven't spoken to him in twenty years. My mother never dated seriously again and she never remarried. She doesn't trust men in general, which means, by default, she doesn't trust Jake. It's not Jake's fault. It's not because of anything Jake did.

After going to the police the other day and filing that missing person's report, it was time to come clean. I didn't want my mother to hear about Jake from someone else, before she heard it from me.

I also didn't want to spend another night in that house alone.

"Just one night so far," I say to Lily. "I picked her up yesterday. She'll stay with me until Jake is back."

Lily reaches for her water. "You should have invited her along for breakfast," she says, taking a sip from her glass.

"It's fine," I say. "I wanted you all to myself. I can never get through a whole conversation with you anymore without us getting interrupted."

"So she's at your house now?" Lily asks.

"Yes."

Lily takes another sip of her water and sets the glass back

down. "Would you excuse me?" she asks and, as she stands up from the table, I see that her face has lost color.

"Yes, of course. Is everything okay, Lily?" I ask, concerned that she might still be sick from earlier in the week.

"I just need to use the restroom," she says. She gets the attention of a waitress to ask where it is. The waitress points her in the right direction. "I'll be right back," she says to me. "Sorry," she says, though there's no reason for her to be sorry. I'm just worried about her.

Lily reaches for her purse before she leaves and I watch as she disappears to the bathroom, weaving between tables. I wait for her to come back. I don't want to eat without her. I keep an eye on the bathroom door, but when I'm not watching the door, I people watch, running my eyes over the vast number of happy people, friends and husbands and wives with kids who fill the crowded restaurant. Everyone seems so happy. Everyone but me.

Eventually Lily comes back. She was gone so long that I was just starting to think I should check on her.

"What were we talking about?" she asks as she lowers herself into the seat across from me, avoiding my eye. She reaches again for her glass of water.

I say, "My mother."

"Oh. Right," she says, and I can see Lily trying to remember what we were even saying about my mother.

I say, "How she's staying with me." I reach for my fork and take a bite of my omelet. Lily isn't eating. I ask, "Are you feeling okay, Lily?"

"Fine. Why?" she asks, but her face is pale and I can see that she's not fine.

"You don't seem fine."

"I am fine. I promise." She sips again from her water.

"You're not eating."

"I'm just not hungry. I'm sorry. Christian made breakfast this morning. He forgot about me meeting you."

"You were in the bathroom a long time. Are you sure you're really okay?"

"Yes," she says. "I'm sure."

I don't know that I believe her. It seems like she's holding something back. I stare at her, worried about her, as she tries to force a bite of scrambled eggs into her mouth to prove a point. It doesn't go well. She winds up chewing the eggs a long time until eventually she swallows. But even then, she has to take another sip of her water to force the bite down.

She scoops more eggs onto her fork, sizes them up, but then gives up. Her shoulders go suddenly slack, she drops her fork and confesses, "I'm pregnant, Nina," and everything that's been happening this week with Lily makes perfect sense. The way she disappeared so quickly the other day after school, to a doctor appointment maybe. Lily's forgetfulness and her absentmindedness. The color of her skin. The extended time she spent in the bathroom, being sick probably. The fact that she's only pushing the food around her plate and not eating, though breakfast was her idea. Lily has always been disposed to morning sickness and I can see in her face, now that I know, that she feels sick. Her left hand is on her abdomen and she keeps sipping from that glass of water, as if trying to squelch a bout of nausea.

"Congratulations," I say, but it's less than enthusiastic because Lily and Christian have had rotten luck when it comes to getting pregnant. Actually, getting pregnant hasn't been difficult for them, it's keeping the baby alive that has been. It's not my place to say, but I don't know why she and Christian keep trying, why they keep setting themselves up for heartbreak.

"Why didn't you tell me?" I ask, my voice softening.

"You know why," she says, and I do. Because the odds that she will lose this baby are high. "Besides, you have so much going on right now, with your mother and Jake. I didn't want to burden you."

I reach my hand across the table for hers. Hers is wet and

icy cold from holding on to the water glass. I've been a shitty friend. I've been going through something hard, but Lily has too. "You're never a burden, Lily. You can always tell me anything. How far along are you?"

"Nine weeks."

I breathe in deeply. Lily has never made it to the second trimester. This is a precarious time for her, Christian and the baby. Life is precious but fragile.

"What is the doctor saying?"

"That everything seems to be fine. So far. But then again, it always is."

It's like with Jake. Things are fine, until suddenly they're not.

In an instant, your world can turn upside down when you're least expecting it.

CHRISTIAN

I go rigid. I hold my breath. I don't breathe.

Above me, things go silent. The water stops running down to the septic tank in the basement. The pipes become quiet and still. I expect to hear the sound of footsteps or a sink running. I prepare myself for it, waiting, but there's nothing, only silence, so that then I start to second-guess what I heard. Maybe it wasn't a toilet flush. Maybe it was something else, like air in the water pipes. Maybe it wasn't caused by something human.

I'd believe it, if it weren't for Lily's text. Thai tonight?

Someone is here.

I slide an open drawer closed without hurrying. It takes everything in me not to slam it shut. I push the chair that I was sitting in back under the desk. I won't make it to the file cabinet or have a chance to look for a safe.

I find my exits. I could use the front door. It's closer, but visible, and I wouldn't be able to lock the door behind myself if I went that way. The office sits less than ten feet from the base of the stairs. I see the wrought iron balusters through the open office doors. There is a window in the office, but to go out that way, I'd have to remove the screen. I couldn't replace it from outside either, meaning it would be impossible to go that way without leaving evidence that I was here.

I have no choice but to go back out through the garage door, the same way I came.

I drag myself across the room. The floors are wood. I wear shoes. It's practically futile to try to be silent. My shoes are anything but light on the wooden floors.

I step hesitantly from the office into the foyer. It's the kind of space that's two stories tall with a coffered ceiling and a giant chandelier. A quarter-turn staircase leads down into the foyer. There's a loftlike space with a railing at the top of the stairs, so that the second floor overlooks the first.

From just outside the open office door, I see a wall-mounted mail holder by the front door. It feels like just the thing I was looking for. The problem is that the mail holder is in direct view of the stairs and the loft. I hesitate, calculating the risk. It's high, but the mail holder is the perfect place for the key. That's exactly where Lily and I would leave it, and I've already come this far. I can't go home empty-handed because without this key, there is no way to move the car. And if we don't move Jake's car, it puts him and Lily together at the same place, on the same day he died. It makes Lily look guilty.

I let my gaze go up the stairs and to the loft. It's still quiet, for now. If I didn't know better, I'd think no one was upstairs.

I pull my way across the foyer floor, feeling completely and utterly exposed. I've done my fair share of disorderly things in my life. I was an insubordinate teenager. I had more groundings, detentions and suspensions than I can count. My mother used to tell me that my behavior was taking years off her life and was going to be the death of her.

But now I'm an adult, and this is breaking and entering. It comes with serious consequences, like jail.

There are slots for mail and bills on the mail holder, but also hooks for keys. I slip my hand into one of the slots, striking gold. The key fob. I pinch the key fob between my fingertips and pull it out. Something else comes too, slipping from my hand and, this time, my reaction time isn't fast enough to catch whatever it is. The object falls to the floor, making noise.

A door upstairs rasps open. "Nina? Is that you?"

The voice belongs to a woman.

I spin around. I don't risk looking up the stairs. I leave whatever fell on the floor. I make my way back toward the garage, as footsteps pad across the hall and a silhouette appears in my range of view.

"Nina!" she calls again.

Footsteps descend the stairs.

I head into the kitchen. I cross the kitchen for the garage door. I set my hand down on the garage door lever and, as deliberately as I can, I pull the door open. I step into the garage and guide the door closed behind me, holding down on the lever, releasing it by degrees so that it doesn't snap back into place.

What I want to do is slam the door and run.

I have no choice but to open the overhead door. It will make noise, but that's inevitable because there is no other way out of the garage other than through that door. I have zero options.

I press the button. The door lifts. It's as loud as a leaf- or a snowblower on a Sunday morning. There is the very real possibility that I've fucked this all up. That I'm fucked. That the police are already on their way and I won't get to my car before they arrive.

As I walk to my car, I risk a glance back and see it.

From one of the front windows, a face is pressed to the glass, looking back at me.

I speed home in such a state of shock that I forget all about the bag of Lily's bloody clothes sitting in the back seat of my car.

"It was her mother," Lily tells me later, when we're both back home. I was home before she got here. She came in to find me pacing, practically running the house from end to end, just waiting for the axe to fall, for the police to show up at the door with a warrant for my arrest. "Her mother is losing her vision, Christian. It's fine. She doesn't see very well. How close were you to her?"

"Maybe ten or twenty feet. The thing is, Lily, even if she couldn't see me, she heard me. She knew someone was there. She spoke to me."

"What did she say?"

"She called me Nina."

"See," Lily says, "there you go. It's fine. She thought you were Nina."

"Except Nina would have spoken to her. Nina wouldn't have run. And it gets worse."

"Why?"

"Because as I was leaving, she got a clear view of my face."

"Not clear, Christian. She doesn't see very well," she says again. "She wouldn't have known it was you. She doesn't even know you. She couldn't identify you. I'm sure it's fine."

The more times Lily says that it's fine, the less I believe it's true.

As the day goes on and the police don't come, I find my anxiety tapering. If they knew it was me, they would have come already. Wouldn't they?

And then, later in the day, just as I finally start to feel safe, the doorbell rings.

NINA

I know that something is different the second I come home.

The garage door is open.

In the kitchen, there is a smell in the air, a woodsy scent like cologne.

I set my bag on the kitchen island and step out of my shoes. I take a sweeping glance of the room, calling for my mother. When she doesn't answer, I take long strides toward the foyer to go check on her.

Just into the foyer, I see that Jake's office door is open. It stops me dead. I draw in a breath. The door is not just slightly open, but entirely open, the frosted glass door flush against the wall. That door hasn't been open in days. I've been keeping it intentionally closed because I kept finding myself looking in this week, expecting him to be there. He never was, but all it took was a lampshade in my peripheral vision, for example, to

JUST THE NICEST COUPLE

make me think that he was. My heart couldn't take any more false alarms.

But now the door is open. Someone has opened it and my first thought is that Jake is home, that he's finally come back home to me. I edge toward it. From the foyer, I don't have a clear view of the inside yet, but there is a part of me expecting Jake to be sitting behind his desk, as if nothing is wrong, as if he hasn't been gone all this time.

I take a breath and step into the room, but it's completely empty. Jake isn't here. I sag against the doorframe to catch my breath, feeling let down by the empty desk chair.

After a minute, I turn away from the office. There is something on the floor by the front door. I go to see what it is and find that it's the extra key card to my Tesla, sitting by the floor register. It must have fallen from the mail sorter, which is where Jake and I keep it. I pick it up and put it back in the pocket of the mail sorter, wondering how it got on the floor and if my mother was looking for something while I was gone.

I reach for the banister. I pull myself toward the stairs. I climb the steps for the guest room, where my mother has been staying. The guest room doesn't get much use because Jake's family and mine live relatively close. When they come to visit, they come for the day, not for the night. Still, I went out of my way to decorate the space. It was wishful thinking, hoping that a beautiful room would bring guests, and it has brought some, old college friends mostly, but not as many as I imagined. For now I'm grateful I have a place for my mother to stay. The room is modern chic, but simple, with dark walls and white bedding and drapes.

I find her sitting in the armchair in the corner of the room with our cat curled up at the end of her bed. She's looking out the window at the street. Her back is to me and she's listening to an audiobook in her earbuds, which is why she didn't hear me calling for her. She's lost in the audiobook. She's consumed with audiobooks these days because it's practically all she can do now that she's losing her vision. She can't read a physical book, she can't watch TV and she can't drive. Because of what's going on with her eyes, she's no longer able to do what she wants to do when she wants to do it. She has to rely on me for everything. It's so hard on her, who's used to being independent.

"Mom," I say and I go to her and set a hand on her shoulder. She turns, taking the earbuds out of her ears. My mother is only sixty-two. She's relatively young, and it shows. Physically, she's fit. She's thin. She used to be a hiker and a backpacker when she was in her twenties. She met my father backpacking through Europe, long before they got married and had me. I forget sometimes that she had an entire life before I was born, when she was once young, adventurous and completely self-sufficient. She's no longer self-sufficient but, even now, she could walk for miles and easily keep up with me. Her age is just starting to show in her face and neck, but her skin is mostly still free of lines, just some around the mouth and between the eyes. I'm envious. I hope that I look half as good as she does when I'm her age.

"Hi," I say, smiling down.

"How was breakfast?" she asks.

"Good," I say. "Did you get along okay while I was gone?"

"Yes," she says.

"Did you nap?"

"A little."

"What else did you do?" I ask.

She shrugs. "I took a shower," she says.

"That's all?" I wasn't gone long, less than two hours. "Did you eat anything? Did you go downstairs?"

"Yes," she says. "I made myself some oatmeal for breakfast."

"Good," I say, glad that she wasn't shy about helping herself to breakfast. But that's not really what I want to know. "Did you go for a walk?" I ask. "The garage door was open."

My mother shakes her head, quiet. I don't think I left the garage door open by mistake, but maybe.

"Did you go into Jake's office while I was gone, Mom? That door was open too. I've been keeping it closed."

My mother hesitates. She knows something but she's reluctant to tell me. I tell her, "It's okay if you did. It's not like it's off-limits. You can go anywhere in the house that you'd like. You know that. What's ours is yours, Mom. I'm just curious, because the door was open and I'd left it closed."

"I didn't go into his office," she says.

I frown. She had to have gone into his office while I was gone, but I don't understand why she would lie to me about it. "Are you sure, Mom?" I ask. The office door was definitely open. I know for sure it was closed before I left. Fully closed. A person would have had to turn the handle to get in, so I can't even blame the cat for it.

"Of course I'm sure," my mother says, but again, she hesitates and I can tell she's holding something back.

"What aren't you telling me, Mom?"

She stands up from the chair. When she does, she rivals my height. "I didn't want to tell you. I didn't want to worry you. But when you were gone, Nina," she says, reaching for my hand, "Jake came home."

My jaw goes slack. It takes a second for her words to sink in. *Jake came home.* Jake is here. My first instinct was right. Someone was here in the house when I wasn't home. It was Jake.

My hand slips from hers. I back away from her, moving in reverse toward the door. "Where is he?" I ask, breathless. Is Jake in our bedroom? Our bedroom is on the opposite side of the upstairs hall. At the top of the stairs, I would have had to turn the other way to get to it, which means I didn't walk past it. I didn't see Jake's car outside. It wasn't in the garage or on the driveway, but if it was on the street, I could have missed it. "Is he in our room?"

I don't know what to feel, that Jake could return home, just like that. That he could be gone all these days, and then slip back into my life as if nothing has happened. Jake would never forgive me if I disappeared for five days, and then came home.

That said, I'm eager to see him. To talk to him. To put this all behind us and move on.

I back toward the open door to go to Jake.

"No, Nina," my mother says, her voice stopping me. "He's not in the bedroom. He left. He's not here anymore."

"He left?" I ask, aghast. "When? Why?" I don't give her a chance to respond. I don't understand. Jake was here and then he left again. Why would he do that? "What did he say?" I ask. "Where has he been staying all week? Is he still mad at me?"

"Nothing," my mother says. "I don't know. He didn't say anything to me."

I can't believe this. I can't believe what I'm hearing. "What do you mean, Mom? You didn't talk to him?"

"No."

"Why not?"

"I tried to. He didn't give me a chance, Nina. He thought he was alone, I think. He didn't know anyone was here. He ran out the door as soon as he found me here."

"How did you know he was here?"

"I heard him, downstairs, just outside his office."

"Doing what?" I ask.

"I don't know," she says. "Looking for something, it seemed from the sound of it. I thought it was you, coming home early. I thought maybe your breakfast plans had changed. I went to the top of the stairs. I called down for you. I must have startled him."

"What did he say when you saw him?"

"I already told you," she says. "He said nothing, Nina. When he heard me, he turned and ran."

"He ran?" I ask. It upsets me, thinking of Jake running away from the home we share, hiding from me. It's even worse than if he hadn't come home at all.

"Yes," she says. "I'm sorry. I didn't want to tell you because I knew it would upset you."

"You should have called me," I say. I would have come home. But it wouldn't have mattered, because it would have been too late. Jake would have already been gone before I could get home.

"I'm sorry, Nina."

"It's not your fault, Mom. What happened then?" I ask. "After you saw him in the foyer and he ran?"

She says, "He went out through the garage, and then I saw him on the driveway, there," she says, turning to point out the window, which faces onto the street. I go to stand at the window beside her, looking out. The day is ugly, windy and gray. Despite the weather, the street we live on is stunning. It's affluent and much sought-after. Jake and I bought a half-million-dollar home only to knock it down because it wasn't the house we wanted, but the land. Land is growing scarce and this is prime real estate. The previous home was dated; it was never our intention to keep it, despite the exorbitant price tag. We knocked it down, and then hired builders to put in the home of our dreams. The street is residential with parks and walking paths and such. The schools, should Jake and I ever have kids, though I'm losing hope of that, are top-notch. Most of the neighbors are rich. It's an ostentatious wealth, though not as ostentatious as Jake's parents', who live in a house with a name—Garrison House, for some Mr. Garrison who lived there a hundred years ago, and was designed by one of the most renowned architects of the time—but something slightly more subtle than that.

Why did Jake come? What did he want? If not me, then what?

What is this game he's playing with me?

Later, I search Jake's office. I don't know what I'm looking for, just for something amiss. I find nothing. Whatever he took from the office, or whatever he was doing in the office, isn't obvious to me.

Our neighborhood has a Facebook page. People are always bemoaning cars driving past too fast, as if none of them has ever once in their life pressed down too hard on the gas pedal. They catch clips of speeders on their video doorbells and post them to the Facebook page for a public shaming. Once the car was mine. Jake and I don't have a video doorbell ourselves. I asked him once if we should consider getting one, but he said he didn't want to be notified every time a squirrel walked past our front door. He said that the video wasn't safe either, that it's being uploaded to the Cloud for anyone to see. Maybe it is and maybe it isn't; I don't honestly know, though I'd teased him at the time, asking if he had girlfriends coming over when I wasn't home that he didn't want me to know about. Video doorbells don't only keep watch on strangers. They monitor the people who live inside the home.

As far as I know, these video doorbells store footage indefinitely. If I ask, I'm wondering if my neighbors with cameras will let me see this morning's feed. I'm sure someone caught something, even just a fragment of Jake's face or the back of his head as he let himself into the house. I want to see him. I need to see Jake.

Because then maybe I'll know why he was here.

CHRISTIAN

My reaction is delayed because I can't believe what I'm seeing when I open the door. I expected to see the police when the doorbell rang. This is no worse, but no better.

Outside it's still gray. The wind has picked up. The trees blow in something like thirty-mile-per-hour winds, the more insubstantial of them bending. You can hear the wind howl as it enters the house uninvited.

Her hair whips around her face. She gathers what she can in a hand and holds it at the side of her head, by her neck.

It's Nina Hayes. I haven't seen her in maybe six months, but she hasn't changed much. She's almost exactly the same as the last time I saw her. She's a brunette. Her brown hair goes just below the shoulders. She's a pretty woman, but she can't hold a candle to Lily.

Nina's expression is flat, if not frowning. It makes me wonder what she knows, if she knows something. It's so unlike her to just show up at our front door like this.

My heart goes wild inside of me and I feel like something feral and caged—a lion at the zoo—trapped and desperate to get out.

"Nina!" I say to her, but my tone and the delivery are too cheerful, too tinny. The smile plastered to my face is fake.

Nina's face is darkened. She stands on the porch in the wind. She has no interest in small talk. She's come for a purpose. "It's windy out here, Christian," she says. "Can I please come in?"

"Oh God, of course. I'm so sorry." I pull the door open more widely. Her arm brushes against me as she steps in, the wind pushing her through.

"Lily told me about Jake," I say, my cheerfulness lessening, becoming almost somber. "I'm so sorry, Nina. If there is ever anything we can do to help, or if there is anything you need—"

"Thank you. I appreciate that, Christian. If you don't mind, I need to talk to Lily, please," she says, cutting me off, and my first thought is to lie, to say that Lily isn't here. Lily's car is in the garage and the garage door is closed, so Nina wouldn't know whether or not she is home. For all Nina knows, Lily had errands to run after their breakfast together.

But then, Lily materializes behind me with a quiet, bemused expression on her face.

"Nina?" she asks, coming around a corner, her voice a whisper, her jaw practically slack. There is a dish towel in her hands. Lily has been doing dishes, cleaning up the kitchen that we've, over the last few days, neglected to clean, so that dishes were piling up on the counter and sink. Nina looks past me as Lily says, "I thought I heard your voice. Is everything okay?"

"Do you have a minute?" Nina asks, her words somewhat curt. Nina has never been the warm and fuzzy type, but this feels almost glacial and makes me uncomfortable. But then Nina says, "I'm sorry to just barge in on you like this," and something about that feels less glacial to me. Maybe I don't need to panic.

They were together not two hours ago. That in and of itself is concerning. Whatever Nina has to say to Lily, she could have said then. But she didn't, which means something has happened since they were at breakfast, something important enough to warrant coming over to our house to speak to Lily in person.

She knows what I've done.

"Yeah, of course," Lily says. "Come in."

Nina follows Lily to the kitchen, as I turn my back to them to close the door, having to shove it closed against the weight of the wind. I turn the dead bolt, trapping us all inside.

And then, for this one regrettable instant, I think I may have to do something to Nina before this is through. Because if she knows something, if she's come to confront Lily and me, then I can't just let her leave, can I? If I do, she'll go to the police. And then I'll go to jail, or even worse, Lily will go to jail. I'll do anything to keep Lily and myself, but especially Lily, out of jail. I have a sudden mental image of my hands coming down on Nina's neck. The image is so real and so crystal clear that I can feel what it would be like to press down, to stop the airflow to the trachea, to strangle her before lowering Nina's lifeless body to the floor. I imagine Nina's arms flailing, her legs kicking, and I wonder how long it would take, how much pressure I would have to put on her neck for her to die.

"Can I get you something?" Lily asks, breaking my reverie, and I feel instantly sick for thinking like that. I'm not a killer. I could never kill someone. Could I?

This whole thing has spiraled out of control, turning me into someone I'm not.

Nina follows Lily to the kitchen. Lily is still talking. "Water, tea?" she asks.

There's this slight tremor to Lily's voice. I hear it, but I wonder if Nina does.

Nina and Jake have been to our house for dinner before. It was after we'd been to theirs and saw the way they lived. Lily was reluctant to have them over; she felt self-conscious, as if our almost three thousand square foot, waterfront home was something to be ashamed of. She went all out getting things ready, cleaning and buying new stuff for the house. I remember saying something to her at the time like, if they're the good friends we think they are, they won't mind our average quality dishes and furniture, but Lily wanted everything just right.

"No. Thanks. I tried calling you," Nina says, still wearing her coat. "You didn't answer."

"Oh?" Lily glances back over her shoulder. "I didn't notice. I'm so sorry. My phone must be on silent. Is everything okay?"

"No. It's not, Lily," she says, and then Nina turns to see me following them into the kitchen. Her expression is unreadable. I force a smile, something that belies my terror and looks more like concern, though inside I'm fucking scared. My heart is a cheetah.

We come into the kitchen. Lily says, "Oh no, Nina," and she goes to the fridge to get Nina water anyway, despite her saying that she didn't want any. "What happened? Is it your mother?"

"No," Nina says. "It's Jake."

Lily says, "Sit, please. Here," while setting the bottle of water on the table. "Can I get you anything to eat?"

"No. I'm fine. Something has happened, Lily," she says, looking again in my direction, and I'm certain that something is me. "Do you mind giving Lily and me a minute, Christian?" she asks, and I'm taken aback by her candor. She stares at me, and then says, "I don't mean to be rude, but I was hoping I could talk to Lily alone."

"Oh yeah, sure," I say. "No problem."

Lily and I exchange a look. She doesn't want to be left alone with Nina any more than I want to leave her alone with Nina. I don't have a choice. I move from the kitchen to the stairs, climbing them and, when I get to the top, I stand there, listening, waiting for Nina to tell Lily that I was in their house this morning, as if Lily doesn't already know that. She came as a courtesy to tell Lily first, because they're friends, before she goes to the police.

I hold my breath. The wind outside is still loud, whipping around the corners of the house. It's begun to rain, the rain spitting against the windows. It makes it hard to hear Nina's voice. The house is dark. We don't have any lights on. It's the middle of the day but, with the weather as it is, it's dim like dusk.

Lily asks again, "Are you sure you don't want to sit?"

"No. I'm sure."

"What's going on Nina? You're scaring me."

"When you and I were at breakfast, someone came into my house," Nina says.

"Who?"

"It was Jake."

My knees practically collapse. I'm floored. Not being able to identify me is one thing, but mistaking me for Jake is something I hadn't expected.

"Jake?" Lily asks. She's unable to keep the shock out of her voice. But it's okay because her shock is warranted. It would be shocking if Jake came home when they were at breakfast, after being missing for all these days.

"Yes," Nina says. "Jake."

"How do you know?"

"My mother. She saw him."

"What did he say?" she asks. "What was he doing there? Is he still there now? Is he home?"

"No," Nina says. "He didn't say anything to my mother. He came, and then left again."

Lily says, "Oh God. I'm so sorry, Nina. What do you think he wanted?"

Nina is exasperated. "Who the hell knows. He was in his

office, my mother said, looking for something. He didn't come for me."

"Oh, Nina," Lily says. It's warm, sensitive. Silence follows and I imagine Lily putting her arms around Nina, embracing her. Thirty seconds or so pass, and then Lily says, "Look on the positive side: You know he's fine, right? He's not hurt. He's not missing, like you thought. Maybe he just needs some time to come to his senses. Every relationship needs the occasional break. What's that they say? Absence makes the heart grow fonder."

Nina is quiet at first. I'd give anything to still be in the kitchen with them. I want to see her face as she considers Lily's words.

"Maybe you're right," she says after a while.

I like how Lily does that, how she turns the conversation into something encouraging. She found a bright spot. Even if it is a bald-faced lie.

The road at night is dark. Lily and I waited until after ten o'clock to leave, knowing the streets would be quieter. In my car, I drive Lily to the place where Jake's car is parked. When we get to it, I pull to the side of the road, directly behind him. I shift the car into Park, and then my hands fall away from the steering wheel. Lily angles her body toward mine, and I put my hand on her knee.

"What are you thinking about?" she asks.

Outside, the rain is through. It never did amount to much. It was over and done within just a few hours. The wind has settled too. The night is perfectly still.

"Nothing," I say.

Lily knows me too well. "You're thinking about something, Christian. I can tell."

"How do you know?"

"You're quiet," she says. "Quieter than usual."

Lily is right. I am thinking about something. I'm thinking about what happened today, how I very narrowly dodged a bullet. "I thought for sure she knew," I say. "When Nina came over today, I thought I was totally fucked."

"But she didn't know, Christian. It's fine," Lily says, setting her hand on mine, holding it.

"I know. I know that now. I just got scared," I say, not wanting to admit that to Lily. I like to be the strong one, for Lily to think I'm indestructible. I want her to feel safe with me, to feel like I can take care of her, of us no matter what happens.

"It's okay to be scared. I was scared too. But Nina suspects nothing."

"I had these thoughts when Nina was at the house today," I confess.

"What kind of thoughts?" she asks. I don't say right away, so that Lily has to ask, "Christian?" as she leans in toward me.

I say, "You're going to think less of me if I say it."

She shakes her head. "I could never think anything bad about you."

I take a breath. I say, "I thought that if Nina knew what I'd done, if she had come to say that she knew it was me in their house this morning, then I wouldn't be able to let her leave. I'd have no choice but to keep her quiet."

"What do you mean when you say keep her quiet?" she asks.

I swallow, hard. I don't say, but I don't need to say it. I look at Lily and she knows from my expression what I mean. She reads it on my face. "You mean killing her," she says.

I nod, dimly. "I thought that if she was dead, then she couldn't tell anyone what I'd done."

"What *we'd* done, Christian," Lily says, reminding me that, "we're in this together. Just like Bonnie and Clyde."

Bonnie and Clyde. I half laugh, which was her intent I think. To lighten the mood. To make me laugh. The only problem is that it's not lost on me that Bonnie and Clyde were killed by the police. They were shot something like fifty times each. It was a terrible and violent way to go.

I like the idea of Lily and me being in this together.

I just don't want to wind up like Bonnie and Clyde in the end.

The thing is that even after Nina left this afternoon, the thoughts about killing her didn't leave. They were intrusive, disturbing and unwanted. I kept thinking how Nina is the only person standing in the way of Lily and me getting off scot-free. No one is really looking for Jake but her.

"Those are just thoughts, Christian," Lily says. "You wouldn't have acted on them. Thinking about killing someone and actually doing it are two different things."

Are they?

"How can you be sure?"

I, myself, wasn't sure. I'm still not sure. The line between right and wrong is getting more blurry with each day.

Lily says, "Just because you thought about doing something doesn't mean you would. You're a good man, Christian."

Am I?

We go quiet. There's something austere about this moment. This, even more than breaking into the Hayes's house for the key, is the point of no return. What we are doing is maybe even worse than breaking and entering. We're tampering with evidence now. For that, you can get something like twenty years in prison. For breaking and entering, it's more like two, assuming you didn't hurt anyone.

Lily says, "I'll follow you. Just don't drive too fast. I don't want to lose you," and it sounds ominous, like a sign of things to come. *I don't want to lose you.* I don't want to lose her either. Ever. I've spent a long time thinking about this in the last few days and I've made up my mind. If we do somehow get caught, I'll say that I did it, that I'm the one who killed Jake. I'll make up a motive. I'll say that I'm the one who broke into their house.

I'm the one who moved the car. Lily did none of it. She knew about none of it. I did it all by myself.

But what Lily said just now wasn't meant as a prophecy. It was a request. I have a lead foot, a tendency to drive too fast. That's all that she meant by it. I need to drive slowly, so that I don't lose her, so that neither of us gets pulled over by the police.

All along this short stretch of street, there are no streetlights, no passing cars. Newcomb is a two-lane road with little to no through traffic. Its only real purpose is to get to the forest preserve and for overflow parking. It's a dead-end street, with no one coming or going. On either side of us are nothing but trees. We're totally secluded.

"You won't lose me," I promise her. "I'll be right ahead of you the whole time."

I lean in toward Lily. She wraps her arms around my neck and I kiss her like it might be the last time I kiss her in my whole life.

"You ready?" I ask, pulling back. She nods. "Switch places with me," I say, so that she can drive my car and I'll drive Jake's. She does. By now, Jake's is the only car here. I slip my hands into a pair of gloves and go to it, letting myself in. I pull out onto the street. Lily follows, her headlights in my rearview mirror. I drive to a budget hotel in Bridgeview not too far from the airport. I drive slowly. I don't go over the speed limit. I never once pass through a yellow light. I use my turn signals unfailingly. But still, I'm fucking scared.

I watch Lily's headlights in the rearview mirror the whole way, to be sure we stay together.

I thought long and hard about where to leave the car after moving it. All I could come up with is somewhere without cameras, which meant that things like the parking lots of big box stores were out of the question.

I decided on a budget hotel in Bridgeview, the reason being that recent reviews alluded to car damage and things getting stolen from the parking lot, and the general lack of security and safety measures. I thought that we would be safe going there. I hope I'm not wrong.

I drive there now. I take side streets so we don't have to risk passing through a toll booth, where there are also cameras. I've never been in a situation like this before but, now that I am, the cameras are endless. They're everywhere. I've read op-eds from private citizens raising privacy concerns about all the surveillance cameras in the Chicagoland area. I thought these people were idiots for feeling the way they did. Why worry if you're not doing anything wrong? But now that I am in this situation, it feels very Orwellian, like Big Brother is always watching, and maybe he is.

I get there, relieved when I see it start to take shape in the distance. I park behind the hotel, in the shadow of the building so that a person can't see Jake's car from the street.

I get back in my car with Lily. I get into the passenger's seat this time, letting Lily drive me home. I'll have to find a way to get the key fob back into the Hayes's house before Nina notices it's missing. I don't know how.

And then, maybe, when that is all said and done, Lily and I can put this behind us and move on.

We can forget Jake Hayes ever existed.

NINA

In the afternoon, after I get home from Lily and Christian's house, I post something to the neighborhood Facebook page. I'm not someone who likes to post often, if ever, but I do enjoy lurking and seeing what other people are complaining and arguing about. It's mostly petty stuff, people in violation of HOA rules and the like. But the page is helpful too, like when people need referrals or general advice or help, like finding a missing dog.

I think for a long time about what to say. Eventually I write:

FedEx says I received a package today. It wasn't on my porch when I arrived home. Wondering if it was delivered to someone else by mistake? If not, would anyone have video of the truck making deliveries this morning so I can see if it did indeed deliver the package to my house? Hoping it hasn't been stolen. Online tracking says it was delivered just after ten this morning. TIA.

I feel confident someone will rise to the bait and check and share the notifications from their video doorbells. Many of my neighbors have them, and they're all too happy to become vigilantes when it comes to minor infractions like speeding and lost packages.

I'm hoping that someone got a video of Jake. I want to see him, on camera if not in person. I miss Jake, maybe not the Jake he is now, but the one he used to be. I'm feeling nostalgic all of a sudden. I find myself going through old photos of Jake and me from the early days of our marriage and from when we were dating. They bring tears to my eyes. Jake used to be such a different man. I loved that man. I loved the relationship we had, before things started to deteriorate, to atrophy, to wilt and waste away like dying flowers in a vase. I want the man I married back, the one who whisked me away to Ibiza, who eloped with me, who I spent days alone with in an oceanfront villa as if we were the last two people on the planet. I hardly remember that man. Jake has changed so much over the years. I blame it on his work because he's so serious, so hardened all of the time, and I think it's because of what he does, how he spends his days trying to bring the dead back to life. It must do something to a person, to know that whether his patients live or die is up to him. There is an unbelievable amount of stress that comes with it, but also power. What must it feel like to pull someone from the brink of death?

As the days go by, I feel more sorry than ever that I argued with him and that I said what I did about him leaving. I put the idea in his head. And then, when he said something about how I'd like it if he left, I didn't object. I watched in silence as he took his pillow and walked from the room, feeling like I'd won at something, when our marriage was not a game to be won or lost.

It's only been five days since I've seen him, but it feels like years.

After I post the message to Facebook, I decide to go for a walk in the neighborhood. It isn't the best weather for a walk, but I need to get out of the house and I need fresh air. I need to breathe. I can't just sit around staring at Facebook, waiting for someone to reply.

The street is quiet because of the weather. It's windy. It rained earlier and there is the threat of more rain in the forecast. The clouds move quickly in, growing thick, turning the sky the color of pewter. I'll have to take a short walk so that the skies don't open up on me and I get drenched.

I sink my hands into my coat pockets and drape the hood over my head. I walk down the long brick walkway for the driveway. The wind comes at me, pushing the hood from my head. I keep having to fix it until eventually I tie the strings so that it doesn't keep coming off. Despite the nasty weather, the movement, the exercise feel good. I need something to do with the angst I've been feeling. As it is, it's just been left to fester.

I've just reached the end of the driveway and turned right onto the street when there, at the fringes of my awareness, I get that feeling that someone is watching me. It's a prickly feeling along my back, that grabs hold of me, and I turn without hesitation, searching over a shoulder and behind me. There is a car much further back. It rolls along the street without headlights on, moving so slowly that I have to wonder if it's moving at all or if it's not just idling in the street. I watch it and decide that the car is definitely moving. I turn my back to it. I keep walking, but the feeling of being watched doesn't leave.

I don't know that I feel afraid, but I notice that, by instinct, I've sped up. I walk with more urgency now. I don't even know that I've done it until my breathing becomes heavy. I throw a glance again over a shoulder, relieved to see that I've put distance between the car and me. Still, I'm overcome with a feeling of seclusion, of the greatest sense of being alone. The street is empty but for me.

If something happened to me right now, no one would know. No one would see.

I try and shake it off, to reason with myself. I'm too old to be scared.

Three houses up is a path through the woods. It cuts between two homes, leading to the neighborhood park. It's a small path, the kind meant for bikes and pedestrians. It's not wide enough for cars which, in this moment, feels advantageous.

When I get to the path, I take it, slipping behind an open chain-link fence. There are quite a few trees as the path cuts through a section of woods. Ordinarily the woods don't faze me, but I feel more restless than usual today. I keep looking back, over my shoulder, to make sure I'm alone. I've lost the car. I don't see it anymore. Still, I'm on edge, thinking about Jake and wondering why he came home this morning. What did he want from the house? What did he take?

What is going on with him?

For a while before our fight, Jake hadn't been himself. He'd been solemn, withdrawn. We'd been fighting. It used to be that Jake and I didn't ever fight. We always got along. But Jake needs to be in control. He isn't used to being told no. Being told no is Jake's kryptonite. It's never been a problem in our marriage because, until recently, when things got so messy with my mother, I almost never told Jake no, to anything. Jake and I had a whirlwind romance. We met, we fell in love. Three months later we were married. Jake asked and I said yes. He didn't want to deal with a big, extravagant wedding, with all that pomp and circumstance. I said okay, that I didn't either though I'd been planning for my wedding day since I was something like six years old, cutting pictures out of magazines and pasting them down in a notebook. Jake and I eloped, which my mother took hard because she'd always imagined walking me down the aisle on my wedding day in lieu of the father I didn't have. Instead, Jake and I got married alone in Ibiza because it was one of those bucket list places he always wanted to visit. I didn't know where Ibiza was at the time. I thought it was somewhere in Mexico, maybe near Cancun. I'd always wanted to go to Mexico. It wasn't. Spain was nice too.

Now, as I pass through the woods, I think again of that night just a couple weeks ago, of Jake glowering at me over his whiskey sour, talking about the gunshot victim who died on the operating table. *Who shot her?* I'd asked. *Her husband*, said Jake.

I remember that it had upset me, thinking of a husband shooting his wife in the head. It was unthinkable. It left me feeling sick to my stomach and I couldn't stop wondering what she did that made him react like that.

But it wasn't Jake saying the husband had shot her that got to me. It was what happened next that really got under my skin. It happened so fast, it was like subliminal advertising: something the conscious mind can't perceive but gets picked up by the subconscious. I didn't notice it at the time. I thought about it later, at night, after Jake was asleep. I lay there in bed beside him and it came to me, what was bothering me so much. What my subconscious had seen was a smile that played on the edges of Jake's lips when he said how this man had shot his wife, as if something about that made him happy.

I didn't know what made me do it, but I got out of bed that night. I leaned over and made sure Jake was dead asleep, and then I crept from the bedroom. I moved unnoticed down the stairs and into Jake's office. Silently, I lifted the painting from the wall. I went into Jake's safe, to be sure our gun was still there, and it was. Only then, when I knew where our gun was, could I sleep.

I leave the woods now. On the other side of the trees, the land opens up into a field. The playground is in the field, though the playground, when I come to it, is completely empty, as if it's been evacuated. There are no happy, laughing kids running across the rope bridge and sliding down the slides. There are no despondent teenagers smoking weed in the little hidey-holes. There is no one. I would have expected someone to be at the park, but there's not and I blame it on the weather. The day has gotten darker in the short amount of time I've been out. It isn't the setting sun—it's too early for the sun to set. It's the incoming storm. The wind has picked up. I walk around the path, in the same direction as the wind, so that it pushes from behind, sweeping me along the sidewalk. I have to fight to keep from going too fast. The swings at the park move in the wind as if driven by ghosts. The carousel spins. It's subtle. I don't know that I would have noticed the carousel spinning if not for the raspy creak of it as it goes round.

The path around the park is hoop-shaped. Trees surround it. I follow the path, wanting to go home, to be home, but realizing there is no point in turning around because the path is spherical. The distance would be the same whether I turned back or kept going, so I may as well keep going. There is only one way in or out of the park, and that's through the woods and the chain-link fence. Eventually I have to go back the way I came.

I pass through the trees again. They darken around me. It takes longer than I remember to get through the woods.

I come out of the trees. At the same time, the car I saw earlier labors down the street going the opposite way as before, as if searching for me.

My mouth goes dry. It's hard to swallow. It's hard to breathe.

I ask myself what exactly I'm afraid of, who I think is in that car. I can't answer. I have no reason to feel afraid, and yet I am. I walk so fast along the sidewalk now, in the direction of my house, that I'm practically running.

The sky suddenly opens and the rain comes, falling in my eyes, making it hard to see.

A car engine vibrates from beside me. I refuse to look—what I want to do is scream—until a voice calls out, "Excuse me," and I'm so completely caught off guard because the voice is a woman's. I don't know why, but I didn't expect that. I turn slowly back to find that the car has stopped on the street beside me. The driver's window is open and this woman is leaning her head out into the rain with a kind but remorseful smile.

The rain comes down sideways, getting into her car.

"I'm so sorry," she says. "I didn't mean to scare you. I'm totally lost. I was wondering if you can tell me where Circle Drive is."

I stand there on the sidewalk, getting wet. My breathing is heavy and my heart races.

She's only looking for directions. I feel silly for being afraid. Of course she's only looking for directions. Who did I think she was? What did I possibly think was going to happen? What did I think she was going to do to me?

"On the other side of Hobson," I breathe. My voice is shaky and this woman can't hear me because of the rain.

She shakes her head. "I'm sorry, what?" she calls out, putting a hand to her ear.

I say it again. "On the other side of Hobson. You have to go back to the stop sign. Cross Hobson," I say, louder now. I point in the direction I mean for her to go. The woman nods, like she knows what I mean. She says thanks. The car window goes back up, and she leaves, windshield wipers whipping back and forth across the glass though her headlights are still off. She turns around in my neighbor's drive before backtracking to the stop sign at the end of the street. I stand there, watching her, trying to catch my breath. I should have told her that her headlights were off.

I run the rest of the way to my house, glad to get out of the rain.

I open the garage and step in, grateful when the door sinks closed and I'm alone in the garage.

I try to breathe, to process what happened. I sink down to the step.

Who did I think was following me?

What am I afraid of?

I take a second to catch my breath before letting myself back into the house. "That was quick," my mother says about my walk, and I blame the weather. "You're out of breath, Nina," she says when I speak.

"It started to rain. I had to run home."

"You're wet. Let me get you a towel," she says. Beneath my coat, I'm not drenched, but my shirt is spotted with rain and my hair is damp, but I think it must be my wet shoes squeaking on the floor that give me away. I step out of them, carrying them back into the mudroom.

"No, it's fine," I say, wiping up the wet footprints on the floor. "I'm going to go change into something dry. I'll be right back," I tell my mother, climbing the stairs for the master bedroom, "and then I'll start dinner."

I get upstairs. I close the bedroom door. I sit on the bed with the laptop. My heart still beats hard. I sit there on the bed for a minute trying to collect myself. Outside, the rain becomes a driving rain, pelting the windows. I take a quick look to be sure the windows are closed and they are.

I go to my Facebook page. Our friends Anna and Damien have announced their pregnancy on social media now. They've used one of those felt boards to do it. On the felt board are the words Coming Soon. Anna holds the board beside her growing belly, while Damien stands beside her, with his arm around her shoulder. Anna is radiant, glowing, wearing this stunning, rust-colored, tiered silhouette minidress, and I feel a stab of jealousy because I don't know if the woman in this picture, happy and pregnant, will ever be me. I'm thirty-eight now. These days, they call that a geriatric pregnancy. In other words, I'm getting too old to be having kids. It makes me feel like I'm ninety years old. Jake and I are clearly not at a place to be starting our family, not when he won't speak to me, I don't know that I trust him and I don't know where he is. Damien looks adoringly at Anna. She looks the same way at him. They're so much in love, it shows. Jake has never once looked at me like that.

I go to the neighborhood's Facebook page. I look for replies to my own post. I need to see Jake's face. I need to know why he was here.

In the comments to my post, someone has told me that sometimes a package is mistakenly marked as delivered, though it hasn't been. *Give it another day*, he suggests, *and then report it*. That's not helpful.

Thankfully his isn't the only reply. A house that sits diagonal from Jake's and mine has shared a video clip with a comment. *Not sure if this helps*, the poster says, *but the timeline fits*.

I expand the video so that it fills my laptop screen. The camera picks up this homeowner's porch and property, but it also gets a view of the street and a partial view of the house on the other side of the street. The quality is better than I would have expected. The only downside is that the view is not in line with Jake's and my house. I can't see our house from this angle.

Still, there's something on the video the original poster thought might be relevant, and so I watch despite not knowing what it has to do with me.

There are potted plants on the front porch. Fountain grass grows in them, with giant plumes that sway and bend in the breeze. The speakers capture the sound of the wind, amplifying it so that the audio is incredibly loud, the wind like a tornado.

I watch. I'm expectant, on edge, knowing something is going to happen but not knowing what.

The sound of a car reaches my ears before a black car, a four-door sedan, enters the frame. I'm not any good with types of cars. Jake would know better than me what it is, if he could get a decent view. The quality of the video is good, but I don't know that the angle is right. You definitely can't see the make or model on the back end of the car, and you can't see the license plate.

The car pulls to the side of the road directly across the street from this doorbell camera. It sits there, idle, the driver sedentary behind the wheel so long that I wonder if he's ever going to get out.

Could it be Jake? Could something have happened to his car? Could Jake be using a rental, or has he borrowed someone else's car?

The door opens. A man gets out. No, I think to myself, disappointed. That's not it. This isn't what I'm looking for. This man isn't Jake and this isn't Jake's car. This man is taller than Jake. He's leaner too. He wears jeans, a jacket and some kind of hat, and I can tell, even just from the way he walks—confident, hands in his pockets, something just short of a strut—that this man is not my husband. Jake is confident when he walks, but it's different than this.

The fountain grass plumes keep getting in the way.

The man walks around the back end of the car, fighting the wind. He cuts across the grassy parkway for the sidewalk. With his hands still in his pockets, he keeps walking along the sidewalk, and then he exits the frame. His face is almost always turned the other way, which doesn't matter because I can tell in a million other ways, without seeing what he looks like, that this man isn't Jake.

The video ends there.

My heart sinks. This is totally irrelevant. Whoever shared it thought they might have caught my package thief. But there is no package thief. This is just some man, stopping to visit a friend. It has nothing to do with me.

I minimize the screen.

I respond to the video. I say: *Many thanks. Anyone closer that has proof of this man actually taking the package?* In other words, does anyone have actual footage of my house or door? That's what I need to see. I want to see Jake. I don't want to see this man.

I'll have to wait and hope that someone else caught something more relevant.

CHRISTIAN

In the middle of the night, I jerk upright in bed. I'm not fully awake. I'm somewhere in that void between unconsciousness and consciousness. I don't know what I heard. I couldn't describe it to save my life. But in some subliminal way—there just beneath that threshold of conscious perception where it was still able to elicit a response—I know there was a noise that pulled me from sleep.

Beside me, Lily is sound asleep. She snores, gently. I don't wake her.

I hold my breath, listening for the noise. My eyes are wide.

I'd been sleeping so well. This was the first night in a few nights that I fell asleep when my head hit the pillow. I was lost to oblivion until now. The digital clock across the room reads 4:12.

I look around the room, searching for something off. The room is dark, like charcoal. It's cloudy and opaque, and it's hard to see much of anything. The door is closed and locked. For the time being, we'll sleep like that. We never used to sleep with the door closed. But it makes Lily feel safer now, though there isn't a reason for her to feel unsafe.

We didn't have a conversation about closing the door, but the other night, before we lay down in bed, Lily watched me close and lock it, and then she just barely nodded as if agreeing it was the prudent thing to do. It's not exactly a robust lock; any little screwdriver can pop the lock. But what I like about it, and what Lily likes about it, is that there is this barrier between us and the unknown when we're out cold. Popping the lock or rattling the door handle would make a sound and wake us.

The noise comes back. I hear it this time, and in some very primal way, I know that it's the same noise that, not two minutes ago, woke me. The sound is a beeping sound, like an alarm. There's a steady beat to it, an unfaltering cadence. It's subdued, making it hard to tell exactly where it's coming from, like when a smoke detector chirps in the middle of the night and you don't know which it is. It's like that. Evasive. Hard to pin down.

I push the weight of the covers away from me. I get out of bed. I let the noise lead me. I follow it around the end of the bed and into the adjoining master bath. With every step, the sound gets louder. Lily sleeps through it. She sleeps much more deeply than me. She always has and we joke how, when the baby is born, I'll get the nighttime feedings because she won't hear the baby cry in the middle of the night.

The porcelain tiles are cold against my feet. Stepping inside the bathroom, my hand instinctively goes to the light switch. I catch myself before turning it on. I don't want to wake Lily, and I also don't want to be visible to the outside.

The sound, whatever it is, is magnified in here. I'm getting close.

There is a window in the bathroom. It sits just behind the

large soaker tub. The window has faux wood blinds on it, which are angled upward and lowered all the way to the sill. Still, I see the gentle flap of the last few slats where the breeze hits them. The window is open a crack, the crisp night air wafting in. It's cold in the bathroom, the night outside thirty degrees colder than it is in the house.

I reach out for the lift cord to pull the blinds open. Before I can, the sound outside goes silent. I stop dead, listening.

I find the sudden silence equally as disturbing as the noise.

I take the lift cord in a hand. I wrap my whole fist around it. Lily and I almost never open these blinds for fear of some neighbor seeing us naked in the bath. I give the cord a gentle tug. The blinds rise by degrees, exposing the open window behind them.

The lights are still off in the bathroom. It's pitchy, the kind of darkness you can only see in once your eyes have had time to adjust. I step carefully into the tub. I crouch down. I stand there in the large soaker tub, pressing my eyes to the part of the window that is exposed, that two-inch gap at the bottom beneath the blinds.

Though it's dark in the bathroom, it's exponentially darker outside. A vast nothingness. The moon and stars are nowhere to be seen.

Our bathroom window faces a neighbor's house. The neighbor has motion activated lights.

I see absolutely no one, nothing outside.

But the neighbor's motion activated lights are on.

Our yard and the yards around us are wooded. We're surrounded by trees and the river. The trees bring wildlife, for food, shelter. It's not unusual to see a deer in the backyard or a fox or a coyote walking down the middle of the street, usually at night, but at any time of the day really. Because of it, neighbors are disinclined to let their dogs, particularly little ones, out unsupervised.

I try and convince myself that something like a coyote could have set off the neighbor's motion activated light.

But coyotes don't wear things that beep.

I run my eyes over the backyard listening for sounds, looking for movement.

I won't be able to sleep until I know for sure that no one is in our yard. I decide to go outside for a better look. I check on Lily first, leaning over her in bed. She's still sound asleep, her breath rattling through her nose.

I get down on my hands and knees beside the bed. I reach under the bed before I leave, to where I keep an old baseball bat, just in case. Lily doesn't know that it's there. I didn't tell her, because if I have a reason to keep a baseball bat under our bed, that means I have a reason for us to be scared.

I take the bat. I go to the bedroom door and unlock it. I pull it slowly open. I coast down the hallway and down the stairs. I'm not worried about being absolutely silent since the sound was coming from outside and there is nobody in the house but Lily and me.

When I get to the bottom of the stairs, I see the alarm's keypad on the wall. It reads Disarmed. System Is Ready To Arm.

I do a double take. I'd bet my life I set the alarm, just as I have every day this week.

But last night was different because I was so tired when Lily and I got home from moving Jake's car. My nerves were shredded. I chugged a beer and then, when Lily went to wash up for bed, I chugged another beer. I collapsed into bed. I don't even know that I brushed my teeth. The yeasty taste is still in my mouth and my teeth feel like they're wearing fuzzy little sweaters. I don't remember falling asleep. It was as if I blinked and the next thing I knew, it was four in the morning.

It's entirely possible I forgot to set the alarm.

I search the first floor, my hand clinging to the barrel of the bat. I played baseball in high school, but other than some adult leagues I've joined for fun since, I haven't picked up a bat in years. Still, I have confidence that, if necessary, I could knock someone unconscious with a swing.

Our house is open concept with large, open spaces. Lily has said how nice it will be when the baby comes. She can cook dinner in the kitchen, while keeping an eye on our baby playing in the next room. It's all about that continuous line of sight, which is advantageous even now because I can see clear across the house without things getting in my way.

There is no one in the house but us.

In the kitchen, I dig around in a drawer for our flashlight. I find it. I unlock and slide open the back door and step outside. Outside, it's cold, something like forty-five degrees. I'm in a pair of pajama pants, but shirtless. I left my T-shirt upstairs and I regret it. The coldness hits like a wall. The brick paver tiles are like ice on my bare feet, but I try to ignore it.

I stand on the step, sweeping the light across the backyard. I don't know how far outside I want to go. I creep across the back patio. It makes me nervous to be out this far, not because I'm worried about me, but because I'm worried about Lily. I don't like putting any distance between the house and me. The back door is unlocked and Lily is in the house alone. The bedroom door is open now. Lily is asleep. She wouldn't hear someone come in.

There is a noise off in the distance to my right. My head snaps in that direction, but it's too dark to see anything. That doesn't matter. Because it's not what I see, but rather what I hear that scares me: the tread of footsteps hitting the trail, the brush of leaves.

I call out, "Who's there?"

Nothing but the skittering of rocks. Whoever or whatever was there has started to run.

I sweep my flashlight over the yard, but the darkness only swallows up the flashlight's beam.

Probably just stupid teenagers getting drunk and high on the trail again. I scared them off. That's what I tell myself anyway, but we've never had kids screwing around in the backyard at four in the morning.

I stand there awhile, watching. But everything quiets. I don't hear any more noise. Eventually, when I'm convinced whoever or whatever was here is gone, I back into the house. I slide the door closed and lock it. I check that all the doors on the first floor are locked. I check the windows. On the way back to the bedroom, I set the alarm. I make absolutely sure it's set. I stand and watch and wait for the sixty seconds while it counts down, and then arms.

The rest of the night, I don't go back to sleep. I lie awake in bed beside Lily, watching out the window as the sky turns from black to blue.

"What are the odds of you and Jake Hayes both being at that forest preserve at the same time?" I ask Lily the next morning. It's Sunday. I slept in, mostly because, from four thirty until six thirty, I didn't sleep, not until the sun started to rise. Only then did I lie fully down beside Lily, curling myself around her, closing my eyes and succumbing to exhaustion. I dreamed about Jake. I dreamed that he was dead and that I was happy.

Lily was gone when I woke up. Her side of the bed was empty, her robe removed from the end of the bed. The bedroom door was open.

I found Lily downstairs, in the kitchen with a mug of decaf coffee, having a stare down with a piece of toast. She was sitting at the table in her robe and bare feet, her hair thrown up in some sort of messy knot.

The world outside looked different somehow, as if nothing was safe anymore.

"I don't know," Lily says now, drawing her eyebrows together. "It was just a coincidence. It happens. Why?" She doesn't wait for me to tell her before she says, "Jim Brady saw me there too. Remember? What are the odds of that? It's popular and it's close. People I know go there all the time."

Some people say there are no such things as coincidences in this world. That everything happens for a reason and is just part of some big, calculated plan.

But whose plan?

"I mean, Lily," I say as I pull out the chair next to her and sit, leaning into her, having to get this out, "how much do we really know about this guy?"

I spent the two hours I was awake thinking about this. The reason I ask is because in the middle of the night, I remembered something he said to me once, about Lily. At the time, it just went to my head and I thought, *Yeah, I am pretty damn lucky.* I don't remember the exact words Jake used, but it was something about me hitting the jackpot with Lily.

While I don't remember the words, what I remember is the look in his eye. It was green with envy. He wasn't looking at me as he said it. He was looking intently across the room at Lily, staring intensely. I followed the gaze of his eye to where she stood, talking to someone who wasn't Nina, so that there could be no mistaking who he was looking at. Lily must have felt our eyes on her because she gazed back, over a bare shoulder. She was wearing this long, strapless black dress that hugged in at the waist, but was otherwise effortless and flowy. It was summer and her skin was a golden tan, flawless, sexy. I can picture it even now, the stillness of her eyes and the way they held mine when she smiled wistfully back, making a face to suggest that this conversation with whoever she was speaking to had gone on too long and she needed me to save her from it, which I did. Gladly.

At the time I was oddly happy that I had something he should envy. He had the fancy house and the fancy car, a lucrative salary and an impressive fucking career.

But I had Lily.

"Not much, now that you mention it," Lily says. "We hung out with them what, maybe ten times?"

"Less."

There were a few dinners at their house and maybe two at ours. A couple dinners out. Maybe three faculty parties. We were friends. We always had a great time together and shared lots of laughs. But it's not like Jake and I were best friends.

Lily nods. She realizes I'm right. "I think because of Nina," she says, standing from the table to pour me coffee, which I take from her, grateful. "Because of all the things that Nina has said to me over the years about Jake. I feel like I know him better than I do."

The reality is that we don't know anything about him.

We only knew what he and Nina wanted us to see.

Later, I walk the property searching for something amiss, for some sign of who was here last night. I find nothing other than an empty can of beer and decide it was probably just some kids or some drunk or homeless person who had lost his way. It's not unreasonable to think. This trail that we live on spans nearly fifty miles, north to south. It runs through something like two counties and a dozen towns. Though the suburb where Lily and I live is middle- to upper-middle-class, each of those twelve towns is not. Some towns that the trail passes through have a pretty decent percent of their population living in poverty. It's sad. The demographics are much different here than elsewhere, where the rate of crime is higher. I've biked the length of the trail before and discovered transient camps—encampments with people living in tents—further down. They're usually single men. The police chase them away, but inevitably, they come back, taking up residence under bridges and in the woods. I never like Lily to run alone too far down the path. If it was a short run, okay, but not her long runs. When she goes for long runs or when she used to go for long runs, I'd bike behind her to make sure she made it home safely.

Ordinarily if I thought someone was trespassing on my property in the middle of the night, I'd call the police and maybe I should have called them last night. But police ask questions, like do I have a reason to believe someone might be trespassing on my property in the middle of the night and why? I don't know that I want them coming to my house anyway, not when I, myself, am guilty of things like breaking and entering and evidence tampering, and have a complete inability to lie.

I didn't think I had a reason to believe someone might be trespassing on my property, not until a few hours ago when my thoughts got the best of me in the middle of the night and I started to wonder if there is any chance, no matter how remote, that Jake isn't dead.

NINA

Monday after school, I have to take my mother for a biopsy of the mass in her breast, so that we'll know decisively if it's malignant or benign. The doctor has already told us not to worry too much yet, that most masses are benign. I know the doctor means well, but with my mother's family history of breast cancer, I have trouble believing hers is. I keep it to myself. I don't want to worry her for now. If the mass is malignant, we'll deal with it.

The doctor's appointment is at three thirty in the afternoon. It takes thirty minutes to get there, and I have to pick my mother up on the way.

I feel rushed as I leave work. I packed my bag during the last period of the day so I could leave as soon as the bell rang. Now I'm hurrying—practically running—to my car in a futile attempt to get out of the parking lot before the buses start to leave and I'm stuck in traffic. My eyes are on my car. I'm not looking where I'm going, so that I trip over a crack in the parking lot and stagger forward, my travel mug getting thrown from my hand, hitting the pavement and rolling under my car. It was empty, thankfully, otherwise the coffee would have sprayed everywhere when it fell. Still, I have to get down on my hands and knees to reach under the car for the mug, which feels like a fitting end to a bad day. I just hope no one sees me. My hand wraps around the mug but then, as I'm about to get up from under the car, something else beneath it catches my eye, and I become motionless, feeling a heaviness in my stomach and in my chest, a sense of dread.

I come up with the coffee mug. I set it aside, on the asphalt. I dig my phone out of my purse, and then I lean back over to shine the flashlight on the object beneath my car for a better look, forgetting for a moment all about my mother's biopsy.

"Should I even ask why you're crawling around in the parking lot on your hands and knees?" a voice banters.

I jump, almost hitting my head on the car. I look up to find Ryan standing there in the glow of the afternoon sun. I shade the light from my eyes with a hand to see him. He looks down in amusement at me, though his droll smile and his raised eyebrows fade away when he sees the expression of shock on my face.

Ryan's words are tempered. "Nina?" he asks, cocking a head and pulling his eyebrows together. "What is it? Is everything alright? Did you lose something?"

My jaw is clenched. "Can you… Could you just look at this for me? Can you tell me if it's what I think it is?"

"Yeah," he says gently, nodding. "Sure." He sets his bag down, and then he lowers himself to the ground beside me, on his knees, asking, "What is it you want me to look at?"

"It's here, under my car," I say, so that he'll bend down to look. It's cramped where we are. When we bend down to look, our heads practically touch. There can't be more than three feet of space between parked cars, which is hardly enough room for one person to fit, much less two.

I use my phone's flashlight to illuminate the underside of the car, pointing toward the small black boxlike thing that sits close to the edge of the car, almost directly beneath the driver's seat.

"What am I looking at?" he asks.

"This," I say, touching it.

Ryan reaches a hand under the car. He removes the object easily from the car's undercarriage because it was just held in place by some sort of adhesive. He comes up with it in his hand, and then he pushes himself to his feet before extending a hand to help me to mine.

"This shouldn't be here," he says as I stand up. He runs his eyes over the object, examining it. His eyes turn soft and pitying and he says, "It's a GPS tracking device, Nina." I feel suddenly weak. I lean back against my car, letting it support me. My fingers go to my mouth. I was right, then. That's what I thought it was, but hearing him say it makes it so much worse. How I wish I'd been wrong.

Ryan reads my face. "I take it you didn't know it was there?"

I shake my head. "No. I didn't know."

Ryan opens his mouth to speak, but then rethinks and closes it.

"What is it?" I ask. "What were you going to say?"

He takes a step closer, bridging the distance I've made. He reaches out with his hand to give my arm a gentle squeeze. "Are you okay?" he asks. I nod, but it's automatic. I don't look at him. I find my eyes locked on the device in his hand, wondering who put that on my car. I don't know that I'm okay. "Is everything alright at home, Nina, with you and your husband?" he asks, treading lightly. I never told him about Jake, about what's been happening with Jake.

But that isn't what Ryan is asking. Ryan isn't asking if Jake is okay.

Ryan is suggesting that Jake put this tracking device on my car.

"Why do you think my husband did this?" I ask, feeling the need to defend Jake all of a sudden. Jake isn't the controlling, jealous type, but he is the type who likes to ask questions. *Where were you? What were you doing? Who were you with?* Once I remember he got upset with me when I got a text from a male colleague in my department, thanking me for a coffee date. It was completely platonic and professional. Something had come up in a department meeting that had upset him and he wanted to talk to someone about it. I remember that, at the time, I'd been put off that Jake was snooping on my phone and reading my personal texts, but instead of telling him that, I found myself defending the reasons I had coffee with a male colleague, apologizing for it, feeling like I'd done something wrong when I hadn't.

I shiver, despite the warm fall day. I wrap my arms around myself to keep me warm. Did Jake think he couldn't trust me?

Ryan is apologetic. He searches visibly for words. "I'm sorry. I didn't mean to insinuate that... I didn't mean to say anything bad about your husband. It just seemed like the logical choice."

"Why?" I ask, my words brusque and I don't mean to take my feelings out on Ryan, but it happens. "Because Jake seems like a stalker or because husbands in general do?" I ask.

Ryan looks hurt. He says, "I've only met him a couple times. I don't know anything about your husband."

"Then why do you assume it was him?"

"Please don't be like that," he says, and I regret the tone I took with him. "You know I didn't mean anything by it. I'm just trying to help."

I shake my head. I put my head in my hands. The only reason I took offense was that he touched a raw nerve, because I was thinking it too.

"I'm sorry. I shouldn't have reacted like that." I try to think, to process what's happening, to make sense of this. "I just don't know why Jake would do something like this."

"But if not him, then who, Nina?" he asks.

"I don't know," I say. "I have no clue."

Ryan bends his knees slightly to lower himself to my height, so he can look me in the eye. "You would tell me if things weren't okay at home?"

"Yes. Of course," I lie.

"Would you?"

Ryan can tell that I'm lying. "No," I say, shaking my head.

"No what?" he asks. "No everything is not okay at home, or no you wouldn't tell me?"

"No everything is not okay at home," I say, my voice and posture crumbling. With my confession come tears. "Shit," I say, swiping at my eyes. I hate to cry. I'm not the crying type, especially not in public like this, with Ryan and only God knows who else as a witness.

He looks around the parking lot first to be sure no one is watching us. Ryan comes closer. He reaches for my shoulders and tentatively pulls me into him. I resist at first, but then I give in, finding comfort in his embrace. His arms wrap around me. He quiets my crying. "Shhhh," he says. My own arms hang stiffly at my sides, but I lean into him, resting my head on his chest, knowing that I haven't been this close to another man except Jake in years.

He runs a hand the length of my hair. It's calming. "Talk to me, Nina. Tell me what's wrong."

I pull back, but we still stand close. The sun is behind Ryan. It's bright. I tent a hand to my eyes as I say, "Jake left me," feeling a sense of shame wash over me. Now that my mother saw Jake at our house the other day, I know definitively that he isn't dead and he isn't missing. He made a choice to leave. He doesn't love me anymore. I went so far as to call the police this morning and tell them what I discovered. There was no point in them searching for Jake when they have truly missing people to try and find.

"What do you mean he left you?"

It isn't that Ryan is confused. It's that he finds it inconceivable that Jake would leave me, which I appreciate.

"We got into a fight a few days ago. These days, it seems we're always getting into fights. I can't do anything right. He left for work Monday morning and never came home. I thought something terrible had happened to him, but no. My mother saw him over the weekend and he's fine. He just left me." More than once, Jake has threatened to leave. He finally made good on his threat.

"Then he's an idiot," Ryan says, reaching for my elbow, his eyes holding mine for a long time.

Noise comes all of a sudden from the school building. I fall away from Ryan, pulling my arm back, turning to look. A cluster of teenage girls has stepped outside, giddy and happy and laughing. I feel my cheeks go red, hoping they didn't see Ryan and me so close. I can only imagine what they'd say about catching Mrs. Hayes and Mr. Schroeder in an embrace. My eyes return to Ryan's. He, too, was watching the girls. He looks back to me.

"I'm sorry you're going through this, Nina," he says.

I swallow. "How does it work anyway?" I ask, wiping my eyes on the back of a hand, eager to change the subject because I don't want to talk about Jake anymore or our homelife.

"This?" he asks, holding up the tracking device.

"Yes."

"I don't know for sure," he says, turning it over again in his hands, "but I think it's a real-time GPS tracker, where someone can monitor your location from their own cell phone."

I imagine a little map with some digital cartoon image of myself, giving real-time updates every time I get into my car to head to work or to the grocery store. I imagine someone watching from afar as a dotted line tracks my movements across town. Work. Errands. My mother's doctor's appointments. A cool wind sweeps across the parking lot and I shiver, hugging myself tighter as the tiny hairs on my arms and on the nape of my neck lift in the breeze. I wish I'd brought my jacket.

"You look cold," he says, his eyes going to my arms, which are spread with goose bumps.

"I am. I have to go," I say, suddenly remembering about my mother's biopsy. I look at my watch. "Shit. I'm going to be late."

Ryan seems reluctant to let me leave. "Do you want me to follow you? Make sure you get home okay?"

I appreciate his concern. There is a part of me that wants to say yes, to ask him to follow me home. This tracker has me on edge, for good reason. But it's more than just this tracking device. It's the anonymous and unsolicited flowers too. Did the same person who has been watching me also send the flowers? "No. I'm fine. Really. For all I know, this thing has been here for years," I say, trying to make light of it, though that's not possible because it was only about six months ago that Jake bought me the car.

"This is yours," he says, handing me the GPS tracking device before he turns to walk around his car for the driver's door. He pauses there on the other side of the car, gazing over the roof at me. "Are you going to be okay, Nina?" he asks.

I nod, but I'm scared to be in my car now, despite the fact that the tracking device has been removed. What if someone is still watching me somehow?

"I'll be fine. Thank you again for your help."

"I'd get rid of that by the way, if I was you," he says, pointing at the device, before he opens his car door and gets inside. As I watch, he starts the engine and pulls away.

I hold the tracking device in my hands. I handle it with care as if it's a bomb or a grenade, about to go off. I turn it over in my hands, feeling exposed even just holding it.

I walk over to the trash can before I leave, and drop the device in. It's heavier than everything else in the can, upsetting it. The device sinks down low, getting buried beneath the rest of the trash.

It's gone. But my mind can't get rid of it so easily.

We're ten minutes late to the appointment, which does nothing for my mother's or my stress. The biopsy is a fine needle aspiration, which I've read is the easiest as biopsies go. There are far worse types. I ask her if she wants me to come into the room with her, she goes in alone.

It doesn't take long. After the biopsy, we go out for dinner, though we're both too worked up to eat, for the same and for different reasons. She is thinking about the biopsy results. I am too, but I'm also thinking about Jake and about the device I found on my car. I can't stop thinking about it.

We go for Mexican, which was once my mother's favorite. From across the table, I can see that she is tired. We eat, or try to eat—it's mostly a wasted effort—and then we go home.

"Don't think about it," I say to her as I drive, reaching for her hand. "Easier said than done, I know, but there's no point in worrying about the results when we don't even know if we have anything to worry about."

The house is completely dark as I approach, so dark it's hard to see. Both the outside and the inside lights are off. It was late afternoon when we left for the doctor's appointment. The sun wasn't anywhere close to setting. I didn't even think to turn a light on, distracted and not thinking how dark it would be by the time we got back home. We were gone for hours and, in that time, the sun went down, night fell.

I press the button inside my car to open the garage door—grateful for the light the garage gives off—and drive my car in.

After turning the ignition off, I get out and go toward the

door, to let myself into the house while my mother is getting out of the car.

But a foot from the door, I become paralyzed. The door into the house is moving. It's open. I can see it bobbing in place from the air outside as a cool breeze wafts in the open garage. The door isn't standing wide-open, but it isn't pulled fully closed either. I could open the door just by pushing on it.

I never would have left the door like this. I didn't leave the door like this.

"Is everything okay?" my mother asks, coming to stand behind me. She sees my reluctance, how I stop briefly before the door, taking a breath, looking at it lapping in the wind against the frame like waves on the shore. "Did you forget to close it?" she asks.

I don't want to tell her what I'm thinking because she's already so stressed and worried about everything. I don't want to make it worse. "I must have," I say, stepping up to the door. I lay my hand flat against it, take a breath and press it slowly open, wondering who or what I might find on the other side.

I slip my hand in first, feeling for the light switch. I find it and turn it on. A flush mount ceiling light shines down, bathing the room in light.

I look for something amiss. I find something.

The cleaning lady was here today. Her name is Martha and she's a godsend. She came this morning when I was at work, when only my mother was home. Martha washes the floors by hand and is always very thorough and conscientious. She came recommended from a friend and is the best. In all the years she's been with us, her work is flawless. She never leaves a speck of dirt or dust behind.

But just inside the mudroom is a partial shoe print. It's a dab of tracked-in dirt on the luxury vinyl tile. My mother doesn't even notice, but I see it right away, sticking out like a sore thumb. It looks like someone stepped through mud or dirt coming in, and then walked into the house with it on their shoe. The shoe print is longer and wider than either my mother's or mine. It's big like a man's footprint, though it's an incomplete print.

Martha would never have overlooked something like this; she never would have left it behind.

There hasn't been a man in my house since Jake.

"I think I'm just going to go up to bed," my mother says as she breezes past me in the mudroom, stepping into the still-dark kitchen just beyond. I can tell from the sound of her voice that she's exhausted from the day and because I slipped her a Xanax before she went in for her biopsy, because she was so nervous about it. I didn't ask the doctor if it would be okay; I did it anyway.

"Okay," I say, finding it hard to tear my eyes away from the shoe print.

Someone has been in the house while we were gone.

Was it Jake?

I shouldn't feel afraid if my husband was in the house when we were gone. I should be happy that he's come back home to me. He's my husband. I love him and he loves me.

But instead of being happy, my mouth is dry and my breathing has become faster, my pulse quickening. I don't like the idea of Jake keeping a low profile all this time, and then concealing himself somewhere in our dark house when I'm not home.

I think of what Ryan asked me this afternoon when we found the tracking device on the car. *Is everything alright at home, Nina, with you and your husband?*

The answer of course is no.

"Wait, Mom," I say, tearing my eyes away from the shoe print and following her into the darkness. I come up behind her, grabbing her gently by the arm and she turns to me.

"Nina. What is it? What's wrong?" she asks, searching my eyes.

I don't have a chance to tell her before something crashes into the ceiling right above our heads from the second floor. I gasp. My mother's eyes and mine jerk in tandem in the direction of the noise. I find my hand clinging to my mother's arm, and hers to mine.

"Just wait here," I whisper. "Let me go see what it is."

"Nina," she hisses once as I pull my arm away.

I reach for the light switch but miss it on the way for the stairs. I bump into the edge of the foyer's console table in the darkness. The table moves, scraping an inch across the floor. It's not quiet. A picture frame on the edge of the console table totters and then pitches forward, falling facedown on the wood. The glass breaks. I leave the broken glass where it is, stepping over it as I approach the bottom of the stairs. My legs are weak and unsteady beneath me. My body trembles. I take the upright post at the end of the stairs in my hand, pulling myself up the steps one at a time. I keep my gaze on the top of the stairs.

Directly above the kitchen is the master bedroom and bath. They're my favorite rooms in the house. Our master bath is mostly stark white, except for the walls, which are covered with a metallic black and gold wallpaper. The bath is stone resin. The shower water comes down like rain. It's practically spa-like.

The master bedroom was once Jake's and my haven, though now when I think of it, I think only of that last awful fight. I don't know that I'll ever be able to separate these things in my mind: our bedroom and that fight. When I think of it, I think of Jake's rabid face, of the way he and I squared off on opposite sides of the bed, screaming at each other. I'd never seen him so angry. I'd never seen him lose his temper like that before.

If you hate it here so much, then why don't you just leave?

I'd called his bluff. I dared him. I lost the dare.

Because by morning, Monday morning, the morning he left, he'd gone to the opposite extreme, to something self-controlled and cold. We got ready for work in silence, saying nothing to each other, just glaring at one another and giving each other a wide berth. The only words he spoke to me were as he left. I spoke first, as he pulled open the door to leave. I said, "Have a good day," and to be honest, I don't know if they were sincere.

Jake froze with his back to me in the open door. He turned slowly back, gazing over a shoulder, his face unsmiling and unkind. He was silent at first, regarding me, his eyes moving up my body to my face to the point of making me uncomfortable and self-conscious. I wasn't sure that he was going to say anything at all, but then he did. He practically huffed, and he said, "Don't wait up," not giving me a chance to reply as he turned and walked away from me, slamming the door so vehemently that the dishes in the kitchen cabinet shook.

When the house was built, Jake and I put so much thought into our bedroom's design. It wasn't just a place for us to sleep, but to spend time. Ours is a Savoir bed, which for some people, costs more than their car. It always felt insulting and overindulgent to sleep in a thirty-thousand-dollar bed, but Jake worked hard for his money and he had an inheritance. He believed that if he wanted a Savoir bed, he should have a Savoir bed. He didn't like me to remind him of all the other more practical things we could do with that type of money.

When I come to it, the bedroom door is only partly open. I don't know whether I left it like that or not, not that it matters because Martha would have been the last one in the room. I reach into the bedroom with a hand, through the open door, holding my breath, being quiet.

As I enter the room, the smell of perfume overwhelms me, piercing my nasal passages.

The light switch is located just inside the door, to the right of it. I run my hands over the wall. I find and flip on the light switch, expecting the room to fill with light, but it doesn't. Nothing happens. The room stays dark.

And then I remember turning the lamp off last night at

the base, which is on an end table beside the bed. I have to walk across the dark room to get to it. I stand in the doorway, working up the courage to step further into the room, picturing this accent chair and ottoman we have in the corner of the room. The chair and the ottoman are velvet. They're the color of marigolds. The chair has a low profile and a deep seat and, for all intents and purposes, is Jake's chair because it's where he likes to sit when he's in the bedroom but not on the bed. He sits back in the chair, kicks his feet up on the ottoman and in the mornings when he's home or at night when I slip into my pajamas, I feel his eyes on me, watching me, following me from his chair.

"Jake," I whisper, practically breathless, out into the darkness, imagining him keeping hidden in his marigold chair, waiting for me to come home. The perfume is mine. I have many bottles of perfume, but this is one I wear all the time. It's Chanel. I'd recognize the scent anywhere. Jake gave the bottle to me. "Are you here? Jake?"

My words are met with silence. It means nothing. It doesn't mean that he isn't here.

I practically have to force myself into the room.

As I cross the room for the lamp, my feet step on something wet and sticky that makes me think of blood.

With the next step, I come down on something sharp. It pierces my feet and I cry out, clamping my hands against my mouth to quiet the sound. I move through total darkness, walking on the edges of my feet where it hurts less, anticipating what it would feel like for someone's hands to come down on me, to touch me, to grab me by the feet.

I come to the lamp. I fumble for the switch. I turn on the light. Light floods the room. I spin around, looking in all the dark corners of the bedroom and bath.

Jake's chair is empty. There is no one in the bedroom but me.

On the floor beside the dresser is a bottle of broken perfume.

Perfume runs along the wooden floors, getting absorbed by a wool rug when the flow of perfume reaches it.

I reach down to collect the glass in my hand.

I see movement peripherally. My head spins in the direction of it.

Shaking, I drop to my knees and look under the bed. The cat is there now, hiding under the bed with its back arched and its tail tucked between its legs, looking scared.

"Did you do that?" I ask, of the broken bottle and the spilled perfume. The cat doesn't answer back. Maybe it did. And maybe it didn't.

I get back up on my feet. Still shaking, I hobble down the stairs with the largest shards of glass in my hand, what I was able to collect. "What happened, Nina? What is it?" my mother asks, cleaning up the picture frame glass in the foyer.

"Nothing. Just the cat."

Cautiously, I search the rest of the house while my mother looks on. I turn on all the lights. I find nothing and no one.

Later, as I sit on the edge of the bathtub, my mother helping me to pick glass out of the soles of my feet, I think how the cat might have knocked the perfume off the dresser either intentionally or by mistake. She does that. She has a tendency to knock things over to get attention or food, or to get a rise out of me.

But the cat didn't leave that dirty shoe print by the door.

CHRISTIAN

Lily likes to feed the birds outside our house. She has two feeders in the backyard, which she hangs from hooks close to the trees and fills with seeds. She loves to stand at the back window and watch them. Even in the dead of winter, when the birds should have flown somewhere south, where it's warm, I wake up to the sound of birdsong. The birds come in droves, and because of it, despite Lily's best efforts, she can't always keep up with feeding them. Eventually the feeders go dry and the birds disappear, and then the backyard becomes quiet and still. Days pass without seeing a bird so that you'd think they were long gone.

Lily goes to the store. She gets more seed. She trudges outside, sometimes in the cold, sometimes through a foot of snow, to fill the feeders.

No sooner does she come back inside than the birds reappear, emerging from the deepest parts of the trees.

We couldn't see them. We were sure they were gone, that they'd moved on to someone else's feeder. But no. All the while they were there, lurking just out of sight, watching Lily, waiting on their next meal.

It makes me think of Jake. It makes me wonder if there is any possibility no matter how remote that he's there, hidden in the background somewhere, camouflaged like the birds in the trees.

If that's the case, the question is why. Why would he do that? Why would he only pretend to be dead?

Late Monday afternoon, I leave work early. The first thing I do is go back to the Hayeses house to return the key. It's around four o'clock when I get there. I park in the same place I parked the other day and retrace my steps, entering the house through the garage. According to Lily, Nina has taken her mother to an appointment and won't be home. The house, she said, should be empty and she's right. It is. I put the key back in its place. I hurry out through the garage door and to my car, and then I make the snap decision to revisit Langley Woods. Once there, I leave my car in the same lot where Lily and I parked, and make my way back to where she and I found blood. It's not easy to find. The ground is soft and wet from the rain this weekend, though, despite the mud, the weather is much nicer today. The sun is finally out and it's warm. Presumably everyone who was cooped up inside this weekend is here, because the place is more crowded than I've ever seen it.

Even having been here before, having found the spot once already where Jake and Lily fought, I don't find it on the first try. It takes three. Three wrong turns onto the wrong unmarked paths until eventually I come to the right clearing in the trees. I've brought a small screwdriver with me, which I found in my car, in a car tool kit. I use it to engrave lines on the trees, to blaze a trail so that I'll be able to find my way out when it's time to leave. I don't want to get lost. Lily doesn't know where I am. No one does. I walk further into the trees, remembering how Jake isn't the only person to ever disappear here. Years ago, a woman named Amanda Holmes also vanished in Langley Woods. She went missing from the area. I remember that she was twenty-two at the time, a senior in college. Her case was strange, the kind that captured national attention. It was all over the news. I followed her story at the time because it was interesting. I didn't think it would ever matter to me on a more personal level.

When Amanda first went missing, her car was found about a quarter mile from Langley Woods. There was a suicide note set on the dashboard. The search for her should have been cut-and-dried. It was anything but. Search parties looked for her for days that stretched into weeks. They used bloodhounds and then cadaver dogs to scavenge the woods and the residential areas around them. Even the dogs couldn't find her. Dozens, if not hundreds, of people searched for Amanda, whose friends called her Mandy, by air and by foot. Her family was devastated. This was maybe five years ago. I remember at the time watching her parents cry on TV. I remember that months passed without finding her. Eventually everyone gave up. People stopped talking about Amanda Holmes. They came to believe that she wasn't at Langley Woods or anywhere even close to it, that something else had happened to her, something far more mysterious and insidious, but no one knew what. There were theories, and unconfirmed reports of Amanda sightings all over the Chicagoland area and around the country. Had someone met her and driven her elsewhere? Was the suicide note just part of a cunning plan? Had she abandoned her life, her family, and was she living a new life somewhere else? But why? No one knew.

The case went cold. A year passed and still she wasn't found, until one day when some hikers stumbled upon her body in the woods.

The medical examiner determined the cause of death: suicide. Amanda Holmes took her own life. She hung herself from a tree. She had been in these woods the whole time everyone was looking for her, and still no one could find her.

I don't know what I'm looking for exactly. Jake, his blood, his wallet, his phone, a shoe. After an hour of searching, walking aimlessly through trees, marking the trees with each turn, I find none of it, and I wonder if I can't find them because I'm not looking hard enough or in the right places, or if I can't find them because they're not here. Because Jake isn't here.

Dusk starts to fall upon the earth. The sun sinks low and the world turns to gold. I look at my watch; it's later than I thought. I need to leave before it's so dark I can't find my way back and before Lily starts to wonder where I am.

I turn around, looking at my inscriptions in the trees, following them blindly out of the woods. I don't notice anything else at first because I'm only looking at my own markings, letting them lead me.

But then I see that there are also dashes etched into some of the trees, with something like paint or chalk. It's white and fading. The dashes are much more elusive than my own etchings, making them hard to see and impossible to follow because some have already been washed away by rain.

I look around and realize what it is I'm seeing. Not so long ago someone else blazed a similar trail so they, too, could find their way out of these woods.

I make my way out of the trees for the path, following the crushed limestone trail back toward my car as the sky starts to get darker. It's late September now. October is only a week away. The sun sets around six thirty, so that now, just shortly before, it's what's referred to as the golden hour, where the sky has a signature soft golden glow. I'll be home later than usual tonight and I'll have to give Lily some reason why, though I wonder if I'll tell her that I was here. It's probably better that she doesn't know.

Up ahead, a man walks his dog. I watch them for a while from behind, thinking how Lily and I used to have a dog before she died. Lily and I always said one day we'd get another dog, but there was never a good time for it. We said kids first and then another dog, but the kids didn't happen like we expected.

The man gets stopped by a little girl who wants to pet his dog. He bends to get a good hold on the leash before he lets her, and then I watch from a distance as the giggling little girl strokes the dog's ears while her mother watches on. When she's had enough, she waves goodbye to the dog. The man stands back up. Something falls from his pocket, but he doesn't notice. He and his dog turn and keep walking.

"Sir," I say, calling after him to get him to stop. I jog to catch up, calling again, "You dropped something, sir."

When I come to it, I stoop over and pick up the man's wallet. At the same time, he hears me and turns around. He's tall like me. He can't be forty.

He shields the fading sun from his eyes with a hand. "Did you say something?" he asks.

"Your wallet," I say, holding it out to him. "You dropped it back there."

"Thanks, man," he says, taking it from me, turning it over in his hands, looking at it as if to make sure it's his. "I can't believe I didn't notice."

I shrug. "It happens." As I get a good look at him, I realize that I recognize this man. I cock my head. "Hey. Do I know you?" I ask, narrowing my eyes at him.

At first he looks at me like he thinks he knows me too, but then that look of recognition fades and he shakes his head. "Sorry," he says. "I don't think so." The dog at his feet starts to bark, tugging on the leash. We both look down at it and he says, "Serena, no." It's a black-and-white dog, something like a border collie. The dog turns and tries walking away despite his command. He tells her again, "No," and this time she listens. "Thanks for this," he says, brandishing his wallet before slipping it into a back pocket. "I don't know what I would have done if I lost it."

I lost my wallet once. Canceling the debit and credit cards and having to go to the DMV for a new license was a pain in the neck. This man is just lucky his wallet didn't fall into the wrong hands.

I say, "No problem."

It's later, driving home, that my brain makes the connection. That man works with Lily. I've met him once or twice. He has a face I'd remember, though, in retrospect, I'm glad he didn't recognize me because then he might have told Lily he saw me at Langley Woods and I would have had to explain what I was doing there.

I might have remembered the man's face, but his name is another story. I beat my brains trying to remember it. I never figure it out, but my best guess is that it's something like Brian or Ryan.

NINA

Wednesday afternoon, shortly after I get home from work, my neighbor across the street sends me a direct message on Facebook. It's a little after three in the afternoon. I've just stepped into the kitchen when the notification comes through. I set my bag on the island, find my phone in the bag and step out of my shoes.

Nina, hi. Been on a social media hiatus but just saw your post to the neighborhood page. Sorry so late. Thought you might like to see this.

It's another video, this one taken from her video doorbell. I sit down on one of the counter stools and press Play. I still have my coat on. There is a timestamp in the bottom right corner of the recording. It's from Saturday morning at 10:07 a.m. This neighbor has a direct sight line to my house, which entices me.

This is what I've been waiting to see. The only thing getting anywhere close to being in the way is a tree, which blocks only part of the frame. You can still see around it.

As I watch and wait for Jake, the same black car from Ellie Miller's video enters the frame. It drives past my house and then exits the frame. Thirty seconds and then a minute pass by while I stare at the video, waiting for something to happen, but starting to give up hope, thinking this is just another wasted effort. Maybe all Emilie, my neighbor, saw was that same black car driving by.

For the longest time, nothing happens. I watch the leaves on the trees move. The leaves are the only way to know that the video hasn't ended or stopped recording because other than them, everything else is static and unchanged. My house. The brick mailbox. The streetlamp and a red fire hydrant.

But then this man in the hat with his jeans and jacket enters the frame. His hands are in his pockets as he walks straight up my driveway, to the brick walkway and to my front door. My attention is momentarily piqued. This man in the black car wasn't going to see some friend. He came to my house after all.

I watch as he stands at my door awhile, with his back to the camera. The video quality isn't great. The man is just small blurry pixels. But I recognize him from Ellie Miller's video. It's the same man. It has to be. He stands at the door for maybe twenty seconds, waiting for someone to come let him in. My mother was home at the time. She didn't say anything about someone coming to the door. She must not have heard the doorbell ring, or she just chose not to answer it. I don't blame her. I don't always answer my door when someone comes.

When no one answers the door, the man turns away from it, so that he would be facing the street, looking straight at the camera, except that his chin is tucked to his chest and the video quality is crap. The brim of the hat is pulled low, too, hiding his face and his eyes. I pause the video to see if I can get a better look at him, but it's too pixelated. The hat looks to be navy blue, but it's hard to say, it might be black. I can't tell what the logo is.

I wonder who this man is. I wonder why he came to our door and what he wanted from us. It was probably nothing, just someone out canvassing the neighborhood, trying to sell us something like a new roof or a year's worth of weed control. Jake and I have a no soliciting sign on the door, but this wouldn't be the first time someone has ignored it.

I watch as the man retraces his steps down the front walkway for the driveway. When he gets to it, I expect him to make his way down the drive for the sidewalk, moving on to another house to try and sell them whatever he's selling. But he doesn't.

The man turns confidently the other way. He goes straight for the garage door keypad. He lifts the cover and I go numb. I stop breathing. I hold my breath. What the hell does he think he's doing? Who is this man? I watch open-mouthed as he presses numbers into the keypad. Nice try, I think, practically laughing to myself. He'll get the passcode wrong. He can't know them.

But he does know them. The door rises up, betraying me. I'm sitting there on the counter stool at the kitchen island, watching this video. My mouth falls open. My eyes are wide and my whole body is frozen still.

I watch in shock as the man lets himself in through the garage and into my home with ease. The garage door sinks closed. From the outside of the house, you wouldn't know that anything was amiss. It looks perfectly peaceful. The only movement is the flapping leaves of the tree.

But inside, there is a stranger creeping around my home, touching my personal things. He's inside the house with my mother.

Ten seconds later, the video ends.

The reality of what's happened plows into me like a tidal wave.

I feel absolutely violated.

It was never Jake. Jake was never in the house. Jake didn't come home. My mother didn't see Jake.

She saw someone else. Someone else came into my home when I wasn't here. An intruder. That's why he didn't speak to her, why he didn't acknowledge her. This man was in the house alone with my mother. He was in Jake's office. He knocked the key card to the floor, which means he was also digging around in the mail sorter for something. Why? What was he looking for? Money?

I should be grateful my mother is alive, that he ran at the sound of her and didn't kill her.

"Mom!" I call, in a panic. I step out of the stool. I slip my feet back into my shoes, going to the mail sorter now to thumb through it and see if anything is obviously missing. "Mom!" I call again, this time up the stairs, my agitation increasing exponentially.

I have my back to the stairs. I hear her feet edge near, and she says, "Nina? What's wrong?" I turn around as she appears at the top of the stairs, coming down in jeans and a shirt that hangs down to her upper thigh.

"I have to run out," I say, "and I want you to come with me."

"But you just got home," she says, looking disappointed. "Don't you want to relax for a while? I can make dinner."

"I know. I'm sorry. I can't, not yet," I say. I stare at my mother, thinking what could have happened to her Saturday morning. When she reaches the bottom of the steps, I go to her and throw my arms around her.

She laughs me off. I'm not usually so demonstrative. But I could have lost her. This man could have killed her. I feel sick when I think about it. "What in the world has gotten into you, Nina?" she asks.

I wish I didn't have to tell her what happened, that she was in danger, that maybe we both still are. I don't want to give her anything else to worry about. She has enough to worry about already. But a strange man was here in the house with her the other day. He let himself uninvited into my home. He was here in my kitchen. He was in Jake's office and in the foyer. He stood where I now stand. He touched our things. I think of all the things he must have touched, and feel desecrated, like the home is contaminated. I want to call the cleaning lady and have everything bleached.

How do I know this man won't come back? How do I know he hasn't already been back? I feel sick when I think just then about the man's footprint in the mudroom the other night and wonder if it was his. I vigorously shake my head, as if trying to dislodge the thought of this man in my house Monday night as well as Saturday morning.

I can't leave my mother alone here.

"It shouldn't take too long."

"Where are we going?" my mother asks, and I tell her then, reluctantly. I tell her about the videos, and then I tell her that we're going to the police. She says nothing at first, but her hand comes slowly to her mouth and her eyes go wide.

We head for the car, going through the garage door. I regret washing the mudroom floor the other night. I should have left the shoe print so there was evidence for the police to see. But the video will be enough.

My mother says, "I'm sorry, Nina. I'm sorry I told you it was Jake."

"Don't be sorry. It was an honest mistake. You didn't know."

But now I'm worried about Jake. He was not here in the home just a few days ago. He's been gone now, missing, for well over a week. And now our home has been broken into twice and random flowers have been sent to me at work. These things can't all be unrelated.

At the police station, I give my mother the option of staying in the car, but she comes in with me. She hangs quietly back, a step behind, saying almost nothing. The front desk officer is a man this time. I tell him, "I need to report a break-in."

"When did this break-in occur?" he asks.

"Saturday."

He asks me to take a seat and tells me that someone will be with me shortly. It's busier today than it was the other day. They have to triage the crises as they come in. Mine isn't an emergency because it isn't a burglary in progress. No one is hurt. No one is in imminent danger, except for maybe Jake. I feel panicky, because the more I think about it, I think he is. Jake is in danger. I'm anxious to speak with someone. I take a seat next to my mother, but it's almost impossible to sit still.

Eventually, another male officer comes. He says that his name is Officer Boone. Officer Boone looks to be in his midthirties, a larger man with a serious face but kind brown eyes hidden behind a pair of glasses. He takes my mom and me to a small room and tells us to have a seat so he can take down our report. He sits across from us, settling into a metal chair, not much better than a folding chair.

"My home was broken into Saturday morning when I wasn't home," I say.

I tell him the rest. I pull up the video from my neighbor Emilie and slip the officer my phone. He takes it into his hand. He removes his glasses and brings the phone close to his eyes for a better look. He watches, intently focused, and I'm grateful for the attention he gives to it.

The police have some of the best technology available to them. They'll be able to enlarge this video, to sharpen the image and to see what I can't see: the face of the man who broke into my home.

CHRISTIAN

Wednesday evening, Lily and I are in the kitchen. Lily is at the table with her laptop grading math assignments online. I'm leaned over the sink, washing dishes. The volume on the TV is turned up high so that I can hear it over the rush of water. There is a basketball game on and every now and then, I look back over my shoulder to see what the score is. I still have work to finish up tonight, a quality check for a colleague that I never got to today because I've been playing catch-up all week.

Lily wears her headphones. She's listening to music while she grades.

I leave the lights mostly off in the house. I've gotten in the habit of doing that and, just like closing and locking our bedroom door, it's one of those things Lily and I do without talking about it, without saying why. But with almost no window coverings on the back of the house, a public trail just outside our back door, and what's happened with Jake, we feel more on display than ever. Fortunately, only the first few leaves of the season have begun to fall so that the trees still hang on to most of them. They give us some coverage, but there is no fence, no physical boundary, which means there is nothing to say that people can't just walk off the trail, past the trees and into our backyard.

In the kitchen, only the stove light is on but the TV and Lily's computer give off light. We also lit a few candles and started a fire in the fireplace. It would be atmospheric and romantic, under different circumstances.

Over the sound of the sink water and the TV, comes a sudden, curt knock on the front door that forces me upright.

I drop the handle on the faucet when I hear it. The water slows but I don't manage to turn it all the way off so that steady drops come from the tap, plunging into the sink.

Plop, plop, plop.

I turn around, drying my hands on a towel. My eyes go to Lily's first. Lily heard a noise at the same time, though it was dulled because of her headphones, and I can see from the expression on her face that she's trying to process the noise, to figure out what it is. She slips the headphones off, looking at me through the semidarkness.

"Shhh," I say, putting a finger to my lips, wrapping my lips around the sound. I hold still, like if I don't move, no one will see me. We're in the back of the house, where the front windows don't reach, but that doesn't mean we're completely unexposed.

My first thought is that if we wait it out long enough, whoever is at the door will go away. But then the knock comes again. "Someone's here," Lily whispers, really hearing for the first time and registering what the sound is. Her eyes widen. Lily is visibly shaken by the knock at the door. Innocent people don't usually worry about things like this, but Lily and I aren't exactly innocent. "Who do you think it is?" she whispers.

"I don't know."

"What should we do?"

I reach for the TV remote and drop the volume. "Just give it a minute. They'll leave," I say, but as I do, the pounding knock comes again for a third time, followed by the chime of the doorbell. Whoever is at the door isn't going to leave by choice.

"What if they don't?"

I say to Lily, "Stay here. I'll go see who it is. It's probably nothing."

I leave the kitchen. I walk through the foyer to the front door, thinking of all the possibilities: a neighbor; some kid selling candy to raise money for his baseball team; a package that needs to be signed for. I turn on the foyer light so that it's not so dark when I open the door.

I pull the door open to find a police officer standing on the stoop. I draw in a deep breath, trying to be nonreactive but, at the same time, telling myself that even innocent people feel nervous from a police officer coming to their door. A police officer at the front door is rarely good news. It either means you're in trouble or that someone has died.

The officer is tall. He's formidable. I'm tall, too, but this man is wide, which I'm not. His chest is broad, filling out his uniform and my front doorframe. His face is long.

"Are you Christian Scott?" he asks, my eyes still taking time to adjust to the foyer light.

"Yeah," I say, raking a hand through my hair, "Yeah, I am. I'm Christian Scott. Is everything okay? Has something happened?"

My mind is all over the place. Someone saw Lily and me move Jake's car. Someone knows that I'm the one who broke into Jake and Nina's house, or that I was back there again Monday night to return the key. I was in and out quickly that time. As far as I know, it was without incident. But I could be wrong. Someone could have seen me. Someone could have known that I was there.

"Is your wife home, Mr. Scott?" he asks, now angling his head to see past me and into our house. I turn around. Lily isn't there, standing behind me. She's in the kitchen, where it's still dark. I can just barely make out the sound of the basketball game on the TV from here. "I was hoping to talk to both of you at the same time."

"Yeah," I say. "Sure. Let me just go get her."

I invite the officer into the house. I don't know that I want him coming in, standing in the foyer alone, trawling the house while I go to get Lily, but it would look suspicious not to, as if I have something to hide.

"Sure," he says, coming into the house and closing the door behind himself. "Take your time."

Lily is at the table when I come back in for her. Her face has gone pale, her limp hair hanging into her eyes. She's been sitting there, listening the whole time. I go to her and she reaches out for my hand. "What does he want?" she whispers. The tension in her voice, her eyes, is palpable.

I whisper back, "I don't know."

Lily and I stare at each other for a second, the fear in my eyes matching the fear in hers.

"What are we going to do, Christian?" she asks.

"Take a deep breath," I say, pulling her into me, feeling her heart beat against me. "Come out when you're ready. It will be fine. I'll take care of this."

When I come back out into the foyer, the officer is still standing by the door. His arms are crossed. My eyes go to the handcuffs and the firearm on his belt before rising to his. "She's on her way," I say. "She'll be right here. Can I ask what this is about, Officer? Did something happen?"

"I need to ask you and your wife a few questions about Jake Hayes."

My stomach turns to a rock.

"Jake?" I say, a question, as if trying to place who he is. My face does that thing where it looks like I'm trying to look inward, to think, to physically pull something out of my memory.

"Yes, Jake Hayes. His wife is Nina Hayes," the officer says.

"Oh yes, of course. Jake," I say as if my brain just made the connection. My eyebrows come together, my forehead tightening. I ask, "Is everything okay? Is *he* okay?"

Lily appears in the space behind me. I don't hear her coming, but I see the officer's eyes go to her, his stance change, and I gaze back over my shoulder to find her looking pale but better than she did a few minutes ago. She comes around the corner, her footsteps delicate and light, her feet bare. She's wearing tight leggings and a baggy T-shirt of mine that slips from a shoulder, revealing the strap of her black bra.

"Lily," I say, stepping aside, making room for her beside me as I slide an arm around her waist, "the officer wants to ask us some questions about Jake Hayes." I'm grateful when Lily's face goes blank and she goes along with what I'm trying to do. "Nina's husband," I explain, as if we only know him peripherally because of Nina, as if he hasn't been the only thing on our minds these last few days.

"Right," she says, "Jake." The concern that manifests on Lily's face resembles mine. "I work with his wife, Nina Hayes," she tells the officer, whose intensity has seemingly diminished since Lily came into the room. Lily has that effect on people. "Nina told me that he hasn't come home in a few days." Lily gazes up at me. "I can't remember if I told you that," she says.

I say, "You did. It's awful." My eyes go back to the police officer's. "What brings you here, Officer? Has something else happened?"

"I'm speaking to people close to the Hayeses, and trying to see if we can't locate Dr. Hayes."

I start to relax because I realize that the officer is only looking into Jake's disappearance. He doesn't know anything more than that he's gone, than that he hasn't come home. He has no clue of Lily's and my involvement or, if he does, he's not letting on yet.

"When is the last time you saw Dr. Hayes?" he asks.

I think back. I look at Lily. "It's been what?" I ask her. "Six months or more? We had dinner together," I say, looking back to the officer, "but that was sometime last spring, I think."

Lily says, "April, yes. We were celebrating Nina's birthday." I had forgotten that it was Nina's birthday, but Lily is right, it was. We met for dinner at a Brazilian steakhouse, the night Jake showed up in his new car and took me for a ride. It had been Lily's idea for us to all get together to celebrate. Nina chose the restaurant. Lily made the reservations.

"Nina said that she and Jake have been fighting," Lily says. It's scarcely audible, like a thought Lily meant to keep in her head, but it slipped out. She's not looking at either the officer or me when she says it, she's looking at her feet, where the pink nail polish flakes off. "I'm sorry," she says then, shaking her head as if realizing her mistake, which wasn't a mistake at all but a brilliant stratagem. "I shouldn't have said that. Nina told me that in confidence, but it isn't something she'd want other people to know. Nina is private."

"Of course," the officer says, like he's really going to disregard what Lily just told him. "Was this something she told you recently?" Lily nods. "How long had they been fighting?"

"For a few months," Lily says. "I'm not sure. I can't remember when she said it began, but it seemed to have been escalating in recent weeks. She told me because it was really beginning to upset her. But I didn't think it would come to this."

"To what exactly?"

"To him leaving. Isn't that what happened?"

"We don't know what's happened to Dr. Hayes. What exactly were Dr. and Mrs. Hayes fighting about? Did she say?"

Lily shrugs. "What any couple fights about I guess."

"How has Mrs. Hayes seemed to you lately?"

"What do you mean?"

"Have you noticed a change in her behavior?"

Lily mulls this over. "Well yes. She's been different. More anxious. More withdrawn. Because of Jake and because she has things going on with her mother too. Her mother's health is failing. I just assumed that's what had her down. But between us, Officer," Lily says, and she looks at me, as if some thought has just surfaced in her mind, but she's not sure she should be saying it.

"Yes, Mrs. Scott?" he asks, encouraging her.

Lily looks back to the officer. Her face is humble. She's soft-spoken, if not meek. "Please don't tell Nina I told you this. I don't want her to be upset with me." Lily looks to me again, dragging this out for effect.

"What did she tell you, Mrs. Scott?"

Lily swallows. Her gaze goes back to the officer. "Nina said once that she thought Jake was going to leave her. She thought maybe he was having an affair. Honestly, I didn't think much about it at the time, because all marriages go through rough times. I said she was probably worried for nothing. I told her maybe marriage counseling would help, if their marriage was struggling."

"Did they go to marriage counseling?"

"No. Their lives are too busy. Jake is a neurosurgeon. He's almost never home. And like I said, Nina's mother is sick. They didn't have time for marriage counseling."

Lily opens her mouth as if to say more, but then closes it. This doesn't go unnoticed.

"Is there something else, Mrs. Scott?"

"She said that if Jake ever did leave, she didn't know what she would do, but that she didn't think she could live without him." She inhales and then exhales deeply. "Nina is a good friend. I feel terrible for saying this, but—"

Lily stops abruptly. She looks to me again, and I find myself spellbound, completely enrapt in her lies.

"But what?" the officer asks, urging her on.

"Nina said something like if she couldn't be with Jake, no one would."

The officer is quiet for a second. "And what did you take that to mean, Mrs. Scott?" he asks.

I watch the news. I read things. I know that in the United States, women kill their husbands more than they do in almost any other country. For every one hundred men who kill their wives, there are something like seventy-five women who kill their husbands, if not more. Some people say it's more like fifty-fifty. When men kill their wives, often it starts with some sort of psychological abuse. Stalking. Manipulation. Gaslighting.

But when women do it, it's usually because she's already determined that she's going to die if he doesn't.

But that's not always the case. Women kill for different reasons other than fear or in self-defense. Sometimes they kill because they're jealous, because they're worried their spouse is going to leave them, for life insurance payouts, or some combination of the three. It's not impossible to believe that Nina could have done this. Implicating someone else feels like a shitty thing to do. I'm sorry about it, but at the same time, I'd do anything to keep Lily and me from getting caught.

Lily shakes her head erratically. Her hair falls into her eyes. "I don't know." She looks to me again, and then at the officer. "I shouldn't have said that. I thought nothing of it, at the time. She was just mad. She was getting her feelings out, you know? Venting." Lily pauses, a pregnant pause, and then she says, "I didn't take it as a threat, if that's what you're asking."

I'm caught off guard, in a good way, by Lily. It's ingenious. She's managed to turn this around, to put the cloud of suspicion on Nina.

NINA

Earlier this evening, I left the police station in a daze, feeling harried and disheartened. It was just after five that we left. I didn't speak to my mother the whole way home. I couldn't speak at all. There were no words because, after that officer watched the video, he slid the phone back to me. His intrigue had lessened. He put his glasses back on his face, and he said, "Doorbell cameras record best between five and thirty feet away. Beyond that, objects can become unidentifiable. Your street is maybe twenty-four to twenty-eight feet wide, which is standard. From door to door, you're talking much more than that because of the size of the property. It's good that your neighbor's camera caught this man entering your home, otherwise you might not have known that he had. I just don't know that the video is helpful to us in finding this man. This image is distorted. It lacks clarity. We can't see this man's face because of the hat. We don't know who he is, unless you recognize him?" he had asked, leading, and I shook my head. I didn't know who the man was, which was why I had taken the video to the police. I needed them to tell me who he is. "There are no discerning features."

"Can you enlarge it?" I asked.

"Not without exacerbating the clarity problem."

I pulled up and showed him the other videos, taken with Ellie Miller's camera, of the man's car. Unfortunately the problem was the same. The car was never at the right angle for the officer to see the front or the back end of it or the car's make and model. He couldn't see the license plate. Even if he could have, he said that he didn't know that he would be able to read it because of the clarity problem. His tech people will take a closer look, but he cautioned me not to get my hopes up. "There are limitations to videos like these. They're helpful," he said. "They're not foolproof."

I had exchanged a glance with my mother before looking back at the officer. "So what do I do in the meantime?" I asked, trying to keep myself from becoming hysterical. "A man broke into my home. He walked right in. He knew the passcode."

"I know," he said. His eyes were sympathetic, which I appreciated. "I'm going to take down your report, ma'am. We'll send an officer out to your home to have a look around. What I suggest you do is change the passcode on your garage door, as well as change the locks on your home. Have you considered installing your own video doorbell or security system?"

"Should I?" I asked.

"That's up for you to decide. We've found that sometimes just having a camera is a deterrent for burglars. Was anything taken?"

"No. Not that I know of. I didn't even know that someone had broken in until my neighbor showed me this."

"Who knows the passcode to your garage?" he asked.

"My husband and me. My mother," I said, looking at her.

She sat in the chair beside me, never once speaking. "The house cleaner." I tried to remember who else. There were more. Jake and I have never been too discriminating in who we give the passcode to, though we haven't been negligent either. The people we've given the passcode to seemed safe. "We had painters in the house not too far back," I remembered. "Neither my husband nor I could be home to let them in, so we gave them the code to the garage. We meant to change it later, but forgot." It felt so stupid in retrospect. There were more painters than I could count in their crew. We were having practically the whole house painted, so there must have been at least ten of them. After I told the officer about the painters, I started to wonder if all of the men in their crew knew the passcode to the garage, or just one, whoever was in charge? Did someone see something they wanted and decided to come back later and get it? Why didn't Jake and I change the passcode after they left?

"Don't feel bad, Mrs. Hayes. It happens," the officer assured me.

"Will they take fingerprints when they come?" I asked, assuming the answer would be yes.

But he shook his head. "No. It's unlikely. That's not something that's typically done in situations like this."

"Why not?" I asked, incredulous. How would they ever find this man if they didn't take fingerprints?

"For fingerprints to yield any results, Mrs. Hayes, we have to have something to compare them to. It's not as easy as one might think or like they make it look on TV. Any prints we lift are liable to belong to someone who has been in your home with your permission. Take these painters you mentioned, for example. If we were to find their fingerprints in your home, it doesn't tell us if one of them broke into your house on Saturday morning or if they were there a month ago, painting. Additionally, we'd need to take elimination prints from every person who has ever had access to your home. It's laborious and most of the time, doesn't generate any reasonable leads to make it worthwhile. You see what I'm saying?"

I did, unfortunately. I thought through the vast number of people Jake and I had welcomed into our home. I couldn't remember them all if I tried.

"But surely there's something that can be done to find this man."

From the look on his face, I knew there was little hope of them ever finding this man.

"Our tech guys will take a closer look at these videos and see what they can find. The other problem, Mrs. Hayes, is that days have passed since this break-in occurred. In that time, you've touched things in your home. You may have unknowingly destroyed evidence. Listen," he said, "if any of your belongings have been taken or if there is damage to your home, you can call the insurance company. They'll send out a claims adjuster."

I nodded, feeling woozy and scared. I couldn't believe this was happening. I still can't. "Okay."

"In the meantime, the best thing you can do is make sure your home is entirely secure. Take steps to protect yourself from future break-ins. As I said, change the passcode on the garage, replace the locks, consider installing a home security system."

"How do I go about changing the code on the garage door?" I asked. It was the kind of thing that Jake would know how to do. Jake took care of things like this.

"They're all different, Mrs. Hayes. Do you have an owners' manual?"

I shook my head. If we did have an owner's manual, I didn't know where Jake would have kept it.

"You can call a garage door repair person. They should be able to help you out." I also didn't know a garage door repair person. I felt so miserably inadequate all of a sudden.

My mother spoke then. She knew how I was feeling. "I can help," she said. "Don't worry, Nina. We'll figure it out." My mother has been single most of her life. She raised me alone. She never relied on a man, but figured everything out on her own. I envy that about her. She's resourceful.

"Okay," I said again. My voice sounded faraway, like I had disassociated, like I was somewhere outside of my body, watching. I felt utterly dazed. I couldn't believe this was happening. Future break-ins. Did that mean this man might come back? Of course it did. I thought then of that footprint in the mudroom and knew there was a chance this man had already been back. I told the officer this. I also told the officer, "The other day, last Thursday, I received anonymous flowers at work. I tried calling the florist to see who they were from, but she wouldn't tell me, not without an order from the police. I'm scared, Officer Boone. What if the same person who broke into my home is the one who sent me flowers? What if someone is stalking me?" I asked. I could feel my mother's eyes on me the whole time, because I'd neglected to tell her about the flowers.

He said, "If it would help, I can call the florist and see if she won't give that information to me."

"Thank you. I'd appreciate that. I'm worried about my husband too," I said. "He's still missing. It's been over a week now since he's been home. Nine days to be exact."

"My understanding," he said, "is that you canceled your missing person's report. I was under the impression that you'd seen your husband since reporting him missing."

I exchanged a look with my mother. I felt awful throwing her under the bus like this, but the officer had to know what happened. "My mother," I said, reaching a hand for her knee, offering a sympathetic smile that she most likely couldn't see, "has trouble with her vision." I looked back to Officer Boone, who was looking at my mother. You wouldn't necessarily know there was anything wrong just by looking at her. "Macular degeneration. She makes mistakes sometimes. She thought she'd seen Jake at our house the other day, but instead she saw this man," I said, making a motion to my phone.

"I see," he said. "So your husband is still missing."

I nodded, remorseful. "Yes," I said, thinking sadly of these last few wasted days when no one was looking for Jake.

"Okay," he said, and then Officer Boone promised to dig more deeply into Jake's disappearance, to continue speaking to the people Jake and I know, to ask around and see if someone knows something they're not telling me.

Because someone, somewhere has to know where Jake is.

It's late at night now. My mother is down the hall, getting ready for bed. I should be asleep, but I don't know that I even want to lie down in bed and let myself sleep. I thought about taking melatonin or a sleeping pill or drinking yet another bottle of wine, but it isn't necessarily that I can't sleep. I haven't tried. It's that I don't know that I want to sleep. I don't want to be vulnerable and unconscious. I can't stop thinking about the ease with which that man let himself into my house. It's only been a few hours since I watched the video of him coming in, but still the shock of it hasn't worn off. I don't think it ever will. Every time I think about it, it's as real and raw as the first time I watched it. I watch the video again and again on repeat, as if to torture myself. I can't stop watching it.

I paid a small fortune for a locksmith to come out. He offered twenty-four hours per day, seven days a week emergency service. It was expensive, but I was grateful he could come on such short notice. He replaced all the locks on the house. I'm the only one with a key.

I got a garage door repairman to come out too. I now have a new garage code that only I know. My mother didn't even want to know it. The repair person turned his back as I programmed it in. I watched him and I made sure he wasn't looking. It was paranoid, but who could blame me?

I spoke to ADT on the phone. I scheduled an appointment for them to come out and install a security system next week, which is the soonest they could get me on the schedule, though I offered five hundred dollars if someone could come tonight. I practically begged, but they couldn't. I'll feel so much better when we have a home security system, when I can arm all the doors and windows before coming up to sleep for the night. On average, ADT responds to an intruder in something like forty-five seconds—that's what the customer service representative told me on the phone—though the sound of an alarm going off is likely to scare him off much sooner and, with any luck, the signs in the yard will deter him from even attempting a break-in. When the security system is installed, no one can get in. No one can hurt my mother or me. We'll be completely safe.

But that won't happen until next week.

I can't shake the thought of someone—specifically the man in the hat and the jeans—letting himself into my house when I'm out cold. For the last few hours, I've thought about almost exclusively nothing but him. I imagine him breaking into my house for a third time. I think about the confidence with which he walked, about the efficiency with which he punched in the garage code and opened the door. He knew the garage code. He knew I wouldn't be home.

What else does he know about me?

That night, I leave the bedroom. I creep downstairs, to find and take Jake's gun from the safe. I'd just feel safer if it was with me. A gun locked in the safe downstairs doesn't do me any good if someone breaks into the house at night. If someone broke in, I couldn't get downstairs in time, much less unlock the safe, load and shoot the gun.

It's dark in Jake's office. The only light is from the moon, coming in the curtainless window. I make my way across the room, the wood hard against my bare feet. I come to Jake's desk, which is massive in size, a charcoal-colored executive desk. It's longer in length than me in height. I feel my way around the edge of the desk, running my hand along the back of his tufted swivel chair. Behind the desk, Jake has two bookcases to match the desk, but between the bookcases hangs an original abstract painting that he bought from a gallery because he liked it, and also because he needed something to hide the wall-mounted safe. The painting is bright orange and turquoise, and if I had to guess, I'd think it was mountains rising out of the ocean, but it's hard to tell.

I lift the painting from the wall. As gently as putting a newborn to bed, I set it on the floor, and then I stand upright and face the safe. The safe has a code. I start pressing the numbers in, remembering how I didn't know how to shoot or even hold a gun until Jake took me to the shooting range for practice. That was years ago, when we were younger, happier. When the future still held promise. I had objected to having a gun in the house at the time. As a rule, I hate them; *no good can come of having a gun in the house*, I tried telling Jake. But what Jake wants, Jake gets. He thought I'd feel differently if I knew how to handle and shoot the gun. He said it wouldn't feel so foreign to me. I went to the shooting range with him. I shot at a paper target. I did quite well. I remember that Jake was impressed. He didn't think I had it in me to shoot at anything, and I think he thought I was going to lose my nerve once the gun was loaded and in my hands. I didn't. Still, punching holes in paper must be far different that shooting at a human.

The safe unlocks. I open the door and reach my hand in, feeling blindly inside for the gun.

I come up empty.

Jake's gun isn't in the safe.

Jake, wherever he is, has his gun.

CHRISTIAN

The next day, I meet Lily in the afternoon for an appointment with the obstetrician. There was blood in her underpants—just a little, from what she said—but enough that my heart stopped when Lily called me at work to tell me. "The doctor said it's probably nothing, just spotting," Lily told me, over the phone, but I could tell from the quiver in her voice that she didn't believe it, that she repeated the doctor's words just to soothe herself and me. She said, "The doctor said it's not uncommon to spot during the first trimester," which I know, I've read practically all the websites on pregnancy, but blood in her underpants has always proven disastrous.

"What time is the appointment?"

"One."

"That's the soonest she can get you in?" I'd asked, wanting to go now. It was ten in the morning when she called. There is nothing worse than waiting, than not knowing. From that moment on, I knew I wouldn't be able to focus on anything today but the baby.

"Yes," Lily had said.

Lily has now made it to ten weeks in the pregnancy. That's about as far as we've ever gotten. The second trimester draws near. That second trimester is a major milestone in that the baby's odds of survival will drastically increase because the majority of miscarriages happen during those first thirteen weeks. It's not foolproof. Miscarriages can happen at any time, and we're still three weeks away from reaching that critical stage. Anything can happen. Anything can go wrong. Lily may have already lost this baby.

Her stress these last few weeks has been high, especially after the unexpected visit from the cop last night. I kissed her hard after he'd left. I took her in my arms and pressed my lips to hers and said, "That was amazing, Lily. *You* are fucking amazing." I couldn't help myself. I was impressed with her quick thinking. But it didn't come without consequences, because Lily felt guilty as hell afterward for what she said or for what she implied about Nina.

There is no actual evidence that stress leads to miscarriage, but doctors don't know everything.

I'm running late to the appointment. The client meeting I was in ran over, and then there was an accident on the expressway. Traffic was backed up for miles. It's eight minutes after one now. I park my car and run into the building.

Lily is already on the exam table when a nurse lets me into the room with her. She has her back to me. She turns and smiles. Lily wears her own red shirt, but she's naked from the waist down, draped with a paper sheet over her lap. She's one of the few people in the world who could ever look gorgeous sitting under sterile fluorescent lights with a paper sheet covering her lower half. Lily is radiant. "Hey," she says. She takes my breath away when she smiles.

"Hey. Sorry I'm late." I walk into the room and close the door quietly behind myself. "What did I miss?"

"Nothing," she says. "You're not late. The doctor hasn't been in."

I come to Lily. I pull her into me, kissing her on the side of the head. I hold her close. "Any more blood?"

She shakes her head. "No."

"That's good, right? How are you feeling?"

"Okay," she says. "Just nauseated. And tired."

I release her. I take a seat on one of the chairs, opposite the exam table. I can see on Lily's face that she's tired. I heard her this morning in the bathroom. She was throwing up. It's not that I want Lily to be sick, but it had come as a relief at the time, as if her being nauseated meant that everything was okay with the baby. It's not a guarantee, because a few hours later, when we were both at work, she saw blood. And last time, even after she miscarried, Lily continued to have morning sickness because of the hormones still in her body. It was a double whammy. As if the miscarriage or the morning sickness wasn't bad enough on its own, she had both.

I feel relieved to see Lily. She looks better than I imagined, and I think if the amount of blood on her underpants this morning was anything like times before, she'd look worse than this.

There's a knock on the door. The doctor comes in. The doctor is a woman. Lily likes her, a lot. I do too. She's been through quite a bit with us and wants us to have a baby almost as much as Lily and I want to have a baby. The last miscarriage, she cried. When we came back months later, pregnant again, she looked about as split as I felt. What were we doing? At what point did we just give up and quit?

The doctor says hi to me, but she focuses her attention on Lily. Today she wants to first try and listen to the baby's heartbeat with a fetal Doppler. The last time we were here, a couple weeks ago, we heard it with the transvaginal ultrasound, which we can do again if necessary, but the Doppler might pick it up and save Lily the discomfort. "Ten weeks is about the soonest a heartbeat can be detected with the fetal Doppler," the doctor says, "so please don't panic if we don't hear it at first."

She has Lily lie flat on the table. I rise from my chair and go to stand beside Lily, at her head, holding on to her hand.

I smile benevolently at Lily as the doctor lifts the hem of her shirt to her ribs. Lily's abdomen is flat and it's hard to believe there could be another life in there, a life that we made. The doctor spreads a glob of gel on her lower abdomen. She turns the volume on the Doppler to high, and then runs the probe across Lily's skin. I hold my breath. Everyone in the room holds their breath. The heartbeat is supposed to sound something like the clippety-clop of horse hooves. I don't hear it. As the seconds go by, the air leaves the room. It gets harder and harder to breathe.

I want to ask questions. I want to ask what's taking so long. But I don't want to speak because then we won't hear the heartbeat when the probe passes over it. Lily's grip grows tighter on mine. I reflect on the events of the week. It's been a hell of a week, and it's not surprising that we're now here, in this position. I should have anticipated this.

After a minute, the doctor says, "Let's try this," as she asks Lily to move to the end of the table, setting the fetal Doppler aside. She helps guide Lily's feet into the stirrups, moving the paper sheet so that Lily is laid bare on the table. Lily's eyes are skittish as the doctor covers the transducer with a condom and gel before guiding it inside her. Lily looks up, her eyes searching for mine. I try and be calm for Lily's sake. I lean in close, stroking her hair. But I'm not calm. I find Lily's hand again—I don't remember letting go—and whisper into her ear, "It's okay," and maybe it is. The doctor just told us this fetal Doppler was a shot in the dark. We shouldn't be surprised it didn't work, and I'm almost resentful she tried.

It doesn't take long this time to find. It's a magical thing.

I exhale. I thank God. Lily's whole body relaxes. She sinks into the table, the tension fading away. The doctor smiles. The mood in the room is completely changed.

An image transmits to the TV monitor. A baby takes shape, undeveloped but there, with a beating heart, a head half the size of its body, and growing nubs for arms and legs.

"There it is," the doctor says, of the heartbeat.

There it is. Our baby.

"Looks like she has your head," Lily jokes because of how huge the head is in comparison to the rest of the body. I laugh. Lily is always teasing me about the size of my forehead.

"It must mean she's going to be incredibly smart."

"Everything looks good," the doctor says as she removes the transducer from between Lily's legs and tells her she can go ahead and sit up. "Spotting sometimes happens during the first trimester. It's scary but is generally not cause for alarm. What matters is that your baby is fine," she assures us, her eyes going from Lily's to mine. "I'll give you some privacy so that you can go ahead and get dressed."

The doctor steps from the room. Lily lowers herself from the end of the exam table to the floor. I hand her her clothes, which were sitting on the empty chair beside me. "What a relief," she says, taking them from me and stepping into her underpants.

She finishes getting dressed. I hold the printout of the ultrasound in my hand. I can't take my eyes off it. But I can't stop thinking: What if this is the closest I get to holding my baby?

We walk out quietly through reception. We're in the elevator now.

"I thought..." Lily says, but she can't bring herself to say the rest, to put those words—*baby* and *dead*—into the same sentence.

"I know," I say, as the doors close. It's with mixed emotions because, just because it hasn't happened yet, doesn't mean it still can't. "I thought so too."

I reach forward to press the button for the lobby, feeling the floor beneath us give as we descend.

Evenings are supposed to be relaxing. Before any of this happened, Lily and I would spend our evenings after work watching TV together or reading. She loves to read. I haven't seen her pick up a book this week. It's because of Jake, and because her attention has been diverted. Like me, she can't focus enough to actually read a book or do much of anything for that matter that requires any sort of mental acuity.

I convince Lily not to grade math homework tonight, but to come sit on the couch with me and relax. She and I nestle side by side on the center cushion. I spread a blanket over our laps. Lily lays her legs on me. She gets comfortable. "This is nice, isn't it?" I say, wrapping an arm around her shoulders, pulling her into me. Lily says that it is. I turn the TV on, wanting more than anything to unwind and to stop thinking about Jake or everything else we've been through this week. I make a concerted effort to think about something else, anything else but him and what Lily did to him.

I'm not so lucky.

We get maybe an hour of peace. But then, during a commercial break, there's a quick plug for the ten o'clock news. It takes my breath away. Neither Lily nor I speak though Lily chokes on her water and it comes back up, through her nose. She presses her hand to it. I offer my sleeve.

The image they show on the TV is of extensive treetops. It's taken from the air, as if from a helicopter or drone.

But it's the anchor's words, not the image, that practically cause heart failure. My mouth falls open. Our heads turn in slow motion to face each other and it's like looking straight into a mirror. We look back in unison at the TV.

The chyron at the bottom of the screen reads: *A body has been discovered at Langley Woods.*

NINA

Despite the new locks and the new garage door code, come the next morning, I still don't feel comfortable leaving my mother alone in my house all day, and I have to go to work.

For as hard as I try, I also can't get the image out of my head of someone breaking into my house. I obsess over it. I fixate on it. And it's not just the break-in because now Jake's gun is missing, and Jake is still missing. I think of how defenseless my mother is in my house all alone all day. What would she do if someone tried to break in again? How could she defend herself? What if she's not as lucky the next time?

It makes my stomach churn to think of something bad happening to her. I consider calling in sick to work and staying with her, but that would only be a one-day reprieve; it couldn't go on indefinitely.

I go into her room shortly after I've woken up. The door is open an inch. I lay a palm on it and press it all the way open, padding lightly across the room to where she lies in the guest bed, sound asleep on her side with the blankets pulled clear up to her neck. I lean down to touch her shoulder and shake her gently awake. "Mom," I whisper. "It's me." She stirs, her eyes opening and focusing on my face, though I wonder how much of me she can see. She describes her macular degeneration as a scribble around her central field of vision so that she has trouble seeing in that direct line of sight, and yet there are times she stares directly into my eyes and I feel the warmth of her gaze, the intense focus, sharpness and recognition. She knows it's me. She can see my eyes. It gives new life to me; it fills me with hope, because I'm not completely lost to her yet.

"What's wrong?" she asks, coming to and pushing herself up into a sitting position. It's still dark outside, too early for the sun to be up. On the other side of the windows, it's black. The only light comes from the bedroom down the hall.

I don't want to worry her and so I say, "Nothing is wrong." I sit on the edge of the bed. I reach for her hand. "It's just that I have to leave for work soon, Mom. I had an idea. I want to drive you to your house for the day. You can stay there, and then I'll pick you up again after school and we'll come back here."

"Why?" she asks.

"I'd just feel better if you weren't alone in the house."

"Why?" she asks again. "What's going to happen to me?"

"Nothing, I hope. But someone broke in the other day, Mom. I'd rather you weren't here alone."

She draws her eyebrows together and says, "No, that's too much trouble for you, Nina," which I knew she was going to say because she never wants to put me out. "I'll be fine."

"It's no trouble," I promise her. "I'll feel so much better if you're not here because, if you are, then I'll worry about you all day. It's easier on me if you just let me take you home. You'll be doing me a favor."

When I say it like that, she acquiesces. She pushes the sheets from her body and swings her legs to the floor. "If it makes you feel better, then okay."

I drive her to her house on the way into work. It's not a long drive. She lives in a ranch on a street with smaller, older homes, each one practically identical to the next. She's lived here for years. She knows her neighbors. She trusts them. She will be safer here while I'm at work.

I drop her off. "Lock the door once you're inside," I say through the open window as she walks away from me. I watch as she struggles to get the key in the lock, but she does, stepping inside and closing the screen door behind her. As I pull away, I see my mother's face from the other side of the door, darkened and disfigured by the fiberglass screen.

I haven't driven a block when I get a call from Officer Boone, asking if I can stop into the police station this morning. "I know you have to work. It will be quick," he promises.

I drive to the police station. He meets me in the front of the station and I ask, feeling anxious, my anxiety coming through in my voice, "What is it? Have you found something out about Jake?"

"No, unfortunately. Not yet."

I follow Officer Boone as he leads me to his desk further back in the police station, in a roomful of desks. He has me sit in a little upholstered chair beside his and offers me coffee, which I turn down, shaking my head.

"What is it, then? What did you want to tell me?"

"I actually have some questions for you, Mrs. Hayes."

"For me?"

"Yes."

"What kind of questions?"

"Well, I've been speaking to a few of your acquaintances," he says.

"And?" I ask, feeling a change come over me all of a sudden because I realize that Officer Boone hasn't called me here to tell me something, to update me on the case, but to ask questions. My walls go up. I wonder who he's been speaking to and what they've been telling him about me. Officer Boone would have spoken to Jake's parents. I've never known how Jake's parents feel about me because they're not the most affectionate or approachable people. They like me well enough. I just don't know that I'm the woman they would have chosen for their son to marry if the decision had been theirs.

"And it's come to my attention that there was some strife between you and Dr. Hayes of late."

His words are unembellished. They're very matter-of-fact, as if he's saying there is rain in the forecast or asking if I take my coffee with cream. They take my breath away.

"Strife?" I ask, my mouth falling open.

"Yes. Strife. Conflict. Marital issues."

"I know what *strife* is, Officer. I'm just surprised that you're asking. Jake has been missing for a week and a half and, in that time, someone has broken into my home. And you want to know if Jake and I ever fought? I don't see why it matters if we fought."

"Had you and your husband been fighting before he went missing, Mrs. Hayes?" he asks.

I don't answer. "Are you married, Officer Boone?" I ask instead, but he just looks at me; he doesn't say whether he's married or not. "If you're married, then you know. Couples fight. Everyone does. It's natural. It doesn't mean anything."

"Did you think he was going to leave you, Mrs. Hayes?"

"Is that what you think happened?" I ask. "That Jake left me."

"Can you answer the question, please?"

I feel like I'm the one under suspicion, that I'm being blamed for what happened to Jake. "I've been entirely candid, Officer. I said from the start that it's possible Jake left me. But that was before I knew he wasn't going to work. I just don't see why, if he was leaving me, he would walk out on his job too. His work means everything to him."

"Did you ever think that he might be having an affair?" he asks.

"Was he?" I ask, wondering if Officer Boone knows something I don't know.

"That's what I asked you."

"How would I know if Jake was having an affair?"

"Did you ever consider that he might be?"

Had I? Yes. I never had any evidence that he was. It could just have been that Jake was falling out of love with me. It might not have had anything to do with another woman, but I could feel Jake's distance from me, those nights when I would reach for him and he would pull away from me in bed, turning his back to me.

"Do I have to answer that?" I ask.

"No. No, you don't *have* to answer it, but it would be helpful if you did. Is there a reason you don't want to answer the questions, Mrs. Hayes?"

"It's just that what you're asking is personal and it has no bearing on where my husband is now. I wish you would focus your efforts on that, on finding my husband, and not whether he and I had fought or whether I thought he was having an affair. Which acquaintances of mine told you that there was strife in my marriage?" I ask.

"I don't particularly like to reveal where I get my information."

"You won't tell me?"

"I'd rather not. But I will tell you, it wasn't just one person. It was a common theme."

I wonder what Jake had been telling his parents and his brother about me.

I stare at Officer Boone. He stares back. The silence goes

on and then, because of it, I ask, "If those are all the questions you have for me, can I go?"

Officer Boone slowly nods. "Yes, Mrs. Hayes," he says, "you're not being held here. You can go whenever you'd like."

I consider his words. I stand up. I slip my purse over my shoulder but before I can leave, he says, "Hypothetically speaking though, if Dr. Hayes was having an affair, how would you feel about that?"

"Excuse me?" I ask.

"Would you be surprised? Would you be upset?"

"Of course I'd be upset," I say. "What woman wouldn't be upset if she found out her husband was cheating on her?"

I watch then as Officer Boone sizes me up, as if trying to ascertain if I would be upset enough to do something to Jake.

He says, "In your missing person's report, you said that you and Dr. Hayes had an altercation right before he disappeared. What were you fighting about?"

I don't answer his questions. Instead I ask, "Are you suggesting that I did something to my husband, Officer?" I don't give him a chance to reply. I go on, saying, "In all the time that he's been gone, I've been the only one looking for him. And now someone has broken into my home. This is more than just some marital spat. I wish you would do your job, and that you would find my husband." I look at my watch. "I have to go," I say, "or I'll be late to work."

I turn and walk away from him, thinking how what Jake and I were fighting about is none of his business.

As I put my head down and walk quickly to my car in the parking lot, I realize that I've somehow just become the prime suspect in my husband's disappearance.

CHRISTIAN

I go out to start Lily's car for her in the morning while she's finishing up her breakfast. It's slow to start. The engine doesn't turn over at first. I blame it on the weather, because it got cold overnight, colder than it usually is in the Midwest this time of year. Last night it dipped beneath forty, and they're saying in the coming nights, it could freeze. I try to start it again, and this time it starts.

"Let the engine run for a couple minutes to warm up," I say to her when I come back in the house. Lily stands at the sink, rinsing out her coffee mug. She overslept this morning because last night, she didn't sleep. She was up for much of the night, like me, because the news didn't say anything other than that a body was found. The rest was left to our imagination, and an active imagination fuels insomnia. I didn't fall asleep until after two. The 5:00 a.m. alarm came as a rude awakening.

I come to stand behind her. I rub her back. I say, "Try not to think about it, babe. Where's your coat? It's cold out."

"On the hook," she says. There's a pulse to Lily's voice. She's crying. She sets her mug in the sink and then wipes at her nose with the back of a hand.

"Hey," I say, turning her around. I look at her. Lily's eyes are swollen. They're red but not bloodshot. The swelling and the redness will go down by the time she gets to school. No one will notice. I wipe a tear from her cheek with my thumb. I don't say anything because there isn't anything I can say that isn't a lie. Instead, I pull her into me. I wrap my arms around her and hold her and, in my arms, she feels like she could break.

I go to find her coat for her, and then I help her into it before she leaves.

At the end of the school day, Lily's car won't start. She calls me at work and says, "I tried to start it, Christian, but nothing happened."

"Where are you?" I ask.

"Sitting in my car."

"Okay," I say, looking at my watch. Thankfully a meeting I had this afternoon already got pushed to the morning, freeing up the rest of the day. "Let me just finish up a couple things and I can leave. I'll come give you a jump. You can take my car home and I'll take yours to get fixed. It's probably a dead battery. Go back to your classroom for a while. Wait there. It's warmer inside."

Lily says okay, that she will go back inside and grade papers. I feel bad for making her wait because I know how tired she is at the end of the day, and how eager she always is to get home.

I leave work as soon as I can. I drive to Lily's high school. I find her car in the parking lot and I pull in, facing it so that it will be easier to jump.

I put my car in Park and turn off the engine. I send a quick text to Lily to let her know I'm here, and then I walk over to her car to pop the hood when I hear footsteps approach. "That was fast," I say, but as I turn to look, it's not Lily, but Nina Hayes.

She says, "Hi, Christian. I thought that was you. What are you doing here?"

"Nina," I say, trying to keep my voice level. I'm not surprised to see her, but I was hoping I wouldn't. I don't know how Lily does this, how she looks Nina in the eye every single day and pretends that everything is okay. I stand at the hood of Lily's car. It's smaller than mine, a little two door coupe that we only intend to keep until the baby comes, and then Lily will need a new car, a family car. "Lily's car won't start. I came to give it a jump."

Nina smiles. "Her knight in shining armor. Does she know you're here? I can get her for you?"

"Yeah. No, she knows I'm here. I texted her."

"Okay," she says, and I know that I should say something about Jake, that I should ask if there is any news or if she's heard anything from him, but I can't bring myself to do it. I wonder if Nina knows about the body they found at Langley Woods. She might, but she also might not. For us, the police finding this body is pivotal. It's practically all I can think about. But bodies are found and people get murdered all the time and most of them, you never hear about.

I unlock Lily's car with my key. I pull open the door and I lean over to pull the lever to pop the hood, and then I come around to the front of the car, find the release latch, open the hood and prop it open with the prop rod, all the while keeping my back to Nina, hoping she'll leave. "Hey listen, Christian," she says.

"Yeah?"

"I wanted to say I'm sorry if I was rude to you the other day at your house. This whole thing with Jake just has me completely undone, and I'm sorry if I took it out on you. I didn't mean to."

I look at her. "No problem, Nina. You weren't rude to me."

"No," she says, "I was."

"Well, I didn't notice. And if you were, you have every right to be. Lily and I feel really terrible about what you're going through with Jake. We're sorry this is happening. We just hope Jake comes home soon. But Lily says that your mom saw him, so you know he's okay at least, that he's not hurt." I step past Nina, moving back toward my own car for the jumper cables. I pop open the trunk with my key fob and the tailgate lifts.

"This is your car?" Nina asks, looking at it, watching the tailgate slowly rise.

"Yup," I say, "this is me," reaching down inside the trunk for the jumper cables. Nina follows me to the car. I feel her come closer and, when I come up with the jumper cables from the trunk, I notice how she's staring at my car in a way that makes me suddenly uncomfortable. Nina walks to the passenger's side, slipping between parked cars, and then she runs her eyes over the outside of my car, before crouching down to look inside. She tents her hands to her eyes to block out the glare, staring into the cabin of the car for a long time. A very long time. Nina takes her time, appraising the dashboard, the leather seats, before moving to look into the back seat.

My mouth goes dry. Because there, on the floor, in the back seat of my car, tucked partway under the passenger's seat where I didn't think anyone could see it, is the bag of Lily's bloody clothes. The bag of Lily's clothes isn't obvious—the floor of the car is dark like a cave—and it's just a bag. It could be groceries, garbage, anything. Literally anything.

But a guilty conscience can take control of a person's mind and make them think and do irrational things.

If I didn't know any better, I'd think Nina was staring directly at the bag, that she could somehow see inside of it, through the opaque plastic.

"What kind of car is this?" she asks. The school backs up to a relatively busy street. Because of it, road noise is loud. Nina and I have to contend with the sound of traffic. We speak over it.

I rub at the back of my neck. "Are you in the market for a new car?" I ask, trying to get her eyes back on me, and also to make light of the situation. I drive a Honda. Nina drives a Tesla. There is no way that, even if she was in the market for a new car, she'd ever consider mine.

She snickers, standing upright, finally tearing her eyes away from the car's interior. "No," she says, with a brief headshake, her mood suddenly changed. "No. It's not that."

"It's a good car," I say, going on. "I've had this for six years. It has over a hundred thousand miles on it and drives just as good as the day I got it. It's never needed any work either, other than your typical maintenance. They say it's one of the most reliable midsize cars on the market."

She deadpans, "I'm not looking for a new car, Christian."

"Right. Of course. Is that your Tesla down there?" I ask, nodding to the Model Y in the distance. She nods. "How do you like it?"

"I like it," she says. "It gets me where I need to go."

Nina goes quiet. I slam the trunk closed. I step around to the driver's side of my car to lean in and release the latch, opening the hood. At the front of my car, I open the hood and hold it open with the prop rod. Nina watches, saying nothing as I connect the jumper cable's red clips to Lily's battery and then mine.

What is taking Lily so long?

"The thing is, Christian," Nina says, and I gaze up at her as she shifts her bag higher on her shoulder, and then pushes the hair out of her eyes, "that Jake didn't actually come into my house that day Lily and I were at breakfast."

In that instant, everything changes. My body becomes stiff. I stand straight, throwing a glance back, over my shoulder at the high school but the parking lot behind me is empty and the heavy school doors are still, the world outside getting reflected in the glass so that if Lily was somewhere on the other side of those doors, I wouldn't know.

"I… I don't understand," I say, looking back at Nina, who's looking again at my car. "What do you mean Jake didn't come into your house that day? I thought that's what Lily said."

"No," she says. "It wasn't Jake. It was someone else."

"What do you mean *someone else*?"

"I mean my mother was wrong. Someone broke into my home."

I clear my throat. "How do you know?" I ask, and she explains that a neighbor had a doorbell camera that captured the break-in.

"This man let himself right in through my garage door," she says. "He knew the code."

"Oh my God, Nina. I'm glad you and your mother weren't hurt."

I grab the black jumper cable clip and attach it to my battery, burying my head inside the hood of the car to avoid Nina's eye.

My heart beats so fast it hurts. I'm fucked. Nina knows it was me that broke into her home.

She's still talking. She says, "The quality of the video wasn't great, unfortunately. I took the video to the police, but even they weren't able to get a clear enough picture of this man, this intruder, to identify him," she says, and it takes a second for her words to sink in, for me to find my voice. If what she's saying is true, then Nina knows an intruder broke in, but she doesn't know the intruder was me.

"That's awful. Did he take anything?"

"Not that I know of."

"What did the police say?"

"Their tech people are looking at the video to see if they can identify the man, but they said not to get my hopes up. It's not likely they'll be able to clean the video up enough to see who the man is. The car in the video, though," she says, running her fingers over my car, as I turn my back to her to attach the last clip to one of those metal struts holding Lily's hood open. I eye the school again. Lily still isn't coming. "It looked like this one. What kind of car did you say it is, Christian?" she asks again, because I never said.

"Honda. Accord. Did you get a look at the license plate?" I ask.

"No. The video didn't pick it up. But it was a four door mid-size sedan, very much like this. Black."

"It's a popular car," I say.

Things go from bad to worse because the next thing I know, Nina has taken her phone out of her bag, and she is pulling up the neighbor's video on her phone so that she can compare my car to the car in the video, which in all actuality, is the same car.

"Hey, Nina," I say, stalling, "you didn't see Lily inside the building when you were leaving, did you?" I need Lily to come. I need for us to get out of here because I don't want my car to be here, for Nina to notice the overt similarities between them when she finds the video.

"No."

"I wonder what's taking her so long."

"I can check if you want," she says, but it's absentminded, and she doesn't mean now, she means after she finds what she's looking for on her phone.

"Could you? I'd appreciate that. I don't know what time the repair shop closes. I want to get this battery replaced tonight."

"Sure," she says, and then I stand helplessly by, watching as Nina sweeps at her phone, navigating to the video. She finds the video, and she holds her phone out for me to see. "See? Doesn't it?"

I swallow hard. Reluctantly I take the phone from her hand. I look at the image.

Predictably I find myself looking at an image of my own

car. It's not a video, but a screenshot from the video, and it's zoomed in on my car parked on the side of her street.

Nina was right; the quality is shoddy.

I pretend to show interest. "Jeez, you're right," I say, staring back to my car as if making the connection. "It is similar."

Nina says, "I thought so too." She regards me and I wonder what she sees, what she's thinking. She takes the phone back from me and slips it into her purse. She's practically morose when she says, "The police called me down to the station today. I think they think I've done something to Jake."

I swallow again. My saliva is thick. My eyebrows pull together and I wonder what exactly Nina knows and if she knows it was Lily who told the police that she may have done something to Jake. "That's ridiculous, Nina," I say, my voice sedate. "Like what?"

Nina's shoulders come up to her ears. "I don't know." Again, she focuses on me, and then she looks at my car, and then she looks back at me until I can hardly breathe. "Let me go see where Lily is," she says, stepping past me.

"Thanks. I appreciate it," I say. I watch as she walks across the parking lot for the school. I sink against my car. Nina doesn't make it all the way to the school building. Before she can get there, the heavy glass doors open and Lily comes out. I watch them talk. They make their way across the parking lot together.

Later, as I leave the parking lot in Lily's car, heading to the auto shop, my hands sweaty and shaking on the steering wheel, I play back the conversation again and again in my mind, fixating on the words Nina used and her facial expression as she said them.

The thing I can't decide is if Nina was saying that she thinks my car resembles the one in the doorbell video, or if she was not-so-subtly suggesting it *is* my car in the video.

NINA

I'm sure I've seen Christian's car at some point in my life, but this afternoon it was as if I was seeing it for the first time.

I took a picture of the car as I pulled past and out of the parking lot. He and Lily were busy giving hers a jump. I wasn't entirely surreptitious about it, but I don't think they noticed. Now I have the picture of his car and a screenshot from the doorbell video on my phone and I toggle back and forth between them at a stoplight, comparing the images. They look the same to me. They might be the same. The car in the video looks lighter, but that could be because the doorbell camera was adjusting to the light, and the sun that day was practically negligible. I disregard the color of the car, focusing on the shape of it instead, the sleekness and the length of it.

The car behind me honks. The light in front of me has turned green and I'm holding up traffic. I have to go, but still

I take one last look at the image, and then I set my phone aside and glide through the intersection.

Why would Christian have been in my house?

At another red light, I reach again for my phone. I know I shouldn't, that I should wait until I get home to look, but I can't help myself. I need to know. I go to the image of that man who broke into my home. I have a screenshot of him too. It's taken from a great distance and every time I zoom in, the man's face and his body get more blurred. There are no discerning features. It's impossible to see something like hair color or the graphics on a hat or shirt because the street is so wide and the distance is far too great for the camera to adequately capture. At best I can see the shape of his body, which is tall and lean like Christian's. Something like this would never hold water in court, but it's tenable to me.

I stare at the imperfect image. I think of Christian.

What I can't understand is why Christian Scott would ever break into my home.

This time when the same car behind me honks, it lays on its horn. In my rearview mirror, I see a woman's angry face silently berate me through her windshield. I coast into another intersection as she gets in the other lane and speeds around me.

I consider calling Officer Boone. I want to tell him what I'm thinking, and yet what I have feels groundless, like I'm grasping at straws. A day ago I didn't know who the man or the car in the video were, and then today, not twenty-four hours after Officer Boone accused me of doing something to Jake, I do. Without proof or a motive, Officer Boone will think I'm making it up, to point the finger at someone else.

I consider that I *am* grasping at straws, that I'm so desperate for answers I'm jumping to conclusions about Christian. Christian had no reason to break into my home, though it dawns on me slowly as I drive toward my mother's house that he could have, that it's possible because Lily knew the passcode to my garage before I changed it. She's watched my cat before. She's been in my house when Jake and I weren't home.

My mother is waiting for me at her house when I go to pick her up. She has on her jacket and she's standing by the door, looking out the sidelight windows, ready to go. As I approach, she pulls the door open and lets me in. My mother is one of those women who wears lipstick all the time, so that even now, when we're just getting in the car to drive back to my house, she stands before me with a bare face but coral lips, her lips pressed together and thin.

"Are you ready?" I ask, forcing a smile.

"What is it, Nina? What's wrong?"

"Nothing," I try telling her.

"You seem upset," she says, and I think it's my body language that must give me away.

I step past her and walk further into the room. She closes the door. I sink onto the arm of her sofa. "That police officer called me this morning. He asked me to come to the police station on my way into work. I thought he had news about Jake, but instead he practically interrogated me, Mom, like he thinks I did something to Jake."

"Oh, honey," she says. She reaches out to stroke my hair. "I'm so sorry that happened to you. That must have been really upsetting."

"It was. And then, after work, I saw my friend Lily's husband at school. She had car trouble and he'd come to help. The thing is, Mom, I saw his car and maybe I'm just jumping to conclusions, but it looked like the car in that video. And Christian, when I really think about it, looks like the man."

"Why would he do that if he's your friend?"

I shake my head. "I don't know."

My mother has never met Christian before. She's never met Lily either but she's heard me talk about her. My mother is the only person who would have gotten a better look at the man that came into my home than the doorbell camera. She was there in my house when he broke in. She saw him from something like ten feet away. "Do you think you would recognize him if I showed you a picture?" I ask.

She says, "I could try."

I dig into my purse for my phone. Lily isn't too keen on social media but I find a picture of her, Jake, Christian and me in my photos. It was taken the last time we were all together, by the waitress at the restaurant where we ate. We'd been drinking that night, and Lily and I especially have a reddish, drunken glow to us though our smiles are wide and without reserve. We're leaned in close, our heads touching. The lighting is terrible. It's not a good picture at all. The four of us had to squeeze together for the picture, so that the men came around to stand behind Lily and me. Jake is smiling but he isn't even looking at the camera.

I show my mother the picture of Christian. I home in on his face. Christian is clean-cut. He has short, dirty blond hair, a narrow nose, and close-set eyes that are either blue or green. Christian isn't shy or an introvert, but he's also not verbose like Jake. He's your typical boy next door: dependable, friendly and kind.

It feels almost unethical to show my mother this picture with her vision as it is. "Was this him, Mom?" I ask, watching as she pulls her eyebrows together, and then stares hard at the image for a long time, searching, exploring, as if trying to see past or through a blind spot.

My mother would tell me anything I want to hear.

"Yes, Nina. I think so. I think it was this man," she says, though the reality is that she was just as sure that it was Jake. "What did he want from you?" she asks, as if having decided definitively that it was Christian who came into our house that day.

I shake my head. I'm at a complete loss. I can't think of one reason why Christian would break into my house, why Christian would do this to me. "I don't know," I say, though I wonder if it was Christian, if he found what he was looking for. On the surface, Christian seems completely harmless. He doesn't seem like the kind of man that would want to hurt my mother and me. But how would I know?

I suddenly don't know who I can trust. Can I trust Lily?

My mother reads my mind. "What if we just stay here for the night?" she asks, gazing benevolently at me, as if allowing me to let my guard down, as if giving me permission to feel anxious about going home, which I do. Outside, behind her, the setting sun comes into the living room with us, through the blinds. The light is golden, disseminating across the carpet in stripes, illuminating my mother from behind. "What if we don't go back to your house? No one knows you're here, Nina. If someone is looking for you, they won't find you here. If someone goes back into your house, we won't be there when they do."

I think of Jake's and my house, the one that is too big and too empty, with all those idle rooms. The security system still won't be installed for a few days. I don't have Jake's gun to protect my mother and me. My mother's house is a small ranch. It has three bedrooms and two baths. There isn't anything particularly charming about the house—it's barely a thousand square feet, is run-of-the-mill and completely lacks character. It's everything I hate in home decor: the wall-to-wall carpeting, small windows and clutter. It's also closed concept, where every room has its own space, separated by walls. There is nothing cohesive about it.

And yet, standing here with her, it feels like home. This house reminds me of homemade cookies and childhood Christmases and, in it, I feel safe and loved.

"Yes," I say, nodding. "That's a good idea. I'd like that, if it's okay with you. I don't want to impose, but I don't know that I want us to be in my house right now."

"Oh, honey," she says. "You could never impose."

As the sun sets, my mother and I walk out to her garage together. We go out through the front door as darkness starts to fall across the earth. She opens the garage and we step inside, under the single, tawdry yellow light bulb that casts shadows everywhere. Now that the sun has set, it's cool, the wind picking up in preparation for another night of rain.

In the garage, we haul storage bins and and move garbage cans to the side of the garage, creating space. As she stands by, watching, I back her car out, and then pull it back in, to the side instead of the center of the garage where she left it last, months ago, the last time she drove before her vision got so bad she couldn't. I pull my own car into the space we've made.

She feels for the the button to lower the garage door, and then we stand on the driveway, watching until it's closed and my car is hidden from view.

I'm safe here. No one can find me now.

CHRISTIAN

"What exactly did she say?" Lily asks.

"Just that my car looked like the one in the doorbell video," I say.

"Do you think she suspects it was your car?"

"I don't know."

"Even if she suspects it, Christian, that's not enough to get you in trouble. She'd need something more substantial than a hunch."

"No, you're right, Lily," I say, trying to make myself believe it.

In the coming days, the details of the body emerge painfully slowly. I look for them online. I watch the news, neurotically, obsessively, waiting for something. And yet, there is practically nothing. It's as if no one's even talking about the body, as if no one is even thinking about the body but Lily and me. All we know at this point is that it was discovered early the other morning by some youth group camping overnight at Langley Woods. No surprise, it was in a lesser-known, hard-to-reach part of the forest preserve. The youth group was searching for some secret waterfall that hardly anyone has ever heard of before and is incredibly hard to reach. It's hidden. The forest preserve doesn't want you to find it because they want to keep the land around it unadulterated. The youth group didn't find it, but what they found was even more memorable. These kids will never forget seeing a dead body.

The body had yet to be identified. On the news that night, they referred to it interchangeably as a *body* and as *human remains*, so there's no way to know what exactly was found, but I've already decided: they found Jake, or whatever is left of him. It's been well over a week, almost two, since Lily ran into him at the park. How much decomposition happens in that time? I don't know and I don't want to know, though I do know that the fresher the body, the more lurid it is. It has probably swollen to twice its size and was likely crawling with maggots. That doesn't matter. What matters is that when the body is identified and Jake's name gets released, it will change everything. He will no longer be missing. He'll be dead. And then people will start to wonder why and what happened to him. The medical examiner will do an autopsy. They'll find a skull fracture, from where Lily hit him with the rock. They will say it was blunt force trauma. I don't know how, but they're pretty good at knowing the difference between homicide, suicide and accidental death.

"When they identify the body," Lily says, "Nina will know where he was when he died. She already knows I was there at the forest preserve, remember?"

Of course I remember. How could I forget? It's all I've been thinking about since we first heard about the discovery of the body: that people know that Lily was there, and soon they'll know that Jake was too.

"Maybe it's not even him," I say, trying to stay optimistic. "Other people have died in those woods."

Lily just gives me a look. Of course it's him.

"It doesn't necessarily mean that you did something to him, Lily. That forest preserve gets a lot of foot traffic. You remember how busy it was when we were there. It was hard to even find a place to park. Anyone could have been there. Anyone could have done it. Anyone could have hurt him, like that Brady guy."

"Jim," she says, the husband of her colleague, the man who saw Lily there that day.

"Right, Jim Brady. He could have done something to Jake."

"Why would Jim Brady do something to Jake?"

"He didn't. I'm just thinking out loud. Creating reasonable doubt," I say because that is all we need. Reasonable doubt. "Or maybe Jake did something to himself. Maybe he slipped and fell and hit his head." I've asked before, but never gotten a clear answer. I try again now. "How many times do you think you hit him with the rock, Lily?" If it was once, maybe twice, a skull fracture could be ruled an accidental death, maybe. There are plenty of things to trip over at the forest preserve, plenty of places for a head to hit, like a boulder or concrete. I went to school with a kid who fell off his bike and hit his head on the curb. He wasn't wearing a helmet because no one did back then. I was there when he fell off his bike. I watched him fall over the handlebars and onto the street. He got up, dusted off his pants, got back on his bike. I laughed at him. We all did. He laughed at himself, too, which later helped lessen my guilt. We went to the store for candy. He thought he was fine. Six hours later he was dead.

"I don't know, a few," Lily says. This whole thing with the body has her visibly rattled. Lily didn't sleep again last night. All night, I felt her tossing and turning in bed. She mumbled in her sleep, things like *stop* and *no*, and unconsciously she whimpered so that I had to shake her awake and tell her she was okay. For a long time, I stayed awake with her, rubbing her back, trying to get her to relax.

"Do you think it was like twice," I ask, "or like six times?"

"I think more than twice." Lily is on the verge of tears. I hate bringing it up because I know it upsets her. "I just, I don't know, Christian, I just reacted. It was involuntary. I don't even remember doing it, but I know that I did because I remember what he looked like after, how he was bleeding."

When I think of Lily fighting back, I picture something wildly uncontrolled.

"Okay," I say. "Okay." That's good to know. Not the answer I was hoping for, but good to know. "Where do you think you hit him? Like here?" I ask, pointing to my forehead, "Or here?" pointing at the base of my skull. I ask because I know that a fracture at the base of the skull can be more deadly because it's stronger there and harder to crack. If you do, you're essentially screwed, which is what happened to my friend from grade school. When he came down on the curb, he came down on the back of his head.

Lily shrugs. "Maybe both," she says. She thinks about it, trying to decide, and then she shakes her head. "I don't know, Christian. I really don't know. It happened so fast. I reacted."

"But if he was coming at you," I reason, "he would have been facing you, right? You probably got him here," I say, pointing again at my forehead.

Lily forces herself to think. I'm quiet. I let her think. I see in her eyes that she's going through it in slow motion, watching it play out all over again. Her face changes. She's remembering now. Something is coming into focus. "I think I hit him in the forehead. And then I remember that he turned around. He started to walk away from me. I don't know why, I think I didn't believe he was really through with me, that he wasn't going to hurt me again. So I hit him again, maybe here," she says, pointing at the back of her skull. "That's when he looked at me, over his shoulder, when his eyes went wide and he fell."

I didn't expect that. Lily hit him when his back was turned, when he was walking away.

I don't blame her. She was scared. She was a quarter mile from help, at least, and there was nothing to tell her he wasn't going to reel back and come at her again. She wanted to make sure he was subdued.

"And then that was it?" I ask. "Then you dropped the rock and ran?"

"Maybe," she says, still noncommittal.

"What do you mean maybe?"

"I don't know, Christian. I just don't know. I can't remember exactly."

She's getting emotional now. There are definitely tears in her eyes. She's no longer just on the verge of crying. She's upset with herself for not remembering. She's upset with me for the way I keep incessantly asking, for the way I keep forcing her to remember something she'd rather forget. "Okay," I say, reaching for her, pulling her close to me. "It's okay, babe. It doesn't matter."

If that wasn't the last time she hit him—when Jake was walking away—then it means Lily hit him again when he was on the ground. At minimum, that's three blows. One to the forehead, one to the back of the head, and a third when he was on the ground. Which essentially rules out accidental death because how likely is it that you fall and hit your head in three different places?

"Christian," Lily says, pulling away from me so that I can see her eyes.

"What?" I ask, looking down at her. We're in the family room. The lights are off. Only the TV is on, the news moving on to other things that are going on in the world, all of which pale in comparison to what's going on with Jake. It's hard to believe there's anything else going on. This, Jake and Lily, is all I can think about.

The TV is bright, the color radiating on the side of Lily's face, making her look sickly and distorted. "Do you know a lawyer?" she asks, her voice cracking. Lily looks small and scared.

I'm quick to respond, flippant, because I, too, am scared, though I'd never admit that to Lily. "We don't need a lawyer."

"We don't," she says, "but I might, Christian, if I'm arrested."

"You won't be arrested."

"How do you know?"

"Why would they arrest you?"

"Because I killed him," she says. She's crying without reserve now, her shoulders shaking.

"Stop saying that," I snap. I don't mean to snap at Lily. I never snap at Lily. It's just that, if she's going to get away with this, she needs to be careful about what she says. "Just because you were both at the same place, at the same time, means nothing. No one saw you together. You had no motive to kill him. Look at me, Lily," I say, setting my hands on either side of her wet face and forcing her to look at me. Her makeup has started to bleed. There's a smudge of black under her eyes. "You were there, yes. But you did not see Jake. Do you understand?" I ask, and she dimly nods. "Say it, then. Say 'I did not see Jake Hayes at the forest preserve.'"

Lily says, "I did not see Jake Hayes at the forest preserve."

It's weak. She's a worse liar even than me.

I've spent a lot of time doing research on the internet over the last week and a half. I know far more about the justice system, forensics and murder investigations than I ever wanted to know. The thing about an autopsy is that the medical examiner won't just say who Jake is and how he died. Once they rule it a homicide, they'll look for things like a killer's fingerprints, his or her DNA. A dead body is a source of invaluable information. They might find Lily's hair on him, fibers from her clothes, traces of her blood on him. Lily was bleeding, too, enough that I put antiseptic and antibacterial ointment on her arms. It could have gotten on Jake. Lily's fingerprints could be on him. Lily is a teacher, which means her fingerprints are in the system.

She would be so easy for the police to find.

NINA

I wake up in my childhood bed. The bed is small, twin-size, so that my legs hang over the spool footrail and my body fills the whole mattress.

The bed hasn't been slept in in ages. Last night, before she went to sleep, my mother washed the flannel sheets for me, so that they were still warm and snuggly when I climbed in, wearing a pair of her own knit pajamas and socks. I drifted right to sleep, though it was a fitful sleep and my dreams were chaotic and illogical. I think I must have had a nightmare because I remember at one point waking up to my mother's shadow perched on the edge of the bed beside me, her warm hand stroking my hair, her indulgent voice crooning, "Shh. There now. You're okay, honey. Go back to sleep."—or maybe that was part of my dream. It rained during the night. There is a skylight in the room, above the bed. For the better part of the night, rain battered the window, though in my dreams, it was the sound of a little boy beating sticks on a drum.

The weekend comes and goes. My mother and I don't leave her house, because there is no need. For two days and three nights, we stay hidden inside.

It's still dark Monday morning when the alarm on my phone goes off. I need to get up and get ready for work. I have to borrow clothes. I feel guilty for leaving the cat home alone, but cats are resilient like that. She has an automatic feeder and a water fountain; she's always fine when Jake and I are gone. I only have someone look in on her if we're gone for more than two days. I'll check on her tonight and pack a bag for myself for the week.

I pull myself from the bed and go to the bathroom. My mother left a few things in the bathroom for me to wear. The shower, like the bed, is smaller than I remember. It's 1980s era with glass block windows that, in daylight, allow the filtered light in. The thick blocks of translucent glass are supposed to provide privacy, but also light. In theory, no one can see in, and maybe it's only the paranoia speaking, but I find it unlikely that if someone was standing in the yard outside the bathroom window, they wouldn't be able to make out the shape of me standing naked in the shower, even if they couldn't make out the details.

I shower in the dark, with the bathroom light off, just in case.

When I'm ready, I leave and drive to work. I get there early so I don't risk running into Lily on the way in. I don't want to see Lily now. I don't know what I'd say to her.

My classroom faces the staff parking lot. Once inside my room, I stand by the window, waiting for her to arrive. When she does, I watch as Lily moves gracefully from her car to the building. She walks alone. She is beautiful, dressed in a black jumpsuit and flats, carrying a bag practically as big as her because Lily is so threadlike and petite. Her hair is braided on the side today. It lies over a shoulder and I think how very naïf-like she looks. I wonder if she truly is or if there is more to Lily Scott than I know.

It's fifth period English. I'm standing in front of the room, leaned against my desk teaching, or trying to anyway. We're reading *Romeo and Juliet* aloud in class. I've assigned parts. Some of the kids are half-asleep, their eyes glazed over and bored. Most of my students don't like *Romeo and Juliet*. They think Shakespeare is lame and they struggle to understand it. I don't blame them. Early Modern English can be hard for high school students. It's the reason we read it aloud, so I can explain what's happening, though I'm practically worthless today because my mind is somewhere else. Listening to my students as they butcher Shakespeare, I feel completely useless. At best, I muster help with pronunciation. At worst, I say nothing as kids stutter and fumble for words. The classroom is quiet now, with the exception of Madison Kief, who's speaking. Madison is Juliet and she's doing lines from the famous balcony speech.

In the middle of the scene, my phone rings. It's in my desk drawer where I keep it during class. It's usually on silent, but I've forgotten to silence it. We have a strict no phone policy at the school, which I enforce. The mood in the room suddenly changes, the kids getting all fired up, turning practically delirious when they realize the phone is mine.

"Ohhhh, Mrs. Hayes," they say, threatening me with a detention.

I look at my phone. It's the police calling. I have to take it.

"Officer Boone," I say, pressing the phone to my ear, ignoring the taunts. But reception is spotty in the classroom and so I step outside, into the hall, to take the call. I drift away from my classroom, walking through the vast blue stretch of lockers for the windows at the end of the hall, where it's quieter and I may have better luck with reception. "Do you have more questions for me? Have you been speaking to more of our acquaintances?" I ask, unable to control my sarcasm.

"No," he says, "I don't have any more questions for you right now. I'm calling to tell you that we've located your husband's missing car."

"Oh," I breathe out. I don't know what I expected Officer Boone to say, but this wasn't it. I reach out to set a hand on the window for support, and then I lean my head against the glass, because the glass is cool and I'm feeling hot all of a sudden and dizzy.

Jake's car. They found Jake's car.

Officer Boone's news is good news, but it brings no relief. If anything, it makes things worse because where is Jake if not with his car?

"Where did you find it?" I ask. Behind me, my classroom suddenly descends into chaos. I turn back, finding Ryan in the hall with me, brought out of his own classroom by the mayhem in mine. He gazes at me from a distance, and then he turns away, going to my classroom door where he stands in the open doorway, keeping watch over my students like a sentry. It works. They quiet down immediately and I'm grateful.

"At a hotel," Officer Boone says through the phone, "in Bridgeview."

"What is it doing there? Is my husband there? Have you found him too?"

"No. Your husband was not with his vehicle."

A hotel. Jake's car was found at a hotel in Bridgeview. Bridgeview is much closer to the city than where we live. As far as I know, he doesn't know anyone who lives out that way. He doesn't have a reason to be there. What would his car be doing in Bridgeview, and where is he if not with his car?

"Can I come get it?"

"Yes."

I ask for the hotel's address, but he says, "You won't find his car at the hotel. It's been towed."

"Towed where?"

Officer Boone tells me that after sitting in that hotel parking lot for over seven days untouched, the hotel called to have it towed, because the car wasn't registered to any guests of the hotel.

"Why was Jake's car at this hotel if he wasn't a registered guest?"

"We don't know. We're looking into that, Mrs. Hayes. It's possible he registered under a different name, but we're not certain. I have an officer headed to the hotel now. We'll be in touch once we know more."

"Where is the car now?" I ask.

He tells me that Jake's car was towed and impounded. He says that I can come claim it.

"Okay," I say, asking where the car is impounded and the officer gives me an address, which I memorize until I can write it down. "I'll be there this afternoon," I say. "As soon as I can."

Ryan is watching me as I end the call with Officer Boone. I come back down the hall, feeling overwhelmed, trying to make sense of this. Ryan comes toward me, meeting me in the middle, somewhere between the endless sea of blue lockers.

"Are you okay?" he asks, his head angled, his features open and soft.

I gaze up at him. I shake my head, breathless, searching for words. When I find them I say, "The police found Jake's car."

"What do you mean they found his car?"

There is so much I haven't told Ryan. The last he knows is what I told him that afternoon in the school parking lot: that Jake left me. He doesn't know what's transpired since, because it's all happening so fast. "There is a lot I haven't told you," I say, feeling guilty, though I don't know why. I have no responsibility to tell Ryan what's happening with Jake. Still, I think of the last time he and I really talked about Jake, standing in the parking lot the same day I discovered the tracking device on my car, with Ryan's warm, tender hand on my elbow and him saying to me, *Then he's an idiot* about Jake. "My husband didn't leave me after all. I was wrong about that. Something has happened to him."

His eyebrows pull together in concern. He tilts his head. "What do you mean something has happened to him?"

"I mean he's missing. I've filed a missing person's report with the police. The police are looking for him."

"Oh my God, Nina. That's terrible. Where was his car?" He reaches forward to give my shoulder a gentle squeeze. Ryan's eyes are solicitous. They're warm. He's attentive, waiting quietly for me to speak, though my mind has gone to a dark place, thinking the worst if Jake has been separated from his car. Wherever he is, Jake has no money, no phone and now no car either.

"At a hotel in Bridgeview," I say, hearing the subtle despair in my voice.

"Bridgeview?" he asks. "What was your husband doing at a hotel in Bridgeview?"

"I don't know. The police say he wasn't a registered guest, but that maybe he registered under a fake name." I practically beg when I ask, "Why would someone do something like that, Ryan?"

He opens his mouth to say something. But before he can speak, my classroom gets loud again. Maybe it's better that way. I don't know that I want to know the answer anyway, that Jake met somebody at this hotel. I throw a glance over my shoulder toward the open door. My student teacher is in there with my class, but any attempts he's made to quiet them are futile.

"I should go," I say.

I feel Ryan's hand come down on my arm, stopping me. "Do you need a ride?" he volunteers before I can leave.

"To the auto pound?"

"Yes."

"No," I say, shaking my head. "I have my car. I can drive myself."

Gently, he reminds me, "You won't be able to drive both cars back, Nina, once you pick up your husband's. Let me take you."

"Oh." My eyes lower. "I'm so stupid. I didn't think of that." I would have driven out to the auto pound only to realize I couldn't get two cars back by myself.

"You're not stupid. I'll take you."

"That's sweet of you to offer. But no," I say. "I can't ask you to do that. I'll just get an Uber."

"Don't be ridiculous. I'll take you," he says again, with some finality. "Those places can be sketchy." I'm not worried about whether I'll be safe. I'm just anxious to have Jake's car back, but I realize there is no use arguing with him about it and so I acquiesce.

I say, "Okay. Thank you. I appreciate it."

I get through the rest of the day, and then, at the end of it, Ryan follows me to my house in his car. I pull into the garage and he waits for me while I run inside to get Jake's spare key fob from the box by the door. I call my mother and tell her I'll be late but I don't say why. I don't want to worry her.

In Ryan's car, I can barely sit still. I fidget with practically everything that comes within reach. He has the radio on and the music is quiet, calming, background noise. "Do you have everything you need to get the car?" he asks.

"I think so," I say. "I have his key, proof of ownership and the vehicle's VIN number. Can you think of anything I might be forgetting?"

"I don't think so. You have your driver's license?"

"Yes."

"Everything is going to be okay, Nina," he says, because he can see how worried I am. I appreciate it. Still, Ryan doesn't know that for a fact. He doesn't know that everything is going to be okay.

"I hope you're right," I say.

We're quiet for a while. I don't feel much like talking. I stare out the window, watching the world pass by. My mind is a million miles away, thinking about Jake and this hotel in Bridgeview. Why would Jake have gone there?

Ryan says, "I'm surprised you didn't tell me what was happening with your husband sooner," as he pulls onto the expressway and toward the auto pound. The auto pound sits just on the outskirts of the city, so that the closer we get, skyscrapers rise up in the distance like LEGO bricks, the street narrowing to a vanishing point.

His voice sounds almost hurt, and again, I feel guilty for not telling him.

I hear myself apologize. "I'm sorry, Ryan. It wasn't anything intentional. I really thought Jake had left me. It's only in the last few days that the situation changed."

"What changed?" he asks.

"My mother thought she saw Jake at our home last Saturday. But she was wrong—it wasn't Jake. Someone broke into my home, which is terrifying, but it also means that no one has laid eyes on Jake in two weeks. He isn't using his phone or his credit cards, he hasn't taken money from the bank. I don't know what he's doing for shelter, for food, or if he's even alive."

"Jesus," he says. "Nina. I'm so sorry." He glances sideways at me. "I wish you would have talked to me. I hate to think that you've been going through all this these last few days alone."

"I'm not entirely alone. I have my mother," I say, "and the police. They've been looking for Jake."

"Still," he says, "I could have done something. I could have tried to help you find him." He's quiet for a beat, and then he says, "I thought you knew you could always talk to me."

"I do," I say quickly. My words come fast. "I've been meaning to talk to you. It wasn't anything intentional, but as it is I've just been trying to keep my head above water. Please don't be upset with me," I say.

Ryan reaches over. His hand comes down encouragingly on my knee. "Hey," he says, softening. "I'm not upset. This isn't about me, Nina. I'm only thinking of you. I just hope you know that you can always count on me. You can tell me anything. I am always here for you."

It's meant to be a bolstering gesture, and at first it is. At first I'm grateful for the kind words and the human touch. Tears prick my eyes and I feel suddenly overcome with emotion. "Thank you. That means so much to me. Really."

But then I look down at his hand. He hasn't moved it. It's still on my knee. I'm wearing my mother's dress and am suddenly aware of how short it is on me because I'm taller than her. When I stood, looking at myself in the mirror at her house, it had come just above the knee. I thought it was completely appropriate and not at all suggestive. I'm always cognizant of this, because I work with teenagers, especially teenage boys. I didn't think what would happen when I sat down, how the skirt would ride up to the upper thigh, though, to be fair, my legs are only ever under my desk when I sit. No one ever sees my legs.

"So where do you think he is?" Ryan asks. He strokes my knee. It's subtle, just the brush of his thumb skinning my leg. I resist the urge to cross my legs, knowing it will only reveal more if I do.

"I don't know," I say, though my throat is dry and it's hard to speak.

"Had he been having trouble with anyone, or was there an issue at work?"

"I don't think so."

"Can you think of any reason why he would go to Bridge-view?"

I swallow against a knot in my throat. "No," I say, risking a glance at Ryan, conscious of his eyes on my thighs.

He catches me looking at him and his eyes shift from my leg to my face, where he stares at me, not blinking. He doesn't move his hand. I feel the thrum of my pulse in my neck and I angle my body suddenly away, turning my knees toward the door. My gaze follows. I look out the window. Ryan's hand slips from my knee, though for a second, in my peripheral vision, I see how it remains suspended midair, his elbow propped on the center console as if debating whether to reach for me again.

Time slows down. I hold my breath in anticipation because once is an accident, but twice is intentional.

But then, he reconsiders. He pulls back, setting both hands on the steering wheel, and I'm left to wonder if he meant something by the physical touch or if I read too much into it, if it was nothing more than a friendly gesture and I'm just being hypersensitive because of all that's going on.

It gets quiet in the car. The car becomes airless and for an entire minute, neither of us speaks. Traffic in front of us comes to a sudden stop. Ryan doesn't notice at first, because he's looking at me and not at the street. But when he does notice, he has to step hard on the brake, just narrowly avoiding a fender bender with the car in front of us. It's not his fault. The car in front of him stopped suddenly, because of something that happened further up ahead, like an accident or a gapers delay. I get pinned in place by my seat belt.

He says, "I'm sorry," keeping his eyes trained to the road now at first.

"It's not your fault. That car stopped too fast."

He looks sideways at me, examining the profile of my face. I can feel his stare. I flick my gaze in his direction. Ryan holds my eyes. He has nice eyes. Kind, soulful eyes, but for the first time, I wonder if there is something insincere and unkind in them too. Traffic begins to flow again and my seat belt unleashes me. Ryan looks away, releasing my eyes. The relief is immediate. When I can, I tug down on the hem of my skirt.

We pull off the expressway and onto some two-lane road with more semitrucks than cars. We drive along the road, quiet, neither of us speaking. Eventually we come to a gravel lot where the words Auto Pound and a phone number are written on a sign on a gate.

Ryan pulls into the lot. "You can just drop me off here," I say, pointing to the office for the auto pound, which is in a trailer.

"Let me park," he says. "I'll come in with you."

But I don't want him to come in with me. I want suddenly, more than anything, to be alone.

"No. Please don't," I say, "I'm fine."

"Don't be ridiculous, Nina," he says, leaning forward in his seat to take in the auto pound. "Look at this place. I can't leave you alone here."

"I'm not alone," I say because there is an attendant in the parking lot though, from the looks of things, I'm not so sure he's not an ex-con. Ryan slows to a stop. I don't wait for him to park. I open the car door and I step outside, leaning my head back in to say, "Seriously, I'll be fine. You've done me a huge favor. Now go home. I'll text you and let you know when I'm safe."

I let the door slam closed. I turn and walk away, hoping he doesn't stay anyway, despite me telling him to leave. I listen to his idling engine, grateful when I finally hear the sound of tires moving across gravel. Only then do I turn back just in time to see him pull from the lot for the street, the gravel upset so that dust rises into the air, obscuring my view of his car.

I exhale. My shoulders relax. I still feel his hand on my knee.

The auto pound is wedged between train tracks in a very industrial part of town. The air becomes reverberant when trains pass by, which they do, many times while I wait for Jake's car. The air smells putrid, like sulfur from nearby factories, as black smoke rises up into the sky.

I take in the broken down and damaged cars around me, conceivably hundreds of them, which have been abandoned by their owners or confiscated by the police.

I don't have any trouble getting the car but, between the impound and the towing fees, it costs me almost a thousand dollars to get it back.

The police searched Jake's car. They didn't need a warrant to do so because it's routine, I'm told, for impounded vehicles to be searched. But they found nothing of concern, nothing indicative of foul play and nothing to tell me where Jake is.

When I finally see it, Jake's car looks so dirty and unfitting in this lot. I gasp at the sight of it before opening the door and letting myself into the car, sinking into the seat where Jake should be.

I drive home, through rush hour traffic. I stay cognizant of the cars behind me, convinced a pair of headlights follows me almost the whole way home. I signal and switch lanes, hoping to lose this other car, but it only mimics my movements, following me into the other lane. Instinctively, I lift my foot off the gas. Jake's car slows, from sixty miles per hour to fifty. I wait for this other car to get impatient and go around me, but it doesn't. Like me, it drops speed, and then, when I speed up again, it drives faster. The car keeps enough distance between us that I can't get a good view of the driver or the car, but not so much distance that it risks losing me.

My exit approaches. I wait until the last minute to signal and switch lanes, and then leave the expressway, spinning down the exit ramp, slowing. This other car does the same. I watch this other car in growing dismay, my eyes more on the rearview mirror than on the street in front of me, so that I drift from the edge of the road and onto the rumble strips, making noise. Startled, I jerk the car back into place, my hands shaking on the steering wheel.

Just off the expressway, I merge onto a four-lane highway.

I signal again and move into the left lane. I watch in my rear-view mirror, as three cars back, this other car copies me, pulling behind a pickup truck.

The cars in front of me slow to a stop. I don't know where I find the nerve. I think it has something to do with all the cars and how I don't think anyone would do anything to hurt me with so many witnesses watching on.

At a red light, I slip the car into Park. I open the door and step out. It's a knee-jerk reaction. I don't think. I just do. I'm out of the car before I can stop myself, stepping onto the pavement. The air around me is overwhelmingly loud with traffic. The noise and the cool air come as a shock to my system, as the hem of my skirt lifts in the wind. I push it down.

I leave the car door open. While other drivers watch on in disbelief, I walk unthinking along the side of the road to where this other car also waits for the light to turn green.

I don't have to see the driver's face to know who it is. As I get close, I recognize the car. I should have known. Still, I feel practically queasy as his face comes into view, though it's a side view only because he's looking down at something and I think that it's probably his phone in his hands or on his lap. He doesn't see what I've done, that I'm standing just outside his car watching him.

I walk forward. I thump on the window with the heel of my hand. He jumps and looks sharply up, my shadow falling over him. His face changes, turning staggered. He laughs to hide his guilt and shock.

The light behind me must turn green because traffic in the right lane starts to move forward though the left lane can't because my car is in the way. It starts with one car honking and then soon, the air reverberates with the sound of car horns.

Ryan looks ahead at the green light. He looks in the other lane, at the moving cars. He lowers his window. "What are you doing, Nina?" he asks, as if I'm the one in the wrong. He looks at me like I've lost my mind.

"What am I doing? What are *you* doing?" I ask back.

"You're blocking traffic, Nina," he says, the voice of reason, as if I don't already know that I'm blocking traffic.

"Come on, lady," someone screams out a car window at me.

"Are you following me, Ryan?" Ryan says no. He tries telling me some bullshit story about how he was just on his way home and how it's a coincidence that we've run into each other like this. "You're lying," I practically shout. "I've been watching you in my rearview mirror for miles. You're following me. Why are you following me? Why are you lying to me?"

Ryan gives in. His posture changes and he says, "I was worried about you, Nina. I didn't like leaving you at that place all alone. I wanted to make sure you got home okay." This means Ryan pulled out of the parking lot and went and hid somewhere, watching, waiting, until I left too.

"I told you I would text you when I got home."

He shrugs. "You can't be mad at me for worrying about you. I just want to be a good friend, Nina."

"Then leave me alone," I say. "If you want to be a good friend, then stop following me."

I move backward and away from him. "Wait, Nina, stop," he says. I say nothing and I don't stop. I turn and jog back toward my car, sliding in the open door. Cars in the left lane are signaling and moving into the right lane to get around me. Some just go but others blast their horn as they pass. The cars directly behind me leave, too, so that soon Ryan's is in my rearview mirror, though there is a gap between us two cars long.

I wait him out. I watch in my rearview mirror for a long time until he finally switches lanes and goes around me. I follow his taillights with my eyes until he gets swallowed up in traffic. Only then do I drive.

I'm still shaking when I get home. I pull into the garage when

I get there. It's after six now and I still have to pack a bag, take care of the cat and drive back to my mother's house tonight. The sun has just dipped beneath the horizon and the sky is a fiery orange. I close the garage door, waiting to get out of the car until it's shut and I know for certain I'm safe and alone, and then I do my own search of the vehicle, shocked by what I find.

"Can we talk about last night?" Ryan asks the next morning. He's standing on the curb as usual, as if this is any other day, which of course it's not. "I tried calling you."

I know that he called. I saw him call, four times between the hours of seven and ten. He was persistent. I let them all go to voice mail, because I didn't want to talk to him last night. Besides, my mind was somewhere else, on what I found in Jake's car. I listened to the messages later, to the increasing agitation in Ryan's voice with each subsequent call when he couldn't get a hold of me.

"I'd rather not. Can we just pretend it didn't happen?" I ask, sidestepping and walking away from him.

The day crawls by. I need to speak to Lily, but I need to do so in private and so I wait until the end of the day, after everyone has left, to go to her classroom. I find Lily sitting at her desk when I come in. I hang back for a minute, watching through the open door. Lily is bent over a pile of papers, grading them. Her long hair falls into her face, so that I can't get a good look at it or her eyes. I feel an overwhelming anger inside of me, though it's not just that. It's also sadness and disbelief. I keep it back. I try so hard to keep the emotion at bay. I've been such a good friend to Lily over the years. I always thought I was a good judge of character, but becoming her friend was an obvious lapse in judgment. I know that now. She isn't the person she pretends to be.

I rap my knuckles on the open door and she looks up from

her papers. "Hey. Nina." She smiles as she says it, but it's the kind of smile that doesn't reach her eyes.

"Hi, Lily," I say, coming in. "Is this a bad time?"

Lily says no. She says that she could use a break and is grateful for the interruption.

"How are you feeling?" I ask. The last time I talked to Lily was days ago when she had car trouble and Christian came to rescue her.

"Okay. Not great, but I can't complain. I've been meaning to come see you, to see if there has been any news on Jake. I'm sorry," she says, "that I haven't been a better friend. This morning sickness sucks. But that's no excuse."

"No, it's fine," I say, waving her off. "I've heard morning sickness is the worst."

"It is. The absolute worst," she says, but then she looks almost embarrassed for saying that because what's maybe even worse than morning sickness is losing one's husband or not knowing where he is. "I'm sorry, Nina. I shouldn't have said that."

"You have to stop being so apologetic, Lily."

She sets her pen down. "So what's going on? Is there any news about Jake?"

"Some. But that's not why I'm here. I have something for you," I say.

"Something for me?" she asks. "What?"

I reach into my pocket. I clasp it in my fingers and pull it out, opening my palm flat. There in my hand is a small silver hoop with a tiny pearl.

"Is that my earring?" Lily asks.

"Yes," I say.

Lily is practically ecstatic. Her face lights up. She's so happy to have her earring back. She pushes her chair back and stands quickly up, coming around the edge of the desk to take the earring from my hand. She wraps her hand around it, and then grabs me by the shoulders and pulls me into an awkward but quick hug. "Thank you so much for finding it, Nina."

"I know how much these earrings mean to you. I know you were upset when you lost it."

"Christian gave these to me for our anniversary a couple years ago," she says, which I know because she's told me before. "I thought it was gone. I didn't think I'd ever see it again."

Lily smiles at me. She clutches the earring to her heart. "Thank you again. I'm so grateful." She turns away from me. She goes back to her chair to sit. She doesn't ask where I found the earring. I thought she would have been more curious but maybe she already knows. She reaches for her pen like she's just going to go back to grading papers.

"Aren't you going to ask where I found it?" I ask. Lily looks up. She reads my face.

"I just assumed the hall or the copy room," she says, knowing the answer is no. She stands slowly back up as if gaining leverage. She crosses her arms. She hangs back, by the whiteboard, keeping distance between herself and me. "No?" she asks.

I shake my head. "No, Lily. That's not where I found it."

Lily is almost afraid to ask, but she does so anyway because it would be strange not to. "Where did you find it?"

Imagine my surprise when last night, I searched Jake's car after getting home from the auto pound. I didn't know what I was looking for, but just any little thing the police might have missed that could provide details of Jake's last day or of his disappearance, something innocuous but revelatory, like a store receipt, that would have told me where he'd been.

I found the earring on the floor in the back seat of Jake's car. At first I didn't know whose it was. I thought maybe it was mine. It was dark in the garage and I couldn't get a good look at it. I got out of the car and held it up to the light. I knew almost immediately then that it was Lily's. Silver hoops are generally unremarkable, but the pearl gave it away. They're pretty earrings, simple but still on trend, and the hoop is minimalist enough to put the small pearl on display.

Standing in the garage, I stared at the earring open-mouthed and at a complete loss. My breath had changed. It was hot in the garage all of a sudden and harder to breathe.

I wondered what it was doing there, how Lily's missing earring had wound up in the back seat of my husband's car.

I could only think of one reason. That Lily had been in Jake's car. Because how would her earring have been there if she wasn't?

I tried to tell myself that it wasn't what I was thinking, that maybe it was something completely innocuous like that Lily's car broke down on the side of the road and Jake gave her a lift home.

Except that now, when I ask Lily, her face goes blank. She stutters and trips over her words, becoming inarticulate. She can't come up with a lie to save her life.

CHRISTIAN

Every day is like New Year's Eve and waiting for the ball to drop. Except that when the ball does drop, we won't be celebrating. Jake's body will have been identified. Everyone will know where he is and that he's dead and, soon enough, they'll know who did it. Identifying a body takes time. The medical examiner might be backed up, or a fingerprint match might be harder to make because of the level of decomposition. I don't ever want them to identify his body. But I also can't stand the anticipation.

Lily calls me that afternoon when I'm at work and she's on her way home from school. It's unlike her to call me at work. Usually she texts because she doesn't like to interrupt me if I'm busy. She'll text and say something like Can you talk? and then waits for me to call her.

I'm sitting at my desk, responding to an email from a client when my cell rings. "Hey," I say, answering. "Is everything okay?"

Lily says, "She found my earring."

It takes a moment to process.

"The one I gave you?" I ask. This is good news, then. I think often of that day Lily sat in the chair in our family room and told me what Jake had done to her, but not before first confessing to the lost earring. *I'm sorry. I lost one*, she'd said, crying, as if I would care. Lily had been upset that the earring was gone. I was upset, too, but not as upset as Lily. Lily loved those earrings, and symbolically they meant something to us. Five years of marriage. Twenty percent of marriages end in divorce within five years. It felt like an accomplishment, like something worth celebrating. I'm not superstitious. I didn't think her losing one was prophetic. But still, it's good to have that earring back because I know how much she loved them and how much they meant to her.

"Yes," Lily says, though I can't help but think that Lily is upset about something. Her words are too cryptic, too clipped.

"That's great news," I say, as if trying to convince her. "Who found it?"

"Nina."

"Where was it?" I ask. There is a hesitation on the other end of the line and I think that I cut out, that Lily didn't hear me. I ask again, "Where was it, Lily? Where did she find it?"

Lily says, "In Jake's car."

The blood drains from my face.

I'm typing the email as we talk, only partially listening. I have the phone balanced on my shoulder so that my hands are free to type.

My hands freeze over the keys. I stop typing. I reach for the phone, holding it in a hand so that I can get up from the desk to go and shut the office door for privacy.

"Whoa," I say, whispering now because even with the door

shut, I don't know what people on the other side of it can hear. "Back up, Lily. What do you mean in Jake's car? Since when did Nina find Jake's car?"

It feels like the walls are closing in on me, like the room is getting smaller.

"Yesterday. The police called her. It was impounded for being illegally parked."

"You didn't tell me."

"I didn't know. Not until today when she told me."

"What exactly did she say?"

"That the police called about the car. She went to claim it, and then last night, when she got home, she searched the car and found the earring."

This is happening fast. I'm having trouble wrapping my head around it. I'm trying not to panic but to process things. Sooner or later the car was going to be found. I knew that. Lily had to know that. It couldn't sit in that hotel lot forever. Our goal wasn't to make it disappear forever, but to take it away from the place where Lily was seen and where Jake was killed.

I sit back down. I ask the obvious question. "How did your earring get into Jake's car, Lily?"

Lily says, "I don't know. I don't know, Christian," and I can practically see her wheels spinning. "I was thinking, could it have somehow been on you when you moved his car that night? Or do you think maybe Jake made it back to his car after I hit him, and the earring was on him, but then…"

Her voice drifts. "But then what?" I ask, thinking it's not possible that he got to his car, and then went back into the woods to die. It doesn't make sense. Why would he do that? And besides, if Jake somehow made it back to his car, for the amount of blood that was on Lily's clothes when I found them, there would have been blood in the car too.

"I don't know. You're right. That doesn't make sense."

"How does Nina even know the earring is yours?" I ask. "Did you try telling her it's not?"

"No, Christian. She sees me almost every day, and every day I wear those earrings. She knows. We talked about them when the one went missing. She was the one who first noticed it gone. It would have looked even worse if I had lied about it."

I think about this. "No, you're right, Lily," I say, meaning it. "It was good not to lie. She would have been more suspicious if she knew you were lying about it. What did you say to her? What was your reason for the earring being in Jake's car?"

"Nothing," she says, and I imagine Lily's shocked expression when Nina revealed the earring to her, which is probably not unlike the look on my face right now. "I didn't have one. I just said it was so strange that it would be in Jake's car. I couldn't explain it. I changed the subject, saying how happy she must be to have Jake's car back, and that, with any luck, the police will soon find Jake too."

This is bad. This is really bad. I can't think of one logical reason why Lily's missing earring would have wound up in Jake's car, unless Lily is right and the earring was somehow attached to me, like on my coat. I tried to be so careful too. I wore gloves. I did research in advance to avoid cameras. I thought of everything, except this, leaving something unintentionally behind.

"Do you think she'll go to the police?" Lily asks.

"And say what? That she found your earring in Jake's car? What does that prove?"

I'm not exactly lying. It proves nothing. It's just an earring. But the earring opens the door to suspicion. It's a piece of the puzzle, like Nina maybe recognizing my car. That's a piece of the puzzle too. If Nina finds too many puzzle pieces, a picture will start to form.

"Where is the earring now?"

"I have it."

"She gave it to you?"

"Yes."

"Good. That's good." I don't know why this is good exactly. But I like the idea of evidence being back in Lily's possession. What I still can't figure out is how it ever got in Jake's car.

NINA

Christian and Lily live on a dead-end street. Theirs is the last house on the block. I've parked in the cul-de-sac at the end, where there are no homes, only trees. There is no through traffic either, which means I'm the only one here. I turn off my car and sit, staring through the dark copse of trees at their home. The porch light is on. It casts a yellow glow on the porch, making it warm and homey and snug, though I have no intent of going to the front door and knocking.

I sit there in the darkness watching. I know they're home because I saw movement on the other side of the blinds, though I couldn't identify them. It was just shadows passing by the windows.

There was only one other time in my life that I considered Jake might be cheating on me. It was early in our marriage. We were out to dinner when Jake and I ran into a colleague of his at a restaurant. The woman was one of the surgical techs at the hospital. She was beyond beautiful; she took my breath away and was the only person in my life that I ever remember making my husband tongue-tied. Even I had never had that effect on him. I remember at the time, Jake saying something along the lines of how he liked working with this woman because not only was she competent and conscientious at what she did, but that she was nice and easy to talk to, which came as a crushing blow because she wasn't just a pretty face, although she was that too.

Jake swore he wasn't flirting with her that night at the restaurant. He said he was only being nice and I let it go, but I never knew if I believed him. The irony was that even though I thought Jake might be cheating on me, I didn't feel angry with him. I felt angry with her. I wondered how any woman could be so horrible as to pursue a married man, and I thought of that woman who had stolen my father from my mother and me and practically ruined our lives. I remember that I went to Jake's hospital once. I sat in the parking lot in my car, waiting for this beautiful surgical tech to leave and when she did, I followed her to an apartment where she lived, and then I sat and watched from that parking lot, fantasizing about ways to ruin her life. I thought of many. I never acted on any of it. It was therapeutic enough just to imagine all the awful things I could do to her if I was so inclined.

My anger is exponentially worse because Lily is supposed to be my friend.

Has Jake left me for Lily? Or did Christian find out and do something to Jake?

I'm sitting in the front seat of my car. The time on my phone reads nine twenty-eight when the front door of Christian and Lily's house unexpectedly opens. I sit more upright in my chair. Christian appears in the doorway, looking out. He lets his gaze run over the street and I think at first that I've been caught. I watch as Christian steps out of the house. He's alone; Lily isn't with him. He turns back to the door to pull it closed behind him, and then he's practically floodlit in the porch lights. Because of the lights, he's easy to see, wearing jeans and a hooded sweatshirt, holding a plastic bag in his hand and, as I watch, he steps from the porch with the bag, making his way toward the trash cans at the end of the driveway.

I sink low in my seat as Christian approaches. My car can't be thirty feet away, though it's shrouded in darkness. The porch lights don't reach this far so Christian is far less conspicuous here, no longer spotlighted. Now he's a mere silhouette. I can only make out the contour of him, blending into the darkness of the street.

Christian doesn't go to the garbage bins to throw the bag away as I expected. Instead, he walks straight past them and I watch, entranced, as he comes to the street, turns and walks along the edge of it with the plastic bag suspended from his hand. I sit motionless, watching through the windshield as Christian grows smaller with the distance. He walks so far that eventually I can't see his silhouette. My curiosity gets the best of me and I decide to follow him. I wait in the car a few more seconds, and then I press the switch on the interior lights so that they don't turn on when I open the door. I don't want to be visible. I slip from my car, pushing the door gently closed and setting it back into place. I don't slam it. I stand immobile after I do, making sure Christian didn't notice me getting out of the car.

Darkness wraps its arms around me. The night air is cool. You can smell fall in the air, the earthy scent of things dying.

I tread softly in the direction that Christian went. Christian and Lily's neighborhood is wooded. Tree branches hang over the street, moving like arms. The homes are old and there are no sidewalks and very few streetlights, which leaves long stretches of blackness where the light doesn't reach. The street itself is uneven and potholed. I have to be careful where I step, so that

I don't trip and fall. I've lost sight of Christian up ahead. Still I follow, listening for footsteps, hearing only the movement of fallen leaves as they scatter across the street in the cool breeze.

Suddenly I'm startled by the low creaking sound of a screen door opening from somewhere behind me. I wheel around as the door slams emphatically closed. I wonder if it's Lily, if Lily saw me or if she's come outside looking for Christian. I stand in the middle of the empty street. My eyes take stock of the homes behind me. It's not Lily. A house back, someone has stepped outside. I wouldn't know it, except that I see the flare of a match and then an amber glow like from the end of a burning cigarette.

I turn back around. I keep walking, catching a flash of Christian in the distance as he climbs a small hill. The land here is rolling, because of the proximity to the river. Christian is about thirty or forty feet up, suddenly manifested in the halo of light that comes from a streetlight. He's there, and then he's gone again, devoured by darkness, descending the other side of the hill.

I pass quietly across the street. I walk along the opposite edge of it, in the grass, taking long strides to catch up, so that my breathing becomes heavy and audible from exertion. I try to suppress it, to hold my breath, to remain invisible and silent.

I catch another glimpse of Christian when the light hits him. I watch from a distance as he comes to a stop, standing at the end of someone's driveway. He takes a quick assessment of the street. He's reached his destination.

I watch as Christian moves toward this neighbor's garbage bin, which, like Christian's, is parked at the end of the drive- way. I'm at a loss. I watch, confused, as he opens the lid and sets the plastic bag he's been carrying inside. He then gently lowers the lid. He sets it closed, so that it doesn't make a sound. He reassesses the street, and then leaves, heading back the way he came. He wastes no time in getting back to his house, walking faster now than he did to get here. He walks past me without even knowing it. I become inanimate as he does, holding my breath, waiting until Christian is gone, and then I pass quietly across the street.

I go to the house where Christian just was. I go to the garbage bin and lift the lid. I use my phone's flashlight to search inside. The bin is practically full to capacity, so that I don't have to reach too far to find Christian's plastic bag.

I take the plastic bag out and set the lid of the garbage bin slowly closed. The bag is knotted at the handle. I pick at the knot, but when the knot doesn't easily give, I take the bag back to my car with me.

Back in my car, I work at the knot. I lose patience after a while and tear through the plastic with my fingernails. I reach inside the hole I've made to pull items out. It's dark in my car. I don't want to turn on the car and risk making myself any more visible than I already am. I try to make do with the negligible light. It's hard to see. I have to feel with my hands, running my fingers over fabric, relying on touch to make out the shape of things. Lying on my lap are items of clothing. I feel buttons and lace. I hold them up one at a time to the inadequate light from the touch screen, which came on when I opened the door.

My eyes, my mind can't process at first what I'm seeing.

Just as I start to make out the reddish-brown stain on the fabric, the quiet drum of knuckles on the driver's window makes me scream.

CHRISTIAN

I think someone is following me as I make my way home.

I don't know what it is exactly that makes me think this, if it's some sixth sense or if it's something I hear or subliminally see. The night is mostly silent. It's still. If you're quiet, you can just make out the sound of someone walking along the river, on the other side of houses. There are voices and then a high-pitched giggle. Kids. You can hear traffic in the distance, too, though it's far-off and subdued. A rabbit darts across the street in front of me as a dog barks, and then there is something else, something closer, slight and subtle but nagging and persistent.

I don't know what that is.

I don't look back. I keep going. I tell myself it's only guilt, that it's my conscience speaking. Lily's and my house sits at the end of the street. The outside lights are on but beyond our home, it's blackness. Lily is inside the house washing up for bed. We didn't talk much tonight. Lily was quiet, shaken from her conversation with Nina. Our stress levels have reached new heights.

I make my way up the driveway, but I don't go inside. I walk around to the side of the house, away from the porch lights, where I lie in wait in the shadows beside our home.

A cool breeze sweeps up out of nowhere, moving my hair. At the same time, a woman walks through a shaft of light coming from the streetlamp, and I would think that it was a neighbor taking a walk or walking a dog, except that as I look, Nina Hayes's face comes slowly into focus. My heart races inside of me as I study her hair and her face, my eyes descending her body until I come to the bag in her hand, the same bag that I just left in a garbage can down the street, to get rid of the evidence of what Lily did to Jake. I didn't want to leave it in our own garbage can in case someone found it.

My thoughts race. Nina was watching me. She was following me. She has the bag with Lily's blood-soaked clothes. I watch in disbelief as Nina walks straight past the end of our driveway, as if to leave with the bag, and if not for the sound of a car door opening and then closing, I wouldn't know she'd parked where the road dead-ends.

I can't let her leave with that bag.

If I do, everything Lily and I have done up to this point is all for naught.

I don't think. I react. It's not conscious. One minute I'm standing on the side of the house, watching Nina, and the next I'm moving down the driveway for the street, feeling like I would do anything, absolutely anything, to get that bag back, to stop Nina from seeing what she's about to see.

I come to her Tesla parked in the darkness. I stand less than three feet from the car. My muscles tighten. Everything feels suddenly more acute. My senses are heightened, honed. I have razor-sharp focus.

Nina's fingers pick at the knot, removing things from the bag.

I'm too late. She's already seen what's inside.

I rap on the window, feeling something inside of me turn stone-cold. At this end of the street, the road narrows and slightly turns. The trees close in on you, making those safe, warm, cozy houselights feel very far away. There is a barricade at the end of the street and then, on the other side of it, nothing but trees. If you forge a path through the trees, you come to the river. The river isn't incredibly deep. Maybe six or seven feet. It's the type of river that's slow and meandering. I hear it from here.

Nina turns at the sound of my knock.

There is this split second of calm before the storm.

In that second, I see myself reach out for the door handle. It's something out-of-body and uncontrolled. A reflex. The door opens and Nina is suddenly aglow in the interior car lights, the open bag on her lap, a look of shock and horror on her face.

I see my hand reach inside the car. I feel myself take a fistful of Nina's clothes in my hand—the collar or the lapels of her jacket, I don't even know what—and pull, dragging her out of the car, while she pushes away with her hands, trying to resist, saying things like "Christian" and "What the fuck" and "What do you think you're doing?"

All I can think about in this moment is undoing this thing that has just happened. Nina got the bag. She saw what was inside. She knows. I have to find a way to negate that because no one can know what was inside that bag.

Nina yelps. She fights against me, but I am either physically stronger than she is or my willpower is stronger. I overpower her. She comes sliding out of the leather car seat as if she weighs nothing. Her feet don't reach the earth first and so she falls sideways out. I make no attempt to stop her from falling or to cushion her blow, so that when she lands, she lands hard on a hip, looking up at me as if hurt, as if offended, as if

MARY KUBICA

I might reach out and help her to her feet, though the expression on her face changes when she sees the expression on mine.

"Please," she begs.

With a foot, I kick her over onto her back. Nina yells but then, as she lies supine on the street beside her car, I fall on top of her. I straddle her between my thighs as she thrashes beneath me, bucking at the hips, arching her back, pushing up on my chin with the heel of her hand, kicking her feet, thrusting backward. I press my hands to her mouth and to her nose, pushing hard, interlocking my hands, so that her eyes are wide and she struggles to breathe, held in place by my body weight. She grabs for my wrists, desperate and scared, her whole body trying to push up against the street. Nina squirms and I count the seconds that she's deprived of oxygen in my head, wondering how long it takes for a person to succumb to oxygen deprivation, to die. I count to five, to ten. To twenty. To thirty.

Nina fights back and somehow in the process, she manages to knock my hands from her face. She arches her back and takes a gasping, sucking breath.

Without thinking, I move my hands to either side of her face, by her ears. I take hold of her face. My grip is tight, squeezing her like the jaws of a vice. Now that her mouth is freed, Nina is able to scream and when she does, it's desperate, full-throated, loud. My only thought is to shut her up. To shut her the fuck up. To make her stop screaming before someone like Lily hears. To make her *stop*. Gravel digs into my knees and my shins as I pull up hard on her head, lifting her neck and torso from the street, bending her forward at the neck, gaining momentum and then propelling her back down to the street.

I pull up for a second time. Nina's hands clutch me by the forearms. Her nails dig in because this time, she knows what's to come. She knows what's happening. She tries to resist but I overcome. I take her head and slam it back down against the street. The sound of her skull hitting concrete is low and dull, sickening. Her body jerks and strains, her desperate scream reduced to a whimper, which is in every way basic and primal, her body dying, the life slowly leaving it. Nina's grip on my forearms loosens. Her hands fall away from me, splaying at her sides, and I could be done. I could haul her into the trees and leave her there to die, though if I do, there is still the chance that she could drag herself along the street for help.

I need to finish this. I need to be done.

I pull back up on Nina's head. I'm able to pull higher this time because there is less resistance. Her body simply gives. Beneath me, Nina still moves, but she no longer bucks and kicks. Instead she wriggles, a slow sliding from side to side like a worm. She moans. Her head hangs heavy, like an infant that can't hold its own head up. It lolls backward as Nina tries hard to gaze up at me disoriented, her eyes drooping, rolling backward, darkness oozing and pooling beneath her. I feel wetness—blood—in my fingers, which are in her hair.

I slam Nina's head down against the street, and this time her whimper becomes a quiet, fading breath. I pick her head back up, cradling it in my hands this time, moving the hair from her eyes. She loses consciousness first. She's peacefully still but I don't think she's dead yet. I watch in anticipation of her death, laying her head gently, tenderly down on the street, like putting a baby to sleep.

This, I think in that moment, suspended on my hands and knees above her, waiting for her to die, is what it feels like to snap.

If I was to sink Nina's body in the river tonight, she'd probably be found by morning in the reeds along the shallow riverbank somewhere just a little further south.

But if I was to weigh her down, that might help slow things down and at least give Lily and me time for a head start out of town.

This is what I'm thinking to myself in that split second of

stillness and silence as Nina turns at the sound of me knocking on her car window, and I find myself looking at her staggered and astonished face in the front seat of her car, as I shine my phone's flashlight on it, turning her into something eerie and incandescent.

I'm thinking about how I could kill her. I'm imagining it. I'm imagining how I would kill her and what I would do with her body if I were to reach in through the window and snap her neck or drag her out of the car and smash her head against the concrete.

I make a motion for her to lower her window. Reluctantly, she does.

"Christian," she says, finding her voice. Her voice lifts as if surprised to see me, like she's not the one running reconnaissance on my house.

"What are you doing here, Nina?" I ask.

Nina blinks. Her eyes search mine. "I... I was just leaving," she says. She steps on the brake and the car powers up.

"Not so fast, Nina," I say, setting a hand on the open window frame. "I think you have something of mine."

"What is this, Christian?" she asks, her voice breathless and desperate. "Is that *blood*?"

Nina bites down on her lip. Her eyes are narrowed, her breathing fast and shallow, and I know that she's thinking the worst, that the blood belongs to Jake and she's right. She's putting the pieces together—Lily's earring, my car, the blood—and coming to the realization that Jake probably isn't okay.

I could tell her what happened. I could go with the truth. I could say that Jake attacked Lily and that Lily fought back, to protect herself, that if she didn't kill him, he might have killed her.

"The baby," I say instead, by instinct, "didn't make it."

Almost as soon as I say it, I wish it back.

I hate myself for going there. It feels like I'm tempting fate, but I don't know what else to say. I don't know what to do. I'm not thinking about what happens thirty weeks from now when Lily gives birth to our baby, or even three weeks from now when she starts to show. I'm just thinking about this moment right now, and how Nina and I both get through it alive.

I'm not a killer. I don't want to have to kill her.

"You're lying."

"I'm not," I say. "Why were you following me, Nina?"

Her face is blank. "I want to talk to Lily. I want to see Lily," she says.

"Lily isn't up for seeing anyone tonight. She's upset."

"Where is Jake? What did you do to Jake?" she asks, her voice turning shrill. "I saw your car on that video, Christian. I know it was you. I know you were in my house. What did you do to Jake?" she asks again.

"Nothing," I say. "I didn't do anything to Jake. He's your husband, Nina. Why don't you tell me where he is?"

She asks then, "Why didn't you throw that bag in your own trash if it's from the baby? Why did you hide it down the street?"

"Because I didn't want Lily to come across it by accident. She's devastated," I say, "as you can imagine."

The first baby we lost hit the hardest for Lily. She cried for weeks. I think it's because we went into it with so much hope and optimism that we didn't consider all the possible outcomes. The only one we considered was that at the end of nine months, we'd have a healthy baby. With each subsequent miscarriage, Lily was less visibly sad, as if somehow accepting of our fate, though she died a little inside every time.

"I don't believe you," she says.

"Believe whatever you want. I'm not lying, Nina. I didn't do anything to Jake."

I reach in through the open window. Nina flinches, drawing back. The street is quiet. It has to be close to ten o'clock. I left Lily in the house. I said I'd be right back. I've been gone much longer than I intended, so that I wonder if she's gazing out into the night, looking for me. People on the street are going to sleep for the night. Interior house lights are switching off, the street becoming somehow darker.

Fully present and completely aware of what I'm doing, I reach in with both hands. Nina sinks back into her seat, recoiling from me. "Stop it, Christian," she says, fighting my hands. Nina's neck can't be three inches from my hands. She's restrained in her chair. Standing outside, I have leverage. I have the advantage of power and height. It would be so easy to strangle her.

But I'm not a killer.

I wrap my hands around the bag of Lily's clothes, lifting it from Nina's lap. It's only in the last second that she tries to resist. Her fingers come down on the bag, but I wrest it easily from her.

Later I wonder if I'll regret letting her leave.

NINA

I call Officer Boone as I drive. He doesn't answer. I didn't think that he would—it's late—but I leave a message and he calls me back almost immediately. I tell him what happened. I'm practically hysterical.

"What were you doing at the Scotts' house, Mrs. Hayes?" he asks.

"I went to see Christian and Lily."

"But you said you were following Mr. Scott. Why?"

"Because I thought he might be up to something. I was curious what was in the bag and what he was doing with it. I think he may have killed my husband, Officer. There was blood in that bag, all over someone's clothes."

"Where is this bag of bloody clothes now? Would you be able to bring it to me?"

"I don't have it. Christian took it from me. Ask Christian where this bag of clothes is," I say, knowing that Christian would have done something with it already. He would have gotten rid of the bag, and then there would be no evidence, nothing for Officer Boone to see.

But the blood. So much blood.

"Talk to him. Talk to Christian Scott. Ask him where he was last Saturday morning when some man was breaking into my home."

The other end of the phone goes quiet at first. Officer Boone's words are deliberate when he speaks. "Are you saying Mr. Scott is the person who broke into your home, Mrs. Hayes?"

"His car is a Honda Accord. It looks very much like the car in the video. Please. I know the quality isn't great, but just speak to him. Ask him where he was last Saturday morning when my home was being broken into. And ask him about this bag of bloody clothes. Ask him why I found his wife's earring in the back seat of my missing husband's car."

My mother is waiting for me when I come home, upset. I tell her what happened.

She wraps me in her arms and holds me close. "You shouldn't have done that, Nina," she says, stroking my hair. "Do you have any idea what could have happened to you?"

"I'm sorry," I say as she releases me. "It was stupid, I know."

"I don't know what I'd do if anything happened to you. You're trembling, Nina," she says, and I am. It's something violent and uncontrolled. She sets her arms on me and asks, "Are you cold, honey? I can turn up the heat."

"No. I don't think so." It's fear, not cold, that makes me tremble.

She gazes at me, her eyes warm and indulgent. "Why don't you come sleep in my room with me tonight?" she suggests, cradling my face in her hands. "Would you like that?"

Nodding, I find and take my pillow from my twin bed and carry it into her room, where, despite being thirty-eight years old, a grown woman, my mother and I lie together on the queen-size bed like we did when I was young and had a nightmare or felt scared. I feel safer beside her like, no matter what happens, as long as she's here I'll be fine.

My mother sleeps, but I don't sleep.

The next morning, my mother has breakfast laid out on the table for me when I step into the kitchen to get ready to leave for work.

"You have to eat something, Nina," she tells me when I try to avoid her breakfast.

"I can't, Mom. I'm not hungry," I say, while helping myself to coffee.

My mother notices how my hands still shake when I fill my cup. I don't know that they've stopped shaking since last night. "Look at you, Nina. Your hands. You're not well. Why don't you stay home today and rest?"

"I can't. I have to work," I say, though the idea of going to work, of risking running into Lily, makes me physically sick. Every time I so much as blink, I see Christian's face in the car window. I see his hands reaching in the open window. I see blood.

My mother is sitting in the large picture window as I leave. It's still dark outside and she's backlit by the inside lights. I worry she won't be okay without me. What if something happens to her while I'm gone?

I'm too busy watching my mother. I'm thinking about what happened last night and wishing that my mother would get away from the window, that she would back up into the house where she's less visible.

I'm not looking where I'm going. I reverse blindly into the street so that I don't see the other car come barreling down the street.

The sound of a car horn blasting gets my attention. Instinctively I slam on the brakes. I don't yet see this other car, and yet I see in the window how my mother's eyes have enlarged to full moons. She presses her hand to her mouth, watching as a passing car, going something like thirty-five or forty miles per hour, far too fast for this residential street, almost crashes into me before I stop. It would have been my fault too. I should have yielded to this other car, despite the fact that it's speeding.

My heart beats hard. My body trembles. I wait for the other car to pass. I wave at my mother to let her know that I am fine, that everything is fine. I'm far from fine.

I take a breath, and then step again on the gas.

It's not yet seven in the morning and already it feels as if there is something very inauspicious about this day.

I hear the sound of a knock on the glass panel of my classroom door. It's the middle of seventh period and I'm standing at the front of the class, before the whiteboard, trying my best to lecture, but I'm not myself today. I can't think. I can't stop seeing blood. I can't unsee Christian's blank face on the other side of the car window. *The baby didn't make it*, he said, cold and unemotional. He snatched the bag from me, and then it was gone, and I never got a good look at what was inside the bag, and either way I don't know if I believe him. Was it the baby's blood, like he said? Or was it Jake's blood? I've stayed in my classroom all day for fear of running into Lily or Ryan in the hall. I haven't eaten. I haven't bothered with the restroom.

"Mrs. Hayes," someone says. A hand rises up in the back of the classroom, waving to get my attention. "Mrs. Hayes, someone is here. It's Dr. Sanders."

A hush falls across the room. I follow everyone's gaze. I look over to see the school principal's face in the glass as he steps back from the door, his hand falling away from the door, going to rest at his side. Through the window, our eyes meet. He holds mine for a second, and then he lets go, looking away, somber.

Someone at the back of the room drops a book and I startle. My gaze darts from Dr. Sanders to the felled book, as the student who dropped it swoops down to pick it up. She rises up, looking at me. "Sorry," she says, and I nod.

There is something very premonitory, almost apocalyptic, about this moment. Outside the classroom windows, a cloud moves past the sun, shading its light. It gets darker in the room, as if someone dimmed a light. The students fall silent, seeing Dr. Sanders through the glass and worrying he's here for them. He only comes when someone is in trouble, and not just the vaping-in-the-bathroom kind of trouble, but the kind that comes with serious consequences like suspension or expulsion. The students look sideways at one another, wondering who he's here for this time, hedging bets on my two biggest troublemakers, who sit on opposite sides of the room toward the back of the classroom, practically frozen, though almost everyone, it seems, based on their reaction, has something to feel guilty for, something to fear. It's human nature.

But somewhere in my gut I know.

Dr. Sanders hasn't come for any one of them. He's come for me.

"Excuse me," I breathe. I move from the front of the classroom to the door. On the other side of it, Dr. Sanders sees me coming. His head lifts and he offers an empathetic smile.

I open the door. "Nina," he says. "Sorry to interrupt."

"Is everything okay, Dr. Sanders?" I ask as I step out into the hall, pulling the door halfway closed behind me.

Dr. Sanders isn't always the most approachable man. He's stone-faced and detached as if by virtue of the job. He has to be, because he can't be falling for every seventeen-year-old's sob story. And yet, he sets his hand on my shoulder, lowers his eyes to me and speaks in a soothing, low tone. "There is someone in my office that would like to speak with you, Nina. You go. I'll take care of your class."

"But—"

"Don't worry about anything here. We'll be fine. You just go."

I nod. I walk through the halls like a prisoner being led to her execution, though I'm all alone, and there isn't even a guard to keep me company as I shamble to my death chamber. There is no one to plead to for a final pardon. The halls are vacant. Behind closed doors, the students are silent as if time has stopped, as if I'm the only one in the universe still moving.

When I come to the office, Officer Boone is there with another uniformed officer. He holds his peaked hat in his hands as I enter Dr. Sanders's office. He says, "Mrs. Hayes. Please. Sit," as someone from the other side pulls the door slowly closed behind me. I turn but it's too late. I don't see the door close but I hear the sound of it as the latch settles into place.

A chair has been pulled out in anticipation of my arrival. It's in the dead center of the room, facing Officer Boone.

"No, thank you," I say, as if by not sitting in the chair I can avoid what comes next. "I'll stand."

Officer Boone tells it to me straight. He doesn't use euphemistic language. He doesn't delay. My worst fears are confirmed. Jake, he says, is dead.

"We found a body a few days ago and the medical examiner has just confirmed that it's your husband, Jake. I'm so sorry, Mrs. Hayes."

I myself go dead, blank, numb. I change my mind and decide that I'd like to sit after all, sinking into the chair by degrees, clutching the arms of the chair with my hands.

"Are you alright, Mrs. Hayes? Can I get you something? Some water?"

"No. When did you find him?" I ask, and he tells me. "Why didn't you tell me sooner?"

"In cases like these, we have to be absolutely certain of a

positive identification before the family is informed. As you can understand, we can't be making any mistakes."

"How did it happen?" I ask. As he tells me, I choke on air, gasping. It's too much. I can't stand to imagine it, to think of what happened to Jake in those final moments before he died.

Leaving the office, I pass vacantly by Pam. "Oh, Nina," she says, and I feel the brush of her warm, trembling hand against my arm, before that same hand rises up to her mouth and she chokes back a sob. Someone has already been down to my classroom to collect my things and, I stand there, like a mannequin, being dressed with my own jacket and purse, my arms shaped to fit into the sleeves. People watch. There is an audience. They gather and collect in the school entrance, just outside the main office, as the assistant dean ushers them along, telling students to get back to class. But there are police here, and everyone is curious. They want to know why there are police here. And then they see Pam with her red face and her red eyes crying and me being attended to, and they make assumptions. There are whispers. People speak behind closed hands. The hallways fill with the quiet susurration of voices, noise, but it's all very distant and I feel dead inside, like this is happening to someone else and not me.

I approach the front doors, walking between Officer Boone and this other officer. The building's entrance has four doors, which are mostly glass. Officer Boone steps in front of me to reach out and open the door. Before it opens, I catch a glimpse of the hallway cast back in the glass. I see Lily in the reflection. She's tucked behind a crowd of people, her body mostly blocked, but her head jutting out, leaning around someone taller to watch me leave.

I feel a gust of wind as Officer Boone opens the door. I stop where I am and turn around slowly to face her. Lily's and my eyes meet.

What I realize is that she doesn't look sad or sympathetic. She looks scared.

★ ★ ★

My mother is standing in her living room window when I pull in, waiting for me, a pair of sheers covering her like a veil.

I park the car in her garage, practically staggering to the door. I didn't come straight here from school. I went to the police station first, following Officer Boone there. I thought they were going to show me Jake's body, but they saved me from that, using his clothes and his shoes as a means of verification, for which I was grateful. I didn't know that I could stand to see Jake's face after what happened to him and after all those days in the woods, though the clothes were hard enough, knowing that they had pulled them from his lifeless body. Officer Boone offered to drive me home but I said no, that I could drive myself. He was reluctant, but he let me, while another officer followed along in his car to make sure I got home okay.

I told them everything I know about Christian and Lily. I told them to speak to Jim Brady, that Jim Brady will tell them that Lily was at Langley Woods the same day as Jake, and then it won't just be my word against hers.

Now my mother pulls open the door. She steps back to make room for me to fit. "Oh, Nina honey, what's wrong?" She throws opens her arms. I walk into them, and she folds them around me. Her body is strong. She's solid and unbreakable against me. I sag into her, letting her hold me, suddenly overcome with emotion that I've been holding back. In that moment, it all comes spilling out. Jake is gone. Jake is dead. My eyes fill, and then tears roll down my cheeks, crying so hard that I can't speak. My mother says nothing at first. She holds me. She strokes my hair, like she did when I was a girl and I was upset about something, a fight with a friend or a breakup with a boyfriend. She would squeeze beside me on my twin-size bed, slip her arm around my shoulders and tell me everything was going to be alright, and I believed her.

"They found Jake. He's dead, Mom," I say, tears stinging my eyes. "He's gone."

Her hands are warm, steady, and her placid voice, when she speaks, is a narcotic. "I know, honey. I know."

As my mother helps me to bed that night, pulling back the covers for me and tucking me into bed, I think about Jake. These last months that I spent with my husband, we were both discontent. We weren't unhappy, but we weren't happy either. It wasn't always that way. There was a time in our lives that we were undeniably happy.

That night, I dream about Jake. I wake up crying for Jake, calling out his name. But Jake doesn't come. My mother is the only one who comes. She is the only one I have left in this world, the only one who cares about me now that Jake is gone.

CHRISTIAN

I leave work. The building I work in is ten stories tall and is easily one of the most recognizable buildings around because of its design. It's cool and unique, postmodern. The building itself is blue with a sloping exterior that is nothing like the squat beige buildings that surround it. It stands out.

I take the elevator down to leave. My office is located on the eighth floor. It's just around five and so the elevator is practically full to capacity, everyone anxious to go home. I'm way back in the elevator because I got on first, which means I'll be the last to get off. Our building backs up to the interstate. From the eighth floor, I always see traffic start to build as late afternoon descends, getting worse the closer it gets to five, which means the interstate is practically a parking lot by now.

Some man and his kid are on the elevator with me. They stand just in front of me, the man carrying the little boy in his arms. The father is turned away, facing the elevator doors, so that I see his son's face over his shoulder. I can't take my eyes off him. He's cute. He settles my anxious nerves as we descend. This wasn't a good day. Despite getting rid of the bag of Lily's clothes, I couldn't stop thinking about them. I couldn't stop regretting letting Nina leave with the knowledge of what was in the bag.

This little boy can't be more than two years old and I find myself thinking how maybe, one day, in the not so distant future, if Lily and I are lucky, this man and his son will be me and mine. I smile at the kid and he smiles shyly back, a toothy grin, before latching on to and burying his face into his father's neck.

The father looks over his shoulder at me. He says, "He's shy," as if apologizing for his kid.

I say, "That's okay."

We reach the ground floor. The doors open and everyone steps out. I walk through the lobby for the revolving doors.

I call Lily on the way home but she doesn't answer. I don't leave a voice mail or text her because I don't want to wake her if she's napping.

Lily is in the living room when I come in. She's not napping like I thought. She stands at the window, staring out into the backyard, so that I just see her from behind. If she heard the garage door opening, if she hears me come in, it's not obvious.

Lily's shoes block the door. Her jacket is on the kitchen island beside her bag and keys. "Hey," I say, stepping over her shoes and setting my own bag on the floor, leaned against the island. "How was your day? I tried calling you."

Lily doesn't reply. She stands, staring out the window as if in a state of suspended animation.

"Lily?" I ask. I come across the kitchen for the living room. When I reach her, I set my hands on her shoulders, looking past her for the backyard, to see what she sees. There isn't too much worth looking at, though the view, as always, is beautiful and serene. It's quiet outside. There is no one there, no one walking along the path. The river is still and the day gray, the sky patchy with clouds. "Is everything okay?" I ask, turning her gently by the shoulders with my hands, forcing her to look at me.

Lily's skin is pale. Her long brown hair falls flat and frames her face. "He's dead," she says, cold and emotionless. "They identified him."

Lily's words reach my ears, but my brain hasn't done anything with them yet. It's slow in catching up.

By instinct, I ask, "Who?" though I know who.

It comes as a complete blow, though it shouldn't, because we've known since they found the body that this was bound to happen. I just didn't know it was going to happen today.

"Jake."

"When?"

"Today."

"Nina told you?"

Lily shakes her head, her words coming out in unsteady bursts. "The teachers. At school. It's all anyone is talking about."

"How do the other teachers know that Jake is dead, that they've identified his body?"

"The police," Lily says. "They came to school to speak with her. Nina was crying. Someone overheard what they said to her. They said that Jake was dead. They found him." Lily's chin quivers. I pull her into me. I wrap my arms around her and, at first, she lets me. At first she sinks against me and she lets me hold and console her.

But then she pulls abruptly back and says, "She looked at me, Christian," her voice changed, becoming stronger and more taut.

I ask, "What do you mean she looked at you?"

"I was there, just as she was leaving. I saw her walk out of the building with the police. She had her back to me. I didn't think she saw me. But then, she stopped all of a sudden. She turned back. She looked right at me. Her eyes," she says, and then she shudders, like she'll never forget the look in Nina's eyes as she was leaving, walking through the foyer, bookended by the police, turning back as with some clairvoyant knowledge that Lily was there, to fix her gaze on Lily's face.

"Did she say anything to you?"

"No," Lily says. "She just stared."

I don't know which is worse. If she had said something or that she didn't.

And then, in a mind-numbing tone, as if telling me dinner is in the oven or asking about my day at work, she says, "The police should be here soon," and I wheel back, squinting my eyes toward a window at the front of the house to see if they're already here.

Lily turns her back to me. She turns around to face the other way, staring back out the window at nothing, as if resigned to her fate.

"Lily?" I gently ask.

"What?"

"What time did the police come to school?" I try to work out how much time we have until the police are here. Now that they've identified the body, they know where Jake died. A witness puts Lily at the scene on the same day that he died. It's too much of a coincidence, though what the police have so far is mostly circumstantial. A person has to infer something from the evidence. They have to presume something. It's not direct evidence, such as if Jim Brady had actually witnessed Lily hitting Jake with that rock or if the police found the rock with Jake's blood and Lily's fingerprints on it. What they have is enough to suspect Lily was there and that she might have done something, but it's not enough to prove beyond a reasonable doubt that she killed him. They have no motive. They have no weapon.

I offer false promises. "It's okay," I say to Lily as I grip her gently by the shoulders, leaning into her, sinking my face into the back of her head, inhaling her scent. "It's going to be okay."

I don't know if I say it for her benefit or for mine.

In my arms, she's stiff. She's quiet. She knows I'm lying.

My hands move down to her abdomen. My arms wrap around her from behind, coming to rest on my child growing inside. "We'll figure this out," I say, and then I hold her and we stand like that for a long time, looking out into the backyard as it gets darker outside, the clouds drifting in the wind, the faint moon rising up over the river, revealing itself intermittently, depending on whether it's behind the clouds.

I think about the first time I saw Lily. We were in college, in a calculus class. Lily was the shy, quiet one, who was also brilliantly smart. She could solve the problems no one else could. I loved her from the very first time I ever laid eyes on her, the first day of the semester when I walked into class and saw her sitting there, bent over her desk. Her hair was even longer then, impossibly long. It pooled on her desk, the color of toffee. Lily must have felt me staring at her because she looked up and our eyes met and, when they did, I felt complete.

I leave Lily standing at the window. I go to look online for information. It's not there yet. We have to wait, which is torture. I hate waiting. I need to know now.

Eventually I convince Lily to move away from the window, though it takes some persuading. We spend the evening in nervous anticipation. I can't sit down. I can't sit still. I try to, but then I find I need to get up, to move, to do something. I mill about the house. Every time I hear a car engine coast down the street, I think it's the police, coming for Lily or me. I go to look and find myself standing in the foyer in the dark, watching the bobbing and weaving movement of headlights down the street. I hold my breath as they come, descending on the house. I think this is it, the beginning of the end. But then the cars stop before they get to our house, going to some other house, and I feel my jaw unclench, my body slacken. I breathe. I go back to sit by Lily, only to return the next time I hear a car in the distance.

I do anything I can to distract myself. I make dinner that neither Lily nor I eat, and then I busy myself cleaning dishes like they've never been cleaned before, taking out all my angst on a pan with a steel wool pad.

If we say anything, it's only to appease ourselves, things like "Just because Jim Brady saw you at Langley Woods, doesn't mean anything. It doesn't *prove* anything" and "It's justifiable homicide, Lily. You acted in self-defense. There is no criminal liability in cases of justifiable homicide. We'll get a good lawyer. The best." I do most of the talking. Lily's eyes are glassy, empty, blank, and her skin is pale. I try to get her to eat—just some crackers if nothing else—but she won't eat. I try to get her to drink. I hand her a glass of water. She takes it from me, she thanks me for it, but then she sets it on the coffee table, where she leaves it untouched.

At some point I say, "I'll say it was me, Lily. Just because Jim Brady didn't see me, doesn't mean I wasn't there." And then, "This isn't something you did alone. We're in this together, Lily, remember? Like Bonnie and Clyde," trying and failing to get a smile out of her. She nods dimly, and I'm not sure what she's nodding at, us being in this together or me taking the blame for what she did.

I force myself to sit on the couch beside Lily. We stare blankly toward the TV, waiting for the news to come on and eventually it does. The lead story is how the body found at Langley Woods has been identified.

My eyes go to Lily's hands in her lap. She's been picking at her nails so that one bleeds. I reach over for her hand. It's like ice. I take it into my own, rubbing it between mine to warm it up.

This moment reminds me of some apocalypse movie. The

asteroid is about to hit Earth and we know we're going to die. It's imminent. It's only a matter of time.

I look back at the TV as they share a picture of Jake, one which I have to think came from Nina, and I imagine Nina going through the pictures on her phone, finding one of Jake to share and giving it over to the police. It's the first time I've paused to think about Nina and what she must be going through. I've only been thinking about Lily and me, and for a second, I get almost choked up, imagining Nina at work being informed by the police that Jake is dead.

In the image, Jake is on a boat. A blue lake surrounds him. Jake looks so easygoing and affable in the image, and I have a hard time reconciling this face and this wide smile with the furious, unhinged man who attacked Lily that day in the woods.

It's almost like they're not even the same guy.

They go to a live shot of a reporter standing in the parking lot of Langley Woods. It's night now. Darkness surrounds her, though with the camera's lights, the trees are still visible behind her. The reporter says, "The body belonged to thirty-nine-year-old Jacob Hayes, a local neurosurgeon. Dr. Hayes was found dead yesterday morning with a gunshot wound to the head…"

I choke on nothing. Everything but the reporter's face fades out. I only see her face.

There is a ringing in my ears.

"What did she say?" I ask, almost to myself. I fumble for the remote. It's on the couch between Lily and me. My hand wraps around it, but my hands are shaking so badly that I drop it the first time, to the floor. The back snaps off the remote and batteries come out, rolling under the coffee table. I reach down to grope for the batteries, snatching them from the floor and forcing them into the little springs that hold the batteries in place. I snap the back on. I rewind live TV. I listen to it again, scooching forward, sitting on the front edge of the couch, leaned into the TV.

"Dr. Hayes was found dead yesterday morning with a gunshot wound to the head…"

A gunshot wound.

Beside me, Lily is limp. I look over at her in disbelief. She has an arm pressed to her stomach and she's folded over it, like she might be sick.

My jaw is slack. My eyes are wide.

I rub at my forehead. I shake my head, trying to mentally absorb what I just heard.

A gunshot wound to the head.

Cautiously I ask, "What does she mean when she says a gunshot wound?"

Lily shakes her head in denial. Some feral sounds rise up to her throat. Her hand moves to her mouth, where she holds something back, a cry or a moan. She utters to herself, "No. No. No," all the while still shaking her head.

"Answer me, Lily," I say, my voice more firm. "What does she mean when she says a gunshot wound?"

"I don't know," Lily says. Her head whirls in my direction. Her eyes are wide and gaping, and, in them, there are tears. She shakes her head harder. It's vigorous, her hair whipping around to slap her in the face.

"I thought you killed him with a rock. Did you…did you shoot him, Lily?"

My words are incredulous.

"I… I did kill him with a rock," she asserts. "I did. She must be mistaken, Christian. She must have her stories mixed up, or the medical examiner got it wrong. Someone must be wrong." She reaches for me. "You have to believe me."

I find myself staring at her. Lily's hair parts down the center. She has high cheekbones, a small forehead and big, round, larger-than-life eyes that remind me of those characters from Japanese anime. I love her eyes. They're a rich, warm brown and always make me think of integrity and goodness.

But what if there is something in those eyes I've failed to see?

I ask, "When is a news reporter or a medical examiner ever this wrong?"

Lily's mouth just falls open.

My chest feels heavy, like there is something weighing it down. It's hard to breathe, to push up against the weight of whatever it is—shock, dread—to let my lungs expand.

There is the taste of something bad in my mouth, like metal.

I wish more than anything that I could go back to five minutes ago, to a state of blissful ignorance, when I believed that what my wife told me was true.

NINA

My mother is standing in the hallway when I step out of the bathroom. I didn't expect her to be there. I thought she was still asleep when I went into the shower a few minutes ago. I barely even see her as I come out of the bathroom, practically running straight into her. Her voice stops me dead. "Where do you think you're going?" she asks, and I startle, throwing my hand to my heart.

"Mom. You scared me. I thought you were asleep," I say.

"Where are you going?" she asks again.

"Work," I say.

"Honey," she says, her voice gentle like a lullaby. "You can't go to work. Jake is dead, sweetie. You're mourning. You're grieving. No one expects you to go to work today."

I hadn't forgotten that Jake is dead. I only thought that if I kept busy, if I kept working I could somehow outrun grief and that the grief wouldn't catch up with me.

There is closure in knowing that Jake is dead. There is resolution, a finality to the events of the last few weeks. With that comes comfort. I know where Jake is now. I don't need to look for him anymore.

My phone has been pinging nonstop with calls and texts from nearly everyone. Lily is practically the only one who hasn't called or texted to express her condolences, which is revelatory. The truth sometimes lies in what we don't say, rather than what we say.

My mother comes to me in the afternoon and gently says, "There are things that we'll need to do, Nina, when you're ready. We'll need to go to the funeral home to make arrangements and pick out a casket for Jake. We'll have to call the hospital and let them know that he's gone, and call the life insurance company." I appreciate that she says *we*. I am not alone. She and I will do these things together, though Jake's funeral will have to wait, because for now, my husband's body is evidence in a murder investigation.

"You just look so tired, Nina," my mother then says, reaching out to stroke my hair. "We don't have to do any of this today. Why don't you go back to bed for a while. Sleep. It doesn't matter if we do these things now or later."

She's right, it doesn't, because either way Jake will still be dead.

CHRISTIAN

That night after Lily is asleep, I search the house for a gun.

I leave the lights off. I don't want to risk waking her. I start in the bedroom, where Lily sleeps less than ten feet from me. I inch open a dresser drawer, though my eyes remain fixed on Lily lying in bed to make sure she sleeps through the sound of it.

I open the drawer only as far as necessary to slip a hand inside, running my hand under and over her clothes and along the niches of the drawer. I feel between articles of clothing, and then I inch the first drawer closed and guide a second drawer open. Lily's is an upright five-drawer dresser. I start at the bottom, working my way to the top, feeling less conspicuous as I search the bottom drawers but then, the higher I go, the more upright I stand, the more fully exposed I become. I don't want Lily to know what I'm doing.

The fourth drawer is open when suddenly Lily flounders in

bed. She's like a fish out of water, suffocating, kicking its fins. I watch her struggle, the white sheet getting tangled around her legs and feet. She mumbles something unintelligible in her sleep. I push the drawer gently closed as Lily bolts upright in bed and she gasps, though I can see in her unfocused eyes that she's not conscious, that she's still somehow asleep and dreaming, having a nightmare.

I go to her. I press lightly against her shoulders and lay her back into bed, where she rolls by instinct onto her side, pulling her knees into her. I draw the blanket over her, and then I lie there beside her, flat on my back, biding time until her breath evens and I can get back out of bed and resume my search.

I finish the last two drawers. I search her bedside table. I check her vanity.

Downstairs I drift around the house. I search in drawers and cabinets. I carry a chair over and search things like above the kitchen cabinets where neither of us go. I lift up the floor registers. I look inside a wide vase, beneath flowers. I come up empty.

I don't find a gun.

But just because I don't find a gun, doesn't mean there isn't one here.

Lily's work bag is on the floor by the garage door. It's a large tan leather tote bag, big enough to hold textbooks and a laptop. I go to the bag. I crouch down beside it and unzip it. It has pockets, both on the inside and the outside of the bag, which Lily was ecstatic about when I bought her the bag for her birthday years ago. Now I run my hand along the inside of the leather, rubbing up against a book, a wallet, keys, feeling for something hard and cold like gunmetal.

I hear the rustle of something from behind me.

"Christian," she says.

I rise up, looking slowly back over a shoulder, blinking the world into focus.

I turn to find Lily behind me. She stands ten feet away, by the window in the moon's infinitesimal glow. She wears a thin white nightgown that hangs to the upper thigh, though in the near absence of light, she's almost translucent, like a ghost. Her hair hangs long. It's tangled, falling into her face where she leaves it, not bothered by the fact that she can barely see past the bangs. I can just make out the whites of her eyes. Her head is at an angle and her hands are hidden behind her back.

I realize that I'm both fascinated by and terrified of my wife.

"What are you looking for in my bag, Christian?" she asks. Her voice is the exact opposite of a balm, whatever that is. It isn't soothing or restorative, though the tone itself is melodious and sweet. But it's in what I know, or what I think I know, that I find it so disturbing.

Lily steps closer. My eyes are on her hands, which I can't see.

Bludgeoning someone to death with a rock in self-defense is one thing. But bringing a gun to a forest preserve requires forethought, and the intent to harm or kill. It means killing someone in cold blood. If Lily went there intending to harm Jake, it means she knew Jake would be there. It wasn't a coincidence that they were both there at the same time.

Maybe Jake didn't lead Lily down that secluded path and into the woods.

Maybe Lily led Jake.

This raises doubt about everything I ever believed about my wife.

"I have to know," I breathe out. "Did you shoot him, Lily?"

Lily watches me, unspeaking.

"Did you?" I ask again.

"That hurts, Christian," she says, her voice quivering, on the verge of tears when she finally speaks. What I can see of her face is pained. Deep ruts form between the eyes. The edges of her lips point downward. She takes another step toward me, her feet so light and airy on the floors that if I didn't know any better, I'd think she had levitated. "Do you really think I could do something like that?" she asks, coming even closer now so that I could touch her if I wanted to, though my arms remain stationary at my sides, while Lily's hands are fixed behind her back.

Twelve hours ago the answer to her question would have been a definitive no. No, I don't believe my gentle, loving wife could shoot someone in the head.

"Answer me," I say, trying to keep my voice calm and level. I hear my heartbeat in my ears. I breathe through an open mouth, my chest rising and falling with each breath. "Did you shoot him?"

"No," she says, her empty hands coming from behind her back to reach for me.

Lily stands on her toes. She presses her body into mine, though mine is straight as a ramrod. Her arms wrap around my neck. "Please," she whispers into my ear, pleading, desperate. "Hold me, Christian. I'm so scared." She presses her face into my shoulder. I feel the wetness of her eyes on my skin. I feel her heartbeat against mine. I wrap my arms around her waist, the cotton of her nightgown thin and insubstantial beneath my hands. I lift her into my arms. I carry her back to bed and lie down beside her, holding her until she falls asleep.

The rest of the night, I don't sleep. I lie in bed, watching Lily sleep.

At some point in the night, I get out of bed and go to watch her from the armchair in the corner of the room.

Eventually, the sun slowly rises. Its light breaches the slats of the wooden blinds, thrusting itself into our room. As the minutes pass, the light grows, disseminating across the bedroom. It spills first across the wooden floors and then climbs the bed to where Lily lies, cocooned in the sheets. The light falls on her face, bathing her in light.

Only then do I slip back into bed with Lily. I lie on my side beside her, facing her, feeling nostalgic all of a sudden, wondering if today will be the day the police come, if today will be the last morning that I wake up with her beside me in bed. Neither of us even thinks about going to work.

Lily feels me come back to bed, though she doesn't know that I was gone. She feels the movement of the bed, of the mattress absorbing my weight. That's what wakes her.

Lily's eyes flutter open and she finds my eyes holding hers.

"What are you looking at?" she asks, smiling momentarily as if half-conscious and blissfully unaware of what's happening, before the knowledge, the memories return to her and the smile disappears.

I say, "You."

Lily presses into me. I reach out and stroke her hip.

"I have something to tell you, Christian," she says, breathing the words into my neck.

I pull back to look at her. "What?" I ask.

Lily pushes herself up into a sitting position, so that she looks down on me. She hesitates, thinking twice about saying whatever she has to say. She gazes toward the window, stalling for time, and I reach for her, setting my hand on her chin, turning her face, forcing her to look at me.

"What is it, Lily? What do you want to tell me?"

She says, "You told me once that there is nothing I could ever say that would change the way you feel about me. Did you mean that?"

I nod, though inside, something has changed. Lily has changed.

"I've been lying to you," she says. "It didn't happen like I said it did."

"Okay," I say slowly, drawing it out as my heart races inside of me. "How did it happen, then?"

"Would you still love me, Christian," she asks, her eyes turn-

ing rheumy and red, her nose starting to run, "if I did something terrible?"

My heart stops. I push myself upright and into a sitting position beside her and ask, "What did you do, Lily? What did
you do?"

What Lily tells me is bad. But it's a different kind of bad
than I imagined.

I feel like someone stabbed me through the chest with a
knife and that when the blade was inside of me, they twisted
the handle.

I wonder if it would hurt less if she said that it happened
once, that one single time she got carried away, caught up in a
moment, that he seduced her, that he practically forced himself
on her, or that she was out of her mind drunk.

But five times. Five times is what she said when I asked her,
which is exactly five times too many. Five times is voluntary
and deliberate and, for two married people having an extra-
marital affair, planned out in advance. It doesn't just sponta-
neously happen. There are things to think about, things to
consider, like how to do it without getting caught by the ones
you're supposed to love.

"Say something. Please," she pleads, biting down hard on
her lower lip.

I can't look at Lily. I can't stop thinking about Jake's hands
on her and hers on him. I feel like throwing up.

Lily reaches for me as I get out of bed. I turn my back to
her, walking away, unreachable to her hands. "How did it happen?" I ask.

"Does it matter?"

"Yes. It does. To me." Lily is quiet behind me. I turn back,
looking hard. "You're not going to tell me, Lily? That's the least
you can do, don't you think?"

It happens as these things almost always happen. It was innocent at first. They ran into each other by accident and they grabbed coffee. But then it happened again, not so accidentally that time.

"Why?" I ask. "I thought you loved me, Lily."

"I do. I love you more than anything, Christian."

In this moment, I find that hard to believe.

"Where did it happen?" I ask. "Here? In our bed?"

"No," Lily insists and it's the one thing she says that I maybe believe. "Not here."

"Then, where?" She swallows. I see the movement of her throat. "A hotel?" I spit out, losing patience. "His car, their house? Where, Lily?"

I can see in her face that I got it right. Lily had sex with Jake in his and Nina's house.

"How?" I ask, aghast. It disgusts me.

"Nina's mother always needs something from her, rides to the store or to church or whatever. She gets lonely. She lives alone and is practically dependent on Nina. It drove Jake mad. Her mother always wants Nina to come stay with her, to keep her company, and Nina obliges. But when Nina was with her mother, Jake was home alone."

I shake my head. That's not what I meant. That's not the answer I was looking for. I say, "What I meant was how could you do that to your friend? How could you do this to me?"

Lily just cries.

"How did you know Nina wouldn't come home and find you with Jake?" I ask.

"Jake would look for her on his phone. He knew where she was and when she'd be home."

"He was tracking her?" I ask, laughing in disbelief, and then I stop laughing. I narrow my eyes at her. "That's fucked-up, Lily. That's really fucked-up." I run my hands through my hair, thinking of those weekend afternoons that Lily would tell me she had errands to run, but instead of the grocery store or yoga like she said, she was stealing away to meet Jake, because Nina had left to take care of her mother for the day and Jake was home alone.

I ask Lily, "What really happened that day at Langley Woods? You didn't just happen to run into him like you said?"

"No," she admits. "I asked him to meet me there. I didn't want to be with him anymore, Christian. I only wanted to be with you." Lily gets on her knees on the bed. She reaches for me, clutching a fistful of my shirt, pulling me back to her. "I'd made a mistake. I was so stupid, Christian. I messed up. I'd been regretting it for weeks, but didn't know how to tell Jake it was through, that I didn't want to be with him anymore. I wished more than anything I could take it back, that it never would have happened in the first place. I asked Jake to meet me there, at the forest preserve that day. He didn't know why I wanted to meet, only that I wanted to talk, and then I told him that it was over, that whatever he and I had was through. I told him that I only want to be with you. He got so upset, Christian. He flew into a rage. He lost his mind. He threw me to the ground, he called me a whore, he said I was leading him on and sending all the wrong signals, and I got scared," she says, crying now, like I should feel sorry for her and maybe I do, a little bit. "I panicked," she says. "It happened almost just exactly as I said it did," she swears, and so help me, I chuckle. I fucking laugh, a demented laugh, though there isn't anything even remotely funny about it, other than that it didn't happen at all like she said it did.

I narrow my eyes. "You lied to me, Lily."

"About some things. Yes. But not about everything. I thought he was going to kill me, and then I saw that rock out of the corner of my eye. I reached for it. I dug it out of the ground and I hit him with it. I couldn't stop myself. I just kept hitting him with it. He tried to fight me off. We fought, and then eventually he fell and I ran away. But I swear on my life, Christian, on our baby's life, I didn't shoot him," she says, clutching my hands as, from downstairs, the doorbell rings following by the sound of knuckles pounding on the door, and Lily's eyes go wide with fear.

"You have to believe me, Christian," she begs, moaning as a pain shoots through her abdomen and she clutches it, folding herself in half over her arm. "I didn't shoot him," she swears, her nails digging into my skin, from the fear, from the pain, leaving slits behind, "but someone else did."

NINA

Ryan has called three times already. He's left three voice mails and texted twice. He wants to know if I'm okay. He wants to know if I need anything. I've heard from Officer Boone, who finally spoke with the florist, forcing her to give up the name of the person who sent me flowers. It was Ryan. It didn't even come as a surprise.

"Please, Nina," he begged on the last voice mail, his voice steeped with empathy and something else, something I couldn't put my finger on but that made me uncomfortable nonetheless, made me get up and go to the windows in my mother's house and pull the curtains closed. "I'm worried about you. Please let me know what I can do to help you through this. You know I'm always here for you."

I stopped listening at that point, and then I went into my contacts and blocked his number so that if he calls, the phone won't ring and if he leaves a message, I won't get a notification, though before I blocked him, one of the two texts that he sent read, Where are you, Nina?

My mother's address is listed in the White Pages.

He knows I'm not home.

I wonder if it's only a matter of time before he finds me here.

One day and then two days pass. There are many things to do when your spouse has died, especially when he has been murdered. My mother and I go to the funeral home and make arrangements for Jake for when his body gets released by the police. I pick out a casket. I pick out a cemetery plot. I call the hospital and Jake's office and tell them the news, listening to complete strangers sob on the other end of the line and having to console them. I call the life insurance company at my mother's reminding. In order to initiate the claims process, I need to fill out paperwork and send in a copy of Jake's death certificate and make a request for benefits. It's all too much to deal with and I'm grateful for my mother's help. Otherwise I wouldn't do any of it.

I feel gutted, like someone tore into me to rip out my internal organs. The visits, the questions from the police are endless, though it's been relatively clear-cut. Lily did this. She says she didn't, but she did. She's confessed to an affair with Jake and an altercation with him in the exact place where he was later found dead, but she swears she didn't shoot him. She's asked the police to do a lie detector test to prove it, though they're not always accurate and not often admissible in court. Even if a lie detector test were to say she didn't shoot Jake, I don't know that I'd believe it.

The police arrested her for murder. She sat in jail for forty-eight hours before the bail hearing, and I hoped they'd never let her out. The bail was set at a million dollars. The police, from what I heard, got a warrant and searched her home, turning it inside out looking for a gun. They didn't find it, but

Lily had plenty of time from when Jake died until now to get rid of it. The gun is somewhere and only Lily and Christian know where.

But even without the gun, the evidence against Lily is incriminating. Jim Brady saw her there. There was physical evidence of Lily on Jake, according to the medical examiner's report, blood, saliva, skin cells and hair.

Almost every night I fantasize about ways to destroy her life.

I've gone to some dark place, where it's hard to find joy in anything. I'm tired all the time. All I want to do is sleep, and most of the time my mother lets me, but then sometimes she comes into my dark cavern of a room, opens the blinds and I squint and thrash and react like a vampire who's allergic to light.

When she leaves, I close the blinds again and slip back into bed beneath the covers.

There is nothing that says I can't go back to my own house. The police did what they wanted with it and now it's all mine. But I don't want to go back there. I don't want to be there with the knowledge that Jake won't ever be coming home, or of what Lily and Jake did together in my house.

"You could sell the house," my mother suggested once as she sat beside me in bed, spoon-feeding me soup because it was the only way I would eat, if she kept shoving the food into my mouth like I was a toddler. "Or we could sell both houses, yours and mine, and move somewhere together." I liked the idea of that. We daydreamed about places we could go because, now that Jake is gone, there is nothing that keeps us tethered here. My mother is the only one who loves me. She's the only person I have left.

"Despite the circumstances," she said to me one night as she sat beside me in bed, "this is kind of nice. It's just like old times," and I agreed that yes, despite the circumstances of my husband being dead, it was just like old times.

One afternoon I sit on my mother's sofa, staring through the gauzy living room sheers at the world outside. She forced me out of the bedroom, saying she wanted to wash the sheets, which I think was just a ploy to get me out of bed and it worked, because being out of the bedroom for just a few hours has brightened my mood. I took a shower for a change. I put on clean clothes.

As I watch out the window now, the mailperson comes tooling down the street in his truck.

"I'm going to get the mail," I call out to my mother, feeling a sudden craving for movement and fresh air. I step outside, pulling the door closed behind me. The sunlight blinds me. It's so bright after all those days of living in darkness.

I make my way toward the mailbox, staying aware of my surroundings. My mother's neighborhood is 1970s era. The houses are all relatively small, mostly ranches like hers with the occasional raised ranch. Her house is just over eleven hundred square feet and is yellow brick with brown trim. The exterior hasn't changed much in forty years. Because of the age of the neighborhood, the trees are mature and yet there aren't many of them because I imagine that before the community was built, the land was razed.

I stay vigilant as I make my way down the driveway. I observe the street, which is remarkably quiet now. Oddly quiet. There isn't a person around. The children are all at school, where I should be. My bereavement leave has officially expired and I'm taking unpaid time off now. I was given four days off from work, four days to grieve the death of my husband. Interestingly enough, there is no law that requires employers to give bereavement leave. I didn't know that before, but I do now. The four days from my school district is considered generous. Four whole days to make funeral arrangements, to call family and friends, to bury a body if I could, obtain death certificates, file life insurance claims and somewhere in there, to actually grieve. Four days isn't enough, though I wonder if any amount of time is enough. I want to get back to work, and yet I can't imagine the way people will look at me when I come back. My mother had told me not to rush things. I worry about money, but she says not to worry about that because Jake has left us plenty of money and soon the life insurance will pay out, and then we will be set for years.

Lily is out of prison on bail, though, under the terms and conditions set by the court, she can't have any communication with me. So far she hasn't tried, but that's not to say it won't happen.

I get to the mailbox. I open the little black door and reach inside for the mail, coming up with it in my hand. There is more than a day's worth of mail. My mother must have forgotten to get the mail these last few days, which have been a blur, every day running into the next until I can't tell them apart anymore.

I flip through the mail. One envelope catches my eye and I stop midstride, as I make my way back up the driveway for the front door. The envelope reads: *Notice of Traffic Violation*.

Ordinarily I wouldn't open my mother's mail but I do because my mother doesn't even drive a car. She owns a car, but only because we haven't had a chance to sell it. For now, it sits idle in her garage, collecting dust and biding time until we do. Someone has made a mistake.

Just inside the house, I slide my finger under the flap. I lift it open, tearing the envelope where it doesn't easily give. I pinch the slip of paper between my fingers and draw it out of the envelope, unfolding and running my eyes slowly over it.

Notice of Violation, it says at the top of the ticket.

Automated Red Light Enforcement System.

It's one of those traffic cam tickets that comes in the mail. I'd think that it was a mistake, but then I see two grainy images of my mother's car on the page, one taken just before and one taken just after the transgression, showing her car turning left through a red light. Another image shows a close-up of the back end of my mother's car, with the car's make and model visible as well as the license plate number.

I would think that someone took my mother's car out for a joyride, that someone borrowed or stole it from her garage, were it not for the fourth black-and-white, low-resolution picture at the bottom corner of the page. In it, I see my mother's face, the picture snapped from the camera on the top of the stoplight through the windshield, the upper bend of the steering wheel slanting across her chin.

The date of violation: September 17

Time of violation: 2:18

There is a location of the violation. I think that's inconsequential at first. It doesn't matter where my mother got this ticket for running through a red light; the bigger problem is that she was driving her car when her vision isn't anywhere close to good enough for her to be driving a car. What was she thinking?

She could have gotten herself killed. She could have killed someone else.

I hear my mother's footsteps approach from down the hall. "Was there anything good in the mail?" she asks, rounding a corner and coming to stand in the living room with me.

"I don't know," I say, turning to look at her. "I didn't look."

I come forward. I meet her in the middle of the room. I hang on to the violation, but I hold the rest of the mail out to her. As she takes it from me, her eyes look down to peruse the mail. I watch for five and then ten seconds as she reads the words on the outsides of the envelopes. I watch the movement of her eyes running from left to right across the page before she catches herself, as if remembering only then that she supposedly cannot see well enough to read.

Her eyes come slowly back up. Our eyes lock. She harrumphs and shakes her head, as if disappointed in herself for trying. She holds the mail back out to me and says, "Can you just tell me what it is, Nina? You know I can't see very well. The words, they're all a blur."

"Of course. I'm so sorry, Mom. I don't know what I was thinking." I take the mail from her, and then I thumb through an electric bill and the cable bill.

"And what's that?" she asks, pointing to the envelope still in my hand.

"You got a ticket, Mom," I say, feeling hot all of a sudden, the room suffocating. "For running a red light."

She doesn't try to argue. She doesn't claim that the woman in the picture isn't her, because it obviously is. She stands quietly, as if waiting for me to speak.

"Can you still drive, Mom?" I ask.

She shrugs. "I have good days and bad days," she tries telling me. But macular degeneration, from what I know, is degenerative and incurable. The progression can be slowed but it can't be reversed, which means that every day should be the same or worse.

I say, "I didn't think you were driving at all. That's why you've been needing me to help take you places."

"I don't do it often," she says. "Hardly ever. I needed something from the grocery store, Nina. You were working. It couldn't wait."

"What did you need so badly that it couldn't wait?" I ask, because every weekend I've been taking her to the store and helping her with her groceries.

She changes tack. "It's not that it couldn't wait. That's not what I meant. It's that I didn't want to bother you. The last thing you need to do after work is to be bringing me a gallon of milk."

"Milk. That's what you needed so badly? A gallon of milk?"

"I was in the middle of baking. I didn't want it all to go to waste."

"But all this time you've been telling me that you can't see well enough to drive."

"What are you suggesting, Nina?" she asks. When I just stare at her, saying nothing, she comes back with, "Do you think that I'm lying? That I've been making it up? You've been to the doctor with me, Nina. He did tests. He diagnosed me." He did. She's right. He dilated her eyes and injected a dye into her arm, which traveled through blood vessels to her eye to look for leakage under the macula, which it found. But as for her actual ability to see, he used a vision test, an Amsler grid, that relied only on what she said she saw, so that I start to wonder if her vision is not as bad as she makes me think it is. My mother was mostly independent until the day the doctor diagnosed her with macular degeneration and then, almost overnight, it was as if she was completely dependent on me. We used to go weeks without seeing one another, mostly because of the way Jake felt when I spent my free time with her and not him. But after the diagnosis, we hardly ever went two days without seeing each other, and every time I was away from her for too long, there would be something she needed that would bring me back to her.

"Truth be told," she goes on, "I shouldn't have been driving at all. See? I couldn't even see that the light was red," she says.

"You have to be more careful. You could have hurt yourself, Mom. You could have hurt someone else."

As I walk away from her, moving down the darkened hall where the sun doesn't reach, I can't stop thinking about how the date of the violation is the same day that Jake was killed.

In my room, I pull up a map on my phone. I enter the intersection where my mother got her traffic violation. I enlarge the map. The grocery store where my mother buys her milk is at best a mile from her house. On a good day, she could walk there.

The traffic violation she received was at an intersection over fifteen miles from her house.

When I see where the intersection is, I go absolutely still. Rigid. Silent. I practically stop breathing. I stop thinking about breathing. I can't feel my body all of a sudden. I feel physically and emotionally numb.

The red light my mother ran through is two blocks from where Jake works. I look back at the images on the ticket, specifically the one taken just before my mother turned left through that red light.

There is just enough shown of the car in front of hers, for me to know that it's Jake's.

Wherever he went that day, she followed him there.

She never liked Jake. She was never coy about it either.

I would say it's impossible. My mother could never kill or even hurt someone.

But then again, I didn't think Lily could either.

My mother knows everything about me, including the code to our safe.

I told her once because I thought it was prudent that someone should know how to get into the safe, in case of an emergency or if something happened to both Jake and me. We keep cash in there. It's where we keep the social security cards, financial documents, passports and our wills. It's where we keep our gun.

She knew the passcode to the garage. She knew my work schedule.

She knew when I'd be gone and she could come over, let herself into my house and help herself to the gun.

That night, after she's asleep, I search what I can of the house looking for Jake's gun. I don't find it. She's in the shower the next day when I search her bedroom.

I still hear the water running when I take her car keys from the hook on the wall and go quickly out to the garage.

I open the garage door. I unlock the car and sink into the driver's seat. I rummage around in the glove box and the center console first, and then I slide my hand under the seats, as far as I can reach. I move quickly, not knowing how much time I have until my mother gets out of the shower and comes looking for me.

From inside the car, I pop the trunk. I leave the car and go around to the back end to search the trunk, which is mostly empty other than a few odds and ends, like an ice scraper and jumper cables.

I lift the trunk's floor panel to reveal the spare tire. I shudder when I see it, falling back from the car.

A second later, my breakfast comes back up. It's spontaneous. There is little warning. I throw my hands to my mouth to try and stop the flow, but end up bending at the waist and vomiting onto the garage floor, because there, in the spare tire well, is the gun.

I force myself to stand upright. I go back to the car. I reach for the gun. I turn it over in my hands, pointing it up toward my own face.

This isn't the first time in my life that I've ever held a gun, but it is the first time I've found myself looking down the barrel of a gun.

I wonder if this is what Jake saw before he died.

I think how somewhere inside that barrel is a cartridge and the firing pin, which is held back by spring tension. All it would take is for the trigger to be pressed, for the firing pin to release. For gunpowder to ignite. For the cartridge to expand, releasing the bullet, spinning it straight toward my face.

What would that have felt like for Jake, I wonder, when the bullet tore through his face?

In the distance, a door creaks open. My range of vision slowly expands. My mother has come outside. I look up just as she lets go of the storm door and it slams closed. I watch as she walks down the small concrete walkway, watching me, her hair still wet, her head cocked and curious as I stand behind her open trunk in the open garage.

"It's getting cool, Nina," she calls out, pulling her cardigan tighter around her body, "and you don't have your jacket on, honey. Why don't you come inside and we'll make some hot cocoa to warm us both up."

I hold the gun in my shaking hand. I reveal it to her. My mother looks unshaken, unmoved, as if she isn't surprised that I've found the gun.

My voice quivers. "What did you do, Mom?"

My mother looks around to make sure her neighbors aren't witness to this, and then she says, "Come inside, Nina, and we'll talk about it."

I still taste vomit in my mouth as I follow her down the walkway and back into the house. I leave the trunk open and my vomit on the garage floor. I carry the gun with me.

In the kitchen, I watch, my stomach curdling, while my mother fills the kettle with water and puts it on the stove, lighting the burner. She reaches into the cabinet for two mugs. With her back to me, she says, "He was cheating on you, honey." She goes to the pantry and pulls out the Swiss Miss and a bag of marshmallows as if a mug of hot cocoa will make this all better.

I stand on the opposite side of the kitchen from her, staring at her from behind, watching her lithe movements.

I mutter, "I know." I feel physically ill. I go to the sink. I turn the water to cold. I let it run, and then I gather a handful of cold water and splash it on my face. I rinse my mouth out, spitting water into the sink. My mother turns around to see what I'm doing. "How did you know?" I ask, standing upright, my face wet.

She hands me a towel. "A mother always knows these things. I did you a favor, Nina. You're better off without him."

"What exactly did you do?"

"I followed him to the woods. It wasn't the first time I followed him. I needed to know what he was up to, for your sake. Someone had to hold him accountable for his actions. That afternoon, I watched what happened between him and that woman. After she went running away, I told him to get up. I pointed the gun at him and I told him to walk, deeper into the woods and that's where I killed him. You remember how your father cheated on me, Nina? He took everything from us when he left. You know that, don't you? You remember that?" I nod, the bile rising up inside of me so that I think I might be sick again. I hunch over the sink as she says, "I couldn't afford the house after that. We had to move here to this little house that I hate, and even then I worried all the time that I wouldn't be able to pay the mortgage and the bank would foreclose on our home. I thought all the time that we'd lose it, that we'd become homeless. Your father should have paid child support, but he never did. He should have paid alimony. I had to work the night shift. I had to take extra shifts whenever I could, to make ends meet. I didn't want the same thing to happen to you."

I push myself upright, aghast. I wipe at my mouth with the back of a hand. My mother reaches out for my arms. I bristle, and then back away from her, going for my phone. "Don't touch me," I say.

"What do you think you're going to do?" she asks as I snatch my phone from the countertop.

"I have to call the police. I have to tell them what you did."

She looks saddened, hurt. "You wouldn't really do that, would you? I'm your mother, Nina."

"Wouldn't I?" I ask. "You killed my husband, Mom."

"I was doing you a favor, Nina. You're far better off without Jake. Think about it," she says. "You have that big house all to yourself and soon you'll have the money from Jake's life insurance policy. You won't want for anything, ever. And besides, Nina honey, that woman was having an affair with your husband. Aren't you mad? Aren't you angry? Don't you think she deserves to be punished for what she did? If it wasn't for her, none of this would have happened."

I am mad. I am angry. More than anything, I want Lily to hurt like I hurt. I want Lily to suffer. I want Lily to sit alone in prison, separated from the people she loves.

But Lily didn't kill Jake.

"Did you lie about your vision, Mom? So that I would have to take care of you? So that we could spend more time together?"

"I didn't lie," she insists. "You heard the doctor, Nina. You were there."

"But your vision isn't as bad as you'd like us to think. You can still drive and go to the grocery store all on your own." My grandmother had macular degeneration. My mother used to take her to her doctor's appointments. She would have known exactly what to say to make the doctor and me believe her vision was worse than it was.

"The doctor said I may go blind one day."

"Yes, one day. But not now."

"It's always just been you and me, Nina," she croons. "Our time together these last few months has been so special to me, honey. I didn't realize how much I missed you."

"What do you mean, Mom? I've always been right here."

"No, you haven't honey. You've been with Jake. Once you married him, you forgot all about me."

"I didn't," I say. "That's not true."

"Oh yes it is. Maybe you didn't mean to do it, but you did. Do you have any idea how lonely I've been? How many times did I ask you to have dinner with me or to go shopping with me but you couldn't because you were too busy spending time with your husband?"

"Why didn't you just talk to me? Why didn't you tell me how you were feeling? Why did you lie?"

JUST THE NICEST COUPLE

"Would you have listened to me?" she asks and I say yes, though I wonder if I would have, if her loneliness would have had the same impact as going blind. As it was, I didn't have a choice but to spend so much time with her. "Would you have? Or would you have let your husband keep you from me?" she asks knowingly. I say nothing because she's right, because, if not for her going blind, I wouldn't have felt compelled to be with her as much as I have.

She says, "Put the phone down, Nina."

I hold the phone in my hand. I look down at it. I've already swiped up to unlock the phone and I stare down at the keypad, paralyzed by indecision. I could call Officer Boone and turn my mother in. But I don't know that my mother could survive prison. The biopsy results came back. Her doctor called me three days ago. I haven't even told her yet, because of everything that's been going on and because I've been trying to work up the nerve to talk to her about it. The cells were malignant. She has breast cancer. There is a chance the cancer has already metastasized to her lymph nodes or the liver or the bones. We don't know. She'll need more imaging tests to determine if the cancer has spread and how far, like a bone scan and a CT scan. She needs surgery soon and radiation and, even with surgery and radiation, she may die. The prognosis for stage four breast cancer is grim, if that's what she has. The five-year survival rate is something like 20 percent meaning there is a measly one in five chance she'll still be alive in five years. I don't want her spending them in jail. I've read things about sick inmates, how they don't get the best treatment if any treatment at all, and how they die in solitary confinement, and spend their last years on earth without ever seeing the sun.

This is happening too fast. I can't catch up. I can't process this.

I look up at her. She comes forward to cradle my face in her hands. She softens, saying, "There is nothing I wouldn't do for you, Nina. I hope you know that. I've only ever wanted what's best for you."

I pull away from her hands. I take myself somewhere out of reach. I look again at the phone, seeing Officer Boone's name in the recent call log. My thumb hovers above his name.

My mother says, "I only did what I did to Jake to protect you. He would have left you, Nina. If not for this woman, then for another. He would have taken everything from you and left you with nothing."

I'll never know if that's true. Would Jake have left me? Would he have taken everything from me when he left?

My mother isn't a monster. What she did is monstrous, but she herself is not a monster. I'm not a mother myself and so I don't know, but I've heard there is no limit to a mother's love.

"I love you, Nina," she says. I know she does. I love her too.

If she wasn't sick, it might be different. But I can't stand the idea of her dying in prison.

I take a deep breath. I set the phone on the counter, facedown. I walk away from it.

CHRISTIAN

I rub the pad of a thumb gently against her cheek to wake her up from sleep. It takes a second for her to come to, and then her dark brown eyes flutter open, coming to rest on my face, exploring it. She smiles and my heart practically explodes out of my chest.

I lean down to slip my hands under her armpits and lift my baby from her crib. Bella is two months old. "We're going to get dressed to go see Mommy," I say to her, and she grins, a big, happy, toothless grin. I support her head as I carry her to the changing table and I lie her on her back, watching as she moves her happy, tiny feet. I can't help myself. I touch them. I wiggle her pale little toes. I kiss them.

I never thought in my whole life that I could love a baby's feet this much.

I get Bella a clean diaper, and then I get her dressed, feeling that same regret that always comes to me when it's time to visit Lily.

It's hard to see Lily now. It's hard to look at her and see how much has changed.

I take Bella downstairs, watching out the window as a flock of geese descends on the river out back. I carry Bella to the window to show her, but at her age they say a baby's vision is still blurry and that they can't see more than a few feet away. There's no way Bella sees the geese, but then her eyes settle on mine and she smiles again and I know she sees me. My heart melts.

I go to the garage door. I lean over to lower Bella gently into her infant seat beside the door, getting ready to leave. I pack the diaper bag with the bottles and the formula, diapers, wipes, pacifier and everything else she might need while we're gone.

I never thought I'd be doing any of this alone.

I hoist the carrier into my arm and we leave. I stare at her as we walk, thinking how, for the most part, she is a miniature version of Lily. I didn't want to be insensitive when Bella was born. I would have raised her either way. I would have come to love her as my own. But as soon as she was born, I had a paternity test done and now I know for certain that her extra-large forehead came from me. Without a doubt, this girl is mine.

I settle Bella in the base in the back seat, and then I get in the car and drive.

Lily is there before us. She almost always is and waiting in eager anticipation of holding her child. The time away from Bella is the worst. I feel it too during the weeks that Bella stays with Lily, which is what she's about to do. She isn't even gone, but I miss her already.

I park beside Lily's car. I get out. I walk to where she sits waiting for us on a park bench. The park where we meet is nice. It's large with a lake, a playground, picnic shelter and walking path. It's never too crowded, but Lily, Bella and I are rarely ever alone. Today, kids play at the playground. Families walk on the path along the lake.

She stands up as we approach. I reach out to hug her and she slips with ease back into my arms, though it's brief. "Can you stay for a few minutes?" she asks. Lily has cut her hair. It's still long, but more like just-beneath-the-shoulder length. I tell her I like it, stopping myself just before I can reach out and touch it, because old habits die hard.

I sit on the bench beside her and we talk while Bella sleeps, lulled to sleep as always from the motion of the car on the drive here.

"I heard Nina's mother was recently released from prison," Lily says, tucking a blanket around Bella's body because the day is breezy but sunny and warm. I nod. She was. I heard this too. From what I heard, she was given a compassionate release because of her quickly deteriorating health. She refused treatment for her cancer and so she's gone downhill fast, faster than anyone expected. She's confined to her home now, where she'll spend the rest of her life until she dies, which shouldn't be much longer.

"Do you ever hear from Nina?" I ask.

Lily shakes her head no. "I never reached out. I just thought it was best that way, if I just let her go." I nod. She's probably right.

We talk for a few more minutes. About nothing and everything. Lily is still teaching, though she's switched high schools and it's summer break, so she has the next two months off. She doesn't keep in touch with many people from the high school where she used to work, though she's heard from the people she does still speak with that Nina returned to work last school year after winter break. At the same time Nina returned, some male colleague of hers resigned, which was a breach of contract—for a teacher to leave in the middle of the school year—and came as a surprise to Lily. He and Nina were close apparently. They were both English teachers. Lily didn't know the whole story, but she thought there was a story there.

She asks how work is going, and I say fine, same. Some things never change.

"Welp," I say after a few minutes, standing up. The standard cue to leave.

Lily goes first. I watch as she lifts the infant seat from the earth and carries Bella away from me for the next week. I stand, watching them go, feeling like they've torn my heart out of my chest and are taking it with them.

Lily gets only a few steps, and then she stops and turns back to me, standing in the shade of a giant oak tree, her hair moving in the warm, gentle breeze.

"I was thinking," she says, tucking a strand of hair behind an ear, "that it might be nice if one day, you would come over for dinner." She swallows. I can see the movement of it in her throat and I know how much courage it takes for her to ask me. Lily asks almost the same question every time I see her. And every time, I say some version of the same thing.

"Can I think about it?"

She offers a half smile. She nods.

Maybe one of these days I'll surprise her and say yes.

★ ★ ★ ★ ★

acknowledgments

Thank you to Erika Imranyi and Rachael Dillon Fried for your constant reassurance and the many brainstorming sessions. Your patience, understanding and your confidence in me were paramount to getting this book written, and I'm so grateful for that and for you.

Thank you to Nicole Luongo, Randy Chan, Heather Foy, Amy Jones, Rachel Haller, Lindsey Reeder, Reka Rubin and the rest of the incredibly hardworking and dedicated Park Row Books team for the feedback and support, copyediting, proofreading and stunning cover art. Thank you to my amazing publicists, Emer Flounders and Kathleen Carter, for helping bring my books into the world. Thanks to the many booksellers, librarians, Bookstagrammers, BookTokers and bloggers who are constantly championing my books; their success is because of you and all that you do! Thanks to Shari Smiley and Scott E. Schwimer for always imagining a place for my books on TV or on the big screen, and to Michelle Brower for your enthusiasm in being a part of the team!

Last, but certainly not least, thank you to my family and friends, especially Pete, Addison and Aidan, for your patience and your willingness to talk about this book—and all the false starts that came before it—again and again (and again) at length, and to my sister Michelle for the brilliant suggestion. I couldn't have done this without any of you!

discussion questions

1. Between Christian and Nina, which of the narrators did you relate to most and why?

2. Christian in particular goes to extremes to protect his wife and unborn child. Did you ever think he crossed a line and, if so, at what point?

3. Are there circumstances where you would be willing to hurt another person or do something awful to protect yourself or someone you love? Explain.

4. Did you expect the final twist at the end? If you were Nina, how would you feel? Would you ever be able to forgive?

5. There is irony in the title of the book, *Just the Nicest Couple*. How do you think it applies to each of the couples?

6. Are you happy with how things are left with Christian and Lily at the end? What do you think will happen to them?

7. What do you think will happen to Nina in the years to come? Do you think it's possible to find happiness after so much trauma?

Read on for a sneak peek at
She's Not Sorry,
the next electrifying thriller from
queen of suspense
Mary Kubica

Prologue

My phone starts to ring as I open the door to walk into the store. It's buried in the depths of my bag and is difficult to find. I shove aside a wallet and a cosmetic bag, knowing the search is likely futile. I will never get to it in time.

My fingers make contact on the third or fourth ring. I fish it out of the bag, but as soon as I do, the phone goes quiet. I'm too late. A missed call notification from Sienna appears on the screen. I'm taken aback. I physically stop in the open doorway and stare down at her number on the display. Doubt and confusion fill my thoughts because it's just after ten o'clock in the morning and Sienna is at school, or rather, she should be. Sienna texts from school sometimes, sneaking her phone when the teacher isn't paying attention—Can I hang out with Gianna today? I lost my water bottle. Did u buy tampons? My stupid calculator won't work.—but she doesn't call. My mind goes in a million different directions thinking how, if she was sick, the nurse would call and, if she got in trouble at school for something, then the dean would call. Sienna wouldn't ever be the one to call.

I don't have a chance to call her back. Almost immediately the phone in my hand starts to ring again and I jump, from the unexpected sound of it. It's Sienna, calling me back.

My thumb swipes immediately across the screen. "Sienna? What's wrong?" I ask, pressing the phone to my ear. I step fully inside the store, letting the door drift closed to muffle the street noise outside, the sound of cars passing by and people on their phones, having conversations of their own. I hear the shrill, unmistakable panic in my voice, and I think how, in the next instant, Sienna is going to ride me for overreacting, for freaking out about nothing. *Geez Mom. Relax. I'm fine*, she'll say, drawing that last word out for emphasis.

That's not what happens.

It's quiet at first. I just barely make out the sound of something slight like movement or wind. It goes on a few seconds so that I decide this must be a pocket dial. Sienna didn't mean to call me. The phone is in her pocket or her backpack and she called me by mistake. She doesn't even know she's called me twice. I listen, trying to decipher where she is, but it's more of the same. Nothing telling. Nothing revelatory.

But then, a man's voice cuts through the quiet, his words cold and sparing, his voice altered as if speaking through a voice changer. "If you ever want to see your daughter again, you will do exactly as I say."

I gasp. My eyes gape. I lose my footing, falling backward into the closed door. A hand rises to my mouth, pressing hard. I can't breathe all of a sudden. I can't think; my mind can't process what's happening at first. I pull the phone away from my ear, looking down at the display to see if I'm mistaken, if it's not Sienna's number that called but someone else. A wrong number. Because this can't be right, this can't be happening. This can't be happening to me.

But it is right. Sienna's number stares back at me from the display.

"Who is this," I ask, pressing the phone back to my ear, "and why do you have my daughter's phone?"

And then, in the background, I hear Sienna's piercing scream.

"Mommy!" she bellows. It's high-pitched, frenzied, desperate, and that's when I know that this man doesn't only have Sienna's phone. He has Sienna.

Pure terror courses through my veins. Sienna hasn't called me *Mommy* in at least ten years. I can't stop thinking what horrible thing must be happening for her to lapse back into her childhood and call me *Mommy*. I'm completely powerless. I don't know where she is. I don't know how to get to her, how to help her, how to make this stop.

"Go away," Sienna commands. Her voice trembles, so that she doesn't sound like herself, who is usually so defiant, so sure. There is no mistaking her fear. "Leave me alone," she demands, crying now. Sienna falters on the words, her voice cracking, so that the execution doesn't carry the same weight as the words themselves.

Sienna is terrified and so am I.

"Sienna, baby!" I shriek. There is the sound of commotion, of muffled noises in the background—this man, I imagine, subduing Sienna, forcing a gag into her mouth so that she can't speak or scream, and Sienna fighting back from the sound of it, resisting him.

I realize that I'm not blinking. I'm not breathing.

Tears sting my eyes. "What are you doing to her? Who is this?" I demand of this man, screaming into the phone so that everyone in the store stops what they're doing to look at me, to stare, some gasping and pressing hands to their own mouths in shock, as if this nightmare is somehow collective. "What have you done with my daughter? What do you want from me?"

"Listen to me," the man says back, his modulated voice unshaken and sedate, unlike mine. I still hear Sienna's desperate cry in the background, a keening, weeping wail, though it's stilted. The sound of it is enough to bring me to my knees, and yet I don't know what's worse: the sound of Sienna's cry or the sound of it as it grows distant and then fades completely away.

"Where is she? What have you done to her? Why can't I hear her anymore?"

"You need to do exactly as I say. Exactly. Do you understand?"

"I want to talk to my daughter. Let me talk to my daughter. I need to know that she's okay. What have you done to her?"

"I have nothing to lose," the man says. "You're the only one with something to lose, Ms. Michaels. Now you need to shut up and listen to me because I don't care one way or the other if your daughter lives or dies. What happens to her is entirely up to you."